All She Wants

. . . for Christmas is him

All She Wants

...for Christmas is him

LESLIE KELLY   TAWNY WEBER   JOANNE ROCK

MILLS & BOON

Published in Great Britain 2014
by Mills & Boon, an imprint of Harlequin (UK) Limited,
Eton House, 18-24 Paradise Road, Richmond, Surrey, TW9 1SR

ALL SHE WANTS... © 2014 Harlequin Books S.A.

Oh, Naughty Night! © 2014 Leslie A. Kelly
Nice & Naughty © 2012 Tawny Weber
Under Wraps © 2010 Joanne Rock

ISBN: 978-0-263-25093-0

025-1114

Harlequin (UK) Limited's policy is to use papers that are natural, renewable and recyclable products and made from wood grown in sustainable forests.The logging and manufacturing processes conform to the legalenvironmental regulations of the country of origin.

Printed and bound in Spain
by CPI, Barcelona

Oh, Naughty Night!

LESLIE KELLY

New York Times bestselling author **Leslie Kelly** has written dozens of books and novellas for the Mills & Boon® Blaze® line. Known for her sparkling dialogue, fun characters and steamy sensuality, she has been honoured with numerous awards, including a National Readers' Choice Award, a Colorado Award of Excellence, a Golden Quill and an *RT Book Reviews* Career Achievement Award in Series Romance. Leslie has also been nominated four times for the highest award in romance fiction, the RWA RITA® Award. Leslie lives in Maryland with her own romantic hero, Bruce, and their daughters.

Visit her online at www.lesliekelly.com or at her blog, www.plotmonkeys.com.

To the younger members of my
big extended family...

Elliott, Kyleigh, Trey, Addison, Isiah,
Christopher, Jordyn, D4 and Baby Lundh...

I hope the holiday memories you're building with
your wonderful parents are as magical as mine
always were. Aunt Loulou loves you all!

1

"THERE'S NOTHING WORSE than having the hots for a sexy guy, and then finding out he has the personality of a turnip."

Lucille Vandenberg—known to her friends and family as Lulu, which wasn't great, but was certainly better than Lucille—didn't try to keep the disappointment out of her voice as she griped to her friends, Viv and Amelia. Honestly, a guy who looked as good as the man holding the guitar at the crowded bar should have boatloads of brains and charm to go with his amazing body. But this one? Ugh. She'd had more scintillating conversations with her houseplants.

"Sorry he turned out to be a disappointment," said Amelia, her pretty, gentle face full of commiseration and support.

Viv wasn't as comforting. "If the turnip's hung like a porn star, you can handle a root vegetable, Lulu. I mean, it's not as if you want a life partner here."

Lulu wasn't convinced, mainly because, once again, she'd set herself up for disappointment. For the past month, since she'd moved to Washington, D.C., she'd been on the lookout for an interesting guy to help break her long romantic dry streak. For what seemed like forever, she had been so focused on getting through grad school, and then on her internship in Rwanda, and then on her new job with a local NGO. She hadn't allowed herself a single date in ages. Of course, that also could have been because her last serious relationship had been with someone who'd been so self-absorbed and career-focused, he hadn't even known her middle name, her favorite color, or much of anything else about her a year after they'd been together.

But now she needed sex. Badly. Needed to have it with somebody who would make her forget she hadn't had it for so long…or at least make her believe the wait had really been worthwhile. She could deal with him not caring about her middle name or favorite colors, at least for one night.

"I just wanted to meet somebody nice, sexy and smart, and have a welcome-to-Washington adventure," she mused.

And when she'd come into this Dupont Circle bar earlier in the week and met the super-hot guitar player, she'd thought she might have found the perfect person with whom to do it.

But when they'd talked tonight, he'd turned out to be as adventurous as a trip to the dentist. Not even a trip for a filling, or a root canal, just a plain old check-up. Yawn. The monosyllabic conversation they'd shared when she arrived tonight had crushed her fantasies completely.

"Who cares about his IQ?" Viv added. "It's his looks and *size* that matter."

"Maybe to *you*," said Amelia, her tone a bit disapproving.

Really, the two former college roommates couldn't be more dissimilar, and Lulu wondered how they'd survived. They were like Oscar and Felix, only female. One was

sexually conservative while the other was a bit of a slut.
A definite odd couple.

"I wish I could be as brutally shallow as you, Viv,"
Lulu said. "But I need conversation to go with the pecs
and schlong."

Viv grinned, impossible to insult. She *was* the queen
of mean. "Fine, forget him. But don't give up. The night
is young."

Maybe. But she didn't want merely smarts, she also
wanted a guy who was honest and direct, who didn't play
games with his intentions. Someone who knew what he
wanted and went after it...not a wishy-washy dude who
couldn't even speak unless the subject was his favorite
band.

Why the hell was it so hard to find somebody like that?

Amelia raised her voice to be heard over the crowd,
which was growing louder with every costumed body that
crammed into the trendy bar. "There will be lots of guys
here tonight. You'll find somebody better."

"I doubt it."

"Have another drink. They'll *all* start to look better
after three of those things," said Viv, gesturing toward
Lulu's glass.

Lulu was already feeling the effects of two. Unfortunately, they were making her more choosy, not less. "I'm
not the one-night-stand-with-a-stranger type."

Viv raised a brow and gestured toward the guitarist.

"He wasn't a stranger," Lulu insisted. "I sorta knew
him."

"You exchanged five words with him before tonight,"
Viv said with a smirk.

"But I knew his name."

"Only his last one."

"Yeah, what's up with that?"

Viv shrugged. "Schaefer's all mysterious about his first name. I bet it's something stupid like Fred or Homer or Ralph."

Amelia, smiling sweetly, said, "Maybe he's just trying to keep some things private, since he's in the spotlight."

Perhaps. But she suspected the broodiness and first-name mystery were intended to heighten interest in an otherwise pretty uninteresting guy. It had certainly worked on her, at least until she'd heard him say more than "Got a request?"

Sighing, she swirled her Devil's Brew—the drink on special for tonight's big Halloween bash—and sipped it. She was careful not to splash any of the red liquid onto the half-mask that covered her face from mid-forehead down to the tip of her nose. Lulu had gone to a lot of trouble with this costume, having fully intended to look as sexy and wicked as she could in hopes of stirring some naughty thoughts in the guitarist. She was a witch, but her green mask wasn't the least bit scary—no long nose or warts. She'd gone instead for a Mardi Gras type facial covering, with sequins and cat-shaped eye openings. Beneath her pointy hat, her hair was curled and teased, wild and untamed. She'd also sprayed a coating of glittery red hairspray onto it, making herself even more unrecognizable.

Schaefer had noticed. She'd seen appreciation and heat in his eyes. His brain might be all vegetable, but his body apparently had some blood flowing through its roots. Er, veins.

That probably would have been enough for most sex-starved twenty-six-year-old women. Maybe it would have been enough for grad-school Lulu. But she'd changed since she'd returned from her internship in Rwanda. Working in a country filled with people who had so little, and then for a nonprofit group that gave microloans to similar, desperately-hopeful populations, would do that to a person.

She supposed she really had grown up. But that didn't mean she didn't still have the desire to go out and cut loose, if only to escape the sadness and deprivation she often witnessed in her job. But not with a turnip.

"Whoa, striptease at eleven o'clock," Viv said, her dark eyes widening.

"Wow, I thought this place was more upscale than that. Maybe we should go someplace else before then," said Amelia, sounding a little shocked.

"I wasn't talking about the time, Miss Literal." Viv pointed. "I mean at *my* eleven o'clock."

Lulu and Amelia both turned, peering through the crowd, trying to see what had caught Viv's attention. At first, Lulu merely spied a sea of devils, vampires, sexy nurses and construction workers. Then she spotted a figure standing alone near the dance floor, facing away from her. And she simply couldn't look away.

The guy had donned a white sheet for the event, going for the age-old ghost outfit that had gone out of style before Lulu was in elementary school. But even a single sheet was apparently too much. As if he'd felt he'd done his holiday duty by appearing in a requisite costume for a little while, he'd begun to pull the sheet up to remove it. He'd already revealed long legs covered in soft, loose-fitting jeans that draped across powerful, muscular thighs. Not to mention an utterly delish male ass lovingly cupped by that faded denim.

As he stretched his arms up, he caught the bottom hem of his shirt, which was now rising with the sheet—perhaps by design, but more likely by accident. Whatever the reason, she, Viv, Amelia and, she noted, every woman around them, watched him with avid attention as he bared smooth, supple skin, golden and slick with sweat from the hot, crowded bar. His jeans hung low on lean hips; his waist was slim, every inch of him hard.

Lulu reached blindly for her drink, sipping, but she didn't take her eyes off the ghost. The sheet and shirt went higher—*oh, God, that back.* It rippled with muscle, every bit of him powerful and sexy. In that body, strength wasn't just implied, it was promised, and though she wasn't a petite woman, she suddenly felt very feminine and fragile in comparison.

Catching a glimpse of ink on the back of his shoulder, she waited for more of it to be revealed. She held her breath, dying to see the broad shoulders and bare, flexing arms.

Unfortunately, he appeared to realize he'd been putting on a show. The man yanked the shirt back into place with one hand, and whipped the sheet the rest of the way off with the other. She almost heard a universal sigh of disappointment from every double-Y chromosome in the joint.

"A blond," Amelia said with a pleased little sigh.

"I like blonds," Viv purred.

Lulu never had before, but she was definitely seeing the appeal. "I'm quickly developing an appreciation for them."

Viv tried to stake her claim. "If he has a face to go with the rest of the package, I'll be poisoning your drinks so I can get to him first."

Lulu waited, sending mental signals for the guy to turn around so she could judge if the front was as amazing as the back. He didn't accommodate her fully, but he did glance toward the guitarist, nodding hello to Schaefer. Lulu got just a brief glimpse of his profile, but it was enough to make her gasp in shock.

Lurching from her chair, she said, "It can't be."

"Can't be who?" asked Amelia.

"Chaz."

Viv frowned. "A guy who looks like that is named Jazz?"

"Chaz," Lulu insisted, shaking the confusion out of her head and slowly lowering herself back down as her two friends eyed her curiously. "No, I'm wrong. I have to be. No way is that Chaz Browning."

"Hmm," Amelia mused, "that name sounds familiar."

"He's a journalist—some of his stuff has been in *Time* magazine and now I think he works for the Associated Press, or maybe Reuters," Lulu said, still trying to get the crazy thought that the Chaz she'd known as a kid could possibly have grown up to be the stud she'd just been ogling.

"Who are we talking about, the guy over there?" asked Viv.

"No, it's just a resemblance." She sipped again, willing her heart to stop thudding. "Chaz Browning was a boy from my hometown in western Maryland, literally the boy next door. Our parents are best friends, but we always tormented each other."

Well, mostly she'd tormented him. She smiled, thinking how silly she'd been to equate Chaz Browning with the red-hot dude across the bar.

"I've barely seen him since he graduated from high school nine years ago. But our families are still close. My mother told his mother that I was moving here, and he emailed me with info about his Realtor. That's how I got my apartment."

"And Chaz is definitely not Mr. Sexy Ghost?" Viv said, still focused on the handsome stranger, now ringed by a trio of costumed women. Lulu frowned, seeing the way they leaned against him, brushing body parts against his thick arms and strong legs.

None of your business, she reminded herself, turning in her chair to face her friend, and not the walking sexsicle.

"No way. Chaz was a total nerd. Skinny, awkward."

He definitely didn't have tons of muscles or an ass that could make a wolf-whistler of a nun. Sweet, quiet Chaz had as much in common with ghost-guy as Brad Pitt did with Elmer Fudd.

"Well, Mr. Ghost is definitely not a wimp," Viv said.

Chaz hadn't been a wimp, either, exactly. Memories flashed through her mind and she felt the same pang of guilt she always felt when she remembered the boy she'd known. She'd harassed him mercilessly—like the time Chaz had gone up onto the roof of the garage to retrieve a football. She'd waited until he was up there, and had then taken the ladder away. Chaz, not wanting to admit defeat to a mere girl, had jumped, landing hard enough on the ground that he fell and cracked his tailbone.

Her mom had accused Lulu of picking on Chaz only because she had a crush on him. She'd denied it, though she'd always thought he *was* kind of cute when he blushed. Which was often.

Suddenly, Viv's eyes went even rounder, and her mouth fell open. "Oh, my God, the front half is even better than the rear."

Lulu spun around on her seat again, wanting a better look. The hot stranger had turned toward them. She saw his face, noted the features—the green eyes with laugh lines beside them, the dimple in one cheek, the small cleft in his chin.

Confusion raced through her. The square, slightly grizzled jaw did not compute, nor did the wide, oh-so-kissable mouth, the flashing green eyes, the utter, rugged handsomeness of the man.

All unfamiliar…yet very familiar indeed.

"No way," she mumbled. "It just *can't* be."

She stared and stared. And gradually, the truth forced its way into her consciousness.

She might not recognize the body, but she knew that face, that smile, that dimple. She could no longer deny that the sexy ghost was, indeed, Chaz, the boy-next-door. The one she'd tormented, the one who'd ignored her until she'd been as rotten as possible to get his attention, the one she'd hoped to meet again here in D.C. if only so she could make up for being such a little snot when they were kids. But she needed to work up to it and wasn't prepared to start tonight. Unfortunately the mask probably didn't hide enough of her face that he wouldn't recognize her.

It was like some kind of morality play or Aesop's fable. She'd been the mean girl to a rather forgettable boy, and Chaz Browning had grown up to be the hottest, most *un*forgettable man she'd ever laid eyes on.

"It's him. It's really him."

"Your old friend?" asked Amelia.

"Something like that." Friend wasn't the word she'd use.

"He's totally checking you out."

Lulu shook off her shock and paid attention again, realizing that Viv was right. Chaz was eyeing her, a smile tugging at the corners of that incredible mouth. So maybe he had a short memory and didn't recall that he had reason to hate her guts. Or maybe he'd just grown up and looked back at their childhood days through a softer lens, as she had.

She gave him a bright, sunny smile back, shoving away her sexual interest, forcing herself to remember this was an old frenemy. No way did she want him to know she'd been drooling over him.

He started to come over, probably to say hello, ask how she was settling in to city life, maybe make small talk about the old days. She glanced away, focusing on her drink, running her fingertips over the condensation on the glass, feigning a nonchalance she definitely did not feel.

"Hi," a man's voice said a moment later. It was Chaz's voice, with many years' worth of maturity added on. He stood behind her, and she felt the warmth of his big, broad body.

Willing her cheeks not to pinken and her voice not to quiver, she glanced up at him. "Hi, yourself."

"Happy Halloween."

"Same to you."

He gestured toward her glass. "I'd offer to buy you a drink, but it seems you're full-up. How's the special?"

"Remember the taste of kids' cherry-flavored cough syrup?"

"Uh-huh."

"That tasted better."

"Think I'll stick to beer."

"Good choice," she said. "I like your costume."

He glanced down at his loose cotton T-shirt and those wickedly worn jeans. "Guy next door?"

Huh. Funny. "I meant the ghost. Why'd you take it off?"

"I'm not so great with scissors. I cut the eye holes too small and couldn't see where the hell I was going."

She laughed. Chaz had never had much hand-eye co-ordination. But she'd bet he could do some utterly amazing things with those hands now, and the heavily-lashed green eyes were enough to make a girl melt.

"Still a fan of the homemade costume, huh?"

"My mother would kill me if I got a store-bought one."

Yeah. She remembered. Their moms had coordinated outfits every holiday, though they couldn't always please everybody. One year, when she'd wanted to be Sailor Moon, she'd had to go as a stupid Power Ranger instead because it was Chaz's favorite show. She'd even had to be the yellow ranger, since his spoiled sister had called dibs on the pink one.

She'd repaid him by stealing every one of the chocolate bars from his trick-or-treat bag and replacing them with raisins.

Lord, she'd been such a little terror.

Chaz hadn't been the only one with a pesky younger sibling—her brother was his sister's age. The four of them had grown up together, squabbling, competing. It hadn't been all-out war, though, until their siblings started dating in high school—and then had a messy breakup. She wasn't sure Lawrence had ever got over Sarah dumping him. But that had happened after Chaz had left home. He might not even realize that his sister was a heartbreaking butthead.

"I had no time to figure out something more elaborate," he explained. "I only decided to come here about an hour ago."

"That's some serious last-minute costume design," she said.

"Hey, cut me some slack. I just got back into town this morning after a long overseas trip. I hadn't even remembered it was Halloween until I got home and saw the decorations. Good thing I had a clean sheet in my linen closet."

"And good thing it was plain white and didn't have Teenage Mutant Ninja Turtles all over it."

He barked a laugh, raising a brow, as if surprised she'd remembered those sheets or those turtles he'd been so obsessed with.

"I think I've outgrown my mutant turtle days."

"Strictly into human ninjas now, huh?"

His eyes twinkled. "Yeah, that's it. Unfortunately, I haven't found a California-king sheet set with little black-cloaked ninja dudes on them."

Mmm. Big bed. For a big guy. With big hands. *And a big...*

"I'm afraid I'm stuck with boring, non-decorative sheets."

She swallowed and forced her mind back to light small talk and away from thoughts of his sheets. Or his bed. Him in his bed... "I'll keep an eye out for ninjas for you. Unless you'd prefer Transformers."

"Nah, I'm good." He grinned and the earth rocked a bit. "Though, if you see black satin, let me know. I might be tempted to play ninja."

She gulped, wondering when on earth he'd gotten so damned confident. He was easygoing, sexy, masculine and totally comfortable in a room full of people. No longer the male wallflower, the kid whose shoelaces were tied together by bullies, or who got picked last for the baseball team because he'd dropped a fly ball and lost the big game in fourth grade.

No. He was all sexy, powerful, enticing, grown-up man. And she just had no idea what to think about that.

"You must be awfully tired," Viv said, interjecting herself into the playful conversation. "After traveling all day."

Funny, Lulu had almost forgotten she was there. Amelia, too. Chaz, while offering the other two women a polite smile, hadn't paid a moment of attention to either of them. That made Lulu feel better—her old childhood nemesis/ friend hadn't come over merely to get Lulu to introduce him to Viv, who usually cast other females in the shade. Lulu wasn't sure whether it was because Viv was so beautiful, or because she was such a stone-cold bitch to most men that they felt challenged to break through the ice. Her costume, a sexy devil, seemed more than a little appropriate. As did Amelia's, who was dressed as a cute rag doll, complete with a yarn wig she'd made herself using supplies from her craft shop.

Hmm. She wondered if Chaz would say she, too, was appropriately costumed for her personality.

"I guess I am tired," he admitted.

"I'll say. Sounds like all you can think of is your bed," Viv said, her smile still knowing, a wicked gleam in her eyes.

Chaz didn't nibble at the bait. In fact, he didn't even seem to notice he was being flirted with. "I probably shoulda crashed, but I was in need of some American holiday fun. There's not a single piece of candy corn in Pakistan. So I decided to come out to combat the jet lag."

"And eat candy corn?" Lulu asked, unhappy Viv was working her vixen magic on her old friend. Well, her old *something*.

"Exactly. Have any on you?"

"I'm all out. I guess you'll have to trick-or-treat through the neighborhood on your way home."

"I forgot my sack."

"Then you're just out of luck."

He sighed. "Day late and a treat short. Story of my life."

Yeah. Because of mean girls who stole his candy bars.

She didn't bring that up, though. No point reminding him of her antics if there was any chance in hell he'd forgotten them.

As if. That'd be like Batman forgetting the Joker's antics. Once an arch nemesis, always an arch nemesis.

Not that she'd ever really considered Chaz her nemesis, arch or otherwise. But he might have one or two reasons to think *she* was. Including a crooked tailbone.

"Well, pull up a chair and join us," said Viv, scooting over to make room for him. She cast Lulu a piercing look, waiting for her to officially introduce them.

She was about to, but he cut her off.

"Actually, I just wanted to see if you'd like to dance," he said, staring down at Lulu, his gaze wavering between friendly and intense. She had to wonder if he, too, had been shocked by the changes nine years had wrought. She didn't much resemble the stringy-haired, braces-wearing seventeen-year-old he probably remembered from his high school graduation party. The one when she'd pushed him into the swimming pool, fully clothed, because he'd called her flat-chested.

To be fair, she *had* been a late bloomer. Of course, he hadn't really needed to point that out in front of all their friends and family.

She sat up a little straighter and thrust that no-longer-flat chest out the tiniest bit.

His gaze shifted. He noticed. She noticed him noticing.

"Well?" he asked, his voice dropping to a more intimate tone. "What do you say?"

"Uh…you really want to dance? With *me?*"

She was pretty sure the only time they'd ever danced together was when they'd had to be square-dancing partners in gym class in middle school. It hadn't gone well. Holding hands with Chaz had been way too weird for her twelve-year-old self. Her hands had gotten sweaty, her breath short, and she'd had the strangest fluttering in her stomach.

She now suspected what the sweating and fluttering had been all about. She *had* liked Chaz's blushes, despite what she'd said to her mother. But back then, never wanting to admit such a thing, she'd convinced herself that holding hands with Chaz Browning was enough to make her want to throw up.

So she'd done what any bratty twelve-year-old would

do. She'd stuck out her foot and tripped him during their do-si-do.

Little bitch.

"You know how to dance, right?" Another green twinkle—how had she never noticed he had the most interesting golden streaks that cut through the irises, looking like starbursts? "I mean, it's pretty easy—you just try to find the beat in the music and move around to it."

She licked her lips, hearing the band finishing "Time Warp," which immediately made her think of pelvic thrusts—not something she should be thinking about when it came to Chaz. Luckily the musicians segued right into a torchy version of "Witchcraft." That somehow seemed appropriate, given her costume, and the fact that she felt as if someone had cast a spell on her. The song was slower, jazzier, and would necessitate close-up dancing, with hands and bodies in direct contact. And though her mind decided that was even riskier than pelvic thrusts, her legs launched her out of her chair immediately.

"Sure."

She let him take her hand and pull her toward the crowded dance floor. When he grabbed her hips and pulled her close, she swallowed hard, trying to maintain her smile. Could he feel her crazily-beating heart or see the way her pulse thrummed in her throat? And was there any way in hell he didn't know that some of her most female parts were standing at attention as their bodies brushed together?

Lulu waited for him to say something—*Welcome to D.C., How's the new place?, How are your folks?* But he remained silent, merely moving his thigh between her legs as they swayed.

Lord have mercy. Though she'd often imagined having Chaz's throat between her hands so she could strangle him for saying something that totally pissed her off, she'd never fantasized about having any part of him between her thighs.

He'd been gone from her life before she'd realized stomach flutters and thigh clenching were definite signs of lust.

But now her body was reacting to him in a way she'd never allowed her mind to. There was no mistaking her reaction for anything except excitement. Her palms were sweating and her whole body felt hot and sticky, as though if she didn't get her clothes off, she would melt right into a puddle of want in the middle of the dance floor.

God, he was so big and strong compared to the boy she'd known. Powerful, male, appealing enough to stop hearts. His chest was so broad it could be used as a life raft. She couldn't help twining her fingers in his longish hair, tousled from the sheet, shaggy from a few months' travel.

The truth slammed into her, hard and life-changing.

She wanted him. Badly. Lulu wanted to go to bed with Chaz Browning and see if all the years of angry tension between them could be erased by erotic tension.

If only he were some random guy she'd just met, and the baggage of an entire childhood of fighting and competing, not to mention family drama, didn't stand between them. If only he were just a sexy stranger like Schaefer, albeit one with charm, easy wit and personality.

Unfortunately, he wasn't a stranger. Despite how closely he held her, Chaz couldn't possibly have forgotten her childhood shenanigans and his own disdain toward her. There was no way he'd look at her as anything but the bane of his youth and the scorn of his adulthood. Plus there was the family-connection burden of looking after her. His email had said he'd promised his mom he'd do exactly that once he was back in the country, like she was some high schooler on a field trip to the big bad city. An inconvenience. A brat.

No, anything remotely resembling a sexual connection between her and Chaz was simply out of the question. She was just going to have to go home and get cozy with her vibrator, or say to hell with it and bang the boring guitar player. Anything to avoid letting Chaz realize he'd affected her so deeply. That would be worse than the sweaty hands/square dancing incident.

"The music's good tonight," he finally said. "Schaefer and his band have improved since the last time I heard them play."

"You know him?"

"Yeah, he's sort of a regular in the neighborhood and he was a soloist for a while. But he was a bit of a hippie. He'd get into trouble, sneaking out of upbeat background music and into some depressing, sixties, psychedelic-mushroom ballad once in a while. Talk about a mood killer. The bar owners threatened to ban him."

"Do you know his first name?"

Chaz grinned. "I do."

"What is it?"

"If I told you, I'd have to kill you. He made me promise."

"Must be a doozy."

He nodded slowly. "Let's just say…it's appropriate."

"Can't I bribe it out of you?"

"What'll you give me?"

"All the Tootsie Rolls from my goodie bag?"

"I'm not interested in candy," he told her, that half smile lingering on a mouth so kissable it made her own go dry.

"I thought you were jonesing for candy corn."

"Maybe I'd rather taste something else sweet."

Whoa. The twinkle in his eye and the flash of that

dimple took the light comment and brought it up to flirtatious—maybe even suggestive—level. It was totally unlike anything he'd *ever* said to her. She had to wonder how many drinks he'd had, or if he'd been drinking them on an empty, jet-lagged stomach. She just didn't believe a sober Chaz would've made that kind of comment—not to her, anyway.

"Like what?" she asked, her tone just as flirty and suggestive, calling his bluff. She knew he'd put a stop to the conversation any second, but couldn't deny she was having fun while it lasted.

"That drink left your lips looking very red and delicious."

Good God, was he going to kiss her? The way his gaze focused in on her face said he was considering it, and her heart pounded in her chest. It was crazy. They hadn't even played doctor as kids, much less snuck even the most innocent of kisses. But he was eyeing her mouth as if he was parched and needed to positively drink from her.

"I have to admit, this conversation is taking me by surprise," she said, hearing the breathiness in her own voice and wondering what he would make of it.

"You can't be surprised that I think you're beautiful."

"I most certainly am," she said with a forced smile. Chaz, the boy who'd once called her a soul-sucking leech, thought she was beautiful?

Yeah. He had to be drunk.

"Every man here thinks it," he said, sounding totally serious. "I saw you the minute I walked in and couldn't take my eyes off you." Glancing down at her body, he smiled wickedly. "You surprised me. I always assumed witches were old and ugly."

"Only bad witches are ugly," she pointed out, catching his *Wizard of Oz* reference.

"And you're a very good witch?"

"Some would debate that. Maybe I'm a little of both."

"Which witch are you tonight?"

"Which witch do you hope I am?"

His green eyes glittered under the dance floor lights. "Maybe a little of both."

Hmm.

"Just remind me not to drop a house on you."

"Or douse me with water," she said with a grin, liking how easy they were with each other. Old friends flirting a little, reminiscing a little. Because they *were* both exploring a shared memory.

It had been her eleventh Halloween. She'd wanted to be a Spice Girl, but in a repetition of the Sailor Moon fiasco, of course the boys wouldn't go for what she wanted, so they'd all done a *Wizard of Oz* thing. Chaz had been the Scarecrow, Lawrence, her brother, the Tin Man, her dog was Toto, and Chaz's dog was the Cowardly Lion. Only, as if he understood his role and wasn't happy about being labeled a coward, the ornery beagle had wriggled out of his lion mane and hidden it in his doghouse before they'd even started trick-or-treating.

As for the rest…well, of course Sarah had been Dorothy and Lulu had been the Wicked Witch of the West. Complete with green flour paste all over her face, a scraggly wig, horrific hat and butt-ugly dress. Not exactly the Posh Spice she'd pictured.

She was pretty sure Sarah was the one who'd gotten raisins in place of chocolate bars that year. Hell, maybe all of them had.

"One thing's for sure, I don't ever remember witches wearing black leather bustiers," he said.

"Or spider-web patterned tights?" she said with an eyebrow wag. She *so* loved the tights.

"The skirt and those heels don't hurt, either."

Yeah, most witches probably didn't wear flouncy, lacy black miniskirts, or screw-me shoes with silver chains around the ankles. All of which she'd donned to attract a guy who now held absolutely no interest for her, and which had instead drawn the eye of one she'd known forever, but had never really allowed herself to *see* until now. Strange, strange world.

"Back to the point. I noticed you, and then you smiled at me."

Yes, she had. A big, friendly, please-don't-figure-out-what-I've-been-thinking smile. "So I did."

"You have an *amazing* smile. Welcoming and uninhibited."

His tone was sincere, his eyes gleaming with something she couldn't quite place. Tenderness? Maybe that. Chaz had always had a nice, tender streak, which other kids had tried to crush. Her included, on occasion.

"When I saw that gorgeous smile, and realized it was directed at me, I figured you felt it, too."

"Felt what?" Right now all she felt was dazed by words she'd never expected to hear from *him* of all people.

He lifted a hand and dragged it through a long strand of her glittery, red-dyed hair, rubbing it lightly, then twining it in his fingers. "Attraction. Heat."

His bluntness shocked her. "Are you serious?"

"Completely."

She couldn't speak, honestly could not find a word to say.

"I've surprised you again?"

Nodding slowly, she admitted, "Just a bit."

"Sorry. I've been out of the country too long. I've lost my manners and forgotten how this game's supposed to be played."

"Are we playing a game?"

"Oh, yeah."

He breathed deeply to inhale the scent of her hair, and lightly, oh, so lightly, kissed her temple, just above the edge of the mask.

She managed to stay upright at this first-ever kiss between them, even though worlds rocked and tides changed and planets skipped out of orbit at the brush of his lips on her skin.

Every instinct she owned was telling her that this wasn't Chaz, that he'd been replaced by a doppelgänger who didn't hate her, who saw her as the sensual woman she'd become and not the mean-spirited kid he'd once known. What other explanation was there? A dream?

This is really happening, isn't it?

"What kind of game?" she finally asked.

Another brush of soft lips on her pulse point, then he inhaled deeply, as if imprinting her scent on his memory. "The kind that ends with us in bed."

"Holy shit."

He laughed. "Shocked you that time, huh?"

"Oh, *hell* yes."

"Sorry. It's just been a long while since I've been with anyone. A long time since I've wanted to, to be perfectly honest. And the minute I saw that smile, I just…wanted you."

How on earth could this sexy, forthright, demanding guy have been born out of the shy, nerdy boy she'd known?

"I know it's quick, and it's crazy. I don't usually do this. Actually, I don't think I've ever moved so fast with a woman in my life. But the truth is, I want to take you out of here and have sex with you like the sun's not gonna come up tomorrow."

Whoa.

This time, she couldn't keep her feet steady. Her ankle twisted and she stumbled in the attractive-but-miserably-uncomfortable high heels. If he hadn't had his arms wrapped around her, she would have fallen right at his feet.

"Okay, point taken. I'm going too fast," he said as he held her tightly against him, so she could feel every rope of muscle, each ounce of masculinity. Including a ridge in his pants that said he was not in any way, shape, or form a boy. He was all, total, 100 percent powerful man.

"Fast? You could be in a car commercial about going from zero to one-twenty in ten seconds flat."

"Sorry," he said with an I'm-not-really-sorry shrug. "Let's back up, play this the normal way, with introductions. I'm not mysterious like the guitarist. My name's Chaz. What's yours?"

Gasping, she stumbled over her own feet again. Chaz tightened his grip on her hips, preventing her weak, suddenly trembling legs from giving out on her. Her head spun, her thoughts pinging around like a ball in a pinball machine until the reality settled in and became something she believed.

Son of a bitch.

"My…my name?"

"Yeah. You have one, don't you?"

She nodded, her brain still scrambling.

He didn't recognize her. Chaz Browning had no idea who she was. That's why he could make those suggestive comments to her—he had no clue he'd been making them to the girl he'd grown up with!

The truth of it settled in, and she went over the past several minutes in her mind. He'd seen her, noting the costume, and of course the mask that covered two-thirds of her face. But he hadn't recognized *her,* Lulu, the bane of his childhood.

Actually, it did make sense. It was stupid of her to think he would have recognized her at a glance, across a crowded bar, after nine years. He'd remember her as a kid, and right now she was wearing a very sexy costume, and her hair was red and curly. Why on earth would he have known her?

She should have realized that. In her own defense, she could only say she hadn't been thinking clearly, she'd been too affected by the grown-up version of the boy she'd known. She was still affected by him, in fact, and growing more so by the minute.

"How potent are those red drinks?" he asked, laughter in his voice. "If they induce amnesia, they should come with a warning label."

"Pretty potent."

She smiled weakly as the truth of the situation continued to settle in to all the most adventurous parts of her brain. A world of possibilities opened up like a long road at the start of an exciting journey. She was a stranger to him. Just a sexy stranger, a hot woman Chaz Browning was trying to pick up.

And, although an hour ago she'd never have dreamed it possible, she was seriously considering letting him.

"Umm...let's hold off on the name thing for a while."

His eyes widened as if he thought she was kidding. When he realized she wasn't, he shrugged. "If you say so."

She did say so, because she was still trying to figure things out. Things like how much she wanted him. Whether she could have him.

Despite the obstacles—their careers, her bratty past that had to have left him hating her, their siblings' angry relationship, their parents' lifelong friendship, and all the stolen candy bars and broken tailbones history that said they could never make a relationship work—she found herself wanting him more than she'd ever wanted a man in her life.

Her curiosity ate at her, of course, and the attraction had been instantaneous. But it was more than that. She had known him as a child, and she greatly wanted to know him as a man. Would the sparks they'd shot off each other throughout their lives transition into a different kind of heat altogether?

Just once, for one wild night, could she have him? Take him, be with him, get the longing and the ache out of her system and then go back to being his friend/enemy without hurting anyone or letting things get complicated? Was that possible?

Catwoman and Batman managed it.

Sure. Nemeses to lovers worked sometimes, if only in the short run. Maybe it wasn't smart, but it was at least possible.

It also sounded very exciting.

There was just one problem. It *had* to be in the short run. There was no way they could have any kind of future, not with all the baggage and the family issues. Besides, he was an internationally traveling reporter—and she intended to stay right here and change the world in other ways.

Meaning if something happened between them, it had to be a one-shot deal. Something with no drama, no angsting, no questions even.

Which meant Chaz could never know the truth.

If she slept with him tonight, she had to make damn sure he never found out who she actually was. And that meant she had to stay in control.

2

CHAZ HAD MET plenty of beautiful women before.

He'd traveled all over the world covering stories of glamorous spies, interacting with powerful politicians and sexy stars. He'd had a few more lovers than a nice small-town-boy should probably ever admit to having. He'd been in love once, infatuated twice, and in lust dozens of times. But he'd never felt his heart stop beating in his chest at the sight of a woman's smile.

Until tonight. Until her.

This stranger, this redhead with a half mask that made her dark eyes gleam nearly black, had a smile that could stop the world on its axis. Her amazing body and mysteriously beautiful face had caught his eye the minute he'd entered. But that smile…nations could rise or fall on a smile like that. And now, having her in his arms, he knew there wasn't much he wouldn't give to make sure this night ended just as he'd told her he wanted it to. Whether he ever learned her name or not.

"Penny for your thoughts?" he asked when she settled back into his arms, her clumsiness an adorable indicator that she was interested, maybe even turned on, by his suggestive comments.

The music changed, the torchy song swinging into something a little faster, but neither of them separated. They continued the sexy, sultry glide of hip to hip, thigh on thigh.

"My thoughts'll cost you a nickel," she said, her voice a bit deeper, throatier than before. As if she was intentionally ratcheting up the flirtation level. She'd gone from sweet to sexy, if only in her tone.

"Inflation sucks."

"Okay, the first one's free. One of the things I was thinking is that I should thank you for preventing me from falling on my ass in front of all of these people."

"Those are some dangerous shoes you're wearing."

"It's not the shoes," she admitted.

"So, it's the company?"

"More like the conversation."

"Should I apologize?"

She snagged a lush lower lip between her teeth, and slowly shook her head. "No. Please don't. I like a man who says what's really on his mind. That's pretty rare."

"Especially in this city. Honesty is a lost art here."

She glanced down toward the floor, toward those oh-so-sexy shoes with the silver chains that resembled handcuffs. Damn, the moment he'd spotted them, they'd put some seriously wicked ideas in his head.

Lately, he'd been living in a high-adrenaline, high-risk zone. People in those situations couldn't hesitate to take risks, even though they never knew what dangers might be lurking around the corner. He apparently hadn't gotten out of that mindset—out of the need to go for what you wanted the moment you spotted it, because you might not get another chance.

Maybe if he'd met her a week from now, he'd never have told this beautiful stranger what he was really thinking. Maybe as soon as tomorrow, he'd regret having done it.

At this moment, though, looking at her luscious mouth and losing himself in those dark, deep-set eyes, he didn't regret a damn thing.

"Are you really not going to give me your name?"

She hesitated.

"Do I have to pay for that, too? I'm not sure I have enough nickels. Or any American money at all, to be honest."

"So I take it I'm buying the first round?"

"Maybe we can go somewhere else where the drinks are cheaper," he said, staring intently into her dark eyes, wishing he could see her whole face without the admittedly sensual mask.

There was something erotic about her anonymity. He had no doubt she was beautiful beneath the mask, but couldn't deny the anticipation of removing it was exciting.

"Where did you have in mind?"

"I live a couple of blocks from here."

She licked those lips, sending another sharp stab of lust surging through him. Damn, the woman was getting to him with every single breath she took. He'd been sexually on edge since he'd left for his trip a few months ago, and certainly hadn't had any relief during it. Now, knowing her all of fifteen minutes, he was ready to rip her sexy bustier open, yank her skirt off, and explore every delicious inch of her.

"That's certainly something to keep in mind," she said. "But didn't you say we were backing up? I think you're directionally challenged. That was pretty forward."

He laughed, enjoying her bluntness, her humor. She was

refreshing, challenging and sharp. He was starting to like her as well as want her.

"Okay. Sorry. Backing up." The music changed, and he said, "Want to go grab a drink? At the bar, not at my place."

She nodded and let him lead her toward the bar. He shouldered his way in, calling their drink orders to one of the harried-looking bartenders.

"Do you need money?" she asked.

He shook his head. "I was kidding. I can cover it."

She stuck out her hand. "Okay, then, where's my nickel?"

Laughing, enjoying everything about her, he dug a coin out of his pocket and dropped it into her hand.

"Ahh, the beautiful feel of cold hard nickels."

Drinks in hand, he led her away from the table where she'd been sitting with her friends. No way did he want to sit with the shark who'd eyed him like he was chum. He had to wonder what this woman had been doing with somebody like that, since she didn't seem at all on-the-make as her dark-haired friend did, or, actually, as innocent as the lighter-haired one seemed.

His witch was just right.

Heading toward a small empty high-top in the corner, he put their drinks on it, and then helped her hop up onto a stool. She crossed one leg over the other. The position revealed a devastatingly sexy length of thigh, and he swallowed hard as he took his seat opposite her.

He sipped the drink, having gotten the special for himself, and grimaced. "Yeah. Cough syrup."

"I warned ya."

"I had to try one holiday-themed drink, and the only other choice was some green, glow-in-the-dark ectoplasm stuff."

They talked drinks for a few minutes, and then music. He realized they had very similar tastes. She was a great conversationalist, but he would never remember half of what she said. He just lost himself staring at her and listening to that sexy, throaty voice—which occasionally tipped up into a more normal tone, one that seemed familiar to him somehow. He was about to ask if she had a cold, or if she'd been around a smoker, but she asked him something first.

"So, Chaz, why were you overseas?" she asked, taking over the conversation. That was a good thing, since he wasn't sure he'd be able to think of anything except how much he was dying to taste that vulnerable spot on the hollow of her throat.

Besides, it was better than *Nice weather we're having.*

"I'm a journalist. I was following a story in Pakistan and ended up staying in Islamabad to help with a new media outfit."

"That sounds exciting."

"It can be. Some days are just routine, but the situation there is just so…unsettled." *Well, that's the understatement of the night.*

"So I hear."

Remembering some of the darker parts of his trip—the things he'd seen and wished he could forget—he admitted, "It's a completely different world."

One where he'd witnessed some of the worst—but also, he had to concede, some of the best—of humanity. Dirt and poverty warred with decency and a strong desire for a better life. He'd met people he would consider good friends…and others to whom he would never have turned his back for fear of them sticking a knife in it. It had been like living on a high wire for two months, but, quite honestly, it was what he lived for. He'd always hated liars as a kid, and now he got to bring down the biggest and worst all over the world. Still, it was exhausting, and he was glad to be back in the U.S. of A. Particularly at the start of the whole holiday season. His parents hadn't expected him home for Thanksgiving and he looked forward to calling them tomorrow to tell them he'd be there.

"Were you in real danger?"

"I never really felt like it, except the two times I crossed over into Afghanistan. Things got a little hairy on the second trip."

She gasped. "Are you crazy? How could you take a risk like that?"

"Chasing a story," he said, amused at her response. She'd reacted as though she were a disapproving family member rather than a woman he'd just met. "Believe me, there wasn't a minute when I wasn't aware of my surroundings."

"Your family must not have been happy about your being there."

That inspired a brief laugh. "You think I'm insane? I didn't tell them!"

He'd swear she was frowning in disapproval beneath that mask. "Maybe it's good you didn't. I'm sure your parents would have been terrified for you."

"Yes, they would have," he said, wondering if she, too, had overprotective parents. "That's why I didn't say anything to them. The trips were in-and-out, neither lasting longer than thirty-six hours. No point in worrying anybody when I was so far away and nothing they could have said would have changed my mind about going anyway."

"I read about some journalists who were attacked there last spring."

His hand tightened around his glass, an instinctive reaction, and a familiar pang of sorrow stabbed him in the gut. "Yes, I knew one of them. She was a wonderful photojournalist." Her death had been part of what made him so conscious of his surroundings for every second of the trip—and so determined to keep doing what he was doing.

Maybe that was also one reason why he was being a little reckless tonight. He'd been tense for weeks, he needed to let loose, shake off the last vestiges of emotional darkness, be around someone exciting and daring. Someone like *her*.

"All I can say is it's great to be home where…"

"Where you can proposition a sexy stranger?"

He smiled, incredibly grateful that she'd lightened the mood again. It was as if she'd read his mind and understood he'd gone as far as he wanted to go on the memory-lane trip.

"Uh-oh, I think you were the one who stepped forward that time."

"Sideways, maybe. The question was related to the subject at hand."

"So it was." He tossed back the rest of his drink, stood, and offered her his hand. "Let's dance again."

She immediately rose, twining her soft fingers with his. He squeezed lightly, wondering why he had such a sudden, shocking feeling of rightness at it being there. Funny, how quickly she was affecting him.

They were back on the dance floor, swaying to another bluesy Halloweenish song, when he remembered what she'd said back at the table. "So, you think you're sexy, do you?"

"I think *you* think I am."

Sexy enough to stop his heart. "Oh? You seem pretty self-assured."

"Well, you gave me a hint with your have-sex-like-the-sun-isn't-gonna-come-up-tomorrow line."

"That wasn't a line," he said, his voice steady, resolute. "It was a promise."

She wobbled again. Damn, he loved rocking her out of her spike-heeled shoes that were more of a sexual invitation than a foot covering.

"Now who's the self-assured one?" she whispered.

"I guess that makes us a good pair."

"I wasn't the one who made suggestive comments about suns not rising."

"But you didn't slap my face and walk away, either."

"No, I didn't."

She lifted her chin and squared her shoulders, so obviously trying to regain the upper hand, he almost laughed. "So, the whole sun-not-coming-up thing. What does it mean, anyway? Aside from the obvious."

He quirked a brow. "Huh?"

"Why would the sun not coming up make the sex better? Is it because it would go on so long since the night would never end?"

She tried to sound arch and noncommittal, but he could already read this woman very well. Part of her was urging him on, another trying to throw up artificial barriers to buy herself time to figure out where on earth they were going with this attraction.

"Or do you need to be in the dark?" She gasped a little, the sound over-exaggerated. "Are you…deformed in some way?"

"Wicked witch coming out to play?" he said with a lazy grin, not letting her get the rise out of him she was trying to.

"Do you like her?"

"A lot."

"Maybe you haven't seen her at her wickedest yet."

He couldn't make it out entirely, but he'd swear he could

see a twinkle in those dark, mask-encircled eyes. She was teasing him. Daring him. *Two steps forward again.*

"I look forward to it. To answer your question, I have no problem in the light or the dark. I'm quite comfortable getting naked and utterly wild in broad daylight."

She quivered the tiniest bit before replying, "You certainly did put on a show here."

He tilted his head to the side, curious as to what she meant.

"When you were taking off your sheet, you pulled your shirt almost all the way off." Wagging an index finger at him, she said, "You had to have noticed. Were you just showing off that back and those shoulders?"

He barked a loud laugh, hearing the compliment hidden within the complaint. "I swear, I didn't realize it right away."

She harrumphed. "Well, every woman in the place did."

Including her. How nice.

"By the way," he said, remembering he'd never answered her question, not surprising given the strange turns they'd taken in this twisty conversation, "I was thinking more along the lines of last-night-on-earth sex."

Her brow furrowed, then she realized what he was talking about. "Ah. We're back to the sun not coming up?"

"Right." Wondering if she would notice his own determined eye twinkle, he took the charm up a notch. "You know, the world's gonna end, you have a few hours left, how else do you spend it?"

"Catching up on *The Walking Dead?* Eating pizza?" *Step back.*

He didn't let her distract him. *Forward. Like dancing.* "I was thinking more along the lines of lying naked in someone's arms."

Another flick of that pretty pink tongue on her lush lips.

She remained silent, not moving in either direction.

So he verbally advanced again…and again.

"Touching, tasting, exploring every erotic possibility. Giving and receiving so much pleasure, the experience leaves a mark on the world that lasts through the end of time."

"Well, I suppose that sounds better than zombies."

"Thanks."

She pulled her hand away and smoothed her hair, lifting it off her neck as if she'd suddenly gotten very hot. Still, she tried her best to regain control. "You know, that mark on the world wouldn't last very long if the world was ending."

Jesus, the woman was killing him here. He couldn't guess which witch he was going to get from one moment to the next. Not that it mattered. He just wanted to kiss her, to screw her, to laugh with her.

"I was speaking metaphorically. I'm a writer. Sue me."

"Do you really think the earth would end if the sun didn't come up?" she asked. "I mean, just to clarify, I realize you're a writer, not a scientist, but it's possible something would survive to…"

He cut her off. "I don't care. I just know the earth might end if I don't get to kiss you soon."

She giggled.

"Cheesy?"

"Maybe a little."

"How's this? If you don't come home with me and let me fuck your brains out tonight, I might never get over it."

Those beautiful lips parted and she breathed across them, breathy sighs in every exhalation. She stared up at him, searchingly, questioningly, and he never broke the stare, letting her see he didn't regret the words and truly meant them.

"You surprise me more and more, Chaz."

"In a good way?"

A slow, deliberate nod as she assessed him, brown eyes glowing. "Definitely. And FYI, I don't think I'd ever get over it, either."

Oh, thank God.

They danced a little more, but now a thick, sexual silence built between them, surging louder and hotter as the music underscored everything they'd said, everything they'd fantasized, everything they wanted. He had no doubt she was thinking the same thing he was—about getting out of here, being alone somewhere. He couldn't wait to find out if these incredible sparks they shot off each other would start a blaze with their first real kiss and become volcanic in bed.

The music shifted again, this time to a faster song that didn't necessitate slow dancing. Both of them ignored that, though, and kept close, swaying, thrusting, mindless and silent. Every brush of her body against his, every shared breath, every stroke of his fingers against the small of her back or press of his thigh against hers was heightening things to ever more intense levels. Her hands did wild and wicked things, riding low on his hips. She kissed his throat, scraping her teeth along his collarbone, which made him groan lightly and repay her in kind until the groan was hers.

Finally, she stopped moving and inched away from him. She distanced herself enough to suck in a few deep, calming, audible breaths. Her lips were full, swollen, her eyes luminous behind the mask. Her whole body was pink and flushed. Her nipples were pebbled, visible even beneath the sexy bustier. A warm, womanly scent rose from her, filling his head, making his mouth water and his brain fog as he realized just how aroused she had become.

Other people on the floor merely moved around them, grinning, casting knowing looks, aware he and his mystery woman had been all but having sex in the middle of the crowd. He'd bet they weren't the only ones.

"Are you okay?" he asked. He wondered if she'd drag him out the door, which was what he most wanted her to do. He mentally held his breath, waiting for her to decide.

"I was getting overheated," she said.

"I noticed," he said, realizing if she listened hard enough, she wouldn't hear teasing, but pure, utter desire in his words.

A long pause. A longer stare.

"I feel like I've known you forever," he admitted, wondering why everything about her appealed to him so deeply.

Wrong thing to say, apparently. She stiffened the tiniest bit. And back she stepped.

"I, uh…look, it's a holiday, we might be acting out of character. I don't want either of us to do anything we might someday regret." Her breaths had slowed, her color returning to normal. "So let's maybe just stay here for a while longer?"

As if he would ever regret making love to this woman? Fat chance. Of course, he'd only met her an hour ago, so he supposed she had a right to slow things down. Again.

He found himself enjoying their sexual dance, the push-and-pull, back-and-forth, a lot. The chase was building his excitement, lifting the anticipation until it hung around them like a vapor.

"I understand. I like dancing with you."

Her relieved sigh told him she'd been holding her breath physically as well as mentally, waiting to see if he was going to agree to cool off or keep up the flirtation.

"Thanks," she said, moving into his arms again, though

he noticed she kept an inch or two of overheated air between their bodies. "Believe me, I'm not a cock-tease. It's just…I don't want either of us to have any regrets."

"I won't," he said, meaning it.

Chaz couldn't help wondering what was making her so skittish. She was hot and sexy one moment, funny and chatty the next. He liked both personalities, but it was the hot and sexy one he wanted to spend the night with. Still, he already suspected he wanted to have breakfast with funny and chatty.

He supposed he wasn't thinking about this in the typical-guy one-night-stand way. Chaz had had a few of those—quick lays, hurried goodbyes before the sun rose, scarcely another thought about the encounter. They were perils of a job that required him to travel a lot, rarely leaving him time to settle down and really get to know someone.

Now, though, he would be stateside for a while, possibly. And within hours of getting here, he'd found someone he really did want to get to know. While he could have taken it slow and played the dating game, the night was too wild, their connection too immediate and his desire for her too insistent. But that didn't mean one night was all he wanted.

Besides, he didn't know her name, and hadn't really seen her face yet. No way was he going to let her get away tonight without being sure of both. The woman could hardly hide behind a mask if they spent the whole night engaged in hot, steamy sex. As for her name and number, he'd kiss the info right off her lips if it was the last thing he ever did.

Whatever the name, he could at least try to start solving the mystery of her identity. "So, what about you? What do you do for a living?"

She relaxed in his arms. "I work for a nonprofit group providing microloans to single mothers in third-world countries."

"I've heard of those organizations," he said, trying to recall the details. "I actually talked to someone about that recently. Can't remember who."

Her throat worked visibly as she swallowed, and he felt her tension rise again "Well, it's a great cause," she said quietly. "But surely not as exciting as what you do."

"It's not about the excitement. Someone needs to hold these liars and fraudsters accountable. Just because they have power, or money or a 'good reason' doesn't excuse the damage they do."

She blanched and he realized he'd gone too far. "Sorry, I get a little wound up. I've been told I have 'trust issues.'"

"I can understand that, after what happened to your friend. Maybe we shouldn't talk shop."

"Okay, no work stuff. So, are you ready to give me your name?"

"Let's say I prefer to be a woman of mystery tonight."

He frowned.

"Is that a deal-breaker?"

He considered it, already suspecting one night with her wouldn't be enough. He'd definitely want to know how to reach her later. But the night was young, and if it ended up where he hoped it would, she'd still be in his arms in the morning. There would be time for details, he had no doubt. For now, the pulsating music, the eroticism of her sultry voice, the lights shining on her red hair, the blood-red remnants of her drink on her lips, the innate hunger... they were enough. Most definitely.

"No. Not a deal-breaker. I doubt you could say anything that would be."

One corner of her sexy mouth curved up in a tiny smile, and she gave a throaty chuckle. "Never say never."

Something came to mind. "You're not married, right?"

"Completely unattached."

He released the breath he hadn't realized he'd been holding. "Good."

"You?" she asked.

"Nope. I've been told I'm not marriage material."

She sneered. "Told by some woman who wanted you to commit before you were ready?"

"That's pretty perceptive."

"It's in the female phrasebook."

"I need to get one of those."

"That'll cost you more than a nickel. State secrets and all."

"I should already have one, considering I had a bunch of girls around growing up."

She stiffened slightly in his arms.

"Is family a touchy subject we are supposed to avoid, like witches and going back to my place for a drink?"

"No. I'm just picturing you as a kid."

"Don't bother. I was a born loser."

"I don't believe that," she said, suddenly vehement.

"If the word 'geek' is in that handbook of yours, my picture's beside it."

"Well, I bet the girls you grew up with feel pretty stupid now," she whispered.

"I doubt it," he replied, remembering his gawkiest years, when he'd been a skinny, uncoordinated sad-sack. "They wouldn't recognize me if they fell over me today."

She mumbled something that he couldn't catch—something like *I know what you mean*—which was interesting. Because he had a hard time picturing her ever being anything but gorgeous, and she was unforgettable. He would *never* forget that smile.

"It's all right," he told her. "Believe me, I'm not carrying around any angst from my childhood. Though, I do avoid going back to my small hometown as much as possible."

She cleared her throat. "You never go home to see your family because of the way other kids treated you?"

"Nah. I go once in a while, not for a few years, though. I'm busy traveling. My parents meet up with me sometimes—last year they came to Berlin when I was on assignment. And I should see my kid sister more now since she just started grad school here in D.C. this semester."

"Your sister is in the city?" She nibbled her lip. "Where does she go to school?"

"Sarah goes to American University."

She stopped dancing. "So does La...um, so does somebody I know. Small world."

"Yeah," he said, meaning it. He'd traveled enough of it to know. "Can we be done talking about our childhoods and our families now?"

"Oh, yes, please!"

"Good. Let's get back to discussing how red your lips are."

"Were we discussing that?"

"If we weren't, we should have been."

Her tongue flicked out and moistened those sensual lips, and he had to clench his teeth as the temperature went up another ten degrees.

"I wasn't lying. I am going to have to kiss you soon."

Her throat visibly worked as she swallowed. "Are you asking me or telling me?"

"Does it matter?"

He didn't give her a chance to answer; he couldn't wait anymore. Those red lips were driving him crazy, and he had to taste her or go completely mental right here on the dance floor. So without warning, he bent and caught her mouth with his. Her lips parted right away, warm, hungry and welcoming, and he kissed her deeply, tasting cherry, whiskey and woman.

She wrapped her arms around his neck, holding him tight, tilting her head and pressing even closer. Her tongue swept against his, thrusting, demanding, and he answered every thrust, each demand. She was sweet and hot, and every cell in his body came to attention, all electricity, fire and need.

Their heartbeats matched, racing, and the kiss went deeper, hotter, wetter. He sunk his hands into her thick, curling hair, and she grabbed his hips, tugging him hard against her, until his hardening cock was nestled low against her belly. They were surrounded in the club, but he didn't give a damn. He felt as though he needed her mouth to provide the very air in his lungs. Kissing her was like diving head first into a deep well filled with nothing but pleasure and excitement, and he had to forcibly pull his mouth away when he realized they were soon going to reach the point where it would be too agonizing to stop.

When it finally ended, they remained close, his forehead pressed against hers, both of them panting. He was rock-hard against her and she ground against him instinctively, as if her body had already made the decision she hadn't yet voiced.

"You ready to go get that drink at my place?" he asked, hearing the hoarse need in his own voice.

If she said no, he might just have to go into the bathroom and jerk off. If she said yes, he wasn't sure he'd be able to make it across the room and out the door without putting a bag over his crotch.

"I don't usually do this," she said, as if worried he might

think less of her. But how could he, when he was barely capable of thought at all?

"Honestly? Neither do I."

"So we're both feeling reckless tonight?"

He scraped his knuckles against her jaw, brushing his thumb over her well-kissed lips. "Maybe it's because there's just magic and madness in the air."

"You might be right," she said, smiling up at him as she twined her fingers in his hair. "Whatever the reason...yes, Chaz, I am ready to go get that drink."

3

LULU DIDN'T QUESTION her decision or second-guess herself. She simply laced her fingers with Chaz's, and let him lead her back over to her table so she could grab her things and say good-night. Viv had gone to the dance floor and was gyrating in the middle of a mosh pile of guys, and Amelia was talking to someone at the next table. As Lulu grabbed her purse and coat, Amelia raised a curious eyebrow but didn't ask any questions, merely wishing her a Happy Halloween and smiling at Chaz. Blessing the more tactful of her two friends, she let Chaz drag her out of the bar, both of them desperate to find someplace to be alone.

Lulu wasn't going to allow herself to think about how crazy this was. Nor could she dwell on how their families might react. She suspected all four parents would like the idea of the two of them together romantically, but they probably wouldn't love the whole one-night-stand thing, which was all this was going to be.

Hell, she couldn't even imagine how Chaz himself would react if he knew who she was! She was just going to do it—take something she wanted, and then let it go, content with the memories of an amazing experience that would be her secret forever more.

They got outside and the sharp October air filled her lungs, redolent with the scent of a log fire burning nearby. Everything about the night revealed the pleasures of autumn—a season she'd missed when going to college and grad school in Arizona. Dry leaves rustled on the trees and blew gently across the sidewalks. The stars filling the sky weren't too dimmed by the city lights, and the air was cold enough so little puffs were visible when they exhaled.

Dupont Circle was an area popular with people her age—young professionals, new grads, maybe a few families, but certainly none were out this late for any candy-begging. Inside every bar and coffeehouse, though, loud music played and voices could be heard even through closed doors. Few lingered on the streets. By now, folks in costume had arrived at their preferred holiday destinations and were staying inside, as an early cold snap had made D.C. a chilly place to be outside at this time of night.

"It's a perfect night for being wicked," she said, keeping her voice low, thick and throaty, as she'd tried to do once she'd realized he didn't know who she was. She might very well see him as herself in a few days and did not want to make herself so easily recognizable.

"I agree. I'm planning all kinds of wickedness with you."

"Are you sure you're not interested in candy corn anymore?" she asked with a flirtatious grin. "You could always try to find an all-night convenience store."

"Definitely not," he replied, dropping an arm across her shoulders, tugging her tightly against his body as they walked. "I wouldn't walk away from you right now if sweet old Lady Larsen from my hometown showed up with a whole box of Snickers bars."

A giggle escaped her lips but she quickly silenced it. As a stranger, she shouldn't know about old Lady Larsen, a neighbor of theirs when they'd grown up. She'd always given out full-size candy bars on Halloween. Every kid in town had hit her house.

"How far away is your place?" she asked, to cover her near-miss.

"Just a couple of blocks away," said Chaz.

Lulu already knew that. When his real estate agent had shown her the available rental properties around here, she'd pointed out the cute townhouse Chaz had bought last year. It was a couple of doors down from the carved-up brownstone in which Lulu had an apartment. They were almost as neighborly as they'd been growing up. Yikes.

That would make things very uncomfortable if he found out who she was, but should also make her getaway easier tonight.

"Will you be okay walking there in those shoes?" he asked, staring down at her feet with a frown.

"I'll be fine," she insisted, ready to run if it meant they could be alone and could get back to that crazy-wild-delicious kissing. And everything that came after it.

She'd walked to the bar, too. But she didn't reveal that, not wanting to let on that she lived around here. She was already being very careful, unwilling to leave him too many clues.

Of course, she might be overestimating her own sexual potency. Maybe tonight would be forgettable, and Chaz would never again wonder about the red-haired, green-masked witch he'd seduced on Halloween night. But she doubted it. Their chemistry was strong. She suspected the encounter would be something they'd both long remember.

"I'm glad it's close," she said. "I don't want to wait too long for that wickedness you promised."

They'd walked for less than a minute, hadn't even rounded the corner to turn onto his—their—street, but Chaz pulled her off the sidewalk into the shadows beside a credit-union building. "You don't have to wait another second."

She threw her arms around his neck and tugged him to her, parting her lips before they met his. They tasted each other as thoroughly as they had on the dance floor, but this was slower, less frantic, more erotic. The pulsing, seething hunger was there, but, as if they both knew it would soon be satisfied, they were content to kiss like pleasure-seeking lovers and not like strangers trying to figure out if one kiss was all they'd have.

Sharing merely one kiss with Chaz would have been a crime for the ages, she realized as he cupped her face in his hands and tilted his head. Their tongues danced. He swallowed down her sighs, tasting her, teasing her. His subtle cologne wafted to her nostrils and she went softer and wetter as the scent imprinted a sense memory in her, one she knew she would recall forever when she smelled his fragrance.

She couldn't wait to touch him. Remembering how easily the shirt had glided over that incredible body, she slid her hands around his lean hips, and pushed up. The shirt moved with her fingers, leaving her free to explore that hot male flesh. His body rippled with muscle, and was slick with desire-stoked sweat. She touched him, explored him, wanting to taste her way along every ridge and line.

"Christ," he mumbled against her mouth when she scraped her nails across his bare back.

Inflamed, he picked her up by the waist, wrapping her legs around his hips and supporting her entire weight. He swung around, bracing her against the building, kissing her more desperately. One big, powerful hand stroked the outside of her thigh, pushing up under the skirt.

The heat and friction of his fingers against the patterned tights heightened her awareness. She was conscious of every single sensation battering at her senses. Being completely in his control, held by him, explored by him, she closed her eyes and enjoyed it. Maybe it was the holiday, or the eroticism, or the drinks…something was making her lose every inhibition and give herself over to him and those magical hands.

Despite the possibility of discovery, he seemed unable to stop himself from touching her. Reaching up under her skirt and tugging at the waistband of her tights, he got them low enough to delve into.

"Naughty girl," he whispered against her mouth when he realized she wore no panties.

"Very naughty. Because right now, I wish the tights were crotchless," she admitted.

"I'd give a year off my life if they were," he said.

He made do by pulling the tights down a bit more, until he was holding her bare ass, stroking, squeezing.

"Mmm," she groaned, wanting more than anything for him to pull her legs even farther apart, opening her to him so he could slam into her right now.

He lifted her higher, shocking her with his strength. Long gone was the uncoordinated, weak little kid. She wondered if he now liked to pick up cars in his spare time.

Holding on to her with one arm, he began a determined, erotic exploration with his other hand. He pushed the tights down farther, until he could slide his hand between her cheeks. He touched her intimately, the sensations wickedly erotic, making her gasp with shocked pleasure. Her gasps turned into needy pleas as his fingers moved deeper, reaching the curls covering her sex and tangling in them.

Lulu arched eagerly toward the touch, wanting everything and more from him.

"I wanna drop to my knees and bury my face here," he said, his need making him handle her roughly, clenching her so tightly she'd probably have bruises tomorrow.

She didn't care, wanting him as hot and crazed and out-of-his-mind as he was making her.

"Yes, oh please," she groaned, wanting him to move those fingers just a tiny bit more so he could slip one inside her.

He shifted her to try to grant her unspoken wish, but the rough brick of the building scraped her hip, scratching her sharply. Lulu hissed in pain.

"Oh, God, I'm sorry." He immediately pulled her away from the wall, still holding her tightly, her legs around his hips. "I wouldn't hurt that magnificent ass for anything— not when all I want to do is nibble it."

"I'm not sorry," she said, pressing frantic kisses on his mouth. "It's worth it, and you can nibble away." Feeling the cold air against her exposed bottom, she giggled. "Though it *is* a little cold."

"I guess we should go."

"Just get me to the nearest warm place and finish what you started," she urged, not sure she'd have the patience to walk blocks at this point. Nor that her legs would carry her.

Chaz turned to glance around. If a seedy, rent-by-the-room hotel had been across the street, she would have raced him to it, but no such luck.

Still, a smile crossed his lips. Lulu followed his stare, seeing his gaze had landed on the door of the credit union. It had an after-hours key-card lock for customers to use the ATM in the vestibule. He studied it for a moment, then looked at her and lifted a suggestive brow.

"You wouldn't dare," she said, her tone amused and

a little taunting. Was she egging him on? She honestly wasn't sure.

"Watch me."

"A *camera* will be watching you."

He glanced back toward the bar they'd left. "Damn. I forgot my sheet. We can't be unidentifiable ghost and witch."

"You would pull a sheet over us, take me in there and...?"

"Oh, hell yes. Right this very minute." He edged closer to the door. "Of course, maybe we don't need the sheet. If we're very careful, and you keep your mask on...."

"Are you an exhibitionist?" she asked, half shocked, more than half aroused. The vestibule was fully exposed right inside the building, and fairly well lit. Though nobody was around to watch, there could be at any moment.

"Honestly, I don't give a flying fuck who sees us. I just want to touch you, get my fingers in you, see if you're as tight and wet as I think you are."

She had to close her eyes as more blood rerouted toward her sex. The man was intoxicating and aggressive, nothing like the boy she'd known, and his demands rang with sexual confidence.

"But there must be cameras," she said, her protest sounding weak to even her ears.

"There's just one in the machine, recording anybody right in front of it. It can't catch all the corners and sides."

"Are you sure?"

"I bank here. I'm pretty sure. But we can go in and check."

She felt herself weakening.

"Just a quick exploration," he begged, kissing her throat, then scraping the tip of his tongue down to the tops of her breasts. "Throw a starving man a bone so I'll have the strength to get us back to my place. I'll carry you home, just like this, and save you from those wicked shoes, if I can just take a tour of your delicious body right now."

She held on tight, her fingers digging into his shoulders as she urged him on. "Do it."

Letting her down, he grabbed her hand and pulled her with him to the front of the building. "I've never been more glad that I bank here," he said as he pulled out his wallet.

He removed his debit card, and swiped it in the card reader to unlock the door. She waited as he pulled it open and ushered her in. They were like fish in a bowl, encased in glass, visible to anyone lurking nearby.

She should have been shocked, nervous and ready to bolt. But the utter wickedness of it thrilled her. She hadn't done anything this daring for as long as she could remember, and the sheer riskiness of it urged her on almost as much as her hunger for him. She needed his hands on her, his mouth on her, but a part of her—the part that had been focused on school and work and hadn't spared a moment for sex—almost *wanted* to be seen.

She didn't spot a soul nearby, and they were surrounded by dark, closed businesses, but they were near lots of parked cars and were only a few buildings up from the bar they'd left.

And then there was the camera. She spotted it embedded in the top of the machine, pointing directly out to catch whoever was standing in front of the ATM. Chaz was already in line with it, and she had to be at least partly visible. No doubt they were already being recorded. But he was right about the tiny neighborhood bank's security. There were no other cameras in sight—no black domes on the ceiling or in the corners, just the one wired within the ATM, facing out, at about eye level.

They might really get away with this.

"Come here," Chaz ordered, beckoning her over. "Stand right there, with your back against the wall."

Understanding what he had in mind, she turned around and backed into the corner directly beside the ATM. It couldn't possibly capture her image; she was side-by-side with the thing. And if there were any inside cameras, she was completely blocked from them by the interior wall between the vestibule and the lobby.

"I think I'll check my balance," Chaz said with a wicked grin as he inserted his card, eyeing her and not the screen.

"I suspect you've hit the jackpot," she teased.

He didn't even look over at her, exploring only by touch. Shifting slightly to further block the camera's view of his actions, he reached for her, scraping his fingers across her jaw, her lips, then tracing a line straight down her throat. She felt the touch down to her very toes, wishing his mouth would follow the same trajectory.

When he reached her bustier, he easily untied it, one-handed. She arched toward him, loving the brush of his warm skin against the sensitive curves. Drawing the laces, he loosened the whole top until it sagged open, and then, only then, did he glance away from the screen to stare at her.

"God almighty," he whispered, sounding nearly reverent. His eyes were dark with want. His muscles bunched under his shirt and his jaw clenched as he struggled to maintain control. Lulu had never seen a look of such pure, unadulterated want in anyone's face before.

She couldn't manage to say a thing as he reached for her breast, cupping it, squeezing gently, stroking his thumb over her hard, sensitized nipple. She was dying for his mouth, but he remained several inches away, pretending to focus only on the cash machine, while secretly pleasuring her just out of sight.

The man's patience stunned her; she was ready to say screw the camera and leap on him, pull his mouth to her breast and beg him to taste her. But he kept his cool, still blocking her from view of the camera, and from anyone who might walk up to the front of the vestibule.

The side, of course, was another story. She was looking right out into the parking lot, and if somebody approached from that way, they'd notice her standing inside, her top hanging open, her breasts freed and heavy, being caressed by a man who definitely knew how to use his hands.

"Damn, I forgot my pin number," he said with a chuckle. "You distracted me."

"Keep trying, you'll get it sooner or later," she whispered as she reached down and tugged her skirt up, inch by inch.

He shifted his gaze and watched, hunger dripping from him as he dropped his hand and stroked his way down her belly and between her legs. He cupped her sex and she arched into his touch, dying, spinning, flying, all at the same time. He felt so good, his touch so possessive, as if he were staking his claim to what lay beneath his hand.

"You're so hot."

"And getting hotter by the minute," she groaned.

"Show me."

He helped her tug the skirt the rest of the way up, and work her tights back down, baring herself from hips to upper thighs.

He couldn't seem to take his eyes off her. "You are gorgeous. I've got to get inside you."

"That might be difficult from that angle."

"My cock is just going to have to wait in line."

Her hips thrust reflexively. "Touch me. Please."

"Thanks, I think I will," he said, smiling wickedly as he again reached between her thighs.

He toyed with her clit for a moment, making the world tremble, bringing an orgasm to within tasting distance. While it rattled and thrummed through her, he slipped between the lips of her sex. She was drenched and ready, and his finger slid easily into her sensitive channel.

"Mmm," she said, closing her eyes and dropping her head back as he pleasured her.

"You are so tight. So wet for me."

"I got wet the minute you made that sun-coming-up comment."

"Thought it made you wonder if the world would end."

"I'm wondering that now—because if you don't make me come, I think it just might."

Masculine laughter rumbled from him as he moved his thumb to her clit and stroked it again. His long fingers pleasured her deep within, and his gentle swirling motion around her clit brought her up higher and higher, even as tension and stormy heat pooled lower and lower.

"Yes, Chaz," she groaned, torn between utter pleasure and a tension that was almost painful. She needed release desperately, and knew it was just a few breaths away.

As if sensing she was so close, he stepped over in front of her and caught her mouth in a hot kiss. Plunging his tongue deep, he stroked her right to the edge of the abyss, until she was almost sobbing against his lips.

"Please," she begged. "I need…oh, yes," she groaned as he gave her the right amount of pressure to send her soaring.

Her hips thrusting helplessly, Lulu gasped as waves of delight washed through her, to the top of her head, to the soles of her feet. Not one molecule was unaffected as she pulsed with satisfaction, and she wanted to cry at how good it felt. She couldn't remember coming so hard before in her entire life. If he could work such magic with his hand, she couldn't even fathom what he would do with his mouth, or with that powerful hard-on pressing against her middle.

Collapsing against him, still savoring his kiss, meeting every delicious thrust of his tongue, she tried to bring herself back down from the incredible high he'd provided.

Easing his lips from hers, he kissed his way down her throat, tasting her skin, sucking gently, biting lightly. He ended up at her breasts. Plumping one in his hand, he covered the tip with his mouth and sucked, hard. More heat sluiced through her, as if she hadn't just had a limb-weakening orgasm. Every inch of her that wasn't already on fire got that way immediately.

"These are beautiful," he told her, moving to pay attention to her other breast, suckling one nipple while he tweaked and caressed the other.

She kept her head back, her eyes closed, loving the moisture and heat of his lips and the stroke of his fingers. Her nipples were so sensitive, every pull of his mouth on her breast was echoed between her thighs. Her clit was pebble-hard again, and she was right on the edge of spilling into another climax.

"I think that's enough for now."

"You think so, do you?" she asked, twining her fingers in his hair.

"Yeah. That took the edge off. Let's let it build up again on the way back to my place."

Fiend. She was so wound up, that first orgasm might have happened a week ago.

Kissing his way up to her face, he stared down at her and gently helped her put her skirt and tights into place again. He left her bustier open so he could continue to play with her breasts, both building the pleasure and denying release with every firm yet gentle caress.

"Are you okay?"

"I'm not sure my legs work anymore."

"I promised I'd carry you. You held up your end of the bargain. I'll hold up mine."

She didn't doubt he could. Perhaps being a world-traveling adventurer equipped him to carry a girl for blocks down a dark, windswept street, after he'd fingered her into oblivion.

"Give me a sec to recover," she told him, not ready to go back out into the cold night and surrender their private—but oh-so-public—chamber. "Finish checking your balance."

He chuckled lightly. "I definitely can't remember my pin now. I'm not sure I can remember my name. That was something to see."

He looked as pleased and cocky as a man who'd made a woman come in under two minutes with just his fingers should look. And while it had been her pleasure to oblige him—most definitely—she also wanted him just as crazed and lost to sensual delight as she had been. "Maybe I can help you remember the number."

"Oh?"

"Sure. Go back over there and put your hands on the keys." She licked her lips. "And keep them there."

He didn't appear to understand at first, but he did as she ordered, stepping into place again and eyeing the machine. "Hmm. Deposit or withdrawal? Or just the balance check?"

"How about ninety minutes of serious deposits and withdrawals," she said. Her smile impish, she added, "Especially if you have a lot to deposit?"

"Find out for yourself."

Unable to wait, she did just that, reaching out to stroke the tented front of his pants. Feeling the massive erection straining against his zipper, she melted, the last bit of strength draining out of her legs. Sliding down the wall, she didn't stop until she sat on the backs of her calves.

Which was a very nice position to be in, indeed.

"What are you…"

"Let me see if I can help jog your memory, and, uh, take *your* edge off at the same time," she said, gazing up at him with wanton sweetness. "Maybe if you relax and don't think too hard about anything, the number will pop right into your mind."

He watched her, looking surprised and excited as she edged between him and the wall, directly below the machine, out of the camera's prying eye. Kneeling face-level with his groin, she grasped his zipper and carefully lowered it, her hand trembling as she acknowledged just how big he was.

"You aren't seriously…"

"Oh, yes, I am," she whispered, moving closer so she could brush her open mouth against the cotton of his tight boxer briefs. She exhaled and then pressed her tongue there, wetting the fabric, tasting the heat and musk of him.

"God almighty," he said, dropping a hand to tangle it in her hair. "Your mouth has been driving me crazy since the moment you smiled at me."

"Did you picture me using it on you…here?"

He groaned as she pressed her lips to the straining cotton again. "Not in the very first ten seconds after I saw you."

"Fifteen?"

"Maybe twenty," he admitted with a boyish grin.

Her laugh was sultry. "Points for honesty. So what did you think about for the first nineteen?"

The rough pad of a thumb scraped her bottom lip. "I thought about kissing you. Tasting you. Swallowing that smile. I figured somebody with a smile like that was somebody I needed to get to know. It brightens a room."

She swallowed hard, trying not to react too strongly to the gentleness of his words and tone. Innate sweetness had always been a part of Chaz's personality; it had been genuine, unfeigned. That kind, earnest streak was potent in combination with the hot masculinity he now possessed in spades.

Needing to return to sexy-and-edgy things and not sweetly-seductive things, she said, "And on the twentieth second?" Pursing her lips, she added, "What did you think then?"

"I plead the fifth."

"Chicken."

Not waiting for him to reply, she licked again while unfastening his belt and unbuttoning his jeans. Seeing that the tip of his erection was nudging out of the elastic at the top of his briefs, she moaned, deep in her throat. He had a lot to deposit, most definitely. More than she'd ever seen in her life, and for tonight, it was all hers.

Dying to taste him, she gently tugged the cotton down, revealing him to her hungry gaze, inch by inch. God, he was beautiful, bold, masculine and strong. She wanted him in every orifice of her body, starting with her mouth.

"Come on, admit it. You imagined this. Me on my knees, sucking you off," she said, still utterly fascinated by the awe-inspiring erection.

"Not on your knees." He sounded hoarse, needy.

She shifted her gaze to see him clenching both sides of the ATM. The tendons in his forearms flexed with the strain. He was dying for her mouth, she knew, but she drew things out, enjoying the sensual torment she was inflicting on them both.

"Where then?"

He scorched her with a glance, his eyes blazing with hunger. "I pictured you lying on top of me, turned around so you could suck my cock while I licked you into incoherence."

He didn't shock her, as he might have intended. "Sixtynine is my favorite number."

"Mine, too."

"Maybe that's your pin number," she said with a saucy wink.

His response was more helpless groan than laugh. "Let's get out of here," he urged. "I'll take you to my place, get you in my bed and we'll talk about all our favorite numbers."

"First, I'd like to do some pleasuring. Now shut up."

He shut up.

Totally in the moment, uncaring of who might pull up outside, or what the camera above her head might record, she could focus only on the masculine perfection before her eyes. Lulu had worked the briefs down low enough to encircle as much of him as she could hold in one hand. Leaning closer, inhaling deeply to create another sense memory—one she would no doubt always associate with pure, driving need and hot, illicit sex—she flicked her tongue across the engorged tip, sampling his essence. His soft skin covered steel, and tasted salty and musky. Delicious.

Widening her mouth, she covered the tip of his erection and gently sucked, her tongue wetting him, her mouth devouring him. His hips instinctively thrust toward her, and she turned her head so he could go deeper. She took him in, sucking until that delicious cock filled her mouth, the end of him hitting the back of her throat, and then she greedily sucked a little bit more.

"Oh, yeah," he groaned, tangling both hands in her hair.

She ignored him, making oral love to him, taking him deep, then pulling away, tormenting him with every stroke. Chaz groaned mindlessly, and his hand tightened in her hair, coming close to the elastic that looped her mask over her ear.

Lulu instantly pulled away, missing the taste of him the moment that powerful shaft left her tongue.

"Huh-uh. You might be willing to risk showing your face, but I'm not," she said, hoping she sounded sexy and mysterious and not slightly desperate. Because, heaven help her, if he insisted that she take off the mask and reveal her true self to him, she wasn't sure she would be able to say no.

Maybe he wouldn't recognize you. Lust has clouded his brain; he might not have any idea who you are.

But she knew better than to think that might really happen. It might take a few seconds, and he wouldn't believe his eyes at first, but he would recognize her.

Besides, in the nearly impossible chance that he didn't, there was no way she could avoid seeing Chaz for the rest of her life, especially since she lived right down the street. He'd eventually find out who his mysterious witch had been.

"Sorry. I got carried away. I wouldn't expose you here."

Here. Right. But later? All bets would be off. It was madness to think that he wouldn't demand she take off the mask at his house. She had no idea why she'd believed she could get him to agree to anonymous, faceless sex. Which meant she might not be able to go through with her reckless plan to go home with the man and take whatever hot eroticisms he would be willing to offer a mysterious, unidentified woman.

Maybe he won't be that curious.

Yeah, and maybe a cop would pull up outside, smile,

and tell them to carry on with what they were doing. Hell, the guy was a reporter. Chaz lived to solve riddles and get to the bottom of stories. He might let her blow him with a mask on her face for her own protection against the camera—typical, protective Chaz—but there was no way he'd let the mask stay there once they were assured of privacy.

Now might be all she had, unless she could figure out how to later reveal every bit of herself except her face.

"Am I forgiven?"

"Yes. But no unmasking, okay?"

"Cross my heart," he said, staring down at her, his hands braced on each side of the machine.

Sure of retaining her anonymity for a while longer, knowing she would probably never have another chance, Lulu concentrated on grabbing whatever illicit pleasure she could. She moved back to him, licking the shaft from base to tip.

"You taste so good, Chaz," she murmured as she shook off any unpleasant thoughts and focused only on the very pleasant task before her.

She reached down and cupped his tight balls, gently toying with them as she devoured his cock, concentrating as much on her own pleasure as on his. She loved how he tasted, loved all that heat and power in her mouth, loved knowing she was bringing him figuratively, if not literally, to his knees.

It didn't take long for him to reach that same state of mindlessness, and his groans signaled his impending release. Ever the gentleman, he cupped a hand around her cheek, trying to stop her. "Wait. No more."

She didn't let him push her away, determined to take him all the way. Gripping his hip, she kept sucking, and with just a few more pulls of her mouth, she got her reward. Shuddering, he came hard, his essence spurting against her tongue. She swallowed every warm, salty drop and licked her lips before releasing him and sagging back against the wall.

They both gasped for a while, and she watched him try to regain his composure. He'd been bracing himself against the machine, his eyes closed, so visibly delighted there could be no doubt something serious was happening out of view of the camera.

She wondered if anybody ever watched the security tapes without there being some kind of crime to investigate. Hopefully not. If they did, Chaz might have to find a new bank.

But right now, she suspected he wouldn't give a damn.

4

ALTHOUGH HE'D CLIMAXED so powerfully he'd thought the top of his head might blow off, Chaz was now even more desperate to get his mystery lover home. He quickly shoved himself back into his clothes, wondering how someone he'd just met could already be the most sexually addictive woman of his life.

She amazed him, thrilled him. Moments ago, she'd taken him to the ultimate heights, but just looking down at her, seeing the heave of her bare breasts as she tried to steady her breathing, he was already hard for her again.

She was stunning. Intriguing. So sexy. He'd never, in his entire life, been as driven by primal lust as he was tonight.

"Let's get out of here."

She busied herself fixing her bustier, not meeting his eye. "Maybe we could just stay here and…"

"Forget it," he bit out. "I want you totally naked and I don't want any interruptions or worries about privacy."

She hesitated, but he wasn't about to give her any time for doubts or regrets. All he could think about was tearing his pants open again, yanking those tights back down, and plunging balls deep into her tight pussy.

Bending down, he hauled her up, shifting them so his back was to the camera, blocking any view of her. "I have to get you home. Now."

"Chaz, I…"

"I doubt we'll even make it past the foyer of my house," he told her. "There's a condom in my pocket and I'm tempted to put it on while we walk so I can fuck you the very second we close the front door."

She gazed at him, the mask still disguising far too much of her face. But the excitement in those eyes was unforgettable. "I like that idea."

Helping her up, he tightened the laces on her top and helped her refasten her black leather jacket. He could feel the thud of her heart as his knuckles brushed her chest. The woman was every bit as aroused as he was.

Leading her outside, he made good on his promise and picked her up, prepared to run home with her now that he knew she was in no way ready to call it a night.

She tried to protest. "This is silly, I can walk."

"Shut up. A deal's a deal."

"Are you always so stubborn?"

"I'm not at all stubborn. I'm the most easygoing guy around. Ask anybody."

"Then why don't you just agree to put me down before you break your back?"

"You're not exactly a wide load."

"I'm not exactly a featherweight, either."

He feigned insult. "You're offending my manliness."

Her responding laugh was cute and feminine. But he had to admit, she might have been right, because, as light as she was, after two blocks, his legs were complaining.

"Put me down, you big idiot. I fully intend to be fucked against your front door, and you won't be able to do that if you can't walk!"

He stopped, liking the way she thought, and really liking that she was so blunt about it. She seemed to be the kind of woman who went after what she wanted and made no apologies for it, which he found incredibly appealing. They might have danced around this a little bit at first, but now that the course was set, she wasn't steering off it.

"Okay, you win."

Pressing a kiss on her lips, he let her slide down his body, loving the instant when her parted legs hugged his hips and they came to within a few layers of fabric of ultimate connection. She ground against him, and he thrust back, his cock painfully hard and desperately in need of hot, wet woman.

Needing another taste before they completed the walk home, he carried her over to the nearest tree and leaned her against it. Bending his face to hers, he kissed her hungrily, exploring the soft, wonderful places in her mouth. Their bodies ground together, mimicking the heated act they'd be completing if not for their clothing.

"I want in," he groaned.

"And I want you in," she whimpered. "Stupid tights."

"They're awesome tights. But right now I'd like to rip them with my teeth."

She hissed into his mouth, bucking a little as she envisioned it. "Why don't you just use your hands instead?"

He stared down at her, wondering what she meant, then getting it. He couldn't decide at first if she was serious. They were not in a brightly lit vestibule anymore, they were half hidden in the shadows of a tree. But still....

"Right here? Right now?"

"Yes," she begged, arching harder against him. "Just a taste, Chaz. Give me something to tide me over for another few blocks."

He reached between her heated thighs, felt the dampness of her crotch and dug his fingers into the weave of the tights, easily pulling them apart. Sighing with relief, with masculine satisfaction, he fingered her, finding her every bit as wet as she'd been before.

Letting most of her weight rest against the tree, he quickly unfastened his pants. His cock sprang hot and hard into his hand. It brushed against her thigh, and she moaned and tightened her legs around him, pulling him close to her heat.

"Please, Chaz," she begged, writhing, thrusting her hips forward to take what he wasn't yet giving her.

It was insane. They were outside on a public street, in one of the biggest cities in the country. But there was something dark and elemental about the night. Maybe it was the late hour. Maybe it was because of the date on the calendar—Halloween night. Maybe it was the bright moon or the long, narrow clouds drifting across the inky sky or the sense of surreal, all-encompassing attraction he'd felt from the moment he'd laid eyes on her. Something just wouldn't let him stop without grabbing this hedonistic, dangerous moment of sin.

He began to slip into her, his cock inching in, gobbled by her silky, wet flesh. From the very first moment of possession, he was shaken by the primitive desire to pour himself into her. He wanted to make a permanent place for himself inside her body, to bury himself so deeply she would never remember what it felt like before he'd taken her.

He'd pushed no more than an inch, barely even the head of his dick, into her, getting nothing but a taste of her sweet tightness, when a car came by, slowing and beeping as someone cat-called out the window.

"Fuck," he groaned, immediately pulling away, lowering her to stand, and tugging her skirt down into place. He quickly spun around, his back toward the street, blocking her from view, and trying to fix jeans that were suddenly way too tight.

"Oh, God, just shoot me now," she groaned.

He glared over his shoulder at the occupants of the offending vehicle, hidden within shadows behind closed windows. The car quickly sped up and tore off down the street with another honk of the horn and a squeal of tires.

"They're gone."

"Did you get that tag number? I'm going to put a hit out on them," she said, sounding tortured by sensual need.

Although it physically pained him, he managed to get his clothes around his steel-hard cock, shoving it behind his seam as he heaved in deep breaths of cold night air.

"It's not much farther to my house," he said, swallowing in an attempt to calm himself down. His heart was racing, his blood coursing hotly through his veins. If he closed his eyes, he could almost feel her still, and it was easy to imagine what it would be like to sink all the way into her and be wrapped in all that silky warmth. "Can you run in those damn shoes?"

"I'll crawl if I have to," she said, her vehemence both cute and flattering. "And FYI, if you'd like to revisit that particular position as soon as we're behind closed doors, I definitely won't complain," she said sounding breathless.

"You've got a deal."

Both anticipating that moment now more than ever, they returned to the sidewalk, walking together, hip-to-hip, thigh brushing thigh. He slid an arm around her waist, tugging her close, and she pressed her cheek against his shoulder, her head fitting there just perfectly. They didn't run, but there was purpose in their strides, a hunger for what would come when they reached their destination.

A chime suddenly interrupted the quiet night. "Crap, let

me turn this off." She glanced into her purse and retrieved her phone, quickly scanning the message on the screen.

"Problem?"

Sighing, she asked, "Are you going to rape me, then murder me and make a lampshade out of my skin?"

He almost tripped over his own feet, coming to a stop and spinning to face her. "Excuse me?"

"My friend Viv, from back at the bar. She finally stopped dirty-dancing with an entire football team and realized I was gone. Now she's harassing me for leaving with you, as if you're Hannibal Lecter's long-lost twin."

"Please assure her that I'm not a rapist, or a killer, or an interior decorator."

It took her less than a second, then her lips twitched. "Ha. Very funny. So I can assure her my skin is going to stay where it is?"

"It seems to be doing a very good job in its present location," he said, casting an appreciative eye over her, from windswept red hair down to her wickedly sexy shoes.

In fact, he wouldn't change a single thing about her. Except for removing that mask. Oh, and the rest of her clothes.

"Thank you," she said, her voice so proper and prim and adorable, he had to tug her close for another quick brush of lips on lips.

Realizing her friend was just being protective, and that she had the right to be, considering this relationship was moving super-fast and had so far involved acts that would probably get them arrested for indecency, he said, "Tell her I'm going to make wild love to you all night, then get up and make you waffles for breakfast."

That sounded like the perfect way to spend his first night and following morning home.

She lowered her eyes and stepped away from him. "Um…"

"You don't like waffles? All right, pancakes it is."

"Listen, the first half of that sounds wonderful." She twisted her hands in front of her, her eyes on her own fingers. "But I'm not looking for anything serious here."

"If I were making Peking duck, I might consider that serious, but we're talking breakfast food here. How about Lucky Charms? How serious can a cereal with marshmallows in it be?"

"They're my favorite," she admitted with a sheepish sigh.

"Mine, too. I once broke up with a woman who told me she wouldn't allow a kids' cereal at her breakfast table."

"Guess she didn't want kids."

"We hadn't really reached that stage yet. But on behalf of any potential future children she might have, I called her bluff and didn't see her again."

"Dumped over a box of cereal. Harsh."

"Hey, don't mess with a man's one weakness."

"I'll remember that."

"Tomorrow morning?"

She immediately realized she'd backed herself into a corner. "Uh, wait, no, that's not what I meant." She tucked a strand of wildly blowing hair behind her ear, visibly stalling. Taking a deep breath, she admitted, "Breakfast implies an all-nighter."

"You doubting my manhood again?" he asked, deliberately misunderstanding her. He knew she was skittish and was backing away from the idea of actually spending an entire night in his bed. Hell, if she thought up-against-the-front-door sex was all he was after, she didn't rate her own appeal very highly. After what they'd already shared, what she'd already made him feel, he wasn't sure he'd be willing to let her out of his sight for a month.

"Not at all," she said, her smile tremulous. "It's just, I'm not thinking long-term here."

"And tomorrow morning is oh-so-far away?"

"Too far away for my taste."

Huh. She'd really surprised him. He hadn't had many one-night-stands, but he felt pretty sure that women got testy if they thought you didn't want them to actually sleep with you once they'd been invited to, uh, *sleep* with you.

"I like you," he admitted with a shrug. "Going to bed with you tonight and waking up with you tomorrow won't exactly be a hardship."

"It might if you knew who you'd be waking up with."

"You mean, the wicked witch?"

"Something like that."

"I'm a big boy. I'll take my chances."

She swallowed, her throat quivering. A gusty wind howled through the night, and she pulled her coat tighter around herself. Chaz stepped closer to block the wind, enjoying the way her hair blew against his face. Not to mention how deliciously soft her skin felt against the tips of his fingers. The memory of sinking just one inch inside that beautiful body made him shake with need, from head to toe.

Yeah. He would definitely take his chances. He'd savor whatever she wanted to give him and then figure out how to make her want to give him more.

He reached for her chin and lifted it, forcing her to look at him. The silly mask remained on her face, and he couldn't wait to take it off. But he sensed they were doing that dance again, like they'd done in the bar. *Forward and back.* He didn't want to do anything to push her away.

"Just come home with me," he urged, "and let the chips fall where they may."

She stared up at him, uncertainty awash in those shaded eyes. "With no promises?"

He sensed she needed an out. Hoping she'd change her mind, he nodded. "No promises." Lightening the mood, he grinned. "And no lampshades."

She visibly relaxed, her stiff posture loosening, her tight mouth softening. "That's a deal."

"Are you going to let your friend know?"

She glanced at her phone, tapped out a brief message, and then turned the device off. "I'm all yours," she said once she'd dropped it back into her purse. "For the next hour or so, anyway."

"There you go, doubting my manliness again."

"Three hours?"

"At a bare minimum."

However long it lasted, he would never forget it. Nothing like this had ever happened to him before, and he was already sure that he was in the middle of something very special. Possibly life-changing. He couldn't say how he knew it—maybe intuition, maybe wishful thinking. It didn't matter. He was just certain, on some elemental level, that he would be irrevocably changed after this night.

They started walking again, but hadn't gone more than a couple of feet before he heard her soft giggle. So maybe she wasn't thinking about anything on an elemental level.

Which was just one more thing he liked about her. She was damned unpredictable.

"What now?"

"I just had this mental image of somebody at that savings and loan watching the video and wondering what in hell was going on when you stood there for so long with your head thrown back."

He thrust a hand through his hair, wondering where on earth the two of them had gotten the nerve to be so outrageous. He could practically see the headlines now: *Local Reporter Charged With Indecency In A Bank Lobby.* Wouldn't his friends and colleagues have a field day with that one?

Still, he couldn't bring himself to regret it. "I suppose that depends on who was watching."

"You might want to change where you do your banking."

He wasn't worried. "I really don't think they watch those recordings unless they have a reason to review them for a crime or something."

"Then let's hope nobody robs the place tonight. I'm so not ready for my *close-up* to be seen by an audience."

"Your *close-up* was my favorite part of the whole banking experience," he admitted, unable to deny it. "But even if somebody does watch, that camera didn't capture anything below waist level."

And if it had, there'd be nothing to see except a mass of glorious, curly red hair.

Christ, the thought of what she'd done to him—how she'd made him feel—was enough to make him want to throw his head back and howl to the moon like a werewolf on the prowl this Halloween night. Her sexual generosity had stunned him.

"You know, I've dated women for months who didn't do for me what you did back there."

"Do you mean going with you to the ATM so you could, uh—" she licked her lips "—make a *deposit?*"

God, she was outrageous. "Yeah. You didn't have to actually let me complete my...deposit."

"I enjoyed it." She shrugged, sounding as though she meant it.

"I thought women only enjoyed it on a guy's birthday or after getting a diamond bracelet or something."

"You calling me cheap for settling for a cherry-flavored drink and a dance?"

"There is nothing cheap about you," he insisted with a squeeze of her hand. "Absolutely nothing."

"I'm kidding. But there was no quid pro quo about it," she said. "I wanted to taste you."

"You didn't have to go for the full-course meal and swallow every morsel."

She stopped and turned on her heel to look up at him. "I told you before, I'm not a cock-tease. I wasn't going to bring you up the mountain and not let you jump off the highest cliff." She lifted up on her tiptoes and brushed her lips against his. "You taste good."

He tugged her close and covered her mouth for a kiss, sweeping his tongue inside to explore her all over again. She twined around his body like a vine around a post, pressing every inch of herself against him. By the time the kiss ended, he was barely able to catch his breath. His heart thudded, his pants refused to stay zipped to the top, and he found himself wishing he hadn't insisted they leave the vestibule. And cursing that stupid honking car to the ninth circle of hell.

Letting her go, he said, "Come on, we're almost there."

She nodded, twined her fingers in his and matched him stride for stride as they headed down the street. They passed one young couple, dressed as a pair of comic book superheroes, who barely managed to stop groping each other as they walked by. He wondered if he and his mystery woman had just interrupted the couple the same way the car had interrupted them. The other couple hadn't seemed to rush to put any clothes back in place, but he would bet they weren't more than a few minutes from reaching that point.

"Happy Halloween," he said with a grin as they passed.

"You, too," the guy said. "Hope you get lots of treats."

Chaz fully intended to.

"That's my place on the corner," he said, nodding toward his townhouse.

"Good thing, these shoes are killing me," she said.

"Serves you right for doubting my manhood."

"I didn't doubt your manhood. Just your wisdom."

That startled another laugh out of him. Damn, how he liked this woman.

"Well, I don't see any toilet paper or eggshells, so I guess the trick-or-treaters didn't punish you for not being home to give out any candy."

"A few knocked before I went to the bar. I handed out a couple of bags of airplane crackers and some Altoids."

"They should've egged your house just for that."

She was probably right. Fortunately, no angry, deprived-of-candy ghosts or goblins had played tricks after he'd left.

Yanking her hand from his, she suddenly stopped. "Who's that?"

"Huh?"

"The woman sitting on the car over there."

Realizing she was looking toward one of the reserved parking spaces directly in front of his house, he followed her stare. A bright yellow Beetle was parked beside his own car, and on the hood of it sat a woman. She was draped in gauzy white fabric that might have been a toga or might have been a ghost-sheet like the one he'd worn.

Chaz scrunched his brow for a moment, wondering why some stranger was sitting alone on the hood of her car at this time of night. Then he spotted the hair, as yellow as the vehicle, and realized who it was.

"Shit." He turned to his mystery witch. "It's my sister."

"Sarah," she whispered.

Taken aback for a moment, he suddenly remembered he had mentioned his sibling's name at the club. "Yes. I have no idea what she's doing here."

"She looks upset." There was a hint of coldness in the tone that hadn't been there all evening. It appeared he wasn't the only one disappointed that someone had delayed them from getting inside for their promised up-against-the-wall adventure. His sister had the worst timing in the universe. Well, second worse. That car honking was number one.

"There you are," Sarah said, sliding off the car and sniffing audibly. *Definitely a toga. Roman goddess?* "Mom said you got back to town today and I just had to see you and you weren't *he-re* when I *neeeeded* you! Where have you *be-en?*"

"Have any cheese you can give her to go with that whine?" his companion muttered.

Chaz smothered a laugh, because, yes, Sarah had sounded like a whiny brat. Which wasn't exactly an uncommon occurrence. She was the baby of the family and relished the role, getting her way in just about everything she'd ever wanted.

"Don't move," he said, reluctantly dropping his companion's hand. "I'll find out what's going on and be right back."

He strode toward his pain in the ass of a sister. "Hey, kid, what's up?"

"I've been waiting for you, big brother. I feel like I'm going crazy!" Sarah threw her arms around his neck, buried her face in his chest and began sobbing loudly. "I'm so miserable!"

So much for *Welcome home. How's it going? I've missed you.*

He returned the hug, smoothing her hair, wondering what on earth the big drama was this time.

"I can't believe you didn't let me know you were home and ask me if I wanted to do something tonight," she said.

"I figured you had plans with your friends."

"I did. I mean, I do."

"So what's the problem?"

"Everything fell apart."

Maybe for her. But things had fallen into *place* for him, and he didn't want anything to change that. "I intended to call you tomorrow. Now what's wrong?"

"You will not believe who I ran into today."

"The president?"

She pulled away and scowled at him. "No! Can you believe Lawrence Vandenberg is going to A.U. for his master's degree and he lives right beside the campus and Mom never warned me?"

Oh. That. "I heard. Lulu mentioned it in an email."

Sarah's jaw dropped. "You keep in touch with *her?* After what her stupid brother did to me?"

"Not regularly, that's for sure. She moved here. Mom gave her my email address so she could get some information on housing and stuff."

That was the full extent of his contact with the girl-next-door, and he wanted to keep it that way. Lulu Vandenberg had been the most annoying next-door neighbor any geeky kid should have to endure, and he was lucky he'd made it out of his childhood with his sanity—and his tailbone—intact.

He did vaguely wonder how she'd turned out. Lulu had,

after all, been one of the prettiest girls he'd ever known, not that he would never have told her he thought so in a million years. Maybe she'd grown up to be a hag, though he doubted it. Her emails had been friendly and chatty, brimming with self-confidence. Of course, Lulu had been that way, too. Always talking, always ready to hand out advice. She'd been a real know-it-all.

Nah. He didn't really want to see how she'd turned out.

"She had the nerve to ask you for help after the way she always treated you when we were kids?" Sarah said, finally thinking of someone other than herself.

To be fair, Lulu hadn't been *all* bad. They'd actually gotten along fine much of the time, usually by ignoring each other. It was just that she was so damned bossy, and good at everything. She'd out-played him on the basketball court, had ridden her bike in circles around him while he still struggled with his first ten-speed. She was the bravest and the toughest when it came to playing truth-or-dare. She was also dangerous—he'd been a witness to the great playground fight, when she, at age eight, had slugged an eleven-year-old boy who made fun of six-year-old Lawrence for still having a teddy bear.

And of course there was the ladder incident. Sometimes, when he sat down just the right way, he still got a twinge out of that forever-cracked tailbone.

"It's no big deal. Mom asked me to help out. Lulu's her best friend's kid. What was I supposed to do, say no?"

"Well, hopefully you told her the safest place in the city to live is Anacostia," Sarah said with a heaping helping of spite, since that neighborhood was one of the most dangerous in the district.

Chaz grunted. "Let it go, little sister."

It was kid stuff, and he'd tried to forget it. That said,

he did hope his Realtor had found Lulu an apartment far away from his own neighborhood.

"What, exactly, did Lulu tell you about Lawrence?" she asked.

"Just that he was coming here to go to school, too."

"Did she mention that he was doing it so he could be close to some girl?"

Chaz stayed quiet, sensing a trap in the question.

Eventually Sarah continued. "Because he happens to have a girlfriend! And I think they might be living together!"

From several feet away, where he'd left his sexy witch, he heard a cough, but he stayed focused on Sarah, knowing he had to hear her out, give her a brotherly word of wisdom, and then send her on her way. "And that's your business...why?"

She sputtered. "Well, he had to have been aware I'm at A.U. He did it on purpose, came here just to get close to me and try to make me jealous."

"Is it working?"

"No, it is not. That's ridiculous."

"Great. Then there's no problem."

She gritted her teeth and literally growled at him. "Of course there's a problem."

He had never found out exactly what had happened between his sister and Lawrence. Nor was he sure he wanted to. Knowing his sister, and well aware that Lawrence was a great guy, he had to assume Sarah had been at fault, not that he was about to say that to her. He valued his eardrums too much; she would scream the neighborhood down if he accused her of being anything but the injured party in that long-ago breakup. The key being *long ago*.

"Sarah, it's been years. Why haven't you moved on?"

Her bottom lip pushed out and her big blue eyes grew

moist. He could see unshed tears, illuminated by the street light overhead. Damn it, his sister really could turn on the waterworks.

"You just don't understand." Sniff. "Of course you'd take his side. You're such a guy."

"I understand breakups and exes. I've had my share."

He didn't add that he was the one who usually did the breaking up, his job being a lot more important to him than anyone he'd ever dated. And most women his age didn't want to wait around for weeks at a time while he jet-setted his way across the globe chasing stories.

There had been one who'd seemed like she could handle it. She'd assured him she could, in fact. Then he'd come home early from a trip and gone to surprise her at her place.

Surprise! She was dating another dude on the side, and had been for a while.

They hadn't had any exclusive agreement or anything, but she'd told him flat-out that she wasn't seeing anyone else. He could take a woman who dated others, but he would not put up with one who lied. In his line of work, where he had to rely on sources, he had absolutely zero tolerance for liars. He'd devoted most of his efforts to tyrants and warlords, but even the lowliest liar could do serious damage. He'd seen friends' careers ruined because of other people's falsehoods, which was bad enough. Worse were the deceptions that put others in harm's way. In some of the darker, more dangerous countries he had visited, deliberate lies had lured journalists to their own brutal deaths, and Chaz was always slow to give his trust and quick to take it back if it were betrayed.

"Listen, why don't you go ahead with your plans for tonight. Go have fun, you'll feel better. I'll take you out for breakfast on Sunday." Seeing that she was considering it, he added the key point. "I'll bet running into you didn't make Lawrence change his plans."

That did it. The crocodile tears dried immediately and her shoulders squared. "You're right. I can't give him the satisfaction of knowing he ruined my Halloween."

"Atta girl," he said, squeezing her arm and gently pushing her toward her car. He opened the door and helped her shove all the loose fabric of her costume inside.

She rolled down the window and blew him a kiss. "Thanks, Chaz. Happy Halloween. Have fun with your… oh, where'd she go?"

"Who?"

"Weren't you with someone?" she asked, craning to look through the windshield at the sidewalk.

The empty sidewalk.

He didn't panic. "She must have gone up to the porch to wait for me."

Sarah sat up higher in her seat and peered toward the front of his house. "Nope, nobody there."

"I'm sure she's around," he said, not worrying…not really, anyway. "Call me tomorrow about breakfast."

Sarah agreed and then backed up the car and drove away. The second she was out of sight, Chaz spun around to return to his companion. He assumed he'd find her in the shadows of one of the large live oak trees that lined the front of the row of townhouses. But she wasn't there.

His heart rate kicked up. He strode toward his own place, searching the porch and the walkway, then retraced his steps.

"Are we playing hide-and-seek now?" he asked out loud, feeling stupid for not having gotten her name. He didn't particularly want to call out, "Hey, sexy witch who just gave me the best blow job of my life, where are you?"

Dry leaves scuttled along the sidewalk and a strong

breeze howled up the empty street, whistling between the cars. There was no other sound. No response.

No beautiful woman.

Not believing his own senses, he looked again, retracing their steps, checking behind each car, going all the way up to the corner. By the time he reached the bank vestibule and saw it empty, something akin to panic made him break into a sweat until he was almost running to the bar. But somehow, he knew even before he went inside and scanned the entire place, table by table, that he wasn't going to find her.

Every minute, every step, every peering glance reinforced in his heart what his head had already begun to accept.

She was gone. His mystery woman, the one he'd been sure was going to become his utter sexual obsession, had disappeared.

5

LULU WOKE UP the day after Halloween to a dull head-ache, but she didn't attribute it to the devilish red drinks she'd consumed at the bar. Oh, no. The ache behind her eyes and the throbbing in her temple had been caused by the long hours she'd lain awake, kicking herself for two things: first, leaving with Chaz and indulging in that wickedly erotic encounter at the bank; and second, running out on him right before they went into his house to have the kind of wild sex she knew would have lived in her memories forever.

Her brain was more regretful about the first, her body the second.

"You are so stupid," she reminded herself as she rolled out of bed and eyed her wild, red-tinted hair in the mirror over her dresser. "Not to mention a damn coward."

She'd been all set to risk it, to take a chance and hope Chaz wouldn't recognize her after they had the kind of sex that was probably illegal in some states.

Then his spoiled kid sister had shown up—to complain about Lulu's sweetheart of a kid brother. It had taken a lot of willpower to stay quiet when Sarah had made the comment about Lawrence living with a girlfriend, which was news to Lulu. She'd gasped so loud she'd had to turn the sound into a cough to cover the reaction.

Plus, not only had Sarah brought reality crashing down on Lulu like a ton of cement, but she'd also upped the risk factor. If Lulu hadn't gotten out of there, it was very possible Chaz would have invited her over to meet his sister. And while Chaz hadn't seen or heard her in years, Sarah definitely had. They had spoken last summer when they'd both been visiting their respective parents. If Sarah didn't figure out who owned the face behind the mask just on sight—by the shape of her mouth or the darkness of her eyes—she would almost certainly recognize Lulu's voice.

Overhearing part of their conversation had added fuel to the fire beneath her feet for another reason, as well. There was just too much baggage between her and Chaz. It hadn't been easy hearing Sarah remind her brother of how much he disliked Lulu, and ask why he'd ever agreed to help her with anything.

Did Chaz really hate her? His sister had made it sound as if he had reason to. Oh, yes, she'd been a little shit to him on occasion, but she'd never been vicious or deliberately cruel. God, she hated to think he might be carrying scars even deeper than the ones she'd taken for granted.

The very idea had made the whole escapade seem tawdry and unkind. She had no business tricking a night of sensuality out of a guy who hated her guts. Going home with him like that was akin to stealing. He had every right to know who she was and shoot her down, and she'd taken away his chance.

So she'd played the coward and darted away while Chaz and Sarah had been talking. She'd slipped around the side of the townhouse row, heading for her own building down the block and entering the back door. Watching through her window as he'd gone looking for her, she had bitten her lip and let tears fall from her eyes as she recognized his frustration.

"Frustration is better than fury."

Right. And Chaz *would* be furious if he found out who she really was. Meaning she had to be more careful than ever not to give him any clue that she was the woman who'd been on her knees giving him the blow job to end all blow jobs last night.

Although she loved her cute apartment, and her neighbors, and the area, she suddenly found herself wishing she'd found a place in another part of the city. Now that he was home, chances were good she would run into Chaz sometime soon. She only hoped she was ready to come face to face with him again, without revealing everything she was thinking.

Trying to put the memories of the night before out of her mind, she went to take a long, hot shower. The spray-in hair color was temporary, but she still had to wash her hair three times before she felt confident the glittery stuff was completely gone. And after she got out of the shower, brushed her hair, and spotted a few incriminating auburn streaks, she went right back in and washed it again.

Finally, when she'd made sure to remove every wisp of color and had thrust her witch costume into the darkest corner of her closet, she pulled on jeans and a sweater, wanting to get out of her apartment. It was a beautiful fall day—sunny, breezy, the sky clear and Robin's egg–blue— and she was determined to stop hiding inside and go out to enjoy the weather. Winter wouldn't be far away now, and while it would never be as bad as the winters in the mountains of western Maryland, where she'd grown up, she knew she'd soon be missing these sunny, cool days.

Heading out her door and down the stairs, she bumped

into the couple who lived in the apartment directly above hers. She hadn't known them long, but she already liked them a lot, appreciating the way the women had immediately been neighborly without being intrusive.

"Hey, Lulu," said Marcia, who was carrying a bag of groceries in one hand and was shoving her glasses up her nose with the other.

"Morning," she replied, holding the front door of the building open so Marcia and Peggy could come inside with their groceries.

"Did you have a good Halloween?" asked Peggy.

"It was…interesting," she admitted.

That was an understatement.

"It must have been if you slept so heavily this morning that you didn't notice all the commotion around here," Marcia said, her voice filled with amusement.

"Why? What happened?"

"Peggy played hero for some kid whose kitty got stuck in the tree out front. She climbed up to rescue it."

Lulu's eyes widened in surprise. The tree was a monster; she'd seen last spring's kites still tangled in its branches. "You didn't go too high, did you?"

Peggy groaned, embarrassed.

"Yes, she did," said Marcia, dropping an arm across the other woman's shoulders. "She made the mistake of looking down."

"I never knew I was afraid of heights," Peggy said, gazing at her feet and scuffing her toe on the tiled floor.

"I had to call 911 and a fire crew came and helped her down."

"Damn, I missed hot firefighters?"

"Well, there was one hot one," said Peggy, "but I don't think she was your type."

"She wasn't yours, either," said Marcia with a smirk as

she held up her left hand, on which glittered a gold wedding band. The two had gotten married this past summer, happy to be in a city that celebrated freedom and let them live their lives exactly as they wanted to.

"And I wouldn't have it any other way," said Peggy, lightly kissing her wife's cheek. Turning to Lulu, she asked, "Where you off to?"

"Just out for a walk. It's too nice to stay inside."

"Definitely. Tomorrow's supposed to be even nicer. Why don't you join us out back for dinner then? We're going to have one final grill-out of the fall. The couple from the first floor is coming. It'll be a BYOM party."

"BYOM?"

"Bring your own meat."

Promising she would join them the next day, Lulu said goodbye to the couple and headed outside. She turned right at the sidewalk, as usual. Then she hesitated. Chaz's house was so close, she'd have to walk right past it. He might be sleeping off his travel jet lag. Or he might be sleeping because he'd been up all night wondering about the woman who'd run out on him. Or he might be wide awake, plotting his revenge.

Hell. It was worth taking a different route today.

She spun around, ready to do exactly that, when a male voice called out, "Hey, you! Wait a minute—stop!"

There was no denying that voice, or the demanding tone.

It was Chaz.

Closing her eyes and taking a deep breath, she turned around to face the music. There was no point delaying the inevitable. She'd have to see him sometime and part of her just wanted to get it over with and stop worrying about it.

Another part was wondering how, exactly, she would react if he recognized her not as his childhood nemesis, but as his almost-lover of the previous night. He'd seen her from behind, but had called out with something that sounded like desperation. So she suspected he'd been searching for his mystery woman, and believed he'd spotted her.

Now the question remained: was this morning's encounter going to end in anger, ambivalence or attempted seduction?

Chaz was jogging up the sidewalk, looking determined, but he slowed to a walk when he got a good look at her. A confused frown tugged at his brow as he studied her, his gaze resting on her long brown hair, then traveling over her face. She knew the exact moment he recognized her, because his mouth opened in a quick, surprised inhalation, and his eyes widened in shock.

"Lulu? Is that you?"

She pasted a smile on her lips. "It sure is. Hi, Chaz!" She cursed herself for sounding giddy—and guilty. "Er, how are you doing? I guess you're home from your trip?" She made sure to keep her voice pitched up a bit, wanting to sound as far from the throaty-voiced temptress of the night as possible.

His long-legged strides brought him to within a few feet of her, and he stopped, staring into her face as if searching for something. Or someone?

Don't find her. Please don't find her in me.

"It's really you?" he asked.

"Yup." She forced the brightest, most unconcerned smile she could manage. "I guess I turned up just like the proverbial bad penny."

"This is a surprise."

More like a shock, judging by his expression.

"A nice one, I hope," she said, just to needle him a little.

"Sure. Definitely."

Deciding to remind him it had been partially his fault

that they'd ended up neighbors, she said, "Oh, thanks bunches for putting me in touch with your Realtor. She was such a big help. She told me this was the best street in the city to live on."

She waved toward the building she'd just left, and Chaz glanced at it, then back at her.

"You live here?"

"Yes."

"Right here," he clarified, tensing. "Three doors down from me?"

"'Fraid so."

He continued to stare, and she shifted uncomfortably on her sneakered feet. She hadn't expected Chaz to bring out the welcome wagon, but yeesh, he acted as if she'd contaminated his street.

Finally she asked, "Do I have dirt on my face or something?"

"I'm sorry," he mumbled. "When I first saw you, from behind, I thought you were somebody else. But of course, I was wrong."

"They say everybody has a double."

He slowly shook his head, and she'd swear disappointment had darkened his eyes. "No, it was just a mistake. She didn't really look like you at all."

Huh. What was that supposed to mean? She felt as if she'd been judged and found lacking. What, exactly, did the green-faced witch have that she didn't, aside from red hair and a mask?

Oh. Right. An untainted history and a name other than Lulu Vandenberg. Even if she were a real redhead, and still had on the dumb mask, she suspected that Chaz would have worn that same expression of disappointment the moment he realized who she truly was.

Shoving aside the sharp feeling of regret, she tried to appear chipper. "So, how's your family?"

"They seem fine. I talked to my dad this morning." He chuckled. "Did you hear? We're all being abandoned for Thanksgiving."

Her jaw dropped. "What?"

"Yeah. My family usually meets up at my grandparents' house down in Virginia for the holiday weekend."

"I remember." That was one reason she hadn't seen Chaz in so many years. He never came home for Thanksgiving, as his family was always traveling elsewhere. And it seemed the two of them had alternated Christmases for the past several years, never making a holiday trip home at the same time.

"Well, apparently our parents—yours and mine—have decided to go on a couples cruise to the Caribbean over Thanksgiving weekend. They're leaving the Tuesday before and will be gone for ten days."

"Nice of them to tell a person," she said, indignant. Then mischief tickled her lips and she grinned. "You'd think they had a life other than us, or something."

"I know, right?" he replied, sounding just as indignant-yet-amused.

Just to rile him up, she smirked. "I bet yours have already turned your room into a sex den like out of that *Fifty Shades* book."

He grimaced. "I know you opened your mouth and said something, but all I heard was mwah mwah mwah mwah mwah."

She couldn't hold back a rumble of laughter. When they were kids, they'd all mimicked their parents—well, all adults—in just that way. Words might be coming out of a grown-up's mouth, but all they'd heard was monotonous noise—like all kids, she supposed.

Funny how the adult world existed so far apart from the kid one, neither believing the other was ever really aware of what was going on. Also funny that she was standing here with a man who'd shared so many years of that world with her.

Yet gazing up at him, she saw nothing of the kid and every inch of the man.

What a delicious-looking man. He was sexy by moonlight, but devastatingly attractive in the light of day. The sun gleamed in his blond hair, and brought out the matching glimmer of gold in his green eyes. Now, clad in sneakers instead of those deadly high-heels, she was reminded just how tall he was, towering over her by several inches. And the long-sleeved T-shirt emphasized those broad shoulders and his powerful chest.

She'd have liked to say that quip about the naughty book hadn't caused some seriously hawt images to invade her brain, but she'd have been lying. Frankly, she'd had those images in her head since she'd seen him pulling off that sheet last night at the bar, and just about every minute since.

"So," he said, "I guess that means I'm going to have to learn how to cook a turkey."

"I hear Stauffer's does a pretty good job of that, and you get the stuffing and gravy right on top of it."

He sneered. "Frozen dinners for Thanksgiving? Forget it. How tough can it be?"

"Just remember to take the insides out of the bird before you cook it."

He paled. "They come with insides?"

"Pretty gross, huh?" Lulu had never been much of a cook, but she was pretty sure they did. "But yeah, I think so. And don't worry, I'll play dumb when my mom calls. I won't let her know you spilled the beans."

"Admit it, you just want to torment her and make her feel guilty."

"Ha. I think I'll call *her* and tell her I'm bringing home my new boyfriend for the holiday."

His smile remained, though she would swear it was a tiny bit tighter than before. She quickly thrust the impression away. Ridiculous to think Chaz would give a damn if she was dating anyone.

"You're seeing someone?"

Okay. So he gave a damn. Interesting.

She thought about implying she was but honestly didn't want to play those kinds of games with Chaz. Last night was as much gaming as she cared to do with the man. Besides, intentionally making somebody jealous was more his sister's style. "No. But I can't come up with a better way to make her sweat."

"You're an evil woman, Lulu Vandenberg," he said, the tone admiring.

"Diabolical, that's me. How could you have forgotten?"

"I haven't. But evil looks a little better on you than it did when you were seven and you tied me up to a telephone pole during a game of cops and robbers, and *left* me there."

Yeah. She'd kind of done that. "If it's any consolation, my mom spanked me after your parents called the police to report you missing and I had to tell the officers where you were."

"You deserved it."

"I guess I did. I'm really surprised you didn't just clobber me."

"I thought about it every day of our childhood." Amusement danced in his green eyes. "But maybe I just always wanted to believe my mom was right."

"About?"

"She used to say you tormented me so much because you secretly had a crush on me."

Lulu's mouth opened and then snapped closed. He

sounded so amused, so damned confident, as if he'd decided his mom was right.

"In your dreams, Chaz Browning."

"You were. Often."

Her brow shot up. So did her heart rate.

"Well, in my nightmares, anyway."

She couldn't help it. She balled her fist and punched his upper arm.

He rubbed at it, giving an exaggerated groan, then broke into a smile. "You still hit like a girl."

"Do you?"

"Uh-uh."

No, she didn't imagine he did, not with those muscle-bearing-muscles.

"I thought you were a lover, not a fighter."

He certainly had seemed that way last night, when he'd been so close, so very close, to becoming her lover. Damn it, why had Sarah shown up and scared her into running away from what she suspected would have been one of the best nights of her life?

"I am. But I sometimes go to some pretty dangerous places. I took up martial arts, just to be on the safe side."

Lulu didn't like to think of him needing to defend himself, though she knew he'd probably had to at one time or another. But it was a reminder of all the reasons why they could never work.

"Did anything like that happen on your most recent trip?" she asked.

"Nah. Totally uneventful. It was pretty boring."

Right. Except for his quick little excursions into freaking Afghanistan. Not that she could tell him she knew about that.

It had been easier when they'd been strangers.

"When did you get back?" she asked, since it seemed to be the sort of question she should ask.

"Yesterday. Just in time to go out and celebrate the holiday." He shook his head, as if clearing it of confusing memories, then managed a friendly, if noncommittal, smile. "It was a pretty long trip."

"You go away a lot?"

"Yes. My job is everything to me, but it has its downsides."

"Like?"

"Like…well, I can't have a dog. I'm away too much."

"I imagine that would be next to impossible."

"Ah, well, I guess I'm a one-dog man, anyway."

She understood, remembering how much Chaz had always adored his beagle.

"I do keep him close, though," he said.

Raising a curious brow, she watched as he pulled his shirt collar down a little, and tugged it away from his skin, just enough for her to make out the ink on his back. Finally, she was able to see what she hadn't been able to make out last night: his tattoo. The image of a cute little dog was etched on his shoulder, a constant reminder and a tribute to a beloved pet.

How very Chaz-like.

Part of her melted, wanting to hug him to commiserate, and wanting to ask him how somebody so utterly gorgeous and so incredibly nice could possibly still be single.

Another part reminded her she needed to keep up as many barriers as she could, if only to prevent him from ever finding out how she'd tricked him the night before. Chaz had always been very forgiving, but she remembered he'd had a real problem with liars—something he'd said had only intensified with the high stakes of his job. While she didn't think she'd actually said anything that was a lie, she was certainly guilty of it by omission.

One thing she knew, however. It was going to be very difficult to keep her secret about how attracted she was to him if he kept doing things like pulling his shirt down to reveal his powerful, muscular shoulders and back.

Damn you, Sarah, for making me realize I was making a mistake about twenty minutes too soon!

"Anyway, enough about me. How are you enjoying the city so far?"

"I love it," she admitted. "The apartment's great, my job's going well, I'm making friends."

"Where is it you're working?"

Uh-oh. He wasn't going to trip her up again. Her job was much too unique to give him the same answer she'd provided last night. So she went for the most literal reply possible. "Up on Mass Ave. I've become a total city girl, I love taking the Metro train everywhere." She glanced at her watch, pretending she had somewhere to be. "Speaking of which, I'd better run."

"Oh, okay. Well, it was good seeing you."

He actually sounded a little disappointed. Considering he'd just admitted she gave him nightmares, that came as a surprise.

"You, too, Chaz. See ya later."

Hoping she'd come off utterly casual and not the least bit like the mysterious woman he'd met the night before, Lulu walked away as if she actually had somewhere to go.

She felt his eyes on her as she strode toward the end of the block, but managed to avoid looking back. By the time she turned the corner and risked a peek, the street behind her was empty. Maybe she'd just been fooling herself that he had any interest in her at all.

6

LULU.

Lulu Vandenberg.

Lulu Pain-in-the-ass Vandenberg was practically his next-door neighbor. And to make matters worse, for a minute that morning, from a few doors away, he'd thought she was his fantasy woman from last night.

Honestly, Chaz wasn't sure which bothered him more—having somebody who'd tormented him during his geeky, embarrassing younger years so close by, or mistaking that girl for a woman who'd blown his mind while she'd blown *him*.

One thing was for sure—he could never tell Lulu that little tidbit. She'd either laugh in his face…or just slap it. It wasn't nice to have those kinds of thoughts about your parents' best friends' daughter. Or about the girl who'd called you a blockhead for the better part of elementary school.

He managed to hide his snicker when he remembered the new urban slang for the word *blockhead*. It definitely didn't mean what it had meant when they were kids.

In any case, he wasn't going to allow any of those thoughts about Lulu. No way, uh-uh. It had been a simple mistake, quickly made, quickly rectified. He'd mistaken her, okay, *amazing* body for the one he'd been seeking since the previous night. But when he got close enough to see the dark brown hair and the familiar face, he'd shoved such images out of his mind.

That didn't, however, mean the realization that Lulu had grown up to be a very sexy woman was easy to forget. Damn, the girl he'd once known was now a stunner, with those long, dark waves of hair falling well past her shoulders and those heavily-lashed eyes. She had definitely grown up in all the right places, developing the serious curves he'd once teased her she lacked. She now had the kind of body that would make a man drop to his knees and beg for her attention. Her jeans had been simple and faded, but had hugged curvy hips and long, slender legs. And her soft red sweater had emphasized full breasts and a slim waist.

Aside from her sex appeal, she was just beautiful to look at. He'd always thought her pretty, with her thick hair and expressive eyes, at least when she wasn't terrorizing him. But her features had been a little sharp, an impression maybe reinforced by her personality. Now, though, everything had softened, from her face, to her smile, to her voice, to her attitude.

He'd actually enjoyed their brief conversation, and would have liked to continue it. But she'd hurried away from him as quickly as she could. So maybe the long-awaited reunion hadn't been as enjoyable to her as it had been to him.

Which irritated him. She'd always seemed to have the power in their relationship, and it seemed some things never changed.

He was just about to go back to his place when he saw

Peggy, his friend and neighbor—and Lulu's—waving from the front door of their building. She gestured him forward.

"Hey, Chaz, can you give us a hand with something?"

"I can try."

"Great. Marcia got a new laptop, and all either of us know about setting it up is pushing the On button."

"I can't guarantee I'll get you much further than that."

"Well, if you can at least get us online so we can stream the newest episode of *Teen Wolf,* we'll pay you back with a steak dinner tomorrow." Peggy wagged her eyebrows up and down and stepped out of the way to let him in the building. "Our pretty neighbor will be joining us. I see you've met her?"

"You mean Lulu?"

"Yeah."

He nodded. "Actually, we've known each other since we were kids."

"Oooh, isn't that interesting?"

"Not particularly." Wanting to nip any matchmaking ideas about him and Lulu in the bud, he asked, "You've lived around here for a few years, right?"

"Yep. We lived one block over until two years ago and right here ever since. Why?"

"I'm just wondering…do you ever remember meeting a really gorgeous redhead? Tall, maybe five-seven, with dark eyes and a great mouth?"

"Hey, I'm a happily married woman."

"I didn't mean for you," he said with a grin.

"Aww, come on, Chaz, you don't need a redhead when you were shooting some serious sparks with our down-stairs neighbor."

Lulu? No way, not a chance. He might agree she was sexy, but the only sparks the two of them would set off each other would be if it was the Fourth of July and she stuck a firecracker down his shirt.

"We're just friends. We literally grew up next door to each other."

"Well, isn't it a funny coinkydink, you two ending up as neighbors again. Like fate."

"No, it's not fate. I hooked her up with my Realtor, who works in this area. No hidden meanings or motives. Lulu and I were childhood playmates, and absolutely nothing else."

Playmates, adversaries, same difference.

"Okay," Peggy said with an exaggerated shrug, "If you say so. But I still gotta tell ya, Chaz, from where I was standing, the two of you looked like anything but mere friends."

As if realizing he was uncomfortable, she changed the subject and led him up to the third-floor apartment. Chaz spent a few hours with Peggy and Marcia, helping them set up the new laptop and hook it to their wireless network. He'd never be called a computer genius, but it wasn't too complicated.

Though he didn't, by any means, expect anything for his labors, he ended up accepting their invitation to a cook-out the following afternoon. He told himself it had nothing to do with Lulu's presence and wanting to even the score with her. He'd simply been out of the country for a while and looked forward to a last outdoor gathering before the doldrums of winter set in. And he'd probably need to relax and have a few beers with friends after what he expected would be a difficult breakfast with his kid sister.

Besides, spending time with everyone who lived in the building would give him a chance to ask Marcia and the couple from the first floor if they knew a sexy, mysterious redhead. That should hammer home to everyone—including him—the fact that he didn't care at all about Lulu.

The next day turned out better than he'd expected, since a much more cheerful Sarah had blown off breakfast in favor of a day with friends. So he had plenty of time to unpack and do laundry, and go shopping for this afternoon's gathering.

He arrived a few minutes after four. Peggy had said they were cooking out early to take advantage of the daylight in the rapidly shortening fall day. He headed around to the back of the building, following the sound of voices and laughter. Marcia and Peggy were there, sitting at a picnic table across from a good-looking African-American man. The middle-aged couple who lived on the bottom floor—Florence and Herman? Sherman? something like that—were at the grill, him cooking on it, her telling him how to do it better. They both looked up at him and smiled in greeting.

Lulu sat away from the group, on a garden swing that hung from a tall, leaf-bare tree, pushing off with the tips of her toes to set the thing in motion. Her eyes rounded in surprise when she saw him. "Chaz?"

"Hi, everyone," he said, setting a bottle of wine and a twelve-pack of beer on the table.

"What are you doing here?" she asked, getting up and approaching him, sounding confused, though not exactly unwelcoming.

"Peggy and Marcia invited me."

"Surprise!" said Peggy. "Chaz told me you two were pals from the olden days, and he did us a solid helping us set up our wireless network."

Marcia piped in. "Plus, well, the more the merrier. We wanted to share some news with our friends and neighbors and figured we'd make this a little celebration."

The two women glanced at each other and then Peggy went around to stand behind Marcia, dropping her hands onto her shoulders.

"What's the news?" asked Lulu.

"First, we should introduce Frankie."

The good-looking stranger who'd been sitting at the table smiled and waved as Peggy ran down everyone's names. "Nice meeting y'all."

"Frankie works with Marcia," Peggy explained. "He recently helped us out with a very special project."

"More special than your internet?" Chaz asked with an eyebrow wag.

Peggy's laughter nearly deafened him. "Oh, yeah. You see…we're going to have a baby."

Lulu squealed, as did Florence. Sherman threw his arms up and shouted congratulations in a language that sounded like Italian. Frankie looked proud, and Peggy and Marcia utterly ecstatic.

"Congratulations," Chaz said, smiling at both women. "I can't imagine a kid having better parents."

Lulu rushed around the table and hugged them both, then said, "Okay, now tell me, which one of you *doesn't* get to drink the wine or beer?"

The two women eyed each other mischievously, then both pointed to Marcia's belly. "Seven months without wine, coffee or junk food. I don't know how I'm going to make it."

"I'm going without, too, in solidarity," said Peggy. "Uh, except for the junk food. There's only so much a Nacho Cheese Doritos addict can do to support the woman she loves."

The dinner then segued from a casual neighborhood thing to a celebration. Through it, Chaz watched Lulu, glad to see how totally cool she was with the whole situation.

They'd both been raised in a pretty small, conservative town. His own horizons had expanded exponentially after he'd left, and it appeared Lulu's had, too. She was completely gracious and genuinely happy for her new friends.

They all talked and joked through dinner, each offering suggestions for names, one more outrageous than the last. Then, after the steaks were finished and they'd moved on to s'mores for dessert, made over the still smoking grill, Marcia asked, "So, Lulu, what was our Chaz like as a boy?"

Lulu had just sipped a mouthful of wine, and she swallowed quickly, swinging her gaze toward him. He gave a not-so-subtle warning shake of his head.

"Remember, I'm a writer. Any story you can tell, I can tell better," he threatened.

She laughed softly, her brown eyes sparkling in the low light cast from the grill and from a small, warming blaze burning in the fire pit. Her lips were stained red from the wine she'd been drinking, and her hair had blown loose of its ponytail, several strands whipping across her face.

Damn, she was beautiful. If she were anyone else—absolutely *anyone*—she might even be tempting enough to console him over the apparent loss of his mystery woman.

"Well, Chaz was…"

"A loser," he interjected.

She glared at him. "A sweetheart. The nicest boy in town."

He made a rude noise and rolled his eyes. "I don't remember you thinking that when you called me a doody-head because I wouldn't let you ride my new bike on Christmas morning."

"I was five," she said. "And I was the doody-head for assuming you should give up your brand-new bike to the brat next door."

"She's right," said Peggy, obviously amused.

"I might not have told you," Lulu admitted, "but I certainly thought you were the nicest kid I knew." She qualified her answer, offering the group a sheepish smile. "At least…some of the time. Other times, I thought he was a butthead."

He raised his glass. "Here's to the first honest thing you've said."

She raised hers, as well, laughter dancing in her eyes.

After sipping, he jumped in, not wanting her to get the upper hand. "As for Lulu, she was a holy terror."

"No," Marcia protested.

"I don't believe that," said Florence. "She's so quiet, barely a peep from upstairs. I worried when she moved in, thinking such a pretty girl would be bringing the men around at all hours of the night, but there's never a sound from her bedroom, which is right above ours." She reached out and patted Lulu's hand. "She's a good girl."

Color rose in Lulu's cheeks as everyone tried to hide their snorts of laughter. Florence, older and maybe a bit naive, didn't appear to realize her compliment had included a back-handed insult. She looked around in confusion, even as Lulu sunk lower in her seat as everyone speculated on her lack of a sex life.

Chaz caught her eye and offered her a genuine smile. Then he mouthed something only she would understand.

Mwah, mwah, mwah, mwah, mwah.

Their stares locked, and she suddenly laughed with him, the sound infectious, her smile breathtaking.

He was seeing her in a much different light than he'd ever expected to, and he didn't just mean physically, though the physical was definitely potent.

Not that anything could come of it, obviously. The family connection alone would make it impossible for them to try anything beyond friendship, if either of them were interested in that, which he doubted.

When the gathering began to break up, he stayed behind to help clean up. Everybody in the building had brought down something, and then left with what they'd brought. Lulu's contribution had apparently been the plates and silverware. The dishes were all dirty now, and there was no way she could carry all of them up to her place, so he stepped in.

"I'll help Lulu take this up," he offered, clearing one end of the table.

"Thanks, Chaz, we're loaded down," said Peggy. She gestured toward her wife. "And that one's not allowed to carry anything more than a spoon."

Smiling at each other tenderly, the other two women headed inside with platters of leftovers, leaving him and Lulu alone to finish up.

"They're great, aren't they?" she mused.

"Yeah, they're the best," he said. "Peggy and Marcia were the first neighbors I met when I moved in, and they helped me unpack boxes for a week."

"They did the same thing for me. I appreciated the help—and I appreciate yours now," she said. "I'd hate to make three trips since I live on the second floor."

He could have been nice and not taken a swing at the pitch she'd thrown. But he just couldn't resist. "Yeah, I heard you lived on the second floor. Your room is right above Florence's."

She scowled and threw a wadded-up napkin in his face.

"Okay, sorry, I didn't hear a word Florence said," he claimed with a wicked grin.

"As if she'd hear anything, anyway," Lulu said, tossing her head, which shook free her ponytail, sending her dark hair tumbling down her back. "I happen to have a very new bed with quiet springs."

He supposed she was trying to salvage her pride, but he wasn't focused on that. For some reason, the idea of Lulu bouncing around in bed with a man was enough to make him stop laughing.

It's just because you're not used to thinking of her as a grown woman. You're still picturing the girl next door, the one who wore angel's wings and a halo in her second grade Christmas pageant, making all the other kids laugh because Lulu was anything but angelic.

Yeah. That was it. Totally.

It had nothing to do with her delicious-looking body, that amazing mouth, all that thick, dark hair that he could suddenly envision being spread across his naked stomach.

Jeez, he really needed to get a grip. More, he needed to find the woman he'd met Friday night. Sexual frustration was making him think the craziest thoughts about someone he should never consider in that way.

"I could give Florence something to listen to," she muttered, still obviously disgruntled about her neighbor's comments. "Something that would have her reaching for her earplugs and praying for my soul."

"Gonna download porn from the internet and set the speaker by the air vent?"

She glared at him. "Some men actually find me attractive, you know."

He didn't doubt it. Physically, she was mouthwatering. It was the nonphysical part that was the problem.

"And I don't need porn."

"Nobody *needs* porn," he said philosophically. "But it can be kinda fun on occasion."

She licked her lips, her lashes dropping over those brown eyes. "Speaking from experience?" she asked, her voice probably not as cool and noncommittal as she'd been going for.

He kept his answer just as cool. "Maybe."

"And here I pegged you as the big stud, women in every town."

He couldn't believe they were having this conversation, but since they were, he decided to finish it. "Porn's not just for lonely guys who have no friends other than Hairy Palmer." Remembering the highlights from Friday night, he added, "You've never thought about watching other people have sex? Or of being watched yourself?"

"You mean, intentional exhibitionism?"

He nodded. She caught her lip between her teeth and shook her head violently. "Never," she swore, though he suspected she was lying to them both.

He had, on occasion, enjoyed watching sex, via hotel movie rentals and adventurous internet surfing. But until the other night in that savings and loan lobby, and then later up against that tree, he'd never even dreamed of someone watching him with a woman. That night had been so wild, so uninhibited and dangerous, he'd half wanted to be caught.

Chaz had never considered himself an exhibitionist, had never toyed with the idea of allowing strangers to peek in on his life, especially during his most personal moments. But somehow, he almost got off on the idea of laying the most earthy, sexual claim on a woman—*that* woman— while others stood watching in envy.

Deep down, the ancient caveman within him wanted to put his mark on her, to proclaim that she was his, and warn every other man not to trespass. He wanted to pleasure her, do wild, erotic things to her that nobody would ever even dare try to repeat because they knew he'd set a bar so high it could never be surpassed. He wanted to show off, to prove he was the ultimate lover so she'd never dream of being with anyone else.

It was sexist, it would probably piss off most women, but it was entirely true.

He didn't think it would anger his mystery witch, though. She'd seemed just as into it as he was. Maybe that was one reason why he so wanted to find her again… to see if she shared the fantasy and wanted to finish what they'd started. In public, in private, it didn't matter. He just wanted to have her.

"Here," Lulu said, interrupting his heated musings by shoving a trio of dirty plates in his hands. "Get your mind out of the gutter."

"You brought it up."

"I most certainly did not!"

"You're the one who mentioned bouncy bedsprings."

"Oh, shut up."

Laughter on his lips at how easy she was to rile, he followed her inside and up the back stairs. A few steps below her, he found himself eye level with an amazing ass and wished he hadn't just been picturing such graphic thoughts.

When, he wondered, had Lulu become so thoroughly feminine? She had curves on top of curves, and he couldn't tear his stare off those amazing hips and thighs as he followed two steps behind her. Thinking about porn and voyeurism and sex ninety seconds before being presented face-to-butt with pure temptation was not a good thing for any guy. Especially not if he wanted to keep his jeans lying flat against his groin.

His weren't.

Holy shit. They *weren't*.

He was hard for Lulu. If he were to be honest about it,

he'd have to admit he'd started getting hard when she'd made that crack about her bedsprings.

This was unacceptable on so many levels, he couldn't even begin to count them. Lulu had made his life hell, she was trouble, she was a part of his past that he didn't much care to revisit. He had no business imagining her body or her bed or anything else.

On the top step, she swung around and caught him staring.

"I knew you were looking at my ass," she said, typical blunt Lulu.

He couldn't even try to deny it. Hell, all she had to do was glance down and see the bulge in his jeans and she'd prove him a liar. Which meant he needed to keep her attention focused above his waist.

"Guilty. You definitely grew up." He stepped up beside her, forcing himself to smile down at her. "When'd that happen?"

"When you weren't looking."

He was looking now, though he shouldn't be. He couldn't even figure out why he wanted to. This was *Lulu* of all people! The girl had poured an entire milkshake over his head once because he'd asked her if she'd been crying. He had no doubt she'd do the same thing again today if she had the chance.

"I somehow suspect you forgot who you were talking to and who you were ogling," she whispered, blinking those dark eyes—familiar eyes, beautiful eyes—and staring searchingly at his face.

"Maybe I did, for just a minute."

Some instinct he couldn't define made him reach up to smooth back a strand of her long, dark hair, which was wind-whipped and soft against his fingers. His fingertips brushed against her cheekbone, and he realized her skin was equally as soft, her peaches-and-cream complexion revealing a flush of color in her face.

Her tongue flicked out and she moistened her lips, exhaling a long, slow breath as the lingering stare continued.

He was hit with the strangest feeling of déjà vu. It was ridiculous, really, because he'd never touched her like this. He'd never even dreamed he might someday have the impulse to lean in and taste that sassy, saucy mouth, to kiss the insults right out of it.

And yet he did.

He suddenly wanted to kiss her, wanted to experience that lush mouth against his own. He wanted to press her soft, curvy body against his and wanted to explore every inch of her.

Of Lulu. Lulu Vandenberg.

"Lulu," he whispered, feeling himself lean closer, drawn by something irresistible and irrevocable, as if he had no strength of will.

Their faces came close. Their lips nearly touched.

Then she took a step back and grabbed the dishes out of his hands. "I can handle it from here."

He blinked, shaking his head hard, wondering whether he'd fallen under some magic spell. How else could he possibly explain his desire to do something as insane as kiss a girl he'd barely tolerated for most of his life?

"Thanks for the help," she said, stepping across the small hallway to the door of her place. "I'll see you later."

Not waiting for him to reply, she twisted the unlocked knob and stepped into her apartment. She shut the door hard, the audible flipping of the lock from within punctuating what she'd been saying to him.

Good night. Goodbye. Go away.

"You're welcome," he whispered. "Goodbye."

He would swear he heard her shuddery exhalation from

inside. Chaz sensed she stood right on the other side of the door, resting her head against it, uncomfortable, unsure.

How very unlike her.

He turned to do exactly as she wanted. He would go away. For now, at least.

But not forever.

Because something had occurred to him when she'd reacted so anxiously to their unexpected chemistry. For some reason, having him around made her nervous. The situation unsettled her far more than it did him. Which meant for once in their long history, he had the advantage.

How interesting to finally have gained an advantage over Lulu Vandenberg.

And how fun it might be to use that advantage to drive her absolutely insane.

7

ALTHOUGH LULU TRIED to keep her mind off Chaz, mere proximity made it impossible. Over the next several days, she ran into him every single morning. It was as if fate kept putting him in her path. Or, well, their work schedules did.

They both left at around the same time every weekday, and both rode the Metro to their respective places of employment. That meant they walked to the station together, waited together, even rode together for a few stops. They talked, at least as much as two coffee addicts could manage to talk at seven in the morning.

And both of them put on a pretty good front, as if they didn't really mind being thrown into each other's company so much, even though she, at least, definitely did. Because being with Chaz—even when she was bleary-eyed and coffee-deprived, focused on work and the shitty commute and the rush of people in the city—still excited her altogether too much for her peace of mind.

She just couldn't go back to thinking of him as good old Chaz. Not when she'd spent one wicked evening with the man, a man more sexually exciting than any she'd ever known. The attraction was eating at her, the pressure to keep her secret intensely frustrating. Every time she saw Chaz swing his head around to catch a glimpse at a passing redhead, she wanted to stomp on his foot, grab his face and order him to look at *her*.

Yes, she'd been masked, yes her hair had been sprayed a different color, yes she'd intentionally tried to change the tone of her voice, but still, couldn't he recognize her scent? The shape of her mouth? The hands, the body, the laugh? Jesus, she would be able to pick him out in a packed stadium, even if she'd never met him before Halloween night, and the fact that he hadn't even begun to connect her to his mystery witch was driving her a little nutty.

She'd told herself she was being stupid, since evading detection was absolutely necessary. But that hadn't helped much. The more her frustration built, the more she realized she needed to steer clear of him.

Hoping to do just that, she'd tried to leave earlier one day…and so had he. She'd wondered if he was trying to avoid her, too. Neither of them admitted it, and he probably felt as dumb as she did. As far as he was concerned, they were old neighbors for heaven's sake, there should be no reason they couldn't chat comfortably.

Well, except for the part that he'd fingered her to an orgasm and she'd sucked his big, hard cock as if it was the world's tastiest peppermint stick. But he didn't know that.

Thankfully, on Saturday she had a break. She wouldn't have to spend another morning pretending to seek nothing but long-standing friendship for a guy whose body filled her fantasies and whose mouth made her weak in the knees—and who would hate her guts when he found out the truth.

She slept in that morning, but her internal clock wouldn't let her stay asleep any later than nine. Getting up, she deliberately bounced the springs of her bed, and stepped a little heavier on her hardwood floors. Now that she was aware Florence was downstairs listening, she felt the need to put up a brave, false front. Hell, did the entire building really have to discuss her sex life...or lack thereof? Oh, that moment had been embarrassing. Bless Chaz for knowing exactly what to do to get her past her immediate humiliation by making her laugh.

Chaz the savior, Chaz the sweetheart, Chaz the good guy. How could she ever have considered him Chaz the loser? She must have been the one with rocks in her head.

Needing to get completely out of the neighborhood today, she was grateful for another weekend of unseasonably warm weather. It wasn't quite as nice as last weekend had been, when she hadn't even required a jacket. Still, it was pleasant enough for some outdoor activities, and she knew how she would spend her afternoon.

In good weather, some of her coworkers and other city residents got together for kickball games near the Washington Monument every other weekend. A coworker had left her a message last night, saying today would be the last game of the year, and urging her to come. Wanting the company and the exercise, and needing the distraction, she'd agreed. She knew better than to ask her two closest friends, Viv and Amelia, to join in. Viv's only physical activity was having sex, and Amelia always worked at her craft shop on Saturdays. Still, it should be fun to work off some energy with some newer friends.

Donning athletic clothes and her sneakers, she headed outside. Turning right would take her down to the Metro station, but would also send her right past Chaz's front door. He was probably busy, almost certainly wouldn't be looking out the window, and, even if he did, and if she saw her, he definitely wouldn't come out to talk to her. He probably felt stalked after their daily interactions during the work week.

But…she turned left anyway. She was taking the long way around, adding a couple of blocks to her walk, but it was worth it, if only for her peace of mind.

"Tell me the truth, are you following me or did you plant a tracking device in my jacket?"

Shocked when she heard a familiar voice, she looked to the entrance of a small cafe on the corner, seeing a very familiar man emerging from within.

"Chaz?"

"Hello, Lulu."

"What are you doing here?"

"I just came out to grab a late breakfast. What are *you* doing here?"

"I'm on my way to the station."

His brow furrowed in confusion and he pointed back the way she'd come. "The station's that way."

She scrambled for a suitable retort. "I mean, well, I wanted to grab a sports drink, then I'm heading to the station."

"Believe it or not, that's where I'm going, too," he said with a helpless shrug. "Where are you off to?"

"Up to the Mall for a game of kickball."

His jaw dropped open. "Seriously?"

Sudden foreboding made her tense. "Yes. Why?"

Shaking his head slowly, he replied, "Well, I'm going to the same place, for the same reason."

Lulu's stomach churned. This wasn't going to be the quick hello-and-goodbye she'd envisioned. "Really?"

"Yep. I'm in an informal league. We play softball in the spring when a lot of people are around. It's more laid-back in the fall and we play kickball for fun. I heard some people were putting together a late-season game and said I'd play."

"Oh. I guess smart minds think alike. I played a few times earlier in the fall, and got asked to come today, too."

Of course, Chaz hadn't been at those previous games, since he'd been out of the country. She cursed her luck, wanting nothing more than to escape him before she did something stupid, like ask, "Hey, still searching in vain for a redhead with an ass you wanted to nibble on?"

She didn't, of course, and mentally slapped herself for even imagining him using that beautiful mouth on any sensitive part of her anatomy. She'd had enough wet dreams over the man this past week, not that any of them could compare to the real moments they'd shared in that ATM vestibule.

They were both silent for a moment, then Chaz said, "So, want to go up to the Mall together?"

Always the nice guy. He'd probably rather be anywhere else, with anyone else. But since she couldn't come up with a logical reason to decline, she merely nodded.

"I'll wait here if you want to go inside and grab a drink."

Again, she couldn't think of any way to refuse. Nodding, she stepped into the café, which sold bottled drinks, and grabbed the first one she could reach. She paid, carried it back outside, smiled and said, "Okay, ready to go?"

"That's not a sports drink."

She glanced at the bottle in her hand and realized she'd picked up a container of milk. Good grief, that was the last thing she needed to drink before running around playing a physical game.

Especially since she hated milk.

"Aren't you going to drink up?" he asked, a sparkle of mischief in his eye.

Damn it, Chaz knew she hated milk. He'd badgered her

often enough about the fact that she liked it over cereal, but wouldn't drink a glass unless she plugged her nose, and she still gagged as it went down.

"No, uh, I think I'll save it for later."

"Don't wait too long, it might curdle."

Yeah, so might her stomach if she tried to drink the stuff.

As they walked to the station, they passed some people with faces that were becoming familiar to her. Dupont Circle was a small part of a big city, and there was a strong sense of community here.

Chaz was friendly to everyone they passed, several of whom appeared to know him. She noted a lot of women gave him appreciative looks, and she suddenly found herself stepping a little closer to him on the cobbled walkway. Close enough that their legs brushed. That faint contact was all it took to remind her of the erotic moments they'd shared the weekend before, and she quickly stepped away.

But perhaps not quickly enough. Chaz was eyeing her, an inscrutable expression on his face. He appeared confused by something. She had to wonder if his own sense memories were working on him, trying to force the truth of her identity into his brain. Wouldn't that be about damn time?

And while she knew that would be the absolute worst thing that could happen in the long run, part of her was very interested in finding out just how Chaz Browning would react if he learned that the woman he'd been seeking had been right under his nose the whole time.

AFTER A WEEK of enforced proximity, Chaz probably shouldn't have suggested that he and Lulu head up to the Mall together. He'd had fun making her a little crazy this week by always making sure they bumped into each other on the way to work or when walking the neighborhood, but he didn't want to push her too far. Actually, when she'd mentioned where she was going, he should have kept his mouth shut about being en route to the same place, and found another way to spend the day.

What he should have said, however, and what he *had* said, were two different things. He wanted to spend the day in the company of the woman he couldn't stop thinking about…in good ways, and in bad.

Because a funny thing had happened during his campaign to rile her up this week—he'd realized he enjoyed being with her. Lulu had changed a lot. Her demeanor was down-to-earth and approachable. She joked around, but there was no real snark. She was just friendly and funny, never going for a dig when a quip would do, her voice holding no edge, her smile no malice.

And Lulu was certainly not hard to look at—sexy and appealing, even when dressed in sports clothes. Hell, *especially* when dressed in sports clothes. Spandex did amazing things for that already amazing ass and those legs.

If only she were anyone but the devil-next-door.

As they took the Metro up to the Mall, getting off at the Smithsonian station and walking past the Washington Monument down to the grassy area where the teams usually played, he and Lulu traded stories about kids they'd known and teachers they'd disliked. They had even laughed over some shared memories.

One topic that did not come up was their siblings. Damn, he did not want Sarah to find out Lulu lived right up the street from him. His hotheaded sister might march to her door and demand that Lulu do something about Lawrence, as if she had the right to order her high school boyfriend out of the nation's capital. But other than avoiding that subject, he and Lulu fell into an easy camaraderie that had been hinted at but never fully realized during their childhood.

Of course, that camaraderie all but disappeared during the game, when they realized they were on opposite teams. Lulu was as competitive as always, while Chaz, who showed up to these games mostly to hang out with friends, barely paid attention to the score.

"Come on, Browning, are you gonna kick it or sit on it?" Lulu called from the pitcher's mound, her tone pissy.

It was his turn to kick, but he'd taken his sweet time getting to home plate. He'd been talking with a colleague, Tonia, an attractive blonde with whom he'd shared a couple of interesting nights a couple of years ago. No sizzle remained between them, but he still liked her well enough.

"We don't have all day."

Lulu's almost angry tone made him finally give his full attention to the game. "Who made *you* pitcher?" he asked, watching her lean over to line up her rolling pitch.

"She's got a mean throw, dude, watch out," said one of his teammates, who'd apparently gone up against Lulu before.

"Chaz knows all about how mean I am," said Lulu, her smile appearing forced. She cast a quick, quelling look at Tonia, then got her head back in the game.

Lulu was all business when she pitched, whipping the rubber ball straight at him. It bounced twice before rolling fast and hard, directly toward the plate, where he met it with the broad side of his right foot. The ball flew up and over the entire field, down into a group of kids playing tag. No way would anybody get it back up here before he rounded all the bases.

As he jogged around the field, he caught Lulu's eye and grinned at her dour expression. "Guess I shoulda warned you," he called, laughter in his voice. "I'm not so bad at sports anymore."

"Does that mean I can actually be on your softball team in the spring and not worry we'll lose one-hundred to nothing?" she asked, her tone sugar-sweet, though her eyes were hard.

Her zinger just amused him even more, and his laughter rang out, simple and joyful. He laughed at her, and at the bright, sunny morning. He thoroughly enjoyed the feeling of being back in a place where he could appreciate a beautiful day like this without a pervading sense of fear or uncertainty.

Maybe someday he'd stop feeling the need to head off to one hotspot or another. At times like this, he could actually envision it. Hell, if he had the right person to make him want to stay, he might never get the urge to leave again.

The thought killed his laughter. He might already have found—and lost—the woman of his dreams on Halloween night. Well, maybe not of his dreams, but she was definitely the woman of his fantasies.

Most of them.

Yeah. Most of them. He wasn't about to admit to anyone—including himself—that Lulu had appeared in some pretty vivid mental pictures on a couple of occasions this week. She and the mysterious redhead both haunted him. That was crazy, since one was an old enemy and he didn't know the name of the other. Nor did he have any idea why she'd run out on him.

Thinking back on their evening, he forced himself to remember the number of times she'd tried to dance away, or put up barriers between them. She'd been on guard, making it clear she was only willing to go so far.

Maybe he'd pushed too hard and scared her off. Maybe she'd been afraid she'd come across too strong. Maybe she had a deathly fear of waffles. Whatever it was, something had made her change her mind. He simply wasn't going to rest until he knew who she was and why she'd left.

After the game, everyone headed for a nearby bar for midafternoon libations. Chaz walked with Tonia, while Lulu fell into step beside Darrell, a guy on Lulu's team. Chaz tensed, remembering Darrell was often called a pig by some of the women because he was such a player.

Lulu probably didn't know that, however, being so new to the area. Whatever the guy was saying to her had to be hilarious because she laughed like she was sitting in the front row of a Def Comedy Jam. Chaz kept his eyes on the back of her head, noting the jaunty bounce of her ponytail, a frown tugging at his mouth.

"What's wrong?" asked Tonia.

"Nothing," he insisted, not wanting to admit yet that the sight of Lulu so enjoying another guy's company bugged him.

His goal had been to drive Lulu crazy, not himself. But now, watching her looking up at Darrell, with a big smile on that beautiful mouth, all he could remember was that moment last weekend when he'd stood outside her door, brushed her hair off her face and wondered what it would be like to kiss her.

"How was your first week back?"

"Not bad," he replied, finally tearing his attention off his distracting neighbor. "I completed the first draft of part one of a series and sent it to editing. The powers-that-be seem to like it and are expecting a wide distribution."

He'd written several short articles while overseas, all of them distributed by the Associated Press and picked up by news outlets all over the world. But he'd also been asked to do an in-depth series with a narrower focus. They were to be longer pieces—five-thousand words—that could end up featured in one of the big print outlets. He sure wouldn't mind a *Time* magazine spot at this point in his career.

"How about you?"

Tonia frowned. "I'm still working on an exposé of that scam charity organization."

"What was that about again?" he asked, not remembering the details, which she'd mentioned to him the last time they'd talked, before his trip.

"It's one of those give-microloans-to-African-mothers things." Tonia sneered. "Another group of bleeding heart do-gooders trying to change the world, twenty-five dollars at a time."

"Those groups make a big difference in some parts of the world."

She rolled her eyes and waved a hand, obviously unwilling to even consider that she might be wrong. "Give me a break. I'm *sure* there's something dirty going on there, I just know it. But it's taking me a while to find it."

Chaz came to a sudden stop, turning to look at her. He suddenly remembered his conversation with his mystery woman, who'd talked about having a job just like that one. There couldn't be that many of those types of NGOs in Washington, could there?

He might have found a solid clue in tracking her down.

"I'm interested in hearing more," he said, meaning it. "Sit with me at the bar and tell me everything you've uncovered, okay?"

Tonia licked her lips as she slid her arm in his and they resumed walking. Something about her expression sent a warning through his brain. God, he hoped she didn't think he was just making excuses to be with her, in hopes of reviving their fling.

Because his mystery witch suddenly seemed more

within reach than ever. Which put a spring in his step and an anticipatory smile on his face.

When they got to the bar, the group spread out, taking up several tables. Everyone ordered beers and sandwiches, chatting loudly and making plans for the spring season. As promised, he sat with Tonia, feeling her out for information on the NGO she was researching, which was called Hands Across The Waters. He took mental notes, determined to research the group as soon as he got home. They might have a staff directory on their website, might even have pictures. He could feel himself edging closer and closer to solving the mystery.

But even as she filled him in, he kept glancing at a table by the door, where Lulu sat with Darrell, and a new arrival. Schaefer, who didn't play kickball, or do much of anything except pluck the strings of a guitar, had joined in. Apparently he was friends with one of the other players, who'd invited him to come over.

Lulu looked as pleased as punch to be sitting between the two men, both of whom were chatting her up. Honestly, Chaz had never seen Schaefer so animated. Or Darrell appearing so innocent.

"So, this Lulu chick," Tonia said with a frown, "I take it you know her?"

He tore his attention off the trio at the other table. "What?"

"Come on, you haven't taken your eyes off her since the two of you got to the game."

"We go back a ways. Grew up together."

"Ah. So you feel brotherly, huh? Because you looked like you wanted to go over there and rip Darrell's arm off when he put it around her."

"He's so sleazy," Chaz said, his jaw tightening. And

the very idea that he felt brotherly toward Lulu was just ridiculous.

"I don't know, I always thought he was pretty hot, and that he'd straighten up for the right woman." Tonia toyed with the condensation on her glass. "Maybe he thinks she's the one?"

That thought just made Chaz's annoyance increase. He couldn't help grumbling, "That booth's plenty big, he did not need to put his arm around her and pull her closer to make room for Schaefer." He took another gulp of his beer. "And is there any reason Schaefer couldn't have sat across from her, rather than next to her?"

"There's another guy sitting across from her."

"What sense does that make, three on one side of the table, one on the other?"

His companion sighed deeply. "How long ago did you two break up?"

He almost spit out his mouthful of beer. "Lulu and I have *never* been a couple."

She didn't appear convinced. "Uh-huh. Sure."

"No, seriously. She is the last woman in the world I'd even think about getting involved with."

"Right."

"She was the bane of my childhood. Our parents are best friends—they went through hell when my sister and Lulu's brother made the mistake of getting involved and then breaking up. I'd never put any of us through that again."

"Okay, okay, I get it," said Tonia, lifting her own drink. Before she sipped it, she added, "But remember that old adage about the guy who protested too much? Well, look in the mirror, dude. 'Cause that's you."

He wasn't quite ready to admit that her reporter instincts were spot on. But before he could even open his mouth, he got a glimpse under the other table and saw Darrell drop a hand onto Lulu's thigh and squeeze it. He was up out of his seat, a growl on his lips, before his brain even engaged.

Fortunately, he came to his senses. Or, Lulu came to hers. She immediately asked Schaefer to get out of the way and removed herself from Darrell's obnoxious grip. Giving him a withering glare that would reduce any guy to a tiny kernel of male ego, she excused herself and headed toward the back of the place, obviously looking for the ladies' room.

Schaefer made some kind of comment to Darrell, then got up and followed Lulu.

Chaz didn't think about it. Something wouldn't let him sit back down and allow Lulu to handle her own affairs. Mumbling an excuse to Tonia, he strode across the place, toward the hallway through which the others had disappeared.

Schaefer was hovering around outside the ladies' room door.

"Is there a line?" Chaz asked, nodding toward the men's.

The guy flushed and swallowed. "Oh, uh, no, go ahead."

He crossed his arms and jutted out his jaw. "You first."

Unable or unwilling to admit he'd been stalking Lulu, the other man ducked into the men's room, leaving Chaz alone in the dark, shadowy corridor. He stood there just long enough to ask himself what the hell he was doing when the ladies' room door opened and Lulu stepped out.

"Oh, Chaz! You startled me."

"Are you all right?"

She nodded, reaching up to tuck a strand of hair behind her ear. It was a little messy from the game. Her cheeks were high with color, her eyes bright, yet, altogether, she looked about as good as he'd ever seen her.

She affected him, deep inside, as all his protective instincts combined with his most covetous ones. He wanted to shield her from some horny guy because she deserved better...but also, he suddenly realized, because he wanted her for himself!

It was totally insane and unacceptable. Sure, he might have been flirting with her this past week to make her sweat, but he'd never intended it to go this far.

Still, he couldn't bring himself to just walk away and pretend he didn't care about what had happened.

"I'm fine, thanks."

"Is the pig bothering you?"

"Who?"

"Darrell. I saw him touch you."

Her lips tightened. "And you felt the need to, what, play overprotective older brother? I'm not Sarah, you know."

"The guy's a creep."

"I'm a big girl."

"I'm just giving you fair warning. You can't trust him."

"You think the third grope under the table didn't tip me off to that?"

Steam built in his head. "Third? He groped you three times? I only noticed him touch your leg."

She crossed her arms over her chest. "That's not surprising. I mean, how could you have been paying close attention to what I was doing when you were so busy trying to score with that ditzy blonde who's been hanging all over you?"

It was his turn to gape in surprise. "What?"

"Come on, Chaz, don't act like you don't know what I'm talking about," she said, edging closer until the tips of her sneakers touched his. "She acted like a toddler learning to walk during the game. *Oh, Chaz, would you teach little old me how to kick like that?* Gag me."

Tension and anger sparked between them, creating a nearly electric current. It crackled between their bodies, and he noticed her chest was heaving with anger and emotion as she struggled to control her breathing.

"Who's the pot and who's the kettle here?" he said, inching even closer, until one of his legs was between hers and their hips grazed. He ignored that, towering over her. "Sounds to me as if you're projecting your own behavior."

"I'm not shaking my tail under some guy's nose and playing the poor-hopeless-girl-can't-kick-a-ball role to try to get his attention," she snarled, not backing down one inch.

They were so close, they shared each breath. Fire snapped in her eyes, and her voice shook with emotion.

"No, you're just playing the creamy filling for a guy sandwich, sitting between two dudes who've been taking turns looking down your shirt."

She gasped audibly, and fisted her hand to punch him. Typical Lulu. Chaz instinctively reacted, reaching up and grabbing her wrist before she could take a swing.

They glared at each other for a loaded moment, and then, somehow, their mouths were together and they were kissing with anger-driven hunger.

Chaz didn't think, didn't plan. He acted on tension and instinct, just wanting to shut her up, to win the argument, to taste her and stop the crazy wondering that had been tormenting him since last week when he'd followed her up the stairs to her apartment.

He moaned, or she did, and suddenly her arms were around his neck, her fingers tangling in his hair and holding him tight. He dragged her body against his, lifting her off her feet and wrapping his arms around her waist.

Their tongues tangled wildly as they gave and took, demanded and received.

The kiss affected him from head to toe. The feel of her soft, curvy form against his drove him slightly mad, and he pushed her up against the wall, loving the way her legs instinctively snaked around his until he was supporting her entire weight. The spandex was slick in his hands, but he had no problem gripping her taut ass, hoisting her even higher until they were lined up at just the perfect angle for wild, intense, up-against-the-wall sex, just as he'd envisioned having on Halloween night.

It made no sense. That night, he'd been with a stranger who'd driven him wild with lust. But this was Lulu, a girl he'd known forever. How could she possibly be even more exciting, more arousing to him than his masked mystery woman?

Kissing Lulu was like leaping willingly into a volcano, aware you might get burned but also sure you'd be in for a hell of a ride when it erupted. It was pure, raw excitement, born out of anger, but quickly exploding into sexual frenzy.

Only the fact that they were erupting in a bar filled with their friends finally brought him to his senses. He ended the kiss, releasing her and staggering back one step. She did the same, her eyes wide and wild, her face red and her whole body quivering. She looked shocked and aroused, but her expression quickly segued into embarrassed confusion.

"What the hell was that?"

He thrust a hand through his hair, which was tangled from her tight grip. "Damn it, Lulu, I didn't mean…"

"Don't. Just don't say another word. This is bad enough."

"Uh, is there a problem?"

They both jerked their attention to the side and saw Schaefer, who'd just emerged from the men's room.

"No, there's no problem," Lulu insisted.

"I don't mean to intrude," the other guy said, "but Lulu, you seem upset."

"I'm fine."

"Are you sure? I could…"

"Back off, Ludwig," Chaz snapped.

Schaefer's eyes rounded into circles and his pale face lost what little color it had held. His spine stiffened, and he looked as though he had been slapped. Chaz closed his eyes, dropping his head, feeling like a complete heel. What the hell was it about Lulu that made all his brain cells dry up and blow away?

Lulu had obviously heard. *"Ludwig?"*

"You dick," Schaefer said, glaring at Chaz before pushing past them and heading straight to the exit. Chaz knew he owed the guy an apology, since he'd promised not to reveal his real name. But right now, that goofy name, and Schaefer's swishy diva walkout, relieved the tension and enabled him and Lulu to recover from their crazy kiss.

She broke first, starting to snicker, and then to laugh.

Equally relieved, Chaz joined her in the laughter. "He's never gonna forgive me."

"His first name is Ludwig? *Seriously?*"

He nodded. "Yeah, I think his parents had a Beethoven fetish along with their hippie lifestyle."

"Poor guy," Lulu said, leaning back against the wall, her laughter fading until just a faint smile remained. "No wonder he goes by his last name and keeps the first one a secret."

When a more comfortable silence descended, he murmured, "Lulu, I'm sorry."

She didn't look at him, merely nodding. "Me, too. That should definitely never have happened."

She was a little too quick to agree that they had no business kissing.

Of course, she was right. He'd wanted to get to know her again, but they did have no business kissing, or doing anything else, for that matter. Not only was there the family issue, there was also the fact that Lulu was new to D.C., soaking up every experience she could get, dedicated to her new job and her friends. She was starting the whole single-in-the-city phase, and the last thing she needed would be to get seriously involved with anyone— especially someone who jetted around the world without even telling his loved ones when he was heading into a war zone.

And he just couldn't see them being involved casually. He might fantasize about taking her home and having steamy sex with her, but considering she lived a few doors down, it sure would make for some awkward mornings after. Not to mention some tense trips home for the holidays. He could just envision the two of them sitting with both their families around a Christmas tree, trying to pretend they hadn't explored every inch of each other's bodies with their mouths.

His own went dry at the very thought of it.

No. Not happening.

He had to forget it and move on. She'd been right the first time when she'd shut the door in his face. There was no point in even thinking about that kiss again…even though he was damn sure he would never forget it.

Their stares locked, and Chaz managed to keep his focus strictly on her eyes. He didn't drop his gaze to those well-kissed lips, or to the amazing body all hugged by spandex.

"Things are way too tangled for us to even consider letting this go anywhere," she said, reading his mind.

"Yeah. Momentary insanity."

"Definitely."

"Never to be repeated."

"Absolutely not. God, if things got so bad with Sarah and Lawrence, can you imagine how it would be for us?"

He didn't really appreciate the comparison, considering their siblings had gone through their nonsense as high-schoolers, but he understood the sentiment. "It could be bad" was as far as he was willing to go.

It could also be good. But neither of them was ready to find out.

"So it can't go anywhere." A tiny sigh preceded her next comment, and she suddenly looked wistful. "I finally feel like you and I are starting to be friends, Chaz. I don't want to screw that up."

That hadn't exactly been his intention, but he agreed. While they'd known each other forever, they had never *really* been friends. Lately, it had seemed as if they'd begun moving in that direction. He didn't want to screw that up, either.

"We won't. For once, I appreciate your directness. I hate playing games. We'll just forget this happened, go back to our own private lives and back to being old childhood..."

"Combatants?"

Her joke lifted the tension even more.

"Something like that."

Agreed, they took another moment to ease back into this new version of normal, then they turned and exited the hallway, heading toward their friends and teammates. Chaz watched her beeline for another table, taking a seat beside one of the women on her team. Darrell, he noticed, had stood up and was lurking near the door. When he saw

Lulu choose another table, he ducked out of the bar without any goodbyes. Which was for the best…it meant Chaz wouldn't have to threaten his life or anything.

Not out of jealousy, of course. But because friends looked out for each other.

Friends. Just friends.

He sat back at his own table, ignoring Tonia's curious stare questioning why he'd been gone so long, and flagged down the waitress for his check. Chaz just wasn't interested in having another beer or socializing. He was too confused to relax and enjoy himself. Confused over that kiss, how he'd reacted to it, and how it had compared to the ones he'd exchanged to the woman haunting his dreams.

Lulu was as familiar to him as a family member, dark-haired, sassy-mouthed, not mysterious. The witch he'd met on Halloween had been entirely different.

So why was he having such a hard time separating them in his mind? And why did the memory of Lulu's kiss have him so on edge and curious?

He just didn't know. He needed to go home and think things through before he found reasons to ignore every decision he'd made regarding Lulu.

Then, something happened that changed everything. The door to the bar opened, bringing in a strong autumn breeze, some dried, tumbling leaves, and three women. A brunette, a blonde, and…

"A redhead," he murmured, unable to tear his eyes off the woman in the middle. The tall one with the long, wind-blown hair, and the dark eyes.

His heart skipped a beat. He blinked, staring at her again, wishing he were closer.

He couldn't be sure, not until he talked to her—heard her voice, got a better look at her mouth. After all, Washington, D.C. was a big city. There had to be thousands of attractive women with red hair. Tens of thousands.

But stranger things had happened.

Maybe fate was tossing him a bone after he'd experienced that momentary insanity with Lulu, and then intelligently agreed to never repeat it. Perhaps his luck was turning. A week ago, the mysterious woman he'd met on Halloween night had captured his full attention. It was now time to put his focus back where it belonged—on a woman who'd intrigued him, who'd wanted him, and who must have had a damn good reason for leaving the way she had.

Not on the woman he'd just agreed he could never—*ever*—have.

8

"HER NAME IS HEATHER, and he thinks she's me. And she apparently is *letting* him think that. Could you just die?"

Lulu threw herself back in her chair, swallowing a big mouthful of wine, waiting for her friends to start commiserating and giving her lots of *You go girl!*s.

They didn't.

Viv merely watched her with a half smirk on her full lips, and Amelia wore a look of sad disapproval.

The three of them had met at a restaurant near Viv's place in Georgetown, Lulu badly needing a girls' night out after the way things had been going the past couple of weeks. She wanted her friends to be indignant on her behalf and rain curses on the evil Heather's head, and do all the things girlfriends were supposed to do when one of them was feeling betrayed.

And she was definitely feeling betrayed.

Men could be so totally dense. Especially when they were being led around by their dicks.

After that insanely erotic, wonderful, sexy kiss she and Chaz had shared, he'd agreed that they couldn't let things go any further, and had gone right back to obsessing over the redhead he'd met on Halloween night.

Which was Lulu.

Only she couldn't let him know that.

And now he thought the redhead he'd met minutes after that wonderful, erotic kiss was his mysterious Halloween witch.

It was too confusing to dwell on for long. All she knew was, the witch—literally speaking, only in her mind she usually referred to Heather with the *b*-word instead—had apparently not made it clear to him that she wasn't the woman he'd been searching for. The two of them appeared to be getting very cozy. *Grr.*

"He even invited her for Thanksgiving dinner, can you freaking believe it?"

That should definitely have earned a few *That skank, bet she's not even a real redhead* comments from her gal pals. But she didn't get them.

"You have to tell him the truth," Amelia said, her pretty blue eyes warm and supportive.

Amelia was the nicest young woman Lulu had ever met. She never had a mean word to say to anyone, and probably did a lousy business of running her craft shop because she believed every sob story she ever heard.

But man, did she have a way of making a person feel guilty about not doing the right thing.

Lulu slunk in her chair, running her finger along the rim of her glass. "It's too late."

For once, Viv, who was as daring as Amelia was conservative, agreed with the other woman. "She's right. It's your own fault he's hooking up with a lying ho-bag instead of you." She grinned evilly. "You lying ho-bag."

"Oh, shut up," Lulu snapped, not in the mood for any ribbing.

"This wouldn't have happened if you hadn't played games with him," said Amelia.

"Exactly. None of it would have happened. I wouldn't have had an amazing time with Chaz that almost led to—" She cut herself off before continuing. Lulu hadn't given them all the details of what had happened after she'd left on Halloween night. She might kiss and tell, but she didn't blow and tell.

"Or," Amelia said, presenting an alternate scenario, "maybe if you'd been honest from the start, you two would have had a drink, caught up on old times, danced, and still left together. Only you wouldn't have felt the need to run out on him and pretend you were someone else."

Viv tossed down the rest of her second margarita. "You never did tell us exactly what happened that night. Did you two fuck or not?"

"Viv!" Amelia exclaimed.

"What? It would help in my advice-giving if I knew how far things went."

Lulu just growled.

"Okay, I take it that's a no on the uck-faying?"

Rolling her eyes as she translated Viv's pig Latin attempt at gentility, Lulu replied, "Take it however you want."

Honestly, she wasn't sure how to answer. "Sort of," seemed a little too ambiguous, and she did not want to go into details. How could she explain that she'd had just a taste of him inside her, but the memory of that heated moment was enough to make her shiver with the need to finish what they'd started?

"It's a no," Viv said with a laugh. "You've been acting like a woman who's been put away wet without having been ridden hard."

She could have had somebody ride her hard. Two or three somebodies, probably. She'd certainly had some offers lately, including from a couple of her kickball pals.

But nobody else interested her. Chaz was the only man she wanted…and he was the only man she couldn't have.

Why was that again? Funny, the more wine she sipped, the harder it was to remember.

"I missed my shot," she mumbled, more to herself than to her friends. "He's dating that red-haired girl and doesn't even remember I'm alive."

"Of course he does," said Amelia. "It was obvious the way he came right over to you that night, not even knowing who you were. There was instant chemistry. Out of the whole, crowded club, he zeroed in on you and never even glanced at anyone else."

That made her feel a little better, because it was true. She hadn't tricked him into approaching her, he'd been the aggressor. He'd truly wanted her.

"Just seduce him and he'll forget all about the bitch," said Viv. "I can teach you a few moves. I'm telling you, lick a guy's balls and he's yours forever."

Screeching, Amelia threw her hands over her ears, but Lulu snorted a laugh, inhaling some wine, then coughing it back up. Viv was over-the-top, but she was certainly always good for a laugh.

"Ignore her," said Amelia. "You don't have to play tricks, or, ahem, do anything gross."

Well, having tasted him, Lulu didn't agree that Viv's suggestion was gross. In fact, exploring his entire body with her mouth sounded like pure heaven. But sweet Amelia didn't need to know that.

"Just be honest. Go up to him and tell him the whole story. The truth and nothing but the truth. You can do it!"

Yes, she could admit she'd been sneaky and manipulative, and that she'd lied by omission on Halloween.

And Chaz would hate her for it. He had put up with a lot as a kid, but he'd never put up with anybody lying. It was his personal line in the sand, one he wouldn't cross and wouldn't forgive in someone else. Now, from a few things he'd said to her, she suspected it was an even bigger issue for him.

Damn it, she had left before things went past the point of no return on Halloween because she didn't *want* to lie to Chaz. She hadn't wanted to take advantage of his own male weakness and use him for great, amazing, world-shattering sex without ever revealing who she really was.

So now this Heather chick was probably using him for great, amazing, world-shattering sex without ever revealing who she really *wasn't*. Namely, Lulu!

It just wasn't fair.

"You know, Lulu," said Amelia, sounding cautious, as though she wasn't sure her comment would be welcome, "you haven't mentioned anything about this being just a fling, like you planned when you were going after Schaefer. Is that still all you want, even with Chaz?"

She stared, unsure how to answer. Yes, on Halloween, she'd been after only a brief, sexual adventure. Now, though, especially having spent the past several weeks getting to know Chaz all over again, she feared she wouldn't be content with that. But was she really ready to try for something real, something honest, that went beyond sex? It wasn't just an issue of Chaz wanting to; she, herself, had to be sure she was ready to trust someone.

You can trust Chaz. You know you can.

With her life, maybe. He'd never physically hurt her, or allow anyone else to. But with her heart? Well, that was a whole other story. His career meant everything to him; she'd only ever be a distant second in terms of importance. She might give him her heart, but he'd never completely give her his.

"I don't know," she admitted. "We're friends, we share

a lot, and he'd never make me feel used or unimportant. But I'm just starting a job here that means a lot to me, and he's never in one place for long. That wouldn't make it easy to build something."

"You deserve someone who knows how you're feeling, knows what your dreams are, what you care about, and who you really are," said Amelia, her eyes misty, as if her heart hurt for Lulu.

"Maybe," she said, thinking about it.

"And if that's Chaz, you've got to wrap your mind around the idea that you have to take some risks," Viv said. "Starting with telling him who you were on Halloween night."

Crap. Back to that again. "He'll be so mad. I've lied, and Chaz always hated liars."

"If you tell him before he finds out some other way, at least he'll appreciate you trying to do the right thing," said Amelia.

"I'll just look desperate, like I'm trying to ruin his new romance with what's-her-face."

"Do you know how far it's gotten?" asked Amelia. "Are they, um…serious?"

"Has he made love to her?" asked Viv.

Lulu frowned at her friend. "Oh, very nice. You ask if he's fucked me but if he's made love to her?"

"I was trying to be ladylike and stuff." Viv waved a hand toward Amelia. "I figure I've burned her ears enough for one night. But if you want to be blunt about it…has he banged her or not?"

"They've gone out the past two weekends." She nibbled her lip. "What do you suppose that means?"

"He didn't seem to be a slow mover on Halloween," said Viv.

Lulu had been trying not to think about that. She

glared at the brunette, who immediately back-pedaled. "Of course, that doesn't mean he's as attracted to her as he was to you. There were some serious pheromones that night. You two might as well have started dry-humping in the middle of your dance."

"Thanks. I guess."

"He really seemed crazy about you," said Amelia, nodding loyally. "For all we know, he's gone out with her a few times specifically because he's trying to figure out why he's *not* feeling that same immediate attraction he felt for you. I mean her. Oh, heck, I have no idea what I mean."

"I understood you the first time," Lulu said. "Do you really think it's possible?"

"Definitely," said Amelia.

Viv merely shrugged and sipped her margarita. "Anything's possible." But she didn't sound very convinced.

Lulu wanted to believe Amelia was right, but Chaz *hadn't* been a slow mover, at least not on Halloween. She'd primed him, gotten him totally worked up and ready, and some other woman had moved in for the kill, taking orgasms that should rightfully have been Lulu's.

Orgasms, and now her holiday dinner, too.

"I still can't believe he invited her for Thanksgiving."

Lulu was kicking herself for having agreed to attend. She wouldn't have if she'd known he was going to invite the redhead, who, upon hearing about the pot-luck holiday meal, had claimed she, too, was being "orphaned" by vacationing family members on Thanksgiving. It sounded to Lulu like the schemer had angled for an invitation the way a pro fisherman went after the biggest carp. And Chaz had acted like a well-hooked fish.

Since all their parents were going to be away, Chaz had decided to step up and host a holiday meal for all his friends who had no place else to go. That included her and

Lawrence, Chaz and his sister Sarah, as well as Peggy, Marcia and Frankie.

And Heather. Blech. Stupid secret-identity-stealing Heather.

Good grief, she was the *last* person Lulu wanted to spend a holiday with. If it weren't for the real possibility that World War Three would break out between Sarah and Lawrence, with pumpkin pies and green bean casserole flying, she'd blow off the whole meal.

But she couldn't. She'd told Chaz she would come, and that she'd help him mediate between their younger siblings. She intended to keep her word, even if it meant smiling across the table at the woman who'd stepped in and taken advantage of the man Lulu had gotten all heated up on Halloween. She wouldn't let on what she was really thinking if it killed her.

She kept reminding herself of that a few days later, on the actual holiday.

She'd arrived at Chaz's place early, having promised to help him decipher the instructions on cooking a twenty-pound turkey. As they'd feared, there were innards to deal with, but fortunately they were bagged, and even more fortunately, Chaz was the one who dug them out.

If she hadn't known that Heather would be arriving later in the day, along with the other, more welcome guests, she might have actually enjoyed the time she spent in the kitchen with Chaz. His house was roomy and nicely furnished, and his kitchen pretty well stocked for a bachelor. Lulu wasn't much of a cook, but she'd paid attention when her mom cooked holiday meals and certainly felt capable of sugaring a few yams and mashing some potatoes. Anything she didn't remember how to do, Chaz was quick to figure out, or look up on the internet.

They made a pretty good team, if she did say so herself.

Since that day a couple of weeks ago, when they'd kissed, he'd gone back to treating her like a friend from back home. There'd been no flirtation. He'd been just a little overprotective but hadn't pried too much into her business. He sure hadn't kissed her, though she had turned around once or twice and caught him looking at her with an intensity he usually kept hidden.

It was at those moments she was sure he hadn't forgotten their kiss any more than she had.

They'd opened Pandora's box. They both knew how good they could be together, and it was impossible to un-remember that delicious, intense passion. They might have shoved it back in the box and vowed to never take it out again, but that didn't mean they didn't both think about it and wonder. And wonder. And wonder.

Usually, though, they managed to behave like nothing had happened. They still walked together to the train every day, still socialized with others on weekends. Lawrence had come over a few times. He and Chaz had become close again, as they'd been when they were kids, when Chaz had served as a big brother figure, before Sarah had come between them.

She and Chaz had so much in common, so much shared history, and truly enjoyed each other's company now. Today had been laid-back and easy, fun and a little silly. He'd teased her about taking as much potato as peel, she'd harassed him for not knowing you had to add sugar to fresh cranberries to make a sauce. They drank a little wine, occasionally exchanging a long, studied glance when their hands brushed over a towel or their legs made contact under the table. The rivalry and tension from their childhood was gone, the awareness warm and unthreatening, and they got along so well it was almost as though they were a couple.

At least, until the doorbell rang.

Heather, who'd called out, "Yoo-hoo," as she passed by the kitchen window, was out front. Heather with the perfect smile and the cutest little upturned nose matched by what Lulu suspected were surgically enhanced upturned tits. Heather who was occupying a place in Chaz's life, in his memories, maybe even in his bed, that rightfully belonged to Lulu.

Chaz was basting the bird and asked her to get the door. Drying her hands on a dish towel, which she whipped over her shoulder, she strode out of the kitchen and yanked open the front door.

"Hello, Heather," she said as she ushered the other woman in. "You're early. Nobody else is here yet."

Heather's smile was small and tight. She'd obviously expected someone else to answer the door. Someone far more susceptible to red hair, a phony smile and equally phony tits.

"Hello, Lulu. I thought I'd come early in case Chaz needed any help."

"I think we have everything under control."

The redhead shoved a foil-wrapped, pie-shaped object into Lulu's waiting hands. "Well, I'll just cheer you two on then, shall I? But first I have to freshen up."

"Whatever," she mumbled, turning and heading for the kitchen. She didn't wait to see if Heather followed or made herself at home, because, frankly, she didn't want the proof that the other women had been here enough to know her way around.

The two women had met that day at the bar, when Chaz had first spotted Heather and made such a fool of himself trying to find out if she recognized him from a former meeting. Like from having given him a blowjob in an ATM vestibule.

The devious woman had played it smart. Being pursued by a gorgeous, successful, charming man, she hadn't immediately denied being the Halloween witch he sought, nor had she confirmed it. She just acted mysterious and coy, and what American man didn't go ape over those kinds of women? She'd played him better than Schaefer played his guitar, and Chaz was too fascinated to notice.

It had been all Lulu could do to not out her for a phony right then and there. Of course, the only way she could have done that would have been to out herself, as well. And that she was not ready to do.

"She brought pie," Lulu said as she entered the kitchen, putting the dessert on the counter. Chaz didn't even look up, busy trying to figure out how to cut into a big, softball-size vegetable. "You'd better be careful, you might lose a finger cutting into that Winnebago."

"It's a rutabaga. I can't believe you don't remember my mom making these every Christmas."

"Guess I always snuck it onto Lawrence's plate when nobody was looking."

"Where is Heather?" he asked, still gazing only at the waxy vegetable and the big-ass knife in his hand. He didn't sound terribly excited about the arrival, and didn't dash off to kiss her passionately in welcome, which made Lulu feel a little better.

"Being nosy and checking the balance in your checkbook, I think."

He lifted a brow at her tone.

"She's in the bathroom," she admitted. "Freshening up her face for you."

"You don't like her, huh?"

"I don't know her enough to like her or dislike her." Licking her lips and pretending to be entirely focused on a recipe for green bean casserole, which she could probably make blindfolded, she asked, "Do *you* like her?"

He thought about it, a confused expression on his face. "Honestly, I'm not sure. Sometimes I think I do. Other times I wonder what on earth it was about her that so fascinated me the night we met."

Lulu's teeth slammed together and she clenched them tightly. She had to pry her words out from between them with brute force. "So, you'd met her before that day we played kickball?"

You idiot, are you totally blind? How dare you think she's me? There's not one real, natural thing about her!

He lowered the big knife he'd been using, glanced toward the doorway, and lowered his voice to say, "I don't know. I thought so, but I'm just not sure. She seems…different than the woman I met, the one I've been looking for. And she's so mysterious about it, she won't confirm or deny anything when I ask her about it."

Lulu swallowed, hard. "This woman you met, the one you're looking for? What was so special about her?"

Chaz shook his head slowly, visibly lost in thought. "I honestly don't know that, either. I'm not even sure the damn night actually happened. Maybe I was so jet-lagged I crashed when I got home from my trip and dreamed up some elaborate fantasy."

She gulped. She didn't want him thinking Heather was the woman he'd been with…but was him convincing himself it hadn't really happened any better?

Well, yeah, if she wanted to keep her secret, it probably was. But part of her wasn't sure about that secret anymore. Okay, so they weren't going to let anything happen between them…would it be the crime of the century if he found out she was the one he'd come so close to hooking up with that night? At least he'd know the truth and wouldn't be driving himself crazy trying to imprint his memories of that night onto the face of someone who didn't even have the guts to tell him he had the wrong girl.

"Well hey there, happy Thanksgiving!"

Heather walked into the kitchen. She'd taken off her jacket. She'd also obviously spent time in front of the bathroom mirror, fluffing up her windblown hair to make it look more artfully windblown. She'd smeared bright red lipstick across her lips, and pulled her sweater down to reveal more of the silicone.

Ignoring Lulu, she walked around to the other side of the kitchen island and lifted her face, pursing her lips for a kiss. Chaz, Lulu noted, hesitated, glancing in her direction before obliging his date. If she had to guess, she'd say he was a little uncomfortable.

Good. Because if he couldn't tell that woman's kiss from hers, he deserved what he got.

"I'm going to double-check the Ping-Pong table," Lulu said, trying to keep the disgust out of her voice. If she had to see Chaz kiss another woman, she might just be the one flinging the pie and green bean casserole.

"Isn't there a lot to still do?" Heather asked, pretending she didn't care that she hadn't gotten her kiss.

But Lulu cared. Oh, hell, yes, she did. She hid her smile, though, not wanting Chaz to notice and interpret it. "Yes, quite a lot," she said.

"If you want to play a game, Lulu, don't worry about it. I'll fill in here."

Lulu smirked. "Uh, the Ping-Pong table is the only thing Chaz had that was big enough to seat everybody around. We're eating on it down in the rec room."

The woman's eyes rounded and her smile faded a tiny bit. Perhaps she was picturing a fancy holiday meal from an internationally published journalist. But she wasn't going to get it.

Frankly, Lulu loved the effort Chaz had gone to for them. Her heart had melted a little bit when she'd arrived and seen him putting a pristine white tablecloth over the huge table, setting it with new dishes he'd picked up just for today. He'd shoved a bunch of mismatched chairs, including outdoor ones, around the table, determined to make it a great holiday, not just for his friends, but also for his bratty little sister, spending her first holiday away from home.

How many guys would go to so much trouble? Not many, she knew. That was just one thing that made Chaz so special.

If Heather didn't see and appreciate that, she didn't deserve him. Hell, she didn't deserve him period!

And somehow, no matter what it cost her personally, Lulu hoped Chaz found out the truth about the other woman, and realized she was not worth his time and trouble. He deserved better.

ALTHOUGH CHAZ HAD worried a lot about the presence of both Sarah and Lawrence at today's holiday dinner, his sister and Lulu's brother managed to surprise him. They'd apparently seen each other on campus and now were both perfectly cordial, if not exactly warm. The younger pair had finally grown up. So in that respect, things were going great.

The problem had come from an entirely different direction. Chaz found his peace of mind most disturbed by having both Heather and Lulu here.

It was crazy. He and Lulu were old friends; they'd both agreed that's what they would remain. End of story. And Heather was a woman he'd just started dating who was new to town and had nowhere else to go. It had seemed perfectly natural for them both to be invited. But now that they were both here, sitting at opposite ends of the Ping-Pong table ignoring each other easily in this big group, he couldn't help comparing them—and realizing he'd made a mistake. Possibly a big one.

Heather *might* be the woman whose memory had tantalized and tormented him for weeks. She *might* be the one who had flooded him with want and erotic fantasy.

But she sure didn't feel like it.

They'd gone out twice before today, and while he thought she was attractive, he hadn't experienced that out-of-breath, heart-pounding, palm-sweating, pant-tenting excitement, not even when they'd kissed. Nor had his usually subtle, but sometimes direct questions about whether she was the one he'd met on Halloween night yielded any definite answers. She hadn't said yes. She hadn't said no. She'd hinted and hemmed and hawed. His sexy witch had hidden her name from him on Halloween night, so she obviously did like being mysterious. But he'd never felt like she was playing games. He wasn't so sure about Heather, who, he suspected, could be a game-player. The only thing he knew for sure was that he felt not only confused but untouched.

Nothing about Heather touched him at his most basic, elemental level, the way it had on Halloween.

He'd invited her for Thanksgiving before he'd come to the realization that she was probably not his mystery/fantasy woman. But since he was no closer to finding that woman, and since Heather was attractive and interested, he had decided to play this out with her.

All that had seemed smart.

Until he'd spent much of the day with Lulu.

Lulu was a brat from his past, the girl next door, the little witch who'd busted his ass, literally.

She was not supposed to feel so natural by his side. She was not supposed to inspire thoughts of hot kisses and sweaty sheets. Her hair wasn't supposed to feel so soft and sensuous against his skin. The sight of her hands shouldn't make parts of his body tense in anticipation of her touch.

What the hell was happening here?

"I still can't believe the parents all went on a cruise for Thanksgiving. But I have to say, you did a really good job today, big brother."

Chaz tore his mind off the confusing women in his life—*woman, one, Lulu is not in your life, not as a woman anyway*—and smiled at his kid sister.

"Thanks. I couldn't have done it without Lulu."

"Well, thanks to you, too, Lulu," Sarah said, sounding sincere and being nice to Lulu, with whom there was usually tension. Then she ruined it by smirking. "I guess we should all just be glad you both survived it. With the track record between you, and all those sharp objects in the kitchen, it's lucky nobody was scarred or maimed."

Lulu picked up her wine glass, bringing it to her lips. "The night's still young," she mumbled before sipping.

"Were these two really nemeses like we've heard?" asked Peggy, who was rubbing her full stomach with one hand, while patting Marcia's with another.

Lulu's kid brother, Lawrence, who looked as a young man exactly as he had when a young boy—a little small, angular face, deep, soulful eyes, and kind smile—answered. "Only because they were in love with each other."

Chaz dropped his fork. It landed with a clatter on his plate. But even that wasn't loud enough to cover Lulu's immediate exclamation.

"That is crazy!"

She sounded like somebody had just accused her of robbing a church, which wasn't exactly flattering.

Of course, his vehemence probably didn't make her feel any better when he snapped, "I doubt Lulu was in love with me when she cut off all my hair with her Fiskar scissors during recess."

"It grew back," she sniped. "And I doubt you were in love with me when you told all your friends that I wet the bed."

"You did."

"When I was three!"

"Nobody ever asked for clarification," he said, his smile taunting. "I never lied."

"No, you never do, Saint Chaz."

"Whoa, whoa, sorry," said Peggy, holding up her hands, palm out, to each of them, acting as referee. "I didn't mean to start a war here."

"Wow, it sounds to me like you two can't stand each other," said Heather, whose sweet smile didn't quite hide the gleam of happiness in her eye. He had to wonder if the redhead had picked up on some of the vibes between him and Lulu.

"Okay, subject change," said Marcia as she licked the last of her mashed potatoes off her fork. "Lulu, I've been meaning to ask you, how's work going? Has our donation been distributed yet?"

"Donation?" Heather asked.

Chaz listened, too. Lulu had never really talked about her job, and he honestly didn't know what she did, beyond working in an office up on Massachusetts Avenue. Her master's degree was in political science, so he assumed she was doing something connected with one of the many embassies up in that part of the city.

"Yes, it has," Lulu said, smiling at Marcia.

"Do you know who it went to?"

"Several women from one family in a village in Tanzania formed a farming co-op, and that's where your donation went." Her posture relaxed and passion came through in her voice. "I am sure you'll be getting a letter from them. All of the participants in the program are so incredibly appreciative."

"What is it you do exactly?" asked Heather, sounding merely polite rather than truly interested.

"Oh, Lulu works for a great organization that puts microloans in the hands of mothers in third-world countries so they can start businesses to support their families," said Peggy. "What's it called again, Lulu?"

"Hands Across The Waters," Lulu said.

Chaz frowned. The name sounded familiar, and it wasn't just because it was from a Beatles song.

Then it clicked. He'd recently been talking to his friend Tonia about that very same organization. She'd mentioned an investigation she was working on that day when they'd played kickball up at the Mall.

He'd been excited to hear about her work because he wanted to pump her for more information in the hopes that he could find his mystery woman from Halloween. Of course, that very same afternoon, he'd met Heather, and had forgotten all about it.

His heart beat a little faster in his chest. An errant thought whizzed through his mind, as quick and directionless as a fly whizzing by. Something insubstantial, something impossible, something that couldn't even fully take shape as an idea in his brain.

He lifted his water glass and sipped from it, unable to take his eyes off Lulu's face. She was happy now, animated when discussing something she obviously cared deeply about. Her dark eyes sparkled, her smile was quick and easy. Her soft, dark hair framed her creamy-skinned face, the thick strands caught in a clip at the base of her neck.

Damn, she was beautiful. Exciting, charming, daring, sexy.

So sexy. So intriguing.

Oh, Jesus.

No. It wasn't possible. That whizzing thought tried to form a picture in his mind, attempted to present an absurd possibility. Chaz just wouldn't allow it. He *couldn't.*

Still, something made his lips form words, and he said, "So, Peggy, you asked if Lulu and I were always nemeses. Did she tell you about the time she swiped all the candy bars out of my trick-or-treat bag and replaced them with raisins?" He caught Lulu's stare, unblinking, cautious, and added, "She was dressed as a *witch* that year, I think. Appropriate, don't you agree?"

Lulu's tiny gasp might have been overlooked by everyone at the table. Everyone but Chaz.

Her dark eyes went as round as silver dollars and color flooded her cheeks. Her lush lips trembled, and her fingers clenched reflexively on the table, squeezing the white tablecloth into her fists.

Son of a bitch.

The truth began to assert itself in his mind. Wheels turned, cogs clicked, and the whole picture assembled, moment by moment, of that strange Halloween night.

It had been her. Lulu had been the mysterious witch.

She'd been the woman haunting his dreams, the woman with whom he'd shared some of the most wild, uninhibited moments of his life. Lulu.

Marcia smiled broadly, completely oblivious, as was everyone else at the table, to the rising tension between Chaz and Lulu. "That's funny. Lulu was a witch this year, too."

"Was she really?" he murmured, his voice low, his eyes glued to Lulu's stricken face. "Was she a scary witch with an ugly wig and mask?"

"Oh, no. She looked so hot in her black leather bustier, with her hair dyed red, and a green Mardi Gras mask, I thought for sure a bunch of guys would follow her home and camp out in front of our building to get a chance with her."

"I can imagine," he said, sounding so calm, so reasonable, nobody else might have even realized that inside he was a seething mask of emotion. Humiliation warred with shock, but anger trumped all.

Lulu was the only one who understood. She had to have seen something in him—a spark of fury he couldn't hide—for she suddenly slapped her hands on the table and launched herself from her seat. Everyone gaped at her, but she didn't look around. She remained focused only on Chaz. All the color that had been rising in her cheeks fell out and she went as white as the sheet he'd worn when masquerading as a ghost.

"I'm sorry, I'm suddenly not feeling well," she said, her voice shaking. She brought a melodramatic hand to her face and covered her mouth. "I have to go."

The others all expressed concern and asked if she needed help, but Lulu had already spun on her heel and raced for the stairs, thumping up them two at a time in her hurry to get away.

Chaz didn't race. He didn't chase her. He didn't yell or hunt her down or demand answers or embarrass her or cause a scene.

He knew where she was going. He knew exactly where to find her.

If she thought her locked apartment door was going to keep him out, she was wrong.

If she thought she could get away with acting as though she hadn't made an utter fool out of him for the past month, she was crazy.

If she thought he wouldn't mind that she'd been lying to him for weeks, she was deluded.

And if she thought he was just going to forget what had happened between them, forget the incredible night they'd almost shared, she was out of her God-damned mind.

9

LULU WAS NO COWARD, but as soon as she got back to her apartment, she locked the door, ran into her room, dove into her bed and pulled the covers up over her head.

"He knows," she whispered, horrifying herself by saying the words out loud.

Chaz had figured it out. She had been so stupid, gushing on about her work. But Marcia had asked her directly, and she'd gotten carried away by the love she had for what she did.

When everything came crashing down around her at the dinner table, she'd half expected him to erupt right there. Steam had practically risen off his head. She honestly couldn't ever remember seeing him so intense as he'd been today. She wasn't sure she could even describe what she saw—rage? Shock? Humiliation? Yes, probably all of the above. Enough to chase her out of there, as if a swarm of wasps was on her tail.

But she'd also detected something else in his eyes— sheer determination. As if he were really looking forward to whatever came next. She just didn't know whether he was picturing something good—like them finally finishing what they'd started; or something bad—like him telling her exactly how much he hated her.

Or worse.

Undoubtedly, Chaz had been furious at having been made a fool of, and probably wouldn't believe her when she told him that hadn't been her intention. With all the dark water under the bridge of their relationship, he might believe the whole thing had been a scheme. He might smell a setup, figuring she'd decided to make him look and feel stupid for not recognizing her.

He was wrong, of course. If anything, she was the one who looked and felt stupid for playing these games...and then getting caught.

But that anticipation could be about something else entirely. And it was the something else that had her literally shaking, every cell in her body awake and sparking with life.

Throughout the evening, she kept watching the clock, flinching at every noise from outside. She felt the way she had when she was a kid and she'd done something bad, and her mother had sent her to her room with the standard, "Just you wait until your father comes home!" warning.

She was on edge, tense, wondering what her punishment would be, listening for that deep voice, or that heavy foot in the hallway. She heard the couple downstairs come in, him yelling about something, her shushing him. When Marcia and Peggy got home and softly knocked on her door to check on her, she remained quiet, wanting them to assume she was in bed.

Nine o'clock swept past. Then ten.

By ten-thirty, she was beginning to think he wasn't coming, and she couldn't decide whether she was relieved or disappointed.

Maybe he was so angry, he couldn't stand to face her yet, wanting to calm down and talk to her tomorrow.

Or perhaps he was so disgusted at wasting a month lusting after *her* that he'd leapt right into bed with Heather, to wash the bad memories out of his mind.

"I'll kill him," she muttered, torturing herself with the mental picture of it.

Ten forty-five.

She glared toward his house through her window, seeing all the lights were off. Had he just gone to sleep, not even thinking about her at all?

Tense, angry, scared, worried, she tore her clothes off and put on a pair of pajamas, prepared for a long night of restless discomfort. But she couldn't go to bed yet. Pacing her small apartment, she considered getting re-dressed and going down to his place. If she and Chaz were going to have it out, she wanted it over with. The tension—the waiting—was killing her.

The knock came at eleven-oh-five.

It was sharp, perfunctory. Two hard raps, then silence.

She ran to the door, her heart in her mouth, her stomach churning with real anxiety now. As she unfastened the lock, she formed explanations and apologies, trying to guess what kind of mood he would be in and how best to handle it.

She was prepared for frustrated Chaz. Or for sad Chaz. Or for confused Chaz.

What she got was wildly sexy Chaz.

The minute she pulled the door open, he pushed his way in and then kicked it closed behind him. He raked a hot, thorough stare over her, taking in the scooped neckline of her silky pajama top, and the flimsy shorts that left her bare from the top of her thighs down to the tips of her toes.

"Chaz, I…"

"To use your favorite expression, just shut up, Lulu."

Then he grabbed her in his arms and pulled her to him, burying one hand in her hair and twisting tightly. He gripped her ass, hoisting her up until the juncture of her thighs met the thickness straining against his zipper. She was groaning with need when he covered her mouth with his, plunging his tongue deep.

He kissed her as if he'd invented kissing. Exploring every corner, every crevice, he licked into her as if he were starving and she his only means of survival.

Strength deserted her. She sagged into him, her legs turning to jelly, her arms too weak to do any more than rest across his strong shoulders.

This was a Chaz she'd never seen before in her life, one she didn't even recognize.

And he excited her beyond all measure.

He scooped her up, swinging her into his arms and striding across the small apartment toward her bedroom. When he reached the bed, he tossed her down on it and followed her. He was heavy, crushing, but she welcomed his weight, wanting his frenzy, needing every bit of his untamed passion.

"Wait," she breathed. "Heather?"

"Gone. For good."

Oh, thank heaven.

He kissed her, and the kiss went on and on. He swallowed her every exhalation, sucking away any possible rejection, his tongue plunging, lapping, devouring. He didn't give her a second to think or consider, making her exist only in this moment of heat and wild desire.

When he drew back to pull in a raspy breath, she reached up to cup his cheek. He ducked away, not in the mood for tenderness, not even in the mood for her to say yes or to welcome him.

He wanted her. He'd wanted her for weeks, after she'd led him on and brought him to a fever pitch of desire. She'd made a fool of him, knowing all along that she was who he sought, and now he was going to have his due.

There would be no turning back tonight. He wouldn't allow it.

She knew Chaz. She trusted him. She had no doubt he would never hurt her. But in this mood, he wasn't going to give her the chance to say a single word, especially if that word was *no*.

She wouldn't have said it—the word didn't even exist in her vocabulary right now. He was making her insane with want, driving her so high, making her quake and writhe on the bed, wanting his mouth and his hands everywhere. How could she possibly form the word *no* when every molecule in her body screamed *yes,* and *yes,* and *yes!*

Lulu reached up to unbutton her top, but he shoved her hands away and caught the fabric in his own. He wrenched the two sides apart, sending buttons flying, baring her to her waist.

Eyeing her hungrily, he fell on her, sucking her puckered nipple into his mouth, drawing hard. Such pleasure, the tiniest hint of pain that only made it that much better.

He went to her other breast—equal time—suckling her, squeezing her, pinching ever so lightly. She felt each sensation down low in her groin, moisture flooding her, the folds of her sex swelling.

He kept going, down, down her body, nipping, licking. When she moved too much, or begged silently with an upward thrust, he put his hands on her hips, holding tight, and pushed her hard against the bed.

He was so strong, his big hands holding her immobile. He would do what he wanted, and the message was clear— she was going to lie there and take it.

Heavens, what woman in her right mind would even consider doing anything else?

Down farther as he tore her silky shorts off. No part of her was left unexplored—his tongue in her belly button, his teeth on her hipbone, and finally, his hot breaths parting the curls at the apex of her thighs. Farther, and now he licked into her most delicate folds, finding unerringly the spot on her body where all sensation centered and seethed.

"Oh, God, yes," she cried when he covered her clit and pleasured her thoroughly.

He didn't stay still. Moving farther down, he buried his face between her legs, looping one leg over his shoulder, opening her fully. She had no secrets, no dignity, could hold absolutely nothing back. And she truly didn't care.

Chaz explored her, inhaling deeply as if he needed to breathe her scent into his lungs and lock it there forever. His lips sank into her, finding her opening, pushing inside, invading her, devouring her. He made love to her with his tongue, slow laps deep within her, mimicking what he would do with his fingers, with his cock.

She began to softly groan, breaking the silence with helpless sobs of pleasure. Tossing her head back and forth on the pillow, she reached for something that was just out of her grasp. The tension was almost painful, the pleasure beyond anything in this world.

He seemed to take pity, as if aware he had to give her something so she could keep going. Moving back to her clit, he scooped all around the base of it with his tongue, gliding, flicking, sucking, until hot bolts of pulsating heat flooded her. She came hard in his mouth, and he lapped at her, taking everything her body threw at him and savoring it.

Lulu was barely even conscious of him standing up beside the bed to pull his shirt off. He tossed it to the floor before unfastening his belt. Unbuttoning and unzipping his pants, he reached in and pulled out that enormous, hard cock. She stared at it, wanting him so badly, knowing she'd die if he wasn't in her soon.

He dropped onto on his knees on the bed, staring down at her, wrapping one hand around his erection and lazily stroking. He was pleasuring himself. Teasing her. Building her hunger.

God, it worked. She wanted him with a desperation bordering on insanity.

"Please, Chaz,"

"Hush," he ordered.

"I need you to…"

"I mean it, Lulu. Not a word."

"But…"

He glared at her. "I waited for hours to calm down, and then came over here, knowing I'd have to either drag you over my knee and spank your gorgeous ass, or kiss you into silence until I was calm enough to talk to you. Say another word and I won't be responsible for which way this goes."

She licked her lips, more turned on than ever by his words and his no-nonsense tone. Lulu had never seen him like this, never even imagined he could be so sexually aggressive. But she knew he meant it. And part of her wanted him to make good on his threat.

She'd never dreamed that fantasy would appeal to her, but she knew Chaz, she trusted him completely. If he put her over his knee and spanked her, she was certain each stinging slap would be followed by a caress.

After the punishment, he would have her lie face down on the bed while he kissed away the pain. She could see it, the fantasy unrolling in her mind.

Then, perhaps, they would both be so aroused by his attention to her bare bottom—which would be thrust up to him in utter invitation—that he'd take her like that, invade her where no one ever had before, introducing her to something new and dark and erotic.

And she wanted it. She wanted all of it. Wanted him to take her in every way a woman could be taken, wanted to give all that she had to give.

Someday. Oh, yes, someday, she would make that kinky fantasy come true. He was the one man she trusted to give her that kind of dangerous, edgy pleasure.

But for right now, she just wanted him to bury himself in her pussy. She'd been tormented by the memories of that tiny little taste of bliss he'd given her outside on Halloween night, and her insides were crying for the full connection.

Chaz had been watching her, as if reading her thoughts, knowing where her imagination was taking her.

She swallowed, but didn't say a word, merely offering him the kind of smile that said she understood what he'd thought about doing to her…and would someday let him do it.

"You drive me insane," he muttered, looking driven past the edge of endurance. "Are you on birth control?"

Remembering not to speak out loud, she simply nodded.

"Good. Hold on."

She reached up and held on, digging her nails into his shoulders. Chaz moved between her parted thighs. He wasn't tender, he wasn't cautious. He'd made her dripping wet and he knew it. So he pushed his cock between the lips of her sex, found her opening, and plunged deep, tearing her apart in the most delicious, most satisfying way.

Gasping, she arched into him, taking him all the way. She hadn't had sex in a long time, and never with someone of such generous proportions. He filled her to her core, and she savored every inch of him.

Dropping down to catch her mouth in another deep, devouring kiss, he began to ease out of her, and then thrust back. His movements were so deliberate and determined, slightly wild. But she still never feared he would hurt her. He was incapable of that.

Instinct took over and she caught his rhythm and matched it. She rose up for every downward thrust, squeezing him deep inside. He might be in the driver's seat, but she felt the shudders of his lean, strong body and knew he was losing himself to this, unable to remain controlled when wracked with such intense sensations.

They never slowed down, twisting and pounding, giving and taking. As if wanting to go as deep as humanly possible, Chaz hooked his arms around her legs and lifted them both over his shoulders. She let out a little scream of pleasure as he gained even more of her. He kissed away her cries of pleasure, driving mindlessly. The position was shockingly fulfilling, and gave her just enough pressure against her clit that she spilled into another climax, throbbing with it. Her obvious passion pushed him past all limits. With one more deep thrust, he threw his head back, his muscles tightening, every inch of him straining, and shuddered as he came deep inside her. Lulu squeezed him, sucking him dry of every drop, clinging to him with arms, legs and body.

Afterward, he collapsed, but even in his exhaustion, he didn't let all his weight fall on her, protective as always. He remained inside her, but moved onto his side, pulling her with him, their legs tangled, her hair still wrapped in his hands.

One more kiss—this one softer, more tender. She returned it with heartfelt emotion, wondering if he had spent all his anger and would now forgive her for her deceit. Or if he'd just gotten started and would now commence with the lecture.

She opened her mouth to ask, but he narrowed his eyes and shook his head.

"Sleep, Lulu. We'll talk tomorrow."

He had offered her a reprieve. A night wrapped in his arms sounded much better than a lot of arguing, and she almost thanked him, but figured she'd better keep her mouth shut. So she merely nodded lazily, smiling, happy and utterly content. Not really caring about what discomfort the morning would bring, she curled even closer, closed her eyes, and drifted to sleep.

WHAT ON EARTH had he done? Twice?

Chaz wondered that as he woke, slowly pulling himself from a wet dream that proved to be reality, since he was still entwined with Lulu, his half-erect dick still inside her. They were wrapped together, limbs, hands, hair, everything, as if neither of them had been able to stand to pull apart while they slept.

Morning light was sifting in through the shades, but it was soft and new. He guessed it was no later than seven. He'd slept soundly for a few hours, after waking up during the night to make silent, erotic love to her again. Neither of them had said a word; they'd simply let their bodies do the talking. He'd held her hips as she climbed on top of him, riding him hard, her fingers digging into his chest, while his hands entwined in her dark hair and toyed with those incredibly sensitive breasts. By the time he was nearing his climax, he was gripping her hips, guiding her, pulling her down onto him with forceful grunts until they'd both cried out their pleasure and she'd collapsed on top of him.

God, he was hard again just thinking about it.

Lulu noticed. She didn't say anything, didn't even open

her eyes. She merely parted her legs and pulled him over onto her. Chaz let himself be pulled, sinking deeply into her wet heat. She fit him like a glove, all soft and welcoming. He'd never felt this kind of life-altering pleasure before. Chaz enjoyed sex, a lot, but had never been driven into an almost animal frenzy, as if he had to mate or die, before last night.

He could become addicted to this.

He cupped her face in his hand, rubbing his thumb across her swollen lips. Her dark eyes drifted open and she smiled up at him. "Good morning," she whispered. Then she sucked her lips into her mouth, her eyes widening as her body tensed.

She'd just remembered he hadn't allowed her to speak last night. He would bet she hadn't been truly afraid of him, knowing he would never really do her harm, but her expression was cautious, worried.

She had reason to worry. He was still bloody furious with her.

But he also wanted to make slow, sweet love to her. So his righteous anger was just going to have to wait a little while.

"Good morning," he whispered, still wondering what had come over him last night. He'd never been so forceful with a woman, never been so torn between desire and anger. Finally they'd swirled together, combining to urge him into the kind of wild sex he'd never had with anyone else.

And never would again, he'd venture. Because Lulu was the only woman he'd ever known who could drive him mad with fury one second and utterly desperate with sexual need the next.

She wrapped her arms around his neck, pressing her mouth to his as they moved together. It was lazy and languorous. He groaned with each slow, deep stroke, not desperate to reach a destination this time, just enjoying the journey.

That wasn't all he wanted to enjoy. She had been ready for him the moment she woke up, but he'd missed out on several delicious steps to get her there. So he moved his mouth away from hers, kissing his way down her chin and her neck, burying his face in the hollow and breathing in that unique Lulu scent.

She was soft everywhere, though not weak—he felt the strength of her, especially in those thighs and the arms that had gripped him close throughout the night. But her body was a wonderland of slopes and valleys, all tender, all sensitive, all waiting to be explored.

He moved lower, licking the curve of her breast, tracing the tip of his tongue around her pink nipple.

"Mmm, yes, please," she sighed. Then she added, "I'm allowed to speak now, right?"

"As long as you focus on telling me how to make you feel good."

"You do," she said, running her fingers through his hair, holding him tight to her breast as he began to suckle her. "Oh, *so* good, Chaz."

He wanted to make her feel even better. And he wanted to explore her more slowly this morning, as the early sun bathed her with light, spotlighting all the delicious places he'd almost attacked the night before. He was slow and deliberate, gentle and insistent as he toured her body. He kissed her from her breasts to her belly, her hip, all the way down her leg to the tips of her toes, and then back up the other way. Her skin was velvet smooth, the intoxicating scent of female arousal pouring off her. By the time he got up to the top of her other thigh, she was trembling.

She arched toward him, silently inviting him to do what he most wanted.

He gently parted her thighs, exposing her to his intimate gaze. She was red and swollen, the wild sex of the night before having left its mark. He pressed his mouth to that tender flesh, licking her gently, wanting nothing but to soothe her into a fever pitch.

It was easy, so damned easy. She rocked against his mouth, hissing when he covered her pert clit and stroked it with his tongue.

"Oh, yes, there," she begged, her desire making her sound a little frantic. He had learned so much about what pleased her during the night, and knew exactly what she needed and where she needed it. He caressed her clit, sucking gently until her whole body tightened and then relaxed as her orgasm washed over her. She was already so wet, so juicy, but her climax brought another flood of moisture onto his tongue, and he drank her up, knowing he could swallow nothing but Lulu for the rest of his life and die a well-fed man.

"Come back to me," she urged, reaching for him, tugging at his shoulders.

He couldn't resist her, and slid up again, returning to his place between her parted thighs.

"That mouth of yours is almost as amazing as *this,*" she said as she reached down and stroked his cock with the tips of her fingers. "I want to explore you that way, too."

"Later," he told her. "I owed you one, remember?"

She sucked in an audible breath, catching her lip between her teeth. He'd reminded her of that night, the one that had been driving him crazy for weeks. They were both thinking of the way she'd gotten down on her knees and sucked him into insanity.

"Chaz, I…"

"Later," he insisted, tensing. He didn't want to spoil this with conversation right now. He just wanted to lose himself in her, one more time, before he got the answers he'd been seeking.

So he did. He sank into her, into hot, creamy Lulu, feeling her adjust to him, welcome him. She wrapped her legs around his hips, her arms around his shoulders, and pressed close. They rocked together, slow, easy, romantic. And when she came again, climaxing right along with him, she whispered, "God, I'm sorry I wasted a month of our lives not telling you the truth."

He was past replying, falling to the bed, tugging her on top of him and holding her as they drifted back to sleep. But the words echoed, and when he woke up an hour or two later, they were the first thing he thought of.

She was already awake. When he opened his eyes, he found her lying across him, staring at him, her fingers tracing the outline of his lips.

"Good morning again," she said, her voice soft, almost shy.

"What time is it?"

"Around nine. Are you hungry?"

He shook his head.

"Oh." Her face fell. "I had hoped I could make you some waffles."

Waffles. Or pancakes. Or Lucky Charms.

He remembered.

Hell, she was intentionally reminding him.

He stiffened. "Can we do this after I take a shower?"

She played dumb. "Do what?"

"Talk about what a fool you made of me?"

"Oh, no!" Lulu sat up on the bed, the covers falling onto her lap, her beautiful body covered by nothing but her long, thick hair. "That wasn't it at all, Chaz, at least that wasn't my intention."

Realizing he wasn't going to get his shower—and, actually, not wanting it, now that his indignation was on the rise again, he sat up, too.

"What *did* you intend, Lulu?" he asked, remembering that night, wondering how on earth he could have spent such intimate moments with her and not seen the truth of it in her eyes when they'd met next. How had he not recognized that mouth, those soft cheeks, that delicate neck?

He shook his head, needing to focus on the conversation, not on how beautiful she was. Not on what a blind fool he'd been.

"I wanted you, so much," she said, her voice trembling with sincerity.

That tremble got to him, shot right to his heart. She'd opened herself to him fully last night, in every way possible, trusting him, fulfilling him, overwhelming him. He had no doubt she was telling the truth—Lulu wanted him. She had on Halloween night, and she still did.

But he couldn't think about that. He couldn't allow himself to soften by looking at her and remembering every heated thing they'd done together. He needed to get a grip, to take a break, splash some water on his face. Calm his racing mind.

"Give me a minute," he ordered, throwing the sheets back and getting out of bed. Ignoring her tiny sound of protest, he strode toward the bathroom, needing to regroup and prepare for battle.

He came out a few minutes later, having slung a towel around his hips, and found her clad in a short bathrobe, perched on the edge of the bed, as if about to flee.

She didn't know what to expect from him, unable to

gauge his mood. He found he liked having that advantage, and jumped right in. "When did you launch this scheme?"

"It wasn't a scheme, I swear. I assumed you'd recognized me from across the bar. That's why I smiled at you. I just figured you came over and asked me to dance so we could catch up."

"How was I supposed to recognize you when I hadn't seen you for half a decade? When your hair was red, your face was masked, and you looked like a sex goddess and not the girl next door I remembered?"

She clenched her hands in her lap, twisting her fingers in the tie of her robe. "I wasn't thinking clearly. I recognized you, but I was pretty stunned. You... God, Chaz, I was so attracted to you! I couldn't believe it, and certainly didn't want you to realize it. I thought we were playing around and that you knew exactly who I was—at least, right up until you told me your name and asked for mine."

He remembered. That had been while they were dancing. To think, a few misplaced words, a few assumptions, and none of this might have happened. Ever.

That sobered him. If he had recognized her, if she'd called him by name the moment he'd come up to her table, making it clear she knew him, he'd have figured out her identity. And nothing that followed would have happened. Including last night. Last-*amazing*-night.

He couldn't let that sway him, though. The ends didn't justify the means. The life-altering sex didn't excuse the lie.

"Once you realized I didn't know who you were, why didn't you say something?"

"At first, I thought it was kind of funny, I wanted to tease you."

"It worked. You teased me. For a damn month." He swept a hand through his hair, stalking back and forth across the room. "Why the hell did you let things go so far? What we did in that bank vestibule..."

"Was incredible," she whispered. "I loved every second of it."

So had he. That wasn't the point. "And then?"

"I intended to go home with you, but every step we took reminded me that sooner or later, you were going to want to take off my mask. I kept envisioning you doing it when you were inside me, and wondering what your expression would be the moment you recognized me."

"Shock, that's for sure."

She wrapped her arms around herself. "Or disgust. Hatred. Humiliation. I was caught in my own trap, wanting you so badly, but terrified you still hated my guts and would regret even touching me once you knew who I was."

Chaz stopped pacing and stared down at her. "I don't hate you."

She looked up at him, her brown eyes luminous, moisture hinting at unshed tears. "I was awful to you when we were kids."

"Kids being the key word. Now that I know the adult you, I'm not about to hold childhood nonsense against you all these years later. And truthfully? I liked the attention, even if it was mostly negative! I wanted to believe my mother, that you did it because you had a crush on me."

She laughed humorlessly. "And I *didn't* want to believe mine, who said the same thing."

"Admit it—you were more scared I'd be furious that you'd tricked me about who you were."

She flushed, looking sheepish. "Well, yeah. That, too."

"Would you have gone through with it, anyway?" he asked, needing to know if she'd been as out of her mind with desire as he'd been.

She nodded easily. "Yes. I would have. If Sarah hadn't

been sitting on her car out front, I would have walked with you into your house and ripped off your clothes right there by the front door, like we discussed."

"*My* clothes. But not *your* mask."

Her cheeks pinkened. "Well, not if I could help it."

Points for honesty, he supposed.

"And then what, you were going to sneak away while my back was turned? Were you ever going to tell me?"

She hesitated. He almost saw the wheels spinning in her mind as she debated how forthright to be.

"Lulu?" he prodded, his tone promising her she'd regret it if she lied.

Finally, she admitted it. "No. At that moment, I just wanted to have you, to store up some amazing memories, and then let us go back to being friends."

He gritted his teeth, crossing his arms over his chest to control his anger. "That's pretty damned cold. As is what you've put me through for the past month."

She leapt up and stalked over. "What I've put you through? How on earth do you think it made me feel when you started sniffing around that red-haired twit, giving her credit for everything you and I had done?"

"Hopefully it made you feel like shit. Because you deserved to."

She stilled, visibly deflating as her anger left her.

"Touché."

They both fell silent for a moment, and he sensed she was as lost in thought as he. The truth had come out, everything was in the open. They'd come so far, shared so much, physically and emotionally. The question was, where did they go from here?

Was it even possible that he and Lulu could have some kind of normal relationship? Did she want to? Did he? And could he ever really trust her after she'd proved herself capable of such dishonesty and stunningly good secret-keeping?

She was the first to speak, and it was as if she'd read his mind. "Chaz, I'll understand if you can't forgive me, but please know I truly am sorry. I have suffered for being such an idiot. I've learned my lesson, and I promise you, I will never lie to you, or keep secrets from you, ever again."

He nodded slowly. "I hope you mean it. Because I really hate liars."

"I know that." She came closer, twining her fingers in the hair on his chest, licking her lips and looking up at him. "But the truth is, I don't want to lose you. I don't want to lose *this* now that we've finally discovered it."

A smile tried to tug at his lips, but he hid it. "Lose what?"

"This…connection," she admitted, gesturing toward the rumpled bed where they'd spent so many wild hours.

"You want to keep sleeping with me?"

"As long as we don't spend all our time sleeping."

More honesty. More points. He liked this adult, open and blunt Lulu Vandenberg.

"What about during the rest of our waking hours?" he asked, aware that was the bigger issue.

How on earth could the two of them develop any kind of real relationship with all the baggage and all the garbage? Awkward enough to have an affair with someone who lived two doors away—they'd never have any privacy, especially with nosy neighbors and siblings.

It was also crazy to try to maintain any kind of real relationship when he could be off for months to another country after the first of the year.

Plus, they were so different now. He was hard-nosed, always after the truth, after the story. She was dreamy, her bleeding heart worn on her sleeve these days. Passionate about her job with a group he'd heard was shady.

And they knew each other too well, had spent seventeen years living next door to each other, jealous of every shared birthday, fighting over stupid crap like Halloween costumes or holiday parties.

Oh, and then there were their siblings. Their parents. Their families. God, wouldn't this affair throw all of their relatives into a tizzy as they began taking sides, tensing up, preparing for the inevitable day when Lulu and Chaz, who had never managed to get along very well, imploded and brought both families down with them?

"Stop trying to figure everything out, at least for now," she whispered, lifting her arms and encircling his neck. She moved even closer, until her bare legs brushed his, and the peaks of those soft breasts pressing against the silk seared his chest.

"What did you have in mind?"

"We're both off work today, and it's a long weekend. We don't have to leave this apartment. We don't have to make plans or think about anything except spending the next three days exploring every erotic possibility either of us has ever fantasized about."

His resolve melted, the arguments drying up and blowing away before he'd even had a chance to verbalize them.

She was right. Outside, the world would give them grief.

In here, at least for the next three days, they could pretend that world didn't exist.

He dropped his hands to her waist and undid the bathrobe tie. "Every single fantasy, huh?"

She nodded slowly, licking her lips, staring at him through eyes glazed with desire.

"Including that one you had last night when I threatened to spank you?"

She sucked in a surprised breath, as if shocked he'd read her mind so easily. Christ, how could he not when she wore her emotions on her face? Well aware what she was imagining—picturing him spanking her, and then making it up to her as erotically as possible—had made it tough to hold onto his justified anger.

"You…you knew what I was thinking?"

"I had a pretty good idea."

She hesitated, a long, heated moment, before whispering, "Good. Then I won't have to take the time being shy about what I want. We can just get started."

10

As promised, Lulu and Chaz didn't leave her apartment for three full days. They barely left her bed for that long.

They slept a lot, talked a lot, made love a *whole* lot.

They laughed and played and indulged every erotic whim. She honestly didn't know where he got his stamina, or how he could get aroused again and again. And again.

He gave her all the credit, which she happily accepted.

Lulu wasn't a great cook, but she had enough food to sustain them, and when they ran out, they ordered in. They turned off their phones and ignored the world.

Lulu did go to the door when Marcia knocked Saturday morning. Chaz stayed in the bathroom, using a new toothbrush she'd scrounged up for him, and Lulu assured her neighbor she was fine. Making an excuse about not wanting the pregnant woman to catch whatever had made her ill at Thanksgiving dinner, she'd thanked her for her concern and then closed the door—and the world—out again. She'd returned, giggling, to Chaz, who immediately joined her, naked, in her bed.

Wrapped in their own secret world, where jobs, histories, childhood grudges, secrets, lies and families didn't exist, they lived only for the pleasure they could give to one another.

But their idyll had to come to an end, and Monday rolled around far too soon. It brought with it jobs, commutes, cold weather, the holiday season and harsh reality.

"I should really go back to my place," he told her as her alarm went off at 5:45 a.m. Monday. "I haven't shaved since Thursday morning and only have the clothes I wore over here that night."

"I like that scruffy look on you." She ran a hand over his stubbled jaw, loving how hot and sexy he looked in the morning, all raw, untamed male. She also liked how that stubble felt on her breasts, her stomach, her thighs. Yum. "And it's not as if you've been wearing your clothes, they're perfectly clean," she said with an eyebrow wag.

"You keep tearing them off me every time I try to get dressed."

"Pot, meet kettle," she said, rolling over and grabbing her shredded pajama top off the bedside table, where she'd tossed it after he'd ripped it open Thursday night. "You did some literal tearing, buddy."

His smirk was entirely male, entirely self-satisfied. "I'll buy you another one."

"Fine. Silk. Victoria's Secret. Wow me."

"That sounds like a challenge."

"Maybe it was." She got up to head to the bathroom, yelping when he swatted her bare backside as she passed him. "Haven't you left yet?"

He grinned wolfishly, trying to pull her down to the bed.

"Go! Get outta here. I can't be late, I'm too new to my job and I'm saving my few days of leave for the week before Christmas."

"Does that mean you don't want to share a shower?"

His tone was so innocent, somebody who *hadn't* showered with him might be fooled into thinking he actually meant bathing. But the last three showers they'd shared had ended up with one or the other of them pinned against the tile wall while they had hot, wet, steamy sex. They'd always run out of water long before they were finished washing.

"No. I'm finished for now. You have serviced me well," she said, tossing her head and sauntering away.

She began to walk away, but he leapt up and followed, grabbing her from behind and putting his arms around her waist. He pulled her back against him, nuzzling her neck, trying to seduce her. "Serviced you, huh? I don't know, there might be a spot left on your body I haven't tasted yet."

She quivered against him, memory assaulting her. "No. There's not. Trust me on this." Oh lordy, there most definitely was not.

He turned her around and caught her mouth in a kiss. She wrapped her arms around him, indulging in the kiss for as long as she dared, then stepped out of his arms and shoved him away.

"Now, beat it. Take that ugly yellow shirt of yours and go home." She offered in a tiny grin. "I'll meet you back here in twelve hours."

He nodded his agreement as he tried to find his clothes, which were strewn around her room. "What's the matter with my shirt?" he asked as he dug it out from under her dresser and picked it up.

"It's hideous," she said. "It makes you look like a bumblebee."

"Gosh, you're so tender and romantic after you've been shagged for four straight nights."

She stuck out her tongue at him, loving that they could go right back to being playful antagonists after being such intimate lovers. The last thing she wanted, when all was said and done, was to lose her newly found friendship with Chaz.

Of course, she didn't want to lose him as her lover, either.

Hell, she just didn't want to lose him. She wanted him in her life, in every way.

They'd pretty much agreed that was impossible, and had hidden out specifically so they wouldn't have to admit to the world what they were doing. As if they could just have a hot, secret fling that was nobody's business but their own.

Now, though, she feared it wasn't going to be that simple. Or that she'd be satisfied with just a hot, mindless fling. Amelia and Viv had pointed the truth out to her last weekend, that she wanted more than that with Chaz, she'd just been forcing herself not to think about it. Especially since he'd given absolutely no indication he wanted more. His world-traveling feet were probably already itching to get back overseas, and her job would only get more demanding as she got more involved.

Still, she couldn't change how she felt. She dreaded him leaving, dreaded going back into her regular life, pretending nothing was different.

The truth was, everything had changed.

He was a part of her now, he'd claimed her, body and soul, and she honestly didn't know how on earth she would ever return to being just Lulu, singular, and not part of Lulu and Chaz.

For all their agreements and discussions the other night…she wanted him in her life permanently. And not just as an old family acquaintance and neighbor.

She was falling in love with her friend.

Lulu let herself think it and accept it as she showered,

glad he'd kissed her goodbye and left before she'd gotten in the water. She doubted she'd have been able to get out and face him without showing everything that was in her heart and in her mind. She needed some time away from him in order to try to decide how to handle this.

She could let it ride, just float along with what they were doing until they were exposed and forced to decide, for once and all, what they might mean to each other.

But that seemed risky, and a little dishonest. She'd just promised him she wouldn't lie or keep secrets. Then again, she hadn't agreed to reveal every emotion the moment she had it.

No, this was too new, too fresh and vulnerable. She had to nurture her feelings, let them develop, and then she'd figure out what to do. After all, she and Chaz had done a really good job over the past few days of starting a clandestine affair. They could keep it up for a while longer.

She was smiling about that as she let herself out of her apartment and locked the door. He was meeting her in front of his house in a few minutes so they could take their usual walk to the train station. She looked forward to walking past the regulars at the station and on the train, knowing the two of them shared a secret unsuspected by anyone else in the world.

"So, you and Chaz, huh? Figured that was coming."

Lulu almost dropped her keys as she spun around to see Peggy on the landing of the stairs, right down the hall. Dressed for work, the other woman had arrived at the perfect time to shock Lulu into utter stillness.

She tried to brazen it out and play dumb. "I beg your pardon?"

"Was it pardon you were begging for at about two o'clock Saturday morning? Because, I heard you yelling 'please' but I wasn't sure what, exactly, you were asking for."

Lulu willed the floor to open so she could sink into it, but the damned wood and carpet remained in place.

"I guess you were also praying for whatever it was you wanted, because I also heard a lot of 'Oh, God's thrown in there as well."

"I hate you."

The woman snorted with laughter. Someone else chuckled, too, and she watched as Marcia descended behind her wife, her smile just as broad, her wink knowing.

"Did you two even come up for air over the past three days?" the petite brunette asked.

Lulu buried her face in her hands. "This sucks."

"In case I haven't made it clear," said Peggy, showing no mercy, "your bedroom is sandwiched between ours above and Florence and Sherman's below. And this old house has some thin walls."

"Has everyone been discussing my sex life this weekend?" she wailed.

"Well, I don't think the neighbors in the next building have mentioned anything, do you Marc?"

Marcia tapped her finger on her cheek, as if in contemplation, and shook her head. "No, pretty sure they haven't. But the day's early yet."

Lulu's eyes narrowed. "You do know that sounds travel both ways, but I've been far too polite to mention it."

"Hey, we're married," said Peggy. "Perfectly respectable. You... Damn, girl, if good old Chaz could make you scream that way, I'm half curious about what it would be like with a dude."

Marcia frowned.

"Kidding honey," said Peggy, slipping an affectionate arm around the other woman's waist.

Finally relenting, Marcia came over and took Lulu's hand. "I'm sorry, she's such a matchmaker, and we wanted you and Chaz together. We were so happy…but we shouldn't have teased you."

"Please, don't let on to him that we had this conversation, okay?"

"Are you kidding? I want to give him a cigar or something," said Peggy.

"Oh, no, I'm begging you. He is adamant that nobody can know about this. It's just so…complicated."

Marcia nibbled her lip. "Um, Lulu, there's no way anybody who was sitting at that dinner table on Thursday didn't know."

"That's impossible."

"Well, maybe Heather. She's as dumb as a brick," said Peggy. "I don't think Chaz's hints that she should leave could have been any broader if he'd said, 'Hey, girl, I want the other one, get out.'"

That made her smile. She hadn't asked Chaz about the specifics of what had happened after she'd burst out of his house the other day. But she was glad Heather wouldn't be coming around anymore.

"The others, though, well, everybody made a pretty obvious assumption about why you skedaddled, and why Chaz got so quiet afterward. Even his jabber-jaw sister shut up and hid her giggles."

"Oh, no, Sarah figured it out? She'll tell his family, and his mom will tell my mom, and then they'll start making in-law jokes, and then when Chaz and I fall apart, they'll start trading insults and defending us. It's freaking Sarah and Lawrence all over again."

Marcia hugged her. "I wouldn't worry. I think your brother and Chaz's sister are staying busy enough to keep their noses out of your business."

That probably shocked her more than anything else. Lulu's jaw unhinged. "No way!"

"If they didn't crawl out of bed to come to Thanksgiving dinner, I'll cancel my membership in the L-club," said Peggy, snorting with laughter again.

Lulu wanted to throw her head back and groan in frustration. That was all she and Chaz needed—more Sarah and Lawrence drama to get the families drawing up battle plans again.

Then she thought about it a little more. If their younger siblings had resumed their relationship, they wouldn't be anxious for anybody to hear about it, either. Meaning they'd have to do some quid pro quo. They couldn't out Lulu and Chaz without risking their own secret.

She hoped and prayed her brother would keep Sarah's gabby mouth shut. Lawrence was very aware that his and Sarah's breakup in high school had nearly ended a whole bunch of friendships, from grandparents on down, since everybody was friends with everybody in their small town. It had practically started a war.

No, he wouldn't risk it. And he'd keep Sarah quiet.

Which meant she and Chaz should be safe for a little while. At least long enough to figure out what on earth they were doing and where they were headed.

CHAZ HAD NEVER been more tired...or more happy.

For the past two weeks, he'd been working his usual schedule, but his nights had been very active and pretty sleepless.

He just couldn't get enough of Lulu. He tried, several times, to go home and spend a normal night, alone, to regain some distance and some sanity. He'd tell himself one night off wouldn't kill him, that she had to be exhausted and getting tired of sex—women did, he'd heard.

But not Lulu. Every time she had him, she wanted him again. Just as he did her. Maybe someday the intensity would wear off and they'd be able to go a few days without touching...but he had no idea when that day might come. For right now, neither of them were anywhere close to sated or tired of their intimate games.

No matter how good his intentions, just the sight of her smiling at him from across the Metro train, or the sound of her laughter as they chatted during their walk home, would be enough to rev his engines. They'd part ways, pretending to be just commuting buddies, going into their respective buildings. Then one or the other would call, and he'd be at her place, or, more often, she'd be at his. They'd fall into bed, or on the floor, or on the kitchen table, and would lose themselves for hours in the kind of intense eroticism he'd never experienced before in his life.

He just couldn't get enough of her. When they weren't in bed, all he thought about was getting her back there.

Like right now.

"Are you sure you don't just want to go home and get naked?" he asked her.

"No," Lulu said, her tone scolding. She cast a look around to see if they'd been overheard in the store where they were shopping. "We have to get this done tonight. I don't want to come back out in *this* again."

She'd invited him out to do some Christmas shopping. He'd said yes, even though he'd rather be back in the Middle East interviewing terrorists than braving a D.C. mall ten days before Christmas.

Still, it had to be done. Plus he'd figured it would be a good chance to do something normal and nonsexual with Lulu. He loved spending time with her no matter what they did, and this seemed pretty laid-back and easy—in contrast to the rest of their relationship.

And then she'd made the mistake of walking that sexy walk right in front of him. And she'd licked that Ben & Jerry's ice cream cone, looking damned orgasmic with every taste.

Hell, she just had to glance at him with that secretive, dark-eyed stare that said she was thinking of something she wanted him to do to her and shopping became the last thing on his mind.

"I'm Christmased out," he told her. "Why don't you just get your mother a gift card?"

"Stop whining, you big baby."

He sighed and shut his mouth, wondering how anybody could be expected to be cheerful here, in this high-end shopping mall filled with desperate-to-get-a-deal revelers.

Cheerful music erupted from every speaker, bells rang, costumed elves darted about giving away prizes and breaking into carols at the least provocation. And the decorations…good grief, it looked like Christmas had crawled in here and died.

But Lulu was smiling. Oh, that amazing Lulu smile.

She passed money to the bell ringers, stopped to listen to every jingling elf's song, had a smile and a "Merry Christmas!" for every clerk and salesperson. She loved the holidays, always had, as he recalled. While he was sick of being here, and bored to tears trying to offer an opinion on whether her mother would like the blue sweater or the gray, he couldn't deny he was enjoying watching her.

Happiness oozed from her, she radiated good cheer, and looked more beautiful than ever. He couldn't take his eyes off her, and noticed just about every man they passed reacted the same way. He wanted to stake his claim on her, but as what? Her boyfriend? Her lover? Her friend with benefits? He had to get her out of the mall and back to the only place their relationship made sense—the bedroom.

"Come on, babe, we've been here for hours. You must be wiped out." He leaned close, putting his hands on her shoulders and gently kneading. "After such a long day of work, and fighting these crowds, don't you want a nice back rub and a hot bath?"

She sighed with pleasure, dropping her head back to lean on his shoulder, and for a second, he thought he had her.

But she quickly jerked away and glared at him. "Stop tempting me! I have to finish my shopping. Lawrence and I are leaving Friday to drive out to my parents' for the holidays, and I don't want to even try to find gifts once we're there."

He understood why, knowing the finest shopping establishment in their tiny hometown was a dollar store. But her comment reminded him of something else. "Are you sure you don't want to wait until Saturday and ride out with me and Sarah?"

She glanced away, studying a cashmere scarf, avoiding his gaze. "I think it's better if we arrive separately, don't you?"

"Not really. Why wouldn't we car pool? The families might think it more strange that we didn't."

Meeting his eyes, she admitted, "I'm not sure I can sit in a car with you for four hours and not let on to Sarah and Lawrence that I'm imagining you naked or remembering what your mouth tastes like."

He swallowed hard. Her tone was utterly sincere, she was genuinely worried. But he couldn't even think that far ahead. He could only think *mouth, Lulu,* and *taste,* and then wanted nothing more than to drag her out of here. He'd maybe get her as far as the car before he had to kiss the taste right out of her mouth.

She read his mind, her face grew flushed, then she

turned and grabbed a sweater—blue—and strode to the checkout counter.

After that, she shopped with less enthusiasm, and he knew she was thinking naughty thoughts. She confirmed that when she led him, casually—but with definite purpose—toward a back corner of the high-end store in which they'd ended up. Chaz followed, seeing that look in her eye—the daring look she'd worn on Halloween night. The look that said she was in the mood to do something outrageous, something dangerous. He could hardly wait to find out what.

They got to a section of the store laden with racks of nightgowns, sexy panties, bras and other undergarments and he began to get the picture.

"We're not shopping for your mother anymore, are we?"

"No, I'm all done. But I might have to buy *you* a present."

"I'll have…this," he said, gesturing toward a green silk teddy. "As long as it's the wrapping and you are the present."

She ran her fingers across the teddy, and Chaz's heart skipped a beat. When she tested the fastening of a garter belt, attached to a silky pair of hose on a mannequin's leg, he gulped down a hearty helping of want.

But then she picked up a filmy nightgown that had a front, a back, a bow connecting them on each hip, and absolutely nothing else. When she headed for the changing room, he walked after her like a panting dog.

It was late on a weeknight, near closing time. The mall had been crowded—packed, actually—with holiday shoppers earlier in the evening. But the place had thinned out a lot in the last half hour. And this lingerie area, in the back corner of a huge anchor store, was deserted, the nearest register closed, the next a whole department away.

Interesting possibilities presented themselves.

"I think I should see that on you," he said as he followed her around a corner and into the changing area. There was a lounge, with sofas and mirrors, where women could come out and view their selections from all sides. Or, he suspected, so men could view them—because the furnishings were masculine, and a sign said men were invited to sit and wait for their companions, but shouldn't proceed past a certain point.

He didn't sit. He proceeded.

Lulu glanced over her shoulder, spying him coming after her, correctly reading his expression, as he correctly read hers.

"Can you help me unzip?" she asked, so innocent, so coy.

"I'll help you out of anything you care to take off."

She nodded, stepping into one of the private changing booths. He walked in after her, pushing the full-length door shut behind him. The area was as big as a decent-size closet, with a mirrored wall and a plush bench seat. Very upscale. Very welcoming. It was as if the store *wanted* their customers' boyfriends and husbands to follow them in here, as if they intended the place to be perfect for trysts and daring escapades.

Well, that's the way he looked at it, anyway.

"Turn around," he said.

She did, waiting patiently as he unzipped her tight skirt. He let his hands slide it down slowly, his knuckles brushing against her rear as he leaned in and smelled her hair.

Their eyes met in the mirror. She was unbuttoning her blouse, easing each tiny, satin-covered button free of its hole with calm, steady deliberation.

She licked her lips. Her eyes were wide and dreamy, her breaths audible in the otherwise silent compartment.

Chaz pushed the skirt off her hips, stepping back a tiny bit so it could drop to the carpeted floor. She finished unbuttoning her blouse, and pushed it off her shoulders, letting it join the skirt.

"Jesus," he said, realizing she must have already done some lingerie shopping before now. He had never seen her in the stunningly sexy getup she wore.

Her black bra was lacy and was meant more to push her breasts up to dizzying, dangerous heights than to cover them. He could see a hint of her nipples peeking out the top, and he growled hungrily at the reflected sight.

But that wasn't all. He almost howled when he lowered his attention and saw the garter belt fastened around her slim waist. Four sexy, lacy seams dropped down to attach to silky stockings, but above the top hem of those stockings, she was utterly bare.

"I think you forgot something when you went to work this morning," he growled, dropping his mouth to the nape of her neck and nipping her.

"I was a good girl. I wore my panties to work."

"Did you drop them somewhere? Should we check the lost-and-found?"

She licked her lips, their stares locked in the mirror. "Maybe you should check your pocket."

Never looking away from her, he reached into the pocket of his jacket, his fingers meeting silky softness. Drawing the tiny clump of fabric out and seeing lacy black undergarments, he lifted them to his face and breathed deeply. "Yeah. They're yours."

"Was there any doubt? Was some other woman dropping underwear into your pocket?"

He dropped his mouth to the nape of her neck and kissed her, sucking lightly, realizing he'd leave a mark but not giving a damn. "No, but I'd know yours anyway. I'm addicted to your scent."

"Is that all you're addicted to?" she asked, arching her back, tilting her bare bottom in invitation until it pressed against the front of his trousers.

He slid his hands down her sides, cupping her hips, then reaching forward to stroke her creamy stomach. Pulling her tighter against him, he watched in the mirror as her eyes flared wide and her face flushed when she felt his rock-hard erection.

God, he liked this, liked coming at her from behind, watching her reflection as he caressed her. She was unable to hide a single thought, a single reaction. She wore her pleasure on her face, and when he smoothed his hand up to cup her breast, she gasped and pushed even harder against his groin.

His hand was big and dark against her pale skin. She looked vulnerable, utterly feminine. Working the front of her bra down, he watched her nipple pop free, and caught it between his fingers. She was so responsive, he knew she felt each tweak throughout her body, knew that him playing with her nipples made her wet.

She leaned back, turning her head to gaze up at him. He bent to catch her mouth in a kiss, remaining behind her. One of her arms came up to encircle his neck, and with her other hand, she reached back for his crotch. When she struggled with his belt, he took over, undoing it, and then unfastening his pants and pushing them down, out of the way.

Lulu lifted her head and looked at his reflection in the mirror again, her face dreamy, hungry.

"Please," she whispered, putting a hand on the glass to brace herself. She made her demands even more clear, bending farther, arching toward him, inviting him to take her from behind.

He had never gotten a better invitation. Nudging her legs farther apart, groaning at the feel of those soft, silky stockings against his skin, he reached down and parted her cheeks. She bent over even more, until he could see the tempting pink flesh between her legs, all slick and wet, just waiting for him. Lulu was utterly aroused; maybe she had been since she'd snuck away to slip her panties off and drop them into his pocket. God knows he would have been hard all night if he'd reached in, felt them there, and realized she was naked beneath her skirt.

"Take me," she ordered, staring into the mirror, watching him eye her lustfully.

"Yes, ma'am," he said, easing his cock into her, watching himself disappear between her welcoming folds.

Wet heat enveloped him; he sank into utter perfection, savoring every bit of her he could take.

When he moved too slowly, she pushed back, taking more, greedy and impatient.

Her impatience snapped the last of his control. He gripped her hips, digging his fingers into her flesh, and slammed into her, plunging so hard his balls slapped her ass.

"Oh, yes!" she groaned. She quickly bit her lip, cutting off her cries of ecstasy.

It was a little late to think about who else might be around. He honestly didn't give a damn if anybody heard them. It would take a gun to his head to make him stop what he was doing.

He thrust again and again, gripping her hips and pulling her back toward him with every forward thrust. He slammed into her with every ounce of himself and her energetic movements and satisfied sighs told him how much she loved it.

It was insane, risky, wild. Like on Halloween night, they were both past caring about niceties, or witnesses, or danger. They were lost to everything but each other.

Only, this time, neither of them were playing games. There was no question of stopping, no possibility of running away.

He had her, she was his to do with what he would.

And he was hers.

11

LULA HAD FEARED things were going too well to last.

Two days later, when she and Chaz were getting on the Metro to go home, they bumped into his reporter friend, Tonia, the blonde who'd monopolized his attention at the kickball game several weeks ago. He'd told Lulu the other woman was just a colleague, which was fine. But, when pressed, he had also admitted they'd maybe been a little more to each other, at least briefly. That wasn't so fine.

Lulu hadn't even been in the picture when he and Tonia had their affair, but she was still jealous of anyone who'd ever had what she considered hers—namely, his body and his sexual attention. She'd staked her claim on Chaz, whether publicly or not. She thought of him as her own, and didn't even want to consider any of the women he'd had before she'd come back into his life. Especially not the pretty, sexy, smart ones. Like Tonia.

Maybe she was being stupid, maybe she had no right. He'd certainly never told her he loved her, never made plans, never talked about any kind of a future. But she had to believe he was thinking along those lines, as was she. She couldn't bear to imagine she'd fallen hopelessly in love with him and he didn't feel the same.

He does. This is real. It's not just the sex.

She mattered to him.

"Chaz, I'm so glad I ran into you!" the reporter said. "I never see you anymore since they moved me to the northern Virginia office."

"How are you doing, Tonia?" His smile seemed forced. Perhaps he, too, was disappointed that he and Lulu wouldn't be able to silently flirt with each other from opposite seats on the Metro train.

"I'm great. And so, obviously, are you," she said, casting an appreciative eye over him.

She was right. Chaz had always been hot, but lately he'd had that well-done look that a man wore when he was getting laid a lot. Something about that look attracted other women. It was as if they could smell sex on a satisfied man.

Lulu cleared her throat to announce her presence, wanting the female reporter to know who'd put that look on Chaz's handsome face.

Tonia turned around and glanced down at her, feigning surprise, although Lulu was sure she'd spotted her the moment she boarded the train. "And you're Lulu, right?" the woman said. "Isn't this a happy reunion?"

"Yes. Nice to see you again." Gee, that had almost sounded sincere.

"Chaz, you are just the man I wanted to meet," the woman said, swinging around and plopping down on the edge of Chaz's seat, blocking him from Lulu's view. She glanced over her shoulder. "You don't mind, Lulu, do you? It's shop talk."

Lulu shrugged, but she glared daggers at the back of the woman's head when she turned to face Chaz and drag him into quiet conversation. Lulu barely paid attention to the subject until she heard Tonia say, "I have a source who's going to give me all the dirt on that shady *Hands Across The Waters* organization."

Her jaw falling open, she looked over Tonia's head into Chaz's face. His expression was strained; he actually winced in reaction. "Tonia, I really don't think…"

"No, seriously. And I know how much you love to expose fraud and shysters. I've sensed for months that there was something going on with that place—those founders are just too squeaky clean to be true. I'm going to bring them down, and I want you to help me."

"Excuse me," Lulu said, "what, exactly, are you talking about?"

Tonia glanced over, gave her a dismissive shrug, and said, "Oh, just a story I'm doing that Chaz helped me with."

"He did, huh?"

"It was a while ago," Chaz said, his tone pointed, his expression begging her not to jump to conclusions.

She was jumping, of course. Lulu was just the jumping sort. And Tonia made jumping so very easy.

"Oh, don't sell yourself short. You're a genius at this stuff."

"Tonia and I bounced some ideas around," he explained. "I gave her some suggestions about researching the story."

Lulu bared her teeth. "Was that before or after you found out that I worked for *Hands Across The Waters?*"

His reporter friend shot up from her seat. "Oh, God, seriously?"

"Yeah. Seriously."

"I had no idea!" She gaped at Chaz. "Did I just ruin this? Is that why you're with her? Were you helping me out, trying to get an in for me?"

"He's been getting *in,* honey, but it has absolutely nothing to do with you," Lulu snapped, fury making her reckless and crude. But oh, it had been satisfying, especially when the other woman flinched. Chaz, meanwhile, looked like he couldn't decide between laughter and shock.

Tonia's mouth got smaller and tighter. "Thank you for being so...blunt. But that's really none of my business."

"Oh, sorry, I thought you were already prying into something that wasn't any of your business. Isn't that what you reporter types do?"

"That's ridiculous."

Lulu cut her off. "Well, it sounds like that's what you're doing to my employers. But let me tell you, Jenna and Felix Bernardo are the most honest, open, generous people I've ever met." She laughed, without humor. "Good luck finding dirt on them, because, frankly, it doesn't exist. You're going on a snipe hunt."

The other woman, who appeared thoroughly jaded, gave her a pitying smile. "Look, you haven't been around the world like Chaz and I have. *Nobody's* that honest, open and generous. When you're a little older, maybe you'll realize people just aren't that good and decent, not unless something's in it for them."

She could have taken a shot at the woman for the age crack, pointing out that Tonia was obviously several years older than she. But that was almost too easy. So she instead said, "Wow, you're really bitter, aren't you? I feel sorry for you if that's your take on life."

"Are you willing to talk to me about your experiences there? Maybe between us we can find out the truth. Wouldn't you like that? I could protect you as a source, keep you anonymous."

"Are you high?"

One of the woman's perfectly plucked eyebrows shot up and she stiffened, more offended than ever. "Look, I'm just doing my job."

"Well, your job sucks."

Tonia glanced at Chaz. "She doesn't have a very high opinion of *us,* does she?"

Her dismissal of Lulu was deliberate and noticeable. Chaz was stiff-jawed, and his angry expression should have sent a warning to Tonia.

She didn't notice it. "This is my stop. I'll talk to you about this later, Chaz, all right?" Her smile was a little too intimate. "Maybe we can meet up before the holiday break at that place we like so much."

She cast a triumphant glance at Lulu. If it hadn't been clear that Chaz had slept with the woman in the past, Tonia's expression would certainly have cemented the fact.

Before the other woman turned away, Chaz said, "Write your own damn story, Tonia. I am not at all interested."

Her smile faded. She flounced toward the front of the car, having to grab a security bar to avoid falling on her ass and ruining her exit. The train reached the station, and she pushed her way through the oncoming crowd to exit.

As the train filled with weekday commuters, everyone was jostled, and Lulu couldn't maintain her footing. Despite being furious, she tumbled into the empty seat beside Chaz.

"Lulu, I didn't set out to do anything behind your back."

"Oh, really? Because it sounds to me like you knew that woman was *trying* to find something bad to report about my employers, people I really respect, and you never said a word to me."

"She mentioned it," he said, "but honestly, I'd forgotten all about it. I haven't seen Tonia in a couple of weeks. I've been focusing on preparing for my next overseas assignment."

If he noticed her shock about that little nugget, he didn't let on.

"Tonia's got this obsession, but I don't share it. Between the time I've been spending with you, the series of articles from my Pakistan trip, the interest from *Time* magazine, and my research to prepare for an investigative trip to Syria after the first of the year, I just haven't thought about her since I saw her last."

Lulu had no idea where to begin. Her head was reeling.

He'd helped another reporter with an exposé on an organization that she knew was doing wonderful work? *Time* magazine? Freaking Syria? Would he again take side trips into war zones and would she be the one who didn't get the call when he was injured since he didn't want to "worry" anyone?

And he had never even mentioned any of this to her?

It suddenly hit her. She'd fallen wildly in love with someone, assuring herself he felt the same way, when the truth was they shared nothing. Absolutely nothing except sex. Amazing sex. Astounding sex. The best sex of her life, hands down.

But nothing else.

He didn't trust her with his ambitions or his dreams. He hadn't even bothered to tell her he was going into yet another danger zone after the first of the year. Come to think of it, she didn't even know where his office was, which damn stop he got off at, who he went to lunch with.

They had sex, and when they didn't have sex, they talked and thought about having sex. Oh, yeah, and they'd shopped once, finishing the shopping trip by, surprise, having amazing sex in a public place.

That was all she was to him, all their relationship was. A wild but secret sexual affair. One he could walk away from without a second glance and nobody would ever be the wiser.

She'd agreed to those terms in the beginning. Now,

though, when she realized just how much of his life he'd excluded her from, she felt small and unimportant. She was fulfilling a need for him—often—but he wasn't giving her a single thought when he wasn't in bed with her or trying to get into bed with her. He'd warned her he didn't trust people, and for some reason she'd assumed she'd be different. But she wasn't. He didn't trust her or care about her any more than he had Tonia. She was just a distraction from his real love, journalism.

She had to be alone. Her chest was tight, her breaths came hard from her lungs. She was dizzy and could barely think, wanting to get off this moving train, away from this crush of people, and far away from *him*.

"Lulu, talk to me," he said, trying to take her hand.

She pulled it away and rose to her feet. Mumbling apologies to the people crowding around, she grabbed a bar and lurched away, moving toward the front of the train.

He got up to follow. She glanced back and snapped, "Don't. Just don't. I need to be away from you right now."

His eyes widened with surprise, and maybe hurt.

Jesus, how could he be surprised that she would react like this? Did he not see her as a person at all? Was she just a sperm receptacle for him?

She knew that wasn't fair. Chaz was a kind person, he always had been. She knew he'd never have set out to hurt her.

No, this hadn't been intentional. He'd just done exactly what they'd both decided to do: have a fling. Keep it secret. Not let it mean anything.

She was the one who'd broken the rules. She was the one who'd wanted something that wasn't there, who'd let herself begin to believe it wasn't the simple, sexual affair it was. She'd seen her own love reflected back from his eyes, but he'd never offered her any such thing.

She was the one hurting so badly she wanted to curl up in a ball and sob.

So she was the one who had to get away from him now, before she broke down in tears and admitted the unthinkable: that she'd fallen in love with Chaz Browning. And that her heart was utterly broken.

"I JUST CAN'T BELIEVE she left without telling me," Chaz mumbled, speaking more to himself than to Peggy, who'd come downstairs to find out why he was knocking and knocking on Lulu's door the next evening. She'd told him Lulu was gone, having packed up and left the city while Chaz was at work.

"Why would she just go like that?"

"Sorry, Chaz, she said she wanted to beat the traffic heading out of the city tomorrow. Her brother was finished with his classes, her boss gave her an extra day off, so they packed up and left."

That all made sense, and he knew Peggy wasn't lying. But he still just couldn't comprehend it. God, had Lulu bought that nonsense Tonia had spewed on the train? Did she have the crazy idea that he had gotten close to her only for a damn story—one that wasn't even his own? How could she have believed that of him?

But there was no other explanation. Because there was no Lulu. She hadn't met him outside for their train ride this morning, hadn't answered his calls, hadn't met him on the way home from work. And hadn't answered his loud pounding on her door.

Now he knew why. She really was gone.

"What'd you do to mess it up?" Peggy asked, blunt as always.

"Honestly? I have no idea." He thrust a hand through his hair, trying to understand. "It was so stupid, a dumb argument over what somebody else said. She got the wrong idea about something, I tried to explain it, and she took off."

Peggy tsked and shook her head. "You shoulda shown up at the door with a dozen roses and a ring last night, before she had the chance to sleep on it, build her anger and take off."

A *ring*? Chaz couldn't hide his shocked reaction to that idea. His jaw fell open and he actually laughed.

"Oh, that's funny? Gee, I think I'm beginning to understand why she left you." Peggy glared her disappointment. "Maybe I shouldn't have bothered to tell you she was gone."

He rushed to explain. "Oh, *I* don't think it's funny. I'm crazy in love with her, and I'd put a ring on her finger in a heartbeat if I weren't sure she'd laugh in my face."

"No woman laughs at a diamond ring. Get her a great big, shiny, ridiculously ostentatious diamond and she'll forgive you anything."

If only it were that easy.

"Not Lulu. She doesn't even want anybody to know we're together. What the hell would she say if I proposed marriage?" Something struck him. "Hell, I wasn't even aware *you* knew about us."

"Good grief, the two of you are so obvious, I'm sure the newspaper delivery guy is aware you're madly in love with each other. Hell, her own brother announced it at Thanksgiving dinner. You two have been in love for years."

"She's never said that. She made it pretty clear that she just wanted a fling, no commitments, nothing serious, absolutely nobody finding out."

"Boy are you stupid, Chaz Browning."

He leaned a shoulder against the wall and waited to find out why he was stupid. He had no doubt she was about to expound.

"From some things she's said, I gathered your families are tight, and your siblings mucked everything up a while back?"

"Definitely."

"And it's not easy for her to trust you, after you've made such a huge deal of your big international career and how it comes before anything else."

Chaz stiffened with shock. Had he been that much of an asshole about it? His career *had* come before everything else in the past. But did it come before Lulu? Had he given her reason to believe that it would?

The very idea made him nauseous.

"So of course she *says* she wants to be discreet, be cautious, keep it all a big secret. No point getting her heart invested if this thing between you is just sex and you're going to walk away after New Year's, right?"

"Actually, that sounds a lot like what she said," he murmured.

"But she didn't *mean* it, not deep down in her heart."

Peggy glanced up as someone came down from above. It was Marcia, who stepped out of the stairwell, eyeing them both.

"I was listening from upstairs. Peggy's right. Lulu is in love with you. Anyone can see it."

"And I'm in love with her," he admitted, acknowledging it himself for the first time. "I guess I always loved her a little bit. Now I love her a lot."

Only, he'd never told her. Never gave her any indication that he was carving out a place for her in his life. He supposed they'd both been keeping things hidden. One thing was sure: if he got her back, they were going to do a lot of talking.

When he got her back.

"I can't lose her," he said. "Not now that I've found her again."

Marcia patted his shoulder. "Then fix it."

"How? With roses and a ring, when I'm not sure which stupid thing I've done made her leave?"

Boy, wasn't that the ultimate male dilemma. He could be the poster child for how-to-screw-up-your-relationship-without-even-trying.

"She left because you let her think that a secret fling was just fine with you, too," Marcia exclaimed.

Peggy piped in. "Duh!"

"What? Wait, I'm in the doghouse because I *agreed* with her?"

"I suspect so," said Marcia. "A woman doesn't want to believe she's only good enough to be your dirty little secret. She wants to know you care enough about her to share your hopes, your dreams, your real life."

"Are you kidding? She knows me better than anyone. We talk for hours every night."

"In bed?"

He wasn't used to such bluntness about his sex life, but nodded.

"Tell me, you ever take her out to a movie? Or dinner? Hell, even a walk?"

"We went Christmas shopping at the mall the other night," he said, sounding defensive.

"And did you sneak her into a maintenance closet and shag her between Macy's and Gap?"

He didn't answer. His flushed face was all the answer the two women needed.

"Yeah. She thinks it's just sex," Marcia said, shaking her head mournfully. "That she's only good enough for you to fool around with, but not good enough to share your life."

"That's ridiculous."

Peggy gave him a pitying look. "We can tell that just by the way you stare at her when you don't think anybody will notice. Your feelings are written all over your face."

Marcia, patting his arm, added, "It's true. Lulu is the only one who hasn't figured out that you love her. She needs you to make it clear. She needs tenderness from you. Words, promises. Not just sperm."

Peggy snickered. "Ew. Sperm."

Marcia rolled her eyes and shook her head. "You're such an infant," she said, fondly scolding. "Remind me not to leave you alone with our child, ever."

"Sorry," Peggy said, growing appropriately serious.

"I have to make her understand that I love her and that I want a real future with her."

"Do you really?" asked Peggy. "Because that might mean you'll have to make some changes in your lifestyle. No woman wants to think she's less important than a job."

The very idea that Lulu would think such a thing shocked him. "She's more important than anything in my life. There's nothing I won't do to prove that to her."

"Even if it means you have to gallivant around the world a little bit less?"

He didn't even hesitate before answering. "If it's a choice between Lulu and the entire world…I choose Lulu."

Peggy patted his cheek. "I knew you were a smart one."

Thanking the women sincerely, and thinking about all the ideas they'd put in his head, he bid them a Merry Christmas and headed home. As soon as he got there, he picked up the phone and called Sarah, asking her if she could be ready to leave for home by tomorrow, and she immediately agreed. Promising to come by campus to pick her up, he told her it wouldn't be until after lunch.

He had somewhere to go in the morning, and a very special present to buy.

But first, he had to call his editor.

_12_

EVER SINCE SHE was a child, Lulu's mom and Mrs. Browning had co-chaired the town's Silent Night, Holy Night holiday festival. It was always held on the Friday night before Christmas, and always in the high school gym.

People would come with crafts to sell, baked goods to share. Practically everybody in the entire town would show up to bid each other a Merry Christmas before folks devoted themselves to their immediate families.

There would be carols sung and eggnog drunk, and the younger children would put on a pageant of the Christmas story. Invariably, some kid dressed up as a shepherd would get the giggles, while an angel lost her halo, and the back end of a camel would scratch his butt.

Hmm. She'd been that angel once, with the dangling halo. And she was pretty sure Chaz had been the ass-end of the camel at least once, though she didn't remember any butt scratching that year.

Being back here, with her family, in her hometown, was so much harder than she'd expected. She'd come home for the holiday season probably every other year since she'd left home, but never had she felt so surrounded by memories, so hemmed in by the ghosts of Christmas past.

Chaz was everywhere she looked. In her backyard, and in his. In the park, where they'd leaped into piles of leaves. On the playground, the baseball field. Every place she went was colored by a memory of something she'd done with him.

Including this festival.

Lulu tried to force her melancholy away, not wanting to spoil anyone else's holiday. She had to be cheerful and find some Christmas spirit as she finished putting the final touches on the manger scene. Her mother had asked her to set it up while she and Mrs. Browning did the other million-and-one tasks for tonight's pageant.

Lawrence was around somewhere, having been roped in to setting up tables or hooking up lights or something. It felt like the two of them were completely alone in the school, which had closed early today for the long Christmas break.

There were a few hours yet before people started to arrive, and Lulu ended up just sitting in a seat in the front row of the auditorium, remembering coming to see school plays in this very place. She smiled as she remembered Chaz's performance in a talent show in freshman year, with a group of his fourteen-year-old buddies. They'd done a Backstreet Boys number, complete with choreography. She remembered thinking at the time that he was cute enough to be a Backstreet Boy, after which she told him the Backstreet Boys were totally stupid and N'Sync was totally where it was at.

Yeah. She probably always had loved him. How on earth was she going to face him when he showed up in town tomorrow? Somehow, they had to get through the holiday season without dragging the family into their situation.

Although she worried about it, she also desperately

wanted to see him. She knew she shouldn't have run away without an explanation. Chaz wasn't the guilty party here; he'd only done what he'd thought she wanted.

She'd realized she couldn't maintain a purely sexual relationship; her feelings were too entangled. But she also couldn't go on treating him like he'd wronged her. Because he hadn't.

"You okay down there, sis?"

She looked up and saw Lawrence standing on the stage. He'd been worried about her since she'd picked him up at school yesterday and dragged him out here, but he hadn't pried. She'd done him the same courtesy, not asking for any details about him and Sarah.

"I'm fine. Just thinking, remembering."

"Good memories?" he asked, brushing back an errant strand of hair, which always dangled in his eyes. He was a young man, but still had a sweet, earnest, boyish look. When they were kids, it had always made her want to pound him, because she'd feared the world would be cruel to tender-hearted boys like her brother. Now, she found him just about perfect, and hoped Sarah realized what she had.

"Some good, some bad. I guess I'm trying to rediscover the joy of Christmas."

"What's not to love?"

This year? "Everything."

"Aww, come on." He stepped to the edge of the stage, his youthful, angular face caught in the spotlights he'd been testing up in the booth. "How can you not love Mom burning the gravy, and Dad cutting too many bottom limbs off the tree so he has to go buy another one, and Uncle Warren drinking too much eggnog and Aunt Shelly complaining that nobody made sugar-free cookies?"

The memories brought a wistful smile to her mouth.

"You used to sneak into my room on Christmas Eve night," Lawrence said. "We would shine our flashlights out the window at Chaz and Sarah's house. They'd flash back so we'd all know we were on guard, waiting to catch a glimpse of Santa Claus."

She nodded. "And all of us would argue the next day over who had fallen asleep first."

"Remember how Dad always read us *'Twas the Night Before Christmas?* I was eleven when you had to explain to me that reindeer have hooves, not paws, and they were really *pausing* up on the roof."

"You dope," she said, actually laughing. "We had some great holidays."

"Definitely. Remember when you convinced me that Chaz would find it hilarious if I wrapped up a box of raisins and gave it to him as a present?"

"You should have quit while you were ahead. Or while I was."

"He loved the attention," Lawrence told her, serious and earnest. "Always. For as long as I can remember, you've both done everything you could to get the other to notice you, neither of you ever realizing why, even if everybody else knew."

"You truly believe we love each other?" she whispered.

"I'm certain of it. You always have, you always will, whether you end up together or not."

"Right at this moment, I'm thinking *not*," she said, sniffing and blinking away moisture that rose to her eyes.

"It's the season of miracles. A time for precious moments that we value because we know nothing lasts forever and we should take whatever happiness we can while we can get it." He came to the edge of the stage and hopped down from it to stand right in front of her. "Christmas is the perfect occasion to do that, Lulu. To be happy, to love and to appreciate all the blessings in your life."

Tears swam in her eyes as she recognized that her kid brother had grown into a remarkable man. Deep and thoughtful, kind and so loving.

She got up and put her arms around him, hugging him tightly. "You're pretty wonderful, you know that?"

"I know somebody who thinks you are, too," he whispered back.

She pulled away and stared at him. But he was looking past her, over her shoulder. Confused, Lulu turned around and saw a man standing there.

It was Chaz.

He walked toward them in the shadowy darkness, saying nothing, his attention glued to her face. As he drew closer, she'd swear she spotted tenderness in his expression, but that might just have been wishful thinking.

"Hello, Lulu," he said.

She didn't reply, for once at a loss for words. She truly didn't know what to say to him. She'd hoped she'd have another day before having to face him, but he'd caught her off guard, caught her emotional and teary. Damn it.

"I'll see you later," Lawrence said, walking by Chaz and fist-bumping him.

And then they were alone.

"Merry Christmas."

She sniffed, finding a stray thought and throwing it out. "Silly, Christmas is a week away."

"For me, Christmas always started with the Friday night pageant."

Yeah, it had for her, too.

He came closer, and then closer still, until she could feel the warmth of his body radiating toward her.

"You left," he said, his expression betraying his hurt.

"I know. I'm sorry, I was being a coward."

"Why did you go?"

She blinked to keep any tears from falling. "I was dumb, blaming you for something that was never your fault."

"Oh, there was a lot that was my fault. Let's start with the article—you don't have to worry. I talked to Tonia and got the whole story, as I should have done from the beginning. Her 'source' was a disgruntled former employee. She can't find a single thing on your employers—they're very good people. There will be no article."

"Oh, thank you," she said, relief lifting her spirits, even though she was still numb about his presence here.

He lifted a hand and cupped her cheek, brushing his thumb across her lips, searching for something in her eyes. Lulu stared back at him, wondering how things could have gone so crazy, how having a wild affair could have led her to acknowledge a truth she'd run from her entire life.

She loved this man. She wanted him for her very own, for as long as she could have him.

When his tender smile widened, she got the feeling he'd found whatever it as he'd been searching for in her face.

"Next, I don't want to have a secret affair with you anymore," he told her.

Lulu flinched, feeling like he'd slapped her. Whatever she'd expected him to say, it wasn't that.

She swallowed, hard, trying to remain calm. Not that Chaz didn't have the right to dump her—she'd acted like a jealous fishwife, when the only title he'd ever offered her was bedmate. Still, a part of her had hoped it wouldn't be that easy for him to give her up. And her heart, which she'd hoped had begun to mend, split apart all over again.

Damn it, loving this man was painful. Especially now that he had come to end things once and for all.

"All right, I understand," she said, wrapping her arms around her waist, suddenly feeling cold. "It's for the best."

"No, you don't understand," he said, brushing his fingers through a strand of her hair, stroking it tenderly. "I don't want to have a secret affair with you, Lulu, because I love you too much to keep hiding it."

She couldn't have heard him correctly. "What did you say?"

He cupped her face in both his hands, tilting her face up to his. "I said I love you," he whispered. "I always have, even when I swore to everyone who would listen that I hated you. I can't imagine myself ever being with anyone except you. You are *all* I want."

"But…but…the families! Your job, the sneaking around…"

"All second to you. I was so intent on finding the truth in dusty, far-off places, but then something Peggy said made me think about what I really want from my life. And it's not travel or a job or a magazine cover."

"What is it?" she asked, almost too afraid to hope she knew the answer.

He brushed his lips across hers, gently, almost reverently, and whispered, "It's you, Lulu. I think, deep down, it's always been you. You're everything I want, and wherever you are will be home to me. I don't need the whole world as long as I can always have one little piece of it where you are."

She trembled, hearing the certainty in his voice.

"So I phoned my boss and told him I plan on working stateside for a while. Do you think you can stand to have me around a lot of the time?"

"I can definitely stand it," she said, relief filling her. Whether they were together or not, she hated the thought of him ever being anywhere that could endanger his life.

He was much too precious, too special, for the world to lose. Someday, she knew, he'd want to go to some far-off place and do his adventuring, but she'd make sure he always knew he had a place to come home to, where he was loved more than life itself.

"I'm glad you're sticking around."

"Just glad?"

"Very glad," she said, her tone and expression solemn.

"I love you," he repeated, brushing his lips against hers, kissing her with such tenderness, she almost melted on the spot. "I won't deny I want to keep sneaking around with you, just for fun. But if we do, we'll have to be pretending we're not wildly in love and that it's all just about sex."

"It's not all about sex?"

"Oh, God, no," he swore, emotion shining in his eyes. "I want you, without a doubt, and you will always drive me absolutely crazy with lust."

That didn't sound so bad.

"But I want *all* of you, not just your body. I want to hear what you're thinking and planning and dreaming. I want you to feel you can tell me anything, and that I can do the same with you."

"You can."

"I know. Because I trust you wouldn't ever betray me."

She believed him. They finally were being completely honest with each other now. Except for one thing. She licked her lips. "You're pretty sure I'm in love with you, huh?"

"Pretty damn sure, Lucille."

"Now you've gone and ruined the moment," she said with a mock sigh.

"Let me make it better." He stepped back. "I want to give you your Christmas present early."

Not sure what to expect, she had to grab the edge of the stage to steady herself when he dropped to one knee in front of her and pulled a small box out of his pocket.

"Think you could sneak around, be a secret lover and have wild, public sex with a guy you're married to?"

"What?"

"Will you marry me, Lulu?"

The world trembled, or else she did, as he flipped open the lid of the box. Inside was a ring, a sapphire surrounded by small diamonds, set in a delicate filigree. It was simple, and beautiful and absolutely perfect.

"I was told I should get you a big, shiny, obnoxious rock," he murmured, watching her closely to gauge her reaction. "But somehow this seemed to suit you better. It's honest, and lovely, just like you."

She nodded, tears filling her eyes. "Yes," she whispered.

"Yes, you like the ring?"

"No. Well, wait, yes, that, too," she said, the tears running now and her thoughts scattering in a thousand directions. "But mainly, yes, Chaz, yes, I love you. Yes, I'll marry you. Yes, I'll be your secret lover and your public wife."

She offered him her hand, noticing it tremble as he slid the ring onto her finger. It was a perfect fit. More, as he'd said, it was honest, and lovely, and had come straight from his heart. And she adored it.

"I love you, I do," she said, not waiting for him to get up, but dropping to her knees in front of him. "I've loved you long before I knew I did."

"I'm not sure you loved me the day you took the ladder away and made me break my tailbone," he said, a laugh rumbling in his chest.

"I did, too," she insisted, "I was just mad because you'd

shared your Capri Sun with somebody else in the playground that day."

He gaped at her, and she blushed.

"What can I say? I'm jealous and I keep what's mine," she said. "Can you handle that?"

He nodded slowly. "I can handle that. And I promise, I will never again share my Capri Sun with another girl." He held her hands, pulling her closer. "Unless she has brown curls and dark brown eyes, just like her mother."

That was a long way off, but the idea of someday having a family with Chaz made her feel light enough to fly up off the floor.

He kept her grounded, though, pulling her close. Crushing her in his embrace, he kissed her with such love, such tenderness, she started to cry all over again, but then to laugh, as well. Emotions surged and filled her, memories washed over her, anticipation of a bright and joyous future swelled within her.

She hadn't been aware she was capable of feeling so much at the same time, and had never dreamed that the boy next door would be the one she'd trust with her heart for all the days of her life.

When the kiss ended, he lifted his head, stroked her cheek and whispered, "Should we go and tell our mothers they're going to be in-laws?"

She nodded happily, picturing it, knowing that she and Chaz had a bond strong enough that it would never break. Their families would be ecstatic, and every one of them would say, *I told you so,* and Lulu wouldn't care one bit, because she was loved and she was *in* love and it was Christmas and life was perfect.

"Yes, let's," she replied.

"Merry Christmas, Lulu, my love," he whispered as he rose to his feet, helping her to hers

She stood before him, staring into soulful eyes that shone with emotion, and replied, "Merry Christmas, Chaz Browning."

* * * * *

Nice & Naughty

TAWNY WEBER

Tawny Weber has been writing sassy, sexy romances for Mills & Boon® Blaze® since her first book hit the shelves in 2007. A fan of Johnny Depp, cupcakes and colour coordinating, Tawny spends a lot of her time shopping for cute shoes, scrap-booking and hanging out on Facebook. Come by and visit her on the web at www.tawnyweber.com.

To my very own Persephone, who really does
climb Christmas trees, but never tears the
heads off teddy bears

1

"Dude, I can't believe your luck with women."

"That's not luck, my friend. That's an abundance of charm," Detective Diego Sandoval offered with a wicked grin. "And the simple fact that I love women."

And with a few painful exceptions, women loved him right back.

Something that came in handy when he was charming information, and a cast-iron frying pan, out of a three-hundred-pound mass of quivering fury.

"I've never seen anyone so pissed, though. When you arrested her old man, I thought she was gonna knock you on your butt. By the time you left, you had her ready to testify against the dirtbag, handing over evidence and offering to make you a bologna sandwich."

Diego shrugged. He was a cop. That was his job, his focus, his entire life. He did whatever it took to break a case. "Try chilling a woman down while she's aiming a sawed-off shotgun at your goods."

"Suspect?"

"Date."

Following Diego up the steps of the large brick building

that housed the Central California Sheriff's Field Operations Bureau, Chris Carson shook his head. In admiration or in disdain, it didn't matter to Diego. He was all about the job and he devoted 100 percent to it. He didn't have time to worry about other people's opinions or doing the buddy thing. That's what made him one of the best.

"Someday, Sandoval, you're gonna meet a challenge you can't charm your way through," Chris said as they strode down the hall toward the patrol and investigation offices.

Diego's grin slipped a notch.

"Someday" had happened at birth. Diego had heard tell over the years about such a thing as motherly love, but he'd never experienced it himself. Hell, his mother had barely tolerated him. His learning to talk had been her breaking point. At three, he'd begun the loser shuffle between the rigid disapproval of his uncle Leon's house and the dismissive foster home's revolving door. Every couple of years, his mom would feel the guilt and haul him back. But those dance breaks never lasted.

No matter. That was then. Diego only cared about now.

"Most women don't need weapons," he told the younger man, leading the way through the bullpen. "Mother Nature made sure they were born armed and dangerous."

Before they reached Diego's desk, one of the other cops shouted his name.

"Captain called down a half hour ago, Sandoval. He wants to see you."

"Yeah?" Diego tossed his leather jacket over the back of his chair, then lifted the stack of file folders off the corner of his desk to find one that Chris had been looking for before they left earlier.

"Immediately."

The room chilled. Chris grimaced, glancing around for an escape route.

Diego flipped through folders anyway. He wasn't oblivious to the potential drama. He just didn't give a damn. The case was what mattered and he was sure he had one that tied in with the bust they'd just made. If Chris moved on it, they could nail this drug dealer for twice as long.

"I can get the file later," Chris muttered. "Kinnison hates waiting."

"He's waited a half hour. Two more minutes isn't going to matter."

The chill in the room turned antsy, nervous.

Diego kept right on flipping files. For a bunch of seasoned cops, these guys were way too intimidated by the new brass. Captain Kinnison had been on the job for three months, but it'd taken him only two weeks to institute a new order in the station house. An order heavy on rules, regulations and protocol. And politics. All things Diego didn't give a rat's ass about.

Something that hadn't earned him any points with his new boss. Despite that, though, word had come down two days before that he was up for a coveted transfer to the San Francisco Sheriff Department, complete with a promotion to Homicide.

For the most part, Diego was the cocky, lone wolf his uncle claimed him to be. One who didn't look for back pats, didn't see the promotion as a big deal. But a little, rarely acknowledged part of him was like a kid on Christmas who'd just found his secretly dreamed-of present under the tree—proof that while he might not be the favorite, Santa still thought he was on the right list.

The move to San Francisco was ideal. Fresno was getting claustrophobic, like the small towns Diego had hated when he was growing up. The promotion to Homicide val-

idated everything he'd done, everything he was. And he
was up for it because he was a damn good detective with
the highest close rate in Fresno County. Not because of
ass kissing and cronyism. Ironic that by insisting on doing
things his way, he'd garnered a file full of commendations
and a fast-track to big-deal promotion. He'd finally done
something that disproved his uncle's and uptight cousins'
assertion that he'd never amount to jack.

"Sandoval, in my office. Now."

The command was quiet. Intense. And seriously pissed.

"Good luck," Chris muttered, knocking a chair into
Diego's desk in his rush to get away.

"Hey," Diego called before he could get too far. The
deputy grimaced, shooting a quick glance over Diego's
shoulder before taking the file folder he held out.

Diego tossed the rest of the stack on his desk, ignoring its precarious slide toward the edge. Then he turned
to face the captain's stony stare.

"On my way, sir."

Diego had a brief vision of walking the plank toward
a very large, very hungry shark. Then he shrugged it off.
What was the worst the guy could do? Take a bite out of
his ass? Diego stepped into the office. The captain, already
seated behind his large desk, inclined his head toward the
door. Shutting it behind him, Diego took a seat. Good. Ass
bitings were always better done in private.

His face as hard as the oak of his desk, Kinnison didn't
waste time with games.

"The D.A. has some issues with yet another of your
cases, Detective Sandoval. Since we've had similar chats
so often over the past few months, I'm sure you're aware
of how much I dislike hearing that you didn't follow procedure. Again. By not playing by the rules, you've com-

promised the prosecutor's chances of getting a conviction. Again."

A dozen arguments ran through Diego's mind, but he clenched his jaw shut and waited.

"You threatened Geoffrey Leeds with—" the captain made a show of looking at the paper in front of him, even though they both knew he didn't need to "—an offer to wrap his large intestine around his throat and choke him with it."

"*Offer* being the operative word, sir," Diego pointed out. "I didn't threaten. I offered."

"And the difference is?"

"He could have said no. He didn't have to tell me the details of the porn ring he and his buddies were running in the high school gymnasium."

Captain Kinnison's stare could have made a polar bear shiver. Before the older man hauled out his lecture on semantics—again—Diego inclined his head toward the file.

"Didn't the D.A. read the letter Leeds signed, stating that he was volunteering the information of his own free will?"

"He read it. But he feels, as do I, that the defendant might have signed under duress," Kinnison said, a small, tight smile puckering his thin lips. "Which puts yet another open-and-shut case in question, thanks to your methods, Detective."

Kinnison had no interest in hearing a defense, so Diego kept his mouth closed and waited.

The captain didn't make him wait long. He set the file down, then held up a letter. With the morning sun shining through the window behind Kinnison, the logo of the San Francisco Sheriff's Department was visible through the thin paper.

Diego tensed.

He'd seen enough of them to recognize a job assessment form.

"Detective Sandoval, you're up for a promotion and transfer."

Damn. Diego tried to tell himself that not getting the promotion wasn't a big deal. He wasn't looking for a ladder to climb. His ego didn't ride on outside kudos.

But, he acknowledged with an inner grimace, he wanted that job. Wanted the challenge of working Homicide. Wanted, intensely, to get the hell out from under Kinnison's watch. Wanted it all so bad he could taste the bitter disappointment as he watched it slide out of his grasp.

"You have a strong record with the department," Kinnison mused, running the letter through his manicured fingers in contemplation. "Your peers respect you. The commissioner feels that your close rate is high enough to offset the cases lost by your roughshod style and disregard for regulations. Captain Ferris in SF Homicide is willing to consider your promotion based on my recommendation."

"But?" There was always a but.

"But there are some issues. The first being that you're not a team player. Add to that your lack of respect for protocol, your inability to follow orders and the way you blithely dance all over procedure. I can't, in good conscience, give you a positive evaluation."

Fury and frustration churned in Diego's gut. It was one thing to lose a promotion because he wasn't good enough, wasn't smart enough or just didn't have what it took. But to lose out because he didn't dot his freaking i's and put tidy crosses on his t's? Screw that.

"So you're going to, what? Withhold recommendation?" The mental image of Diego's uncle, wearing the same smug, arrogant expression as the captain, flashed through his head. The old man had always said that Diego's rebellious attitude would be his downfall. Maybe he should drop him a note, let him know he was still right.

"No. Denying you recommendation might be appropriate in this situation, but it wouldn't serve me in the long term."

In other words, while Kinnison would love to screw him out of the promotion as a punishment, he'd given up on making Diego toe the line. So he'd rather get him out from under his command. He just wanted to mess with him before he did.

"Then what's the deal?" Diego asked, wondering how the guy was going to reconcile the two.

"You're going on special assignment."

And there it was. His punishment. And his last chance. That promotion was close enough to taste. And it tasted mighty sweet. But even more appealing was the chance to work under a different captain.

"What assignment, sir?"

"You'll be reporting to the mayor of Diablo Glen in the morning to investigate their little crime wave."

Diablo Glen. Tiny town, nestled in the foothills of Sequoia National Park. Too small to have its own police force, towns like that usually rented out a deputy now and then or had a low enough crime rate that they could rely on the occasional sheriff patrol.

"I don't do small towns," Diego stated, his throat tight. The truth was, he hated small towns. Close-knit, judgmental and unyielding. "My skills are better suited to cities. There isn't a whole lot of vice in the boonies."

"Oh, you'd be surprised." His smile about as friendly as a shark's, the Captain leaned forward to hand a file across the desk. Smelling a trap, Diego hesitated for a second before taking it.

"Diablo Glen has need of your services, Detective. This

crime is right up your alley. It seems they have a series of rather odd burglaries."

"My specialty is vice, not burglary."

"The line is blurry in this case." The captain inclined his head again, this time toward the file.

Trapped, Diego opened it. Thirty seconds later, he shook his head. "No way. Absolutely not."

"You're refusing a direct order from a commanding officer, Detective?"

The older man didn't have to voice the threat. It hung there over their heads like a swinging blade, glinting right over Diego's neck. As much as he wanted Diego out from under his command, the guy would veto the promotion if he didn't get his way. Fury and frustration battled for supremacy in Diego's belly as he glared.

"I have no choice at all?"

"None," the captain verified with a smile as wide and satisfied as a cat in a fully stocked mouse house. "You are now assigned to the tiny little town of Diablo Glen until their mayor is satisfied that you've solved this case. And you will solve it by the book. No hotdogging, no skirting the system. To do so, you'll have to play nice with the locals. And you'll have to show the utmost respect for the department's rules and procedure."

Diego's jaw ached from the effort to hold back the furious rant. Finally, when he was sure he wouldn't spew swearwords and abuse, he inclined his head. "I'm going out on a limb here and guessing that my closing this case, your way, is mandatory if you're going to sign off on my promotion."

"Exactly, Detective. You want your promotion, you need to catch a panty thief."

2

"WHAT DO YOU THINK of a sheer peekaboo red nightie with white fur trim paired with over-the-knee patent boots?"

Cringing, Jade Carson shook her head so hard she almost dumped a whole spoonful of red sugar on cookie Santa's jolly face.

"I think those are three things that should never go together, Beryl," Jade told her younger sister decisively. "It's like mixing beer, chocolate truffles and mashed potatoes. They're all fine on their own, but together they're every kind of wrong."

"Ew," her eldest sister, Ruby, said in agreement.

"What's wrong with beer and mashed potatoes?" Beryl asked. "I mean, I wouldn't have the truffle at the same time, but maybe afterward for dessert?"

"Are you sure we're related?" Jade asked Beryl, shifting her focus from lining the chocolate jimmies around Santa's boots to peer at her sister.

A silly question.

Nobody peeking through the greenery-festooned garden window could take them as anything but siblings. Any of the Carson sisters could have graced the top of the

Christmas tree, with their flaxen hair, wide green eyes and dimples. But when it came to personalities, they were as different as their hairstyles.

A CPA, Ruby was labeled the smart sister. Her hair was as practical as she was. She wore a sleek pageboy long enough to be pulled back for exercise or tax season, both of which she claimed kept her in prime shape. Beryl was deemed the sweet sister by the good people of Diablo Glen. Her blond curls waved to her shoulder blades. The romantic look, combined with her soft heart and slightly ditzy personality, gave her a fragile air.

The creative sister, Jade was neither practical nor fragile. Her hair was long, edgy and razor straight with low-swept bangs sassy enough to counteract her dimples. Her style was more rock-star than small-town, and she often said that her attitude was her best accessory.

"You are the one with the degree in fashion," Ruby pointed out, just this side of snickering. "Why don't you explain to her why the style doesn't work."

That was the thing about fashion, though. It was all subjective. What made one person feel fabulous would make another cringe, and yet another feel as if they were dressed in an alien costume. And though most people would cry foul over tennis shoes, a tank top and a tuxedo together, she'd seen it pulled off with panache. Fashion always depended on the person, and whether they had the attitude to pull the look off or not.

"Maybe I'm just a prude when it comes to my sisters," Jade muttered, shrugging away her odd discomfort. She, herself, didn't know why the idea of Beryl dressing as a slutty Santa for her fiancé was so cringeworthy. So there was no way she could explain it to her sisters.

"Right," Ruby agreed as she slid the spatula under a chocolate reindeer to transfer it from the baking sheet to the cooling rack. "Except you were the one who threw my lingerie-themed bridal shower four years ago. And you helped me get ready for my wedding night, remember?"

"Didn't Jade buy you that black satin merry widow with red lace trim?" Beryl asked.

"She did. She also showed me how to adjust it so my boobs looked their perky best," Ruby acknowledged. She wiggled her brows at Jade and tossed a melting chocolate chip into her mouth before adding, "Ross appreciated your artistry, by the way. Anytime you want to work your magic again, feel free."

Jade grinned.

"That is just so sweet," Beryl said with a happy sigh, licking peppermint frosting off her knuckle before rinsing the bowl in the wide country sink. "Four years married, and you and Ross are still all googly over each other."

"Googly and giddy," Jade agreed, just as thrilled as Beryl over that fact. She loved seeing that happy-ever-after was actually possible.

The sisters had lost their dad five years ago. Their mother, who was diagnosed soon afterward with multiple sclerosis, had taken his death really hard. As they did with everything, the girls had found a way to share the care of their mother while keeping her life as normal as possible. As Opal's MS progressed, Ruby had taken on her mother's finances and responsibility for the general upkeep of everything. Beryl chose a local college so she could live at home, always there to help with her mom's needs. And Jade, after her dreams of turning her fashion degree into an awesome, exciting career in a big city went kaput, had returned to Diablo Glen, moved into a cottage near the family home and taken a job at the library where Opal was head librarian.

"That's what I'll have with Neal," Beryl predicted. "Years and years of googliness."

Jade's smile dimmed. She didn't know why. Instead of commenting, she dropped her gaze to the tray of sugar cookies, as if messing up the decorations meant the end of Christmas as they knew it. There was nothing wrong with Neal. Maybe he was a little boring, and not quite the type Jade would have picked for her flighty sister. But he was a nice enough guy who earned a decent living and most of all, he treated Beryl like a princess.

A princess he planned to make his queen in the new year, and haul off to a castle of her own.

Beryl, like Ruby, would be married. Off living her own life. And like Ruby, who'd moved to Santa Clara for better job opportunities, Beryl would likely be fleeing the Diablo Glen nest, too. Neal was already talking about where he wanted to go. Leaving Jade trapped in this small town, with the full responsibility for their mother's care falling on her shoulders.

And on top of it all, Beryl would be getting regular sex.

Which was probably the part Jade was most jealous of.

And didn't that make her quite the ultra bitch. Horny ultra bitch, she corrected. A sad, sad combination.

"You need googliness too, Jade. But you're so picky," Beryl decided, her voice muffled because she had her head inside the refrigerator.

Jade frowned. Was that any better than horny ultra bitch? Instead of denying it, she made a humming sound that could be agreement. Or "Jingle Bells."

"Oh, I know," Beryl exclaimed excitedly. The younger woman bumped the fridge door shut with her hip, then set the batch of cream-cheese cookie dough on the counter for the next round of treats and gave an excited clap of her hands. "I'll have Neal set you up with someone. He's got a huge family, with people always in and out of their house. He has a whole slew of cousins visiting for the holidays, even. I'm sure he can find a great date for you. What do you think? Maybe we can double this weekend?"

"God, no!" Shock and horror sped through Jade's blood at equal speed. A blind date, set up by her little sister's boyfriend? Why not just force her to parade through town naked, wearing ugly discount-store shoes? That sounded a little more fun and much less humiliating.

"Why not? It'd be fun."

"I'm not interested in dating. And if I were, I definitely wouldn't need my little sister's boyfriend finding me a pity date."

"Fiancé, not boyfriend," Beryl corrected, smiling softly as she tilted her hand from side to side so the diamond glinted. "And you should be interested in dating. It's been four years since that jerk, Eric, ran off to join the circus. You've hardly dated, and when you did, nobody lasted more than a month. C'mon, Jade. Give it a chance."

Join the circus was her sisters' disdainful dismissal of Jade's fiancé ditching her at the altar to follow his dream of being a big-city attorney. She knew he figured he'd done her a favor by not making her choose between him and her responsibility to her family. So she tried not to be bitter.

But being a good sister—and hey, a girl's got the right to be a little bitter about losing her wedding night—she never bothered to correct their nasty comments about Eric. Why ruin the fun?

"Don't nag, Berry," Ruby chided as she arranged the last of three dozen chocolate-peppermint sandwiches in a decorated tin for the bake sale. "If Jade wanted to date, she would."

"Well, she's got to want sex," Beryl argued, giving Jade an arch look of inquiry. Unable to deny that she hated this long dry spell, Jade just shrugged. "Aha. See! So unless you're planning to call Horny-for-Hire, you have to do some dating to get to the sex."

"Horny-for-Hire?" Jade asked, laughing too hard to be offended. Besides, Beryl was right. She was a big fan of sex and seriously missed the opportunity to enjoy it on a regular basis. It just wasn't worth going through the dating drama to get it, though.

"You know what I mean."

"I know that you're a sweetie who wants everyone to have what you do," Jade said, truly appreciating that her sisters cared enough to want her as happy as they were. "But it's not that simple. Nor is it something I have the time—or the inclination—to deal with right now."

"Aren't you the one who's always saying that it's the everyday choices that count most? Or that there's no time like the present to get off your ass and fix your life? Or, you know whatever those other feel-good sayings are that you're always quoting from those empowerment classes you teach?"

"You're paraphrasing the message just a little, there." Jade grimaced. Still, Beryl was right. That was pretty much the message Jade included in all her presentations.

The classes had started out as a simple Dress for Career Success talk for teenagers that she'd offered at the library. Somehow midtalk, she'd sort of drifted from making an impression through clothes to why every woman deserved to pursue her dream career. Since Jade was currently working in a library—where, let's face it, fashion was closer to a word in the dictionary than an actual trend—she'd felt a bit like a fraud. But the kids—and many of the parents— had loved the presentation. So much so that the following month, she'd been asked to tweak the presentation for the ladies' club.

A year and a half later, Jade still felt like a fraud, but her workshop repertoire had expanded from Fashion and Career Empowerment to Embracing Sexuality, The Art Of Saying No, and Lingerie for All Ages. Not too bad for a woman who wasn't living her dream career *or* getting any regular nookie.

Still, it was enough to make her want to dig into the bowl of chocolate chips for a little comfort.

"Isn't being empowered about creating a life that makes you happy?" Beryl prompted. "And for that, you need a man, of course."

Shocked, Jade dropped the chocolate morsels back in the bowl and stared. She couldn't have heard that right.

"Of course?" Ruby repeated, so offended her voice hit five different decibels. "Nobody needs a man to make them happy."

"They do if they want sex," Beryl countered with a gloating smile only a sheltered and slightly spoiled twenty-two-year-old could pull off.

Ruby and Jade exchanged eye rolls, but neither was willing to delve into the ins and outs of self-pleasuring during their baking marathon. But Jade made a mental note to add a Sexing Solo workshop to her spring-workshop offerings.

"Part of being empowered is being able to say no," she pointed out gently instead. "It's also empowering to accept someone else's decision with grace."

Beryl's lower lip poked out for a second as visions of fun double dates burst in her head. Then, in her usual cheerful fashion, she shrugged it off. "Fine. If you don't want to date, that's your call. So, where's the cookie press?"

Used to Beryl's verbal one-eighties and non sequiturs, they all scanned the kitchen. The three large green-and-red bins they'd hauled in that morning to start preparing for the Carson Holiday Open House were stacked against one wall. Held every year on the twenty-third, it was a little over two weeks away. Just enough time to make and bake every delicious holiday treat in Mom's cookbook. Jade sighed.

"We're missing one bin," Ruby realized. "It's probably still in the garage."

"I'll get it."

Jade waited until the kitchen door shut behind Beryl before shaking her head.

"A blind date," she breathed in dismay. "Seriously?"

"The mind boggles at the horror," Ruby agreed. Then she gave Jade a long, considering look. "She's right, though. You do need a date. Just not a blind one."

"I don't think so. In the first place, I have no interest in dating. In the second, even if I did have an interest, one of the joys of small towns is that there is nobody here to date. The men are all too young, too old, too married or just too icky."

"Not all of them," Ruby objected. "There are one or two nice single guys within your optimal age-dating range."

"Optimal age-dating range?" Jade repeated with a laugh.

"You know what I mean."

Sliding the tray of decorated cookies toward her sister and accepting a new one of raw shapes, Jade sighed. "Sure. Charlie Lake is home for the holidays and asked me out last week. Mark Dinson is managing the bank now and he's invited me to dinner a few times."

"But…?"

"But while they might be within the optimal dating-age range, and non-icky, they just don't do it for me." Jade gave a discontented shrug.

"You're not still holding on to—"

"No!" Jade interrupted, knowing exactly where her sister was going. "I'm not hung up on Eric. I'm not letting his leaving me at the altar affect my trust in the opposite sex. And believe me, the sex with him wasn't so great that it ruined me against orgasms for life."

"How long's it been since you got lucky?" Ruby asked, not looking convinced, but obviously not wanting to argue.

Her last block of resistance crumbling, Jade scooped up a handful of mini milk chocolate chips and tossed a few in her mouth.

"It's been a while," she acknowledged, figuring that sounded better than admitting it'd been eighteen months, long enough to make her feel almost virginal. "But what are the options in Diablo Glen? I mean, it's not like I can just go up to one of these guys who live here and say, 'Hey, I'm not really attracted to you, you don't melt my panties and I don't want a future together. But d'you suppose you could scratch an itch for me?', now, can I?"

Coming over to sit at the table with Jade, Ruby pushed the sleeves of her red sweater up before carefully counting out twelve chocolate chips for herself.

"You know, most of the guys around here would probably go for that just fine."

"Which brings us back to icky," Jade pointed out.

Yet another reason to wish she lived in a big city. The anonymity offered so many sexual possibilities. Not that she was looking to turn her life into a series of one-night stands. But a chance to scratch an itch, a few delicious orgasms here and there, and the freedom of not having to see the guy again unless she actually wanted to?

That dream appealed to her almost as much as the dream of a career as a fashion stylist. Ever since she'd been old enough to dress her Barbies, she'd loved creating looks, putting together outfits and developing signature styles. By eight, she'd even taken her Ann doll from raggedy to bohemian with just a little tie-dye and tiny pair of faux-leather boots.

"Speaking of icky," Ruby said, finishing off her measly dozen morsels and getting to her feet as the timer dinged. "Did you hear the latest in the Panty Thief Caper?"

Jade wrinkled her nose. "There's nothing caperish about a creep who sneaks into women's bedrooms and steals their undies."

"Men's, too," Ruby said, setting a tray of cookies on the cooling rack and putting another in the oven. "I heard old Ben Zimmerman was having a fit. He won't say what was stolen, but he's still screaming up a storm."

"He's going to scream louder when his unmentionables end up paraded through town. This creep left the latest pair of panties hanging from the top of the cart corral at the grocery store this morning, along with a note that said 'No Peeking.'"

"What do you think it's all about?"

"It's a nuisance." Jade shrugged.

"That's it? A nuisance? Don't you worry, living alone like you do? How do you know your panties are safe?"

"Oh, please," Jade dismissed with a laugh. "Just a few minutes ago you were trying to get some guy into my panties."

"Don't joke, Jade. This might not seem like a big deal now, but you don't know what could happen. Someone this unstable could easily shift from stealing when people aren't home to sneaking in when they are. From taking panties from the dresser to tearing them right off women."

Jade wrinkled her nose. It was hard to be scared of something that screamed prank.

"I think you're reaching a little."

Ruby got that stubborn look on her face. The one that

said she'd made up her mind and wouldn't let it go until she'd made up everyone else's, too.

"I hear that Mayor Applebaum is bringing in a detective to solve the case," Ruby added, her tone triumphant. As if that proved her right for worrying.

"A cop? For this?" Jade laughed. "And not for the pumpkin-smashing spree from a few months ago? Or the spate of dirty phone calls everyone was getting last summer? I mean, talk about sexual harassment."

"Or Persephone's holiday-property destruction binges?" Beryl said as she returned with another green bin.

"Hey, now," Jade chided with a laugh. "Leave my cat out of this."

"Well, you have to admit, she is a nuisance," Beryl pointed out, setting the bin on the floor by the others.

"But she only breaks into holiday displays and drags decorations around town," Ruby defended tightly, clearly upset that her sisters—who, unlike her, still lived in this town—weren't taking the situation seriously. "The pumpkins were tossed by kids on a dare. And those dirty phone calls, didn't someone trace them to an out-of-town number?"

"And this is someone with a panty fetish," Beryl said, laying out the cookie press and accessories. "No big deal. It's not like he's keeping them and doing pervy things."

"That we know of," Ruby snapped.

Beryl's chin lifted, her posture echoing Ruby's angry one. Time to change the subject.

"Let's switch jobs for a while," Jade suggested to Beryl, waving her hand toward the table full of deliciously tempting edible decorations. "I'll press spritz cookies, you dress Santa."

"You sure?" Beryl said with a frown as she glanced from the cookie disks she'd spread across the counter to the decorations. "You're usually so territorial about making the cookies look just right."

"Yep, I'm sure." She glanced at Ruby, then asked, "We have two weeks until the open house. What else do you want to make today besides cookies?"

While her sisters debated fudge or pumpkin rolls, she filled the press. She needed the distraction. Not because she was worried about a creep with a panty fetish. But all this talk about panties, dating and sexual droughts was making her crazy.

If she wasn't careful, she'd start eating to numb the sexual frustration. She'd done that after Eric had left, putting on twenty pounds as she tried to deal with the emotional blow. For a girl who topped out at five-four, that'd been a quick wake-up call in how fast things could get out of control if she wasn't careful.

Still, it was a better option than finding herself a real Horny-for-Hire.

As Jade pressed out the first dozen starshaped cookies, she pretended they were flying across the sky and made a Christmas wish.

Please, let a sexy, gorgeous man sweep into her life just long enough to fulfill her every sexual fantasy. Give her enough good loving to last until she'd sorted out the rest of her life, then scootch on out without any hard feelings, leaving things simple and complication free.

And if she couldn't have the latter two parts of the wish, she'd settle on having a few of those sexual fantasies come true.

After all, she'd been a really good girl.

Wasn't it time she had a chance to be a little bad?

3

HER MIND FILLED with images of sexy guys all wrapped in bright red ribbons and nothing else, Jade strolled past the twinkling lights and animated Santa's workshop scene in Diablo Glen's version of winter wonderland, better known the rest of the year as Readers Park. One of the few perks of living in a small town was being able to walk everywhere. The library was only two blocks from her cottage, her mother's house a block to the east and the shopping district—if a dozen buildings could be considered a district—a block to the west.

The houses surrounding the park were dressed in their Christmas best, trees sparkling with festive decorations and eves strung with lights. Nobody did the holidays like people in a tight community.

But tonight, the quaint appeal and homespun warmth couldn't keep her attention. Jade couldn't get her sister's words out of her head. Was she only paying lip service to being empowered? Eighteen months was a really long time to go without sex. Well, it was if it was good sex. Maybe that was the problem. All the sex she'd had was pretty much mediocre. She scrunched her nose, remembering her ex-fiancé's fumbling fiver, as she'd nicknamed his lovemaking style.

She was only twenty-five. Too young to accept a sexless life. Not that she'd admit it to anyone—especially since it'd put a major dent in her tough, empowered image—but she wanted the kind of sex she read in those books so hot their covers were a blazing red. Just once, she wanted to experience that headlong rush of desire. To be overcome by passion. To need someone so badly, she could forget everything.

But unless star cookies had the power to make Christmas wishes come true, all that passion was going to stay between the pages of a book.

A little dejected and a lot frustrated, she crossed the street that ran between the park and her cottage. Left to her by her paternal grandmother, it was cozy, comfortable and cute. She'd just opened the latch on the white picket fence when a blur of black fur shot across her feet.

Yelping, Jade jumped back. Her book bag hit the ground, paperbacks sliding across the sidewalk like a colorful rainbow. Heart racing, she pressed her hand to her chest and tried to catch a breath.

"Persephone?" Jade's confused gaze slid from the now-smug cat pushing her way into the book bag to the front door of the cottage. It was closed tight. Glancing right, then left at the multipaned windows, she noted the sheers were still, indicating the windows were closed, too.

"How'd you get out?"

Thanks to her habit of viewing the neighbors' holiday decorations as enemies to be destroyed, Persephone was forced to be an indoor cat in December. Last week she'd escaped when Jade was hauling out the trash. Ten minutes later she'd found the cat batting foam presents at the tin soldiers on Mr. Turner's front lawn.

Kneeling to scoop books back into the cat-filled bag, Jade took a second to scratch Persephone's purring head. Brow furrowed, she craned her neck to get a glimpse of the side of the house. There, from her open bedroom window, fluttered a sheer white curtain.

"Uh-oh."

Her heart pounded so loud that her head throbbed with every beat. Forgetting the bag, the cat and books, Jade reached for her purse instead. Straightening slowly, she sucked in a shaky breath, telling herself there was nothing to be scared of. Yes, the town had experienced a rash of break-ins. But they were petty thefts. Not assaults. Despite Ruby's paranoia, there was nothing to be afraid of.

Still, she'd watched too many horror movies to be stupid enough to walk in there alone. With fingers that were only trembling a little bit, she fished her phone out of her purse.

It took her three tries to dial the mayor's office. It took the phone seven rings to go to voice mail.

"This is Jade Carson, and I think I've had a break-in. Can someone call me right back, please."

Applebaum was a hands-on kind of mayor, proud of always being available to the townspeople. His voice mail would forward to both his and his secretary's cell phones. Sure she'd hear back within five minutes, Jade took a deep breath and debated. She couldn't go inside. But that didn't mean she couldn't look around. Sweeping the books into her bag, she set it on the porch steps, but kept her purse—and cell phone—with her.

Careful not to step in the flower beds, she leaned forward to press her face to the living room window. Everything looked normal. Nothing to worry about, she assured herself as she continued around the side of the cottage. Her fingers curled around the windowpane, she shifted to the tiptoes of her four-inch-high boots. Squinting through the dusk-shadowed sheers, she peered into her bedroom.

And wanted to cry.

"Holy shit."

Jade would be the first to admit that she had a lingerie addiction. But seeing every piece she owned thrown around the room, tossed over the bed, dresser, floor and even the curtain rods, she wondered if she should look for a 12-step program.

Just as she was imagining herself standing in front of a bunch of strangers declaring her name Jade and confessing her love of tiny pieces of silk and lace, her phone rang.

"H'lo," she answered morosely.

"Jade, dear, this is Mrs. Clancy," greeted the mayor's secretary. "Are you okay? You think someone broke into your home?"

"Either that, or the Victoria's Secret Fairy had a tantrum in my bedroom."

"Oh, dear. The Panty Thief got you, too. Poor thing. You didn't go into the house, did you? You're not supposed to."

"No, ma'am. I'm looking through my bedroom window."

"Good, good. Mr. Applebaum is meeting that detective the sheriff sent. He's due anytime now. Not that I have much faith that he's any good. I overheard the mayor talking to the person in the county office. It sounded like the detective has some issues. And to be sent out here, on a case like this? Clearly that means he's bad at his job, right?"

Such a comforting thing to say to the most recent victim of the crime that the said detective had been sent to solve.

"Mrs. Clancy," Jade interrupted, leaning her forehead against the cool wood of the windowsill. She closed her eyes, but couldn't block out the image of her ran-sacked room.

"Did you hear they found another pair of underpants this evening? Sheer, red with little pink roses sewn around the sides. Imagine that, sheer undies. I'll bet they were ordered from one of those catalogs. Not sure who they belong to, since the news hasn't traveled much yet. But someone will step forward, I'm sure. Panties like those didn't come cheap."

"Mrs. Clancy—"

"Not to worry, though. With a detective on the job, even if he's not a good one, I'll bet this is solved before your undies are left out in public somewhere. He should be here soon, too. I was making up a plate of cookies to take over. I imagine the young man is hungry after his long drive. And as he'll be staying at Mary Beck's bed-and-breakfast, you know he's not going to find anything good to eat there."

"Mrs. Clancy," Jade interrupted, louder this time. She blinked hard to clear the frustrated tears from her eyes, but couldn't push the feeling of angry embarrassment away as easily. "Please. Can you let the mayor know about my break-in now? It's getting chilly out, and Persephone is on the loose."

There was a loud gasp, then the sound of cookies tumbling and crumbling onto a plate. "There we go. Sugar cookies are just as good in pieces. I'll run this over right now, and the mayor will be there within ten minutes. You go catch that cat, Jade. If she gets into Carl's train one more time, he's going to be furious."

"Only if she eats the head off his teddy-bear ballerina again," Jade muttered to the dead phone. A new layer of nerves danced through her tummy. Thanks to some creep, her favorite pink silk thong was dangling off her vanity mirror. And now a strange, possibly incompetent cop was going to paw through her stuff.

And her cat, the scourge of Christmas decorations everywhere, was on the loose.

With a grimace and one more pained glance through the window, Jade turned, calling, "Persephone?"

So frustrated she was ready to cry, Jade made her way to her postage-stamp-size front porch, still calling for her pet. Usually the cat responded instantly. But Persephone wasn't stupid. She knew the minute she got within grabbing distance, Jade would lock her in the house.

Then she saw her across the street. Right on top of Carl's six-foot inflatable Santa snow globe. Jade squinted, then moaned. Yep. That was a teddy-bear head dangling from the black furry mouth.

DOUBLE-CHECKING the address, Diego parked his Harley in front of a two-story house that looked as if it'd been puked on by Christmas. Santa waved from a sleigh on the roof, danced with an elf on the lawn and flashed in lights, Vegas style, from the front porch.

This was the mayor's house? Why couldn't they have met at his office? This was so…small-town. Diego sighed. He wrenched his helmet off and scanned the view with a grimace. A tree glittered holiday cheer from the front bay window, and a beribboned pail of candy canes hung off the mailbox, inviting people to share one.

But it wasn't the effusive ode to holiday cheer that had him massaging his temple.

It was the man, probably in his sixties, romping around on the lawn while three kids clung to his back as if he was a bucking bronco. Or—Diego squinted at the brown sticks tied to the guy's head—maybe a flying reindeer?

Kinnison really knew how to twist the knife, shipping

Diego off to a modern-day Mayberry. Small towns were
worse than a gang-run ghetto when it came to trying to
solve a crime. The residents banded together like glue, protecting their own. And while the ghettos had drugs, guns
and prostitution, small towns had closed minds, uptight
attitudes and suspicion of outsiders. And mayors who saw
their citizens as beloved children to be protected.

It took all Diego's resolve to swing his leg over the
bike and step onto the sidewalk. His tension didn't shift
any when the older guy pulled out a friendly smile instead of a gun.

"Well, hello, there," the man said from his prone position, looking none the worse for wear as a fourth kid
came barreling around the corner to latch onto the guy's
neck like a demented squirrel monkey. "Can I help you?"

"I'm looking for Mayor Applebaum."

"That'd be me."

Of course it would. Diego didn't bother to sigh.

"Sir, I'm Detective Sandoval with the Central California Sheriff's Department."

"Ah." The mayor nodded, then with a few tickles, a
hug or two and a direction to head on home for cookies,
he dispersed the children and got to his feet. He watched
them scurry over his lawn and up the steps of the house
next door before giving Diego his full attention.

As long and lanky as he was graying, the man towered
over Diego's own six feet. Brushing grass off his ancient
corduroys, he came forward and offered his hand.

"Welcome to Diablo Glen." He gestured toward the
matching detached garage next to the house, just as nau-
seatingly decorated as the house. "My office is in the town
hall, of course, but I seem to get more work done here at
home. Less interruptions, I suppose. Come in, we'll talk."

On edge, Diego followed.

"Kinnison sent you, then?" the mayor asked, opening the unlocked door. Following him in, Diego felt his shoulders relax for the first time since he'd got his new orders that afternoon.

Despite once being a garage, and the outside decor, this place was all business. The desk might be polished oak and the law books on the shelves leather, but it wasn't intimidating. Diego grinned at the life-size oil painting of the Three Stooges as he took the seat the older man indicated.

"Nice office," he said. This wasn't going to be so bad, he decided. He hadn't been looking forward to dealing with another micromanaging tightass like Kinnison, but this old guy seemed pretty chill.

Eyes twinkling, the mayor nodded his thanks as he took his own seat behind the large desk. As if just realizing he had it on, he pulled the reindeer-antler hat off and tossed it on the desk.

"I didn't get word who Kinnison was sending until an hour ago, which means all I have to go on is his assessment and a cursory check of your record." Before Diego could do more than frown, the mayor continued. "Kinnison would see a case like ours as an irritant. So I figure this goes one of two ways. Either you have a lot of potential, but somehow got on his bad side so he sent you here as a warning. Or you're too good to fire, but you regularly piss him off and he's trying to break you."

"You know the captain pretty well?" Diego sidestepped.

"We've served on a few of the same boards."

It didn't take years as a detective to read his tone and realize the mayor wasn't a fan of the new captain. Score one for the old guy's good taste.

All traces of teddy bear gone now, Applebaum tapped a finger on the stack of files on the corner of his desk. "Punishment, lesson or hand slap aside, I don't care that this sounds like a joke of a case. I expect it to be handled with tact, delicacy and a tenacious resolve for justice."

Kinnison's threats echoing through Diego's mind, he debated for all of three seconds. Then, unable to do otherwise, he opted for the truth. "I can only guarantee one of the three, sir. I've got the highest close rate in the county. I'm a damn good cop."

"But?"

"But I failed the course in tact, and have no idea what delicacy is when it comes to solving crimes."

"Then we might have a problem. This case involves a number of women, all embarrassed over the violation of their privacy. You're a stranger, a man, and a good-looking one at that. To solve this case, you're going to have to get them to talk to you about their unmentionables."

Diego grimaced.

Kinnison was probably laughing his ass off.

"I'll work on the tact, sir."

Applebaum's bushy brows rose, but he didn't mention delicacy again. He gave Diego a long, searching look. The same kind his uncle had always wielded, the kind that poked into the corners of a guy's soul. Uncle Leon had always come up disgusted after his searches.

Diego wondered how he'd convince Kinnison that being kicked to the curb before he even started the case wasn't the same as failing to solve it.

Before he could figure anything out, though, the mayor reached across his rosewood desk and lifted a thick file. Frowning, Diego took it without looking. His eyes were locked on the older man instead. What? No lecture? No warning about not causing trouble in his town?

"Well, then, let's see what you can do. Here are my files. They're probably a great deal more detailed than the ones you've seen. You go ahead and look through these, then we'll get to work."

We? Diego shifted. He didn't do partners. Especially not ones who saw the townspeople as friends instead of potential suspects. Still, the sooner he started, the sooner he could get the hell out of here. Small towns made Diego claustrophobic. Punishment cases just pissed him off. Not a good long-term combination.

"I'm ready to get to work, but I have a request first."

"You need a dictionary to look up the word *delicate?*"

Diego smirked. It was hard not to like a guy who'd honed his smart-ass mouth to such a sharp edge. "I realize this is your town, and your focus is on protecting your citizens. But I'd like permission to handle the case my way."

Eyes narrowed, Applebaum leaned back in his chair and studied Diego over steepled fingers. "Your way. Which means what, exactly?"

"I'll follow procedure, stick with the rules and regulations." Even if it choked him. "But I prefer to work a case alone. It's easier to form an unbiased opinion, to dig for and sift through information solo. I'm not asking you to stay completely out of it or to give me free rein. It'd just be easier if the victims, the townspeople, see me as the lead on the case."

"You don't want me breathing over your shoulder while you grill one of the ladies of my town about her underwear?"

Diego hesitated. Nothing said he had to let Applebaum ride shotgun. But edging him out could be seen as smudging that line the captain was crazy about.

Diego shoved a hand through his hair, noting that he'd forgotten Kinnison's order to get it cut.

Before he could address the tact Applebaum had mentioned, the door flew open. Surprised, both men watched a plump woman in a red Rudolph sweater hurry in, a plate in one hand and a sticky note in the other.

"I'm so sorry to interrupt. I brought cookies, but they're a little, well…" She set the red-and-white-striped plate on the desk so fast, at least a cookie's worth of crumbs hit the floor. Ignoring them, the woman hurried around the desk to hand the mayor the sticky note. Since she looked like the kind who chased crumbs like they were minions of the devil, Diego figured that note was damn important.

The frown on Applebaum's face confirmed it.

"Thank you, Clara," he said. Brow furrowed, he gestured to Diego. "Clara, this is Detective Sandoval. Detective, my secretary, Clara Clancy."

"Nice to meet you, ma'am."

"Likewise," she said with a quick smile before poking her finger at the note again. "You should go now. Jade can't enter her house until you get there, and Persephone's out."

The mayor rose quickly. He grabbed a couple of cookie pieces off the plate and gestured Diego toward the door. "You can read the files this evening. For now, we have another theft."

"Sir?" He did a quick replay of the conversation. "What's the significance of this burglary? Who is in danger?"

As he always did before approaching a volatile crime scene, Diego did an automatic weapon check. Surprised at how quick the older man moved, Diego lengthened his stride.

"Jade Carson is our librarian," the mayor said, hurrying around the back of the garage-slash-office. Diego was just about to point out that he preferred to use his own transportation and that his GPS was perfectly capable of finding the address.

Then they reached the carport and his mouth was too busy drooling to get the words out.

"Climb in," the older man said, sliding into the driver's side of the cherry-red '66 Corvette. "And buckle up."

Diego didn't see it as capitulation to follow orders. It was more like expedience. And—he breathed deep the smell of rich leather—appreciation.

"Sir, is there a reason why the current victim being the librarian necessitates the rush?" Noting the sheepish look on the mayor's face, why did he feel as if he was getting the runaround? In fine style, he acknowledged as the powerful roar of the engine kicked to life. But style or not, he didn't go into a scene blind. It wasn't a violent crime, the victim hadn't entered the premises. So what was going on?

"We're hurrying because, well, because of something that has nothing to do with the crime but a lot to do with keeping the peace." Applebaum's words were as tight and controlled as his hands on the steering wheel.

Diego sighed. Adrenaline, so high and intense a second ago, started dissipating. "Is this one of those small-town things?"

Applebaum gave him a look that was part warning, part amusement. "Jade's cat got out. That's how she knew someone had been in her house. The cat is likely causing trouble, so while you investigate, I'll be rounding it up, assessing the damage and pacifying the neighbors."

Applebaum parked the car, then gestured to the cozy-looking cottage. Slate-gray with soft pink trim, it looked like something out of a fairy tale. Diego's gaze scanned the neighboring houses. A crowd had gathered across the street in front of one lit so bright, it dimmed the stars. Squinting, he could make out a pair of feet dangling from the roof. Part of the decorations?

"This is it," Applebaum stated. "You go on in, do your job. I'll send Jade in after a few minutes."

Diego's eyes followed when the mayor gestured to the crowd. Only one looked to be a woman. Older, plump and wrapped in a bright pink tracksuit. The librarian?

"I'd solve this as soon as possible, Detective," the mayor said as they both exited the car. Frowning, he glanced at the crowd again. "People deserve to enjoy their holiday without this kind of thing hanging overhead."

"I'll do my best, sir. I'm hoping to have the case resolved before the weekend, and leave you and the town to your holiday celebrations in peace."

Diego glanced at the crowd again and shook his head. Yep, the sooner he got himself back to the safe anonymity of a city, the sooner he could celebrate the holidays the way he always did—by ignoring them.

4

CROUCHED ON CARL'S SHINGLED ROOF, the heels of her favorite boots digging into her butt, Jade shoved a frustrated hand through her hair, pushing it from a sassy tousle to a freaked-out mess. Fitting. After all, she was on a damn roof.

"Mayor Applebaum," she said to the man at the top of the ladder, trying to sound grateful instead of hysterical. "I appreciate your help, but I don't think you should be climbing on a roof to get my cat. Persephone is my responsibility."

And the mayor was pushing sixty. If one of them was going to fall two stories and land on Carl's nativity scene with a splat, it should be her. Younger bones healed faster.

"You didn't let her out, Jade. A burglar did, so nobody is going to blame you for her escape." When Jade snorted, the mayor sighed. "I'll deal with Carl. You go deal with the unfortunate reason the cat's AWOL."

Jade eyed the furious mountain of a man pacing the lawn below, his beefy arms waving in the air. In one hand was a headless, tutu-wearing teddy bear. In the other, a very large, very flat sheet of plastic that had once been a blow-up globe. Which was worse? Facing the devastation of her bedroom, or facing the fury that was Carl?

She glanced at the top of the roof where her bratty cat perched, a teddy-bear head still dangling from the black furry mouth. Maybe she'd just wait here for a while.

"Come on," the mayor ordered. "Detective Sandoval is already on the scene."

"Aren't you coming?"

"Nope. The detective would like to run this on his own. I'll lure Persephone in with Clara's sugar cookies. Then after I've pacified Carl, I'll bring the cat and see how our fine detective is holding up."

She followed him down the ladder, grateful when he planted himself between her and the still-shouting Carl. Avoiding her neighbor's eyes, she gave a guilty wave and scampered across the street. As she approached her front door, she pressed one hand against her churning stomach. She really shouldn't have taste-tested so many cookies.

She'd seen how trashed her bedroom was through the window. Nobody else hit by the Panty Thief had mentioned their undies being tossed around. Was this an actual burglary instead? And why was the mayor worried about how the detective would hold up? Was he as bad as Mrs. Clancy thought he'd be?

Knowing she was stalling, she took a deep breath. For the first time in her life, Jade had to force herself to cross the threshold of the tiny cottage, her feet dragging across the polished wood floors. She could hear movement at the end of the hallway, indicating that the cop was already back there.

Maybe she could wait here for him? She could call her sisters over for moral—and housekeeping—support before she had to face the destruction of her bedroom. Her fingers inched toward the cell phone in her pocket. The temptation was so appealing. But so was the voice in her head, clucking like a chicken.

Get a grip, she ordered herself. Tossing her black leather duster over the back of a chair, Jade tugged her tunic smooth over her hips, rubbed a scuff off the toe of her boot, then headed down the hallway.

Chin high, she stepped into her bedroom. And for the second time that evening, froze solid.

Only this time the reason had nothing to do with fear.

Nope, this was lust. Pure, sticky lust.

It was like a million sweaty, hot dreams. The kind that woke her in the middle of the night, aching with need and frustration. He stood in front of her dresser, one hand filled with little scraps of nothings she called underwear.

Intense need swirled through her. Her legs were like jelly, her stomach clenched with an edgy sort of desire. The kind that made her thighs tremble and her nipples tighten against her silk bra.

A bra, she realized, that matched the hot-pink panties dangling from his index finger.

Her breath knotted in her throat, Jade tried to clear her head. Her home, her undies, had been violated. But her brain was busy stripping the man naked. And from the look of him, naked would suit him just fine.

He was gorgeous. At least, he was from the backside.

She took a visual inventory. Tall, an inch or so over six foot. Broad-shouldered and slim-hipped with a butt so tight and hard her mouth watered. Arrow-straight black hair covered his collar and invited her fingers to test the weight of those strands to see if they were as soft and silky as they looked.

Then he turned, just his head, and met her gaze.

Heat poured through Jade so fast, she swore she had a

tiny orgasm standing there in front of a complete stranger with his hands in her panties.

His eyes were like midnight. Dark, intense and searching. As if he could see all the way into her deepest fantasies and clue in to her every secret. Nerves, the kind she'd never felt around a man before, assailed her. Jade bit her lip, trying to figure out what it was about him that was so enthralling.

"Can I help you?" he said. His voice was as sexy as the rest of him. Deep and throaty, with just a hint of a Hispanic accent. The kind of voice made for sexy pillow talk.

"Ma'am?" It wasn't the verbal nudge that yanked her out of the sexual stupor. It was the amusement in his tone that told her that he was not only aware of her overwhelming interest, he thought it was funny.

Nothing like being laughed at to clear a girl's head.

He turned to fully face her, offering the perfect view of his wide, sculpted chest hugged lovingly by a black T-shirt. Trying to ignore this new enticement, she kept her gaze on his amused face. Big mistake. Chiseled cheekbones, a full bottom lip made for nibbling and eyes so deep and dark she knew if she fell in she'd never climb back out. Her heart, already racing, tripped over itself.

"This is a crime scene. I'm going to have to ask you to leave until I speak with Miss Carson." His smile was a grin now, just this side of mocking.

"I'm Jade Carson," she said stiffly, stepping farther into the room. Her foot caught one of the pieces of fabric strewn over the floor, sending a black lace demibra across the hardwood, just inches from his motorcycle boot.

Her face burned as red as the silk panties dangling from her vanity mirror.

His smile faded. His gaze traveled from the small notepad in his hand to the black lace bra on his toe, then back to her.

"You're Jade Carson? The owner of this house, and—" his finger swirled to indicate the room "—all of this lingerie?"

"Yes." What? She might not have the overblown curves of a centerfold, but she looked damn good in her unmentionables. Maybe she could yank down her jeans and show him the dove-gray lace of her thong.

"You're the librarian?" he asked slowly. His gaze took a slow stroll over her body, his expression making her tingle with both nerves and desire. Those dark eyes met hers again, the look in them hot and intense before he shuttered his gaze.

Jade shivered a little, missing the heat and wondering what'd turned it off. And what it would take to turn it back on. After all, he'd already seen all her underwear.

"I'm Detective Sandoval," he said, that whisky-smooth voice official and just a little stiff. Like he'd just swallowed a rule book. "I'm investigating the Panty Thief burglaries."

Jade's gaze swept the room before she gestured with her chin to his little cop notebook. "No kidding?"

His lips twitched. But he didn't drop the official routine. Jade arched a brow. A man both sexy *and* disciplined? The mind boggled at the possibilities that combination inspired on a fantasy level. Throw in endurance and attention to detail and he was a dream come true. Or at least inspiration to come.

"Ma'am?" he prompted, frowning as if he was trying to figure out where her mind had wandered. She'd be glad to tell him. "I'd like to ask you a few questions, if that's okay."

"Sure." Even though she doubted any of those questions would involve dinner, dancing or a bottle of wine, her stomach still swirled in anticipation.

"Given the state of the rest of your home, I figure it's safe to assume your room didn't look like this when you left it. Can you tell me what time you left the house today and how much of this disorder is due to the break-in?"

"Since I had to be at the library at ten, I left around nine so I had time to stop at my mother's, then at the bakery to get pastries for the ladies' club. They hold their meetings at the library and we like to provide a snack for them."

And while she'd been out doing those regular-life things, someone had invaded her home and wreaked havoc.

Jade finally looked, really looked, at her bedroom. Her sanctuary.

Unlike rumors of the other thefts, which were simple cases of an underwear drawer being dumped on the floor and a pair of panties taken, Jade's room was trashed. Lingerie strewn about like confetti after a drunken bachelor party, her possessions knocked over, books not only thrown from the shelves but ripped in half.

Who the hell ripped up books? Forgetting that she shouldn't touch anything, she knelt down to gingerly lift the ravaged pages she immediately recognized as *Madame Bovary.*

This was a complete and utter nightmare. Swallowing hard as the full impact hit her, she straightened and pressed one hand against her churning gut, trying to see through the swirling black fogging her vision.

"It's not that bad," he said. He didn't sound distant anymore. Instead, his voice was soothing and mellow, almost friendly. She wished he'd stuck with the uptight tone.

"Compared to what?" she asked, furious at the tears clogging her throat. She didn't cry. Tears were useless, stupid. Even angry tears.

"Compared to what my place would look like if someone did this," he said, his words teasing. "Car magazines ripped apart, boxers dangling from the lamp. A Speedo hanging in the window for all to see."

His mock shudder made her laugh.

"Speedo?" Her now-clear gaze skimmed his body, from the T-shirt tight over hard, flat abs down his narrow hips. For just a second, she let her eyes rest on his zipper, imagining what he looked like in a teeny-tiny piece of spandex. She grinned, somehow sure he could make the fashion faux pas sexy.

"Really?"

"A gag gift from the guys at the station house. These thieves have no respect for quality, low or high."

Her eyes soft with appreciation for how easily he'd pulled her back from the edge of hysteria, Jade nodded. Well, well. Looked like Hottie Cop was more than just a gorgeous face and rock-hard body. Which qualified him as the hottest fantasy material she'd ever encountered.

An empowered woman would go for it, right?

Nerves danced the cha-cha in her stomach. She wanted hot sex. She wanted a fling. And she was empowered, dammit. But could she actually chase a perfect stranger with the intention of getting him naked?

It was as if Santa had heard her wish, decided she'd been such a good girl that she deserved a chance to try her hand at being really, really bad. But only if she was brave enough to play.

She wanted to be brave. She really did. But as she told the girls in her workshops, some things you had to work up to. Small, consistent steps. She swallowed hard, looking around the mess. Maybe she should clean up her underwear first. Then she could work on being brave.

DIEGO'D FIGURED that life's little ironies were what kept things interesting. Or provided the best torture. It was always a toss-up which was which. Letting his gaze cruise over the woman in the doorway, he figured this was proof yet again. Without the intense four-inch studded boots, maybe five feet and four inches could be measured between her toes and the top of her pale blond head. Mussed and a little wild, her hair looked as if she'd shoved her hands through it a few times, letting the bangs flop down in a long sweep over her eye and down to her shoulders. Sharp, angled features, huge green eyes and lips made to give a man sweaty dreams rounded out the fairylike looks.

Her body was a series of slender lines and soft curves. Legs nice enough to make his mouth water were tucked into boots that had enough edge to assure him that, despite her sweet face, she and the plethora of seductive lingerie were, indeed, well suited.

"I know it's difficult to tell, given the state of the room," he said, trying to bring his focus back to the case instead of wondering how it'd feel to have her wrap those gorgeous legs of hers around his waist. Or better yet, over his shoulders. Diego closed his eyes for a second, trying to find control. Kinnison, he reminded himself, letting the name work like a cold shower. "But can you tell if anything's missing?"

"Not without going through it all," she said. She took a deep breath, her breasts pressing against the heavy weight of that purple sweater and making his palms itch. "Can I touch anything?"

A list of possibilities, all better fondled while naked, flashed through his mind. Diego blinked twice trying to clear the deliciously tempting images away.

"Yeah, sure. Just touch the fabric, though. I need to dust the hard surfaces for prints. But I'll wait until you get your delicates picked up."

Diego slid the black silk he'd picked up earlier between his fingers, luxuriating in the softness. He'd bet the blonde's skin was even smoother, softer.

Suddenly the crappy assignment took on a tempting sort of appeal. The kind of appeal that was likely to get him in trouble. Because he was pretty sure charming a victim into bed was on the Don't list in Kinnison's rulebook.

Still...

"Nice panties," Diego said with a smile as lethal as the weapon strapped to his side. "I'm impressed."

"Yeah?" Kneeling on the floor to scoop up an armful, she gave him a teasing look from beneath lush lashes. "You're impressed by my underwear?"

"The quantity is a little awe-inspiring," he said, side-stepping the truth—and his interest—by keeping his words cool and distant.

A tiny frown creased her brow, as if she was disappointed he hadn't taken the flirtation bait. Then she focused on her lingerie again. And growled. The sound was low and sexy. The kind of sound a woman might make during sex. Wild sex. Wild, mind-blowing, "do it two more times to see if it was really that good," sex. Good thing this was a temp assignment and an easy case to wrap up. Because he was pretty sure this was a woman who could actually make him whimper.

"What kind of lowlife dirtbag treats silk this way?" the blonde muttered, cussing under her breath as she held a teeny-tiny pink leopard-print nightie. "What's the deal? I thought this creep was all about stealing panties. Why would he mess with my nightgowns?"

Forcing his attention away from the curve of her ass as she bent over to scoop armfuls of cotton nighties and sleep shorts, Diego considered the question. It was a good one, the same he'd been wondering himself when she'd walked in.

"Were they in the same drawer?" Unless her drawer was the size of a closet, he already knew the answer was no.

"I keep my lingerie in the armoire, my nighties and pajamas are in the chest of drawers."

Diego frowned, noting the two pieces of furniture she'd indicated were on separate walls. It'd be easy to assume the destruction was the result of frustration from not finding her panties right off. But it felt like more. This felt personal.

"We're probably dealing with a kid or some perv with an underwear fetish," he mused, rocking back on his heels. That'd been his—and the deputies' who'd written the previous reports—assumption of the case. But he'd learned years ago to listen to his gut over assumptions, his or anyone else's. "You don't have much in common with the other victims, though."

"You don't think so?" Dumping her armload of delicates into a laundry basket at the foot of her bed, she gave him an amused look with those cat eyes. "I don't know about that. We're all female. We all live in the same town. We all wear underwear. Well, there is the rumor floating around this evening that Ben Zimmerman had his undies snatched, too. Now, Ben does have a habit of dressing up as Little Bo Peep for Halloween, and I avoid hoopskirts like the plague. But other than that, I'd say we all have quite a bit in common."

Diego'd always had a hell of a time resisting a woman with a smart mouth. He eyed the white eyelet bedspread and collection of hardback books lining the shelves on either side of the curved iron bed. The shelf filled with family photos was untouched, other than a leopard-print bra dangling from one frame. Despite the abundance of sexy underwear, he hadn't come across a single sex toy. And given the feel of the scene, if there'd been one to be found, the culprit would have tossed it in the mix.

Diego glanced back at the petite blonde, looking like an irate fairy as she plucked her lingerie from furniture, curtain rods and shelves where it hung like the fruits of temptation.

She was hot. No question about it.

And he'd seen the look in her eyes. Sexual speculation, mixed with a whole lot of lust. He figured it was close enough to an invitation to move on, even if she had snatched it back pretty damn quick.

Except for two things.

One, she was on the other side of that hard line Kinnison had warned him not to cross.

And two, despite her lusty looks and fabulous taste in what she wore against her skin, she was obviously a nice girl.

And while he might risk Kinnison's wrath on the first, he never risked the heartbreak that came with messing with the second.

Still…

"You got a boyfriend?"

"Why, Detective, is the sight of my lingerie tempting you?" she teased, her tone flirtatious and light. But he saw that look in her eyes again. The "wouldn't it be interesting to strip you naked and climb all over your body" look.

Was she trying to kill him? Diego hadn't been this uncomfortably hard since he'd found a crack in the dressing room wall of the local strip club back when he was a teenager.

"Mixing business and pleasure is against regulations." And right now, he figured those regulations—and the promotion riding on them—were the only things keeping him from trying to find out just how nice a girl she was. He cleared his throat. "In cases like this, a boyfriend, an ex or a rejected admirer all fit the bill for crimes of this nature."

He couldn't help but grin when she ducked her head. Skin that fair sure blushed easily. There. Temptation handled. Now she'd think twice about flirting. Nice girls were easy to handle, he decided.

"No boyfriend, no ex, no rejected admirer," she told him, her words a little tense. Embarrassment? Then she met his eyes again. His brows shot up. Nope, that wasn't shyness in the green depths. It was irritation. Did the fairy have a temper?

"I hope you have more to go on than that to solve this case," she said, separating the clothing she'd gathered into tidy piles on her bed. Panties in this one, nighties in that. Diego swore a drop of sweat ran down his temple when a sheer red thong missed its pile and landed on her pillow. "Then again, rumor has it you might have a few problems with that."

So she could bite back. When had temper become sexy? Maybe when temper had such great taste in lingerie. Eyeing the tiny roses decorating the red thong, he asked, "Problems with what?"

"Solving the case."

Diego's gaze snapped to hers. "What are you talking about?"

Jade tilted her head to one side. The light caught on the row of tiny gold hoops piercing her ear. "Word on the street is that you're here because you've got a problem with your boss."

God, he hated small towns.

"And you shouldn't give too much weight to rumors," he added. "Small towns might thrive on them, but they're rarely rooted in fact."

"So you weren't sent here as punishment?" she asked,

her tone as friendly as her face was curious. Whether it was a ploy to garner gossip fuel, or whether she was actually interested, Diego couldn't tell.

He'd been about to write her off as a sexy nice girl. Sweet, but not much of a challenge. Now he wasn't so sure of anything but the sexy part. That bothered him. His gift for reading people was one of the keys behind his success.

"I was sent here for two reasons," he said slowly, measuring just how much to share with the town pipeline. He might be having trouble getting a gauge on the pixie, but he knew how to finesse information. "I'm up for a major promotion. Solving this case is the last step to ensure I get it."

Diego had no problem lying to solve a case, but it was always easier to go with the truth if possible.

"And the second reason?"

It only took two steps for Diego to cross the room, standing close enough that the scent of her, light and airy, wrapped around him. For a second he forgot what he was doing. Forgot why he was there. Forgot everything except the sudden discovery of just how appealing sweetness could be.

Her lashes fluttered, thick and dark, hiding those expressive eyes. He watched the pulse quiver in her throat, wanting nothing more than to lean closer and press his lips to the soft flesh. To feel her heart race beneath his tongue.

As if reading his mind, she gulped. Then, as if she was trying to make it look casual, she moved over to the armoire, putting breathing distance between them.

Dammit.

"You were telling me the second reason you were sent here," she reminded him breathlessly.

To find out how many different sounds she could make while he brought her to orgasm? Diego gave himself a mental head slap and tried to shake off the sexual fog.

"The second reason? Because I'm good," he promised. Her eyes widened, fingers clenching the wicker handles of the laundry basket so hard it made a loud snap. Grinning, Diego nodded. "I'm damn good. I close cases, and I put criminals away. Whoever did this, their ass is mine."

And there ya go. Toss in a little intimidation, and he'd be home by the end of the weekend. Before he did anything stupid, like give in to the need to find out if the pretty little blonde's naughty side was reserved for her lingerie.

"You promise?" she asked, looking around the mess of her bedroom. "You'll find out who did this. And why?"

Diego didn't do promises. Growing up, he'd had too many broken to ever want to cause someone else that kind of disappointment.

He looked around the room. The deputies who'd been called in on the previous burglaries had dusted for prints and come up bust. Despite the shift in M.O. from snatch-and-run to destruction, there was no reason to think this time'd be any different. This was either a copycat with a grudge against Ms. Carson, a totally unconnected case, or all the other thefts had been smoke. Which meant the green-eyed pixie was the real target.

He'd have to work the case as if all three were fact. But his gut said it was the latter. He just had to find enough evidence to pull all the pieces together. And he would. Because that's what he did.

But the pretty little blonde was looking at him as if he had a superhero cape tucked under his leather bomber jacket. Diego was a good cop. A damn good one. But no one had ever considered him a hero.

It was weird. And very appealing.

And probably his downfall, since he couldn't resist leaning closer and reassuring her.

"Babe, I guarantee it."

5

THREE HOURS AFTER he'd made that promise to Jade, Diego tossed his gym bag onto a creaky bed in a cramped room and sighed. His stomach ached from cookie overload. His head hurt from holding back his investigative instincts and trying to follow Kinnison's damn rules.

He would bet his Harley that Kinnison didn't realize how badly he'd screwed over his recalcitrant detective. Dumping him in a town so small, they didn't even have a cheap motel. Instead, he was stuck holing up in some old guy's spare room. Because, apparently, as much as the ladies of the town might like the safety of having a man around their home for a few days, *it wasn't proper*.

So now, he eyed the twin bed with its threadbare Speed Racer comforter and stingy pillow. It looked as if he'd have a backache to round it all out.

And what did he have to show for it?

Five interviews with four victims and one interested party—namely, a grizzled old woman by the name of Mary Green. Two tins of cookies, one of fudge and a questionable fruitcake—again from Mrs. Green. And a lecture on the lost art of saying please and thank-you.

What he didn't have to show was any more information. None of the women had been home during the thefts. None had recently been involved in any sort of conflict, either alone or with each other. They didn't wear the same brand underwear, do laundry at the same place or shop together.

Other than living in the same small town, and as Jade had pointed out, all wearing feminine underthings—which had been painful for all parties to learn during his interview with Ben Zimmerman—there was no common thread.

Not even the type of underwear stolen. Everything from white cotton to something named after spankings—which neither he nor the mayor had been willing to ask about. If the selection left behind at Jade's was anything to go by, the thief had added supersexy to the collection.

Jade.

Diego dropped to the bed, wincing as springs that were likely as old as he was creaked loudly. It all came back to her. Every victim he'd talked to, he'd thought of her. Of how devastated she'd been when she'd seen the destructive mess in her bedroom. The other burglaries had been obvious, all with an open dresser drawer, rumpled contents.

The other victims were older. Not elderly, but all over forty. Except Jade.

Finally, now that he was alone and out from under the constraints of rules and protocol, Diego let his instincts have free rein. Risking his eardrums to another squeak from the bedsprings, he lay back on the bed, folded his hands behind his head and closed his eyes.

In the course of his questioning, he'd asked each of the victims about their ties to one another, and to Jade. As he'd expected, they all knew one another. But he had been surprised at the effusive praise they'd all had for Jade—even Mrs. Green of the rock-hard fruitcake.

The familiar tingle sped down his spine as intuition, finally cut loose from regulations, flared to life.

That was it, he realized.

Respect.

Unlike Jade, the other victims had been shown respect.

Not just in the lack of vandalism they'd faced. But in the clear purpose of their break-ins. Their underwear had been found on display, but more as a joke. In a rolled-up newspaper left on the diner counter, in someone's mailbox, hanging from the barber pole. He didn't think the display of Jade's panties would be quite as unassuming and nonthreatening.

He didn't know how—yet. But Jade Carson was definitely the center of this case.

Both because the boring, by-the-book investigation logically suggested it, and because his spine was tingling.

That wasn't all that was tingling. He still had the remnants of a horny hangover. Unlike most hangovers, two aspirin, hot coffee and a nap wouldn't do anything to relieve this particular tension.

Nope. This tension required one of two things.

Jade.

Or a more of a hands-on, do-it-yourself kind of remedy.

Not willing to give in to his body's screaming urge for one or the other, he got to his feet. Maybe he could pace off some of the pressure.

On his third trip around the sparse bedroom, his cell phone rang. Diego pulled it from his belt, glanced at the display and rolled his eyes.

The captain could tell it to voice mail.

Diego tossed the phone on the bed and kept on moving.

His pacing ended at the tiny, narrow window. He glared out at the view. With the black sky aglow with overexuberant Christmas lights, the tiny town was like something off a postcard. Or one of those irritating movies with their saccharine moral messages.

Then his gaze shifted. He stepped closer to the window, angling himself along one wall, and located Jade's cottage on the next street.

His body went into hyperalert mode.

The same way it did when he knocked on a door and was greeted with the barrel of a shotgun.

Two hard thumps of his head against the wall weren't enough to keep him from looking again.

At his direct view right into the lingerie sprite's bedroom.

It was too far away to see details. The room was a shadow. But Jade? She was vividly clear. Her skin glowing as if she was fresh from the shower, she wore a tiny pair of candy-cane-striped shorts and a tinier tank top.

His mouth watered when she bent down to touch her fingers to her bare toes, making the fabric of her sleep shorts stretch across the best ass he'd ever had the pleasure of peeping at.

She slowly rolled her spine upright. Arms stretched overhead, she twisted to one side. The candy-cane-striped material pulled tight over breasts gloriously full for a woman so tiny. She twisted to the other side, then she slid her foot up to her knee, straightened her leg, and caught ahold of her calf.

He almost whimpered when, her hands wrapped around her ankle, she raised her foot overhead.

Damn, she was limber.

When she did the other side, his body hardened to a painful state. He needed to stop. He was a cop. Not a peeping pervert.

Before he could force himself away from the window, though, she bent over again. Then, in a sleek move, she flipped into a headstand. Her tiny tank top slid up her torso. Diego's mouth dried up like the Sahara. The top bunched up just above—below? Which was it with her upside down?—her breast.

He wasn't sure what to wish for. That the fabric finish its slide south. Or that it stop, safely there so he could keep his professional sanity.

Slowly, as if she knew he was watching and she wanted to torture him, she spread those gorgeous sleek legs of hers into the splits. Diego's dick was so hard, he was afraid he'd bust his zipper. The woman was doing upside-down splits.

Before he could cry, or explode, she dropped back to her feet. A quick finger tousle of that pixielike hair and she padded over to the bed. Then, because someone somewhere had the tiniest bit of mercy for his sanity, she snapped off the light.

Show over, the room pooled black.

Diego threw himself on the rickety bed with a groan. Who said Christmas wishes—especially the kind that earned a guy a truckload of coal—didn't come true.

PERCHED SO LONG on the wooden stool that her butt was numb, Jade leaned her elbows on the high library counter, scrolling through photos on the computer. Her focus in life might be fashion first, followed closely by empowerment in all its forms. But if five years in the library had taught her nothing else, they'd taught her the art of research. There was very little by way of information that Jade couldn't find.

Including, it seemed, photographs and information on a certain sexy detective. She sighed as she enlarged a newspaper shot of Diego Sandoval in track shorts, sneakers and little else. His bare chest was partially obscured by the T-shirt he was using to wipe his face, but the grainy black-

and-white photo did lovely justice to the rounded muscles of his biceps and shoulders.

Oh, baby. She waved her fingers in front of her face. She'd been right. He was built beautifully. Like a male underwear model.

He came across as a loner. All the information she'd found, which, admittedly, wasn't a lot, seemed to support the message of a guy who did life solo. But he participated in the Cops and Kids Olympics?

Winning, she noted after forcing her gaze off the photo and on to the text, in four different events. Her eyes actually teared up when she saw one event was swimming and they hadn't included a photo of him in swim trunks. Or—she licked her lips—maybe he'd worn a Speedo like the guys in the real Olympics. He had one, after all.

His name was mentioned in a few crime-beat articles, his commendations touted in the county newsletter, and that was about it. No Facebook page. No Twitter account. Nothing else coming up on Google. So unless she tiptoed across the line and checked one of those pay-to-stalk sites, that's all she was getting to aid her in figuring him out.

That, and her own impression.

Which was admittedly clouded by lust.

Still, she got the feeling that Diego Sandoval was exactly what he said. A good cop, who was definitely sexy as hell. And his sexiness had nothing to do with vanity, she figured. No, he seemed to regard his sexy body as a tool.

A tool she'd love to use a few times.

Without taking her eyes from the photo, she reached for her tea. She grimaced as the rich honey-laced caffeine slid down her throat. Lukewarm was so…tasteless. Boring, even. Honey was best heated up. Maybe drizzled over a set of rock-hard abs. She'd bet it tasted extra sweet licked off that body. Was he one of those "service me and be grateful" kind of guys? She didn't think so. She'd got the "best sex of your life" vibe from him. Which meant he'd be the kind who'd reciprocate with the honey licking.

Oh, to be licked by a man who knew what to do with his tongue. Who could use it gently, in soft swirling enticement. Or roughly, with voracious hunger. Or, oh, please, yes, with plunging strength, in a scream-inducing rhythm.

"Sweetie, are you sure you should be in this morning? You could have taken the day off, you know."

Crap.

Her face flushed and breath a little shaky, Jade ripped her gaze from the computer screen and her mind from its fantasy over Diego Sandoval licking warm honey from her naked body.

"I'm fine, Mom. I don't like laundry enough to take an entire day off to do it," Jade said, trying to lighten the worry lines etched in her mother's forehead. Opal Carson had seen enough stress in the last five years. She didn't need to be worrying about creeps fondling her daughter's undies.

"Still, you don't look like you got much sleep." Opal frowned up at her daughter from her motorized scooter. "You could have taken a half day, slept in a little."

"I'd rather be here, keeping busy," Jade said with a cheerful smile, hoping to redirect the conversation. "Besides, if I stayed away today, I'd have to come in tomorrow. And tomorrow's crafts day."

She gave an exaggerated shudder, rubbing her hands over the billowing sleeves of her shirt as if trying to overcome the horror.

"You know how I feel about crafts day, Mother. Don't make me face glue sticks and glitter. And sequins. Oh, the sequins."

Opal's lips twitched and she shook her head. "It's beyond me how a girl as creative as you could hate crafts."

"I have no imagination," Jade said, shrugging as she slid from the stool. Time to quit drooling in the name of research and get to work.

"Darling, you have the best imagination of anyone I know."

"That's because you're the best mother of anyone I know," Jade said, coming around the counter and bending to plant a loud kiss on her mother's cheek. "And I'm not at all biased."

"Jade—"

Dammit. Tension spiked through Jade's system, swirling through her temples as if it wanted to take up residence and start pounding away. Before it could, and more important, before her mother could voice whatever motherly concern had her frowning at her middle child, a voice interrupted.

"Excuse me, ladies?"

Jade turned, automatically stepping aside so her mom could maneuver the scooter around the desk to face the speaker.

Well, well. Look who was turning into her very own knight in leather armor. Detective Sandoval stood just inside the entrance, the morning sunlight filtering in behind him doing nothing to soften his bad-boy edginess.

She offered a wide, welcoming smile. It was only her mother's presence that kept her gaze from dropping to the front of his jeans to see if they fit as well as she remembered. Checking out a guy's package was definitely a nonparental event.

"Good morning, Detective Sandoval. This is my mother, Opal Carson." Just a little breathless, she introduced them with a wave in what she figured was her mom's general direction. Her mom might have been perched on the roof for all she could tell, though, she was so fixated on the sexy detective. "Mom, this is Diego Sandoval. He's the detective that Mayor Applebaum brought in to deal with the underwear thefts."

"Detective, it's nice to meet you."

"Ma'am," Diego greeted, shaking her hand with a quick smile that flashed enough warmth and charm to make Jade wish she was the panting type.

"I hope you're taking this case more seriously than the rest of the town."

"I take every case seriously. This one is no different." He had that perfect "just the facts, ma'am" tone. "I won't stop until I've found the creep who broke into your daughter's house."

His words were intent enough for Jade to settle against the counter, pretty sure her mother wouldn't send her to the Religious Studies section to get a bible for him to swear on.

"And you're good at your job?" Opal asked, making her daughter groan.

"The mayor has access to my service history. He's spoken with my captain, who I'm sure gave a full and honest reference." He paused, an indecipherable look flashing across his face. Then he tilted his head toward the phone on the counter. "I have no problem with you taking your questions to the mayor. Actually, I'd appreciate it. The quicker people cooperate, the quicker I'll solve this case."

"I'll be talking with Mayor Applebaum this afternoon."

Even though he'd told her to do just that, Jade cringed at her mother's words. Diego smiled, though, and gave a satisfied nod. Then his gaze flicked toward Jade. "I'll be happy to answer any questions you have after your discussion. In the meantime, I need a few minutes with your daughter. I have some follow-up questions pertaining to last night's burglary."

"Take her home," Opal directed, waving her hand toward the door. "I've been trying to talk her into going, but she doesn't listen to me. You're an officer of the law, so you can force her to listen to you."

"Mom!" Jade exclaimed.

"It would actually be a lot more convenient if I could take another look at the crime scene."

Take him back to her bedroom?

Images of the two of them, naked and covered in honey, slid through her mind. She tucked them into the corner, knowing she couldn't enjoy them or their yummy effect while in the same room as her mother.

"I'll be back after lunch," Jade muttered, grabbing her purse from the cubby beneath the counter and slinging the long leopard-print strap across her chest. Diego followed her up the steps. She reached for the door, but before she could pull it open, his large hand covered hers. Warm, callused, intense, his touch sent shivers of desire spiraling through her body. Her legs tensed, heat pooling between her thighs.

Oh, please, let it be a honey-drenched lunch, she wished as the cool morning enveloped them.

DIEGO GRATEFULLY SLID his sunglasses onto the bridge of his nose. Not in defense against the winter sun's weak rays. But because he needed something between him and the pretty little pixie. Her mouth was as clever as her looks were sweet.

He hadn't been able to get her—or those stretching moves she'd unknowingly tortured him with the previous night—out of his mind. A first for a noncriminal.

"So how does a detective go about solving a case like

this?" she asked, pulling him from his thoughts. "Visit each house in town and inspect their underwear drawers?"

Although he'd ridden his Harley to the library, he didn't mention it as they walked past, toward the sidewalk. Walking was better. More exercise, a safe distance between their bodies. And, he noted as a set of curtains twitched when they passed a quaint A-frame, lots of witnesses. On the Harley, she'd have her arms wrapped around his body, her chest pressed to his back, and he'd likely drive right out of town to the nearest motel where he could beg her to switch positions.

Behind the pseudo safety of his dark glasses, he let his eyes eat her up. Her hair was just as tousled today as it'd been the day before, spiked ends thick around her shoulders and the bangs a sweeping tousle across one eye. Green earrings, a perfect match for her eyes, dangled to her jaw. Under the weathered leather jacket, she wore a black cotton shirt, the collar flipped up to frame her throat. Red lace peeked through the unbuttoned front of the shirt.

The black shirt was huge, hanging halfway down her denim-clad thighs. She'd wrapped a skinny red belt twice around her waist, so despite its size, the fabric followed her curves instead of hiding them. But it was the boots that held his attention. The woman had a way with boots. Black, again, these were flat-heeled and the suede over-the-knee style.

Sexy bohemian, was all he could think.

Very, very sexy bohemian.

His gaze met hers again.

"What're you doing here?" he wondered aloud.

Both her brows arched as she gave him, then the holiday-festooned neighborhood, a questioning look.

"I mean, you don't seem like a small-town type of woman."

Her eyes dimmed. Lashes fluttering, she slid her gaze toward the ground as if she was afraid the sidewalk was going to buckle at any moment. After a second or two, she gave a one-shouldered shrug.

"This is my home. I was born here, grew up here. My family is here."

Wondering why any of that would tempt someone to stay in a place that clearly didn't suit them, he looked around. Old houses, old people, no nightlife, more twitching curtains. Nothing worth sticking around that he could see.

"So that's it?" he clarified. "Roots and family ties?"

He almost wanted to hand her his sunglasses so she could hide the stricken look that swam in her bright gaze. Not so much for her sake, but for his. Seeing it made him want to slay dragons, kick asses and offer hugs. Clearly he was going crazy.

Then she puffed out a breath as if she was blowing away the urge to run, and shrugged. "It is what it is. The why doesn't matter."

A sentiment he usually lived by.

So why did it bother him so much to hear it from her?

Then she gave him a big smile.

"But hey, the upside is I know everyone in town. And I know everything about everyone in town," she said, her words rising with excitement. "You know what that means, right?"

"That privacy is a myth in Diablo Glen?"

Her laugh was like a bell, bright and cheery.

"Well, yeah, but that's a good thing because it means I can really help you out," she offered, placing an enthusiastic hand on his arm. "I'll introduce you around, lay the groundwork so people will talk to you, let you know if you're getting the facts or works of fiction. It'll be great."

Great?

He glanced at her hand, so small and slender on his arm. He couldn't feel her warmth through the leather of his sleeve, but he swore tiny sparks of electric heat shot from her fingers through his body, setting fire to all his erogenous zones.

Was she trying to kill him? First she made him think he was a superhero, making the first promise of his life. Then the almost-naked stretch session the night before that'd given him more aches than the too-uncomfortable-to-be-believed Speed Racer bed. Now this? As much time with her as he wanted, all in the name of solving a case?

"Thanks, but I work alone."

"Well, sure. But this is a special circumstance, right? I have something you need, and I'm happy to share it." Her smile teetered somewhere between sexual temptation and friendly encouragement.

"I appreciate the offer, but I'll be fine without help."

With a look somewhere between exasperated and amused, Jade shrugged. "Okay. But if you want easier entry, a smoother experience and quicker satisfaction, you just give me a yell."

His body hardened as heat flashed, forbidden and sweet.

Yep. She was trying to kill him.

6

DIEGO HAD NEVER ACTIVELY, desperately craved a woman the way he craved Jade at that moment. Had never needed to bury his face in the tender curve of her throat and breathe in her essence to see if it was as sweet as he thought. Resisting her when they were alone in her house would put all his cop training to the test.

"Holy crap," she breathed, stopping so fast he was surprised she didn't slam face-first into the sidewalk. Had he thought that out loud? He watched her eyes round in slow, horrified increments.

"What?"

Jade sprinted down the sidewalk so fast, Diego didn't know if she even heard him. As he stepped forward, the huge tree no longer blocked his view of her front yard.

He winced. "Holy crap, indeed."

Her house looked as if it was waving its sexy flag. The front lawn, porch and a few bushes were all sporting lingerie. Panties here, bras there. A single black stocking dangled from a wind chime.

Another hit? Diego didn't change his pace. No point since the apparent culprits were still in the front yard, both gathering lacies before the chilly wind could grab them away.

Jade didn't seem too worried about her lingerie blowing in the wind, though. She stormed right past the pretty little blonde trying to pluck a bra down from a naked tree branch.

"What the hell are you doing?" she snapped at the guy on her porch, one tennis-shoe-clad foot propping the screen open while he quickly tossed handfuls of undies inside. The guy straightened so fast his shaggy brown hair hit him in the eyes.

"We're sorry," the blonde said before Shaggy could defend himself. "I felt horrible when I heard what happened to your lingerie. I knew you'd be totally ooked out, so I came over this morning to take it to Mom's to wash. I was bringing it back and had my hands full."

Mom's? Reaching the front yard, Diego studied the other woman. Twenty at the most, she was as blonde and tiny as Jade, but softer. Girlie curls tumbled around a face rounder, but no less striking, than her sister's. A pale blue skirt floated around her feet, matching the cloud-soft-looking sweater peeking out from her long, white wool coat. There was a third Carson sister, wasn't there? Diego scratched his chin, wondering if the gene fairy had been just as generous with that one, too.

"I tripped going up the steps, though," the pretty blonde said, almost in tears as she rose to her feet and angled one leg to show the dirty rip at the hem of her skirt. "The basket flew out of my hands and your unmentionables went everywhere. Oh, Jade, I'm so sorry."

"I'm not worried about the underwear, Beryl. I want to know where my cat is," Jade snapped, not looking pacified at all. Diego was impressed. He considered himself hardened and tough, but he'd have had trouble resisting the pleading sweetness in the younger woman's look. Must be some kind of sibling immunity.

"I thought I was helping," Shaggy excused sullenly from the porch. Ignoring Diego, he crossed his arms over his expensive ski jacket and gave Jade a look just as pouty as his girlfriend's. Diego couldn't help grinning. The pair of them looked like the last two sad puppies in a pet-store window on Christmas Eve.

"Helping? I'm under strict orders by the mayor, and by Mom, to keep Persephone inside for a reason," Jade scolded as she swept her hand toward the house next door. Diego followed the gesture, then winced. The cute wooden gingerbread house was lying on its side, tinsel shredded around a mangled foam candy cane.

"Neal didn't mean to let her out," the other woman explained quietly as she drew herself up. She gave Diego a curious look, but kept her focus on pacifying her sister. Tilting her chin so the curls slid over her shoulder, she waved her hand in a move worthy of any prom princess. "Neal was carrying some gift boxes that I wanted to hide here so Mom couldn't find them. Suddenly Persephone got all crazy. Growling at him and hissing and stuff. Then I tripped and when he came out to help me, she just sort of took off. You know how she is this time of year."

Was the cat really that bad? He cast a quick, suspicious glance around the bushes, glad to be wearing thick leather motorcycle boots. Just in case.

"She's supposed to stay inside," Jade said stiffly, as if she was having to filter her words through her teeth to keep the cussing at the back of her tongue.

Diego knew the feeling.

"We'll catch her," the princess offered. "I promise, we'll haul her back before she does any damage."

"She headed for the park. She'll probably go straight for the gazebo. I'll get her before she can haul any decorations off. Don't worry, I'll fix it," Neal said, his words conciliatory, despite the flash of anger in his eyes. He brushed a quick kiss on the princess's cheek, then sprinted down the steps and across the street without glancing left or right. Arrogance? Or that small-town lack of basic caution necessary to survive in the city?

"I'm so sorry," Jade's sister said again. "I wanted to have this done before you got home. I knew you were upset after the break-in. I didn't mean to make it worse."

"I know, sweetie," Jade said with a sigh, shoving her hand through her hair so the ends danced every which way. "I appreciate you trying to help. Especially since laundry's your least favorite chore. But you know how unreasonable everyone gets about Persephone this time of year. I'm going to be hearing complaints for days now."

"People overreact," the princess dismissed. "Just because she rearranges a few displays, they get all bent out of shape."

Diego arched a brow at the mangled tinsel and broken gingerbread display. Rearranges?

"She's only bad in December," Jade excused with a worried look at the park. Then she glanced at Diego and winced. "I'm so sorry. Detective, this is my sister Beryl. Berry, this is Detective Sandoval. He's the panty cop."

"Nice," Diego said with a grin. He glanced at the black silk panties caught on a bush and quit smiling. His body tightened as he considered how many ways he'd like to conduct an in-depth investigation of Jade's underwear.

Oblivious, the younger woman gave Diego a quick smile, then cast a nervous look toward the park where her boyfriend had disappeared. She bit her lip, before giving her sister a beseeching look. "I'm sorry, but I've got to go help him. I'm afraid Persephone might be hard to catch. She doesn't like Neal very much for some reason."

With that and another quick hug for Jade, she rushed toward the park. As if her sister's departure had let the air out of her, Jade seemed to deflate. Her smile dropped, her shoulders sank and her sigh was pure stress.

"Your cat isn't the friendly sort?" he asked, not because he cared but because he hated seeing that look of distress in her eyes again.

"Actually she is, usually. There's something about this time of year, though," Jade explained. "She was a feral I rescued when she was three months old. In January it'll be four years. I don't know what she went through over Christmas, but it seems to have made a lasting impression and she's been trying to dish out paybacks ever since."

Diego laughed.

"You wanted to ask me some questions, though, not to hear about my crazy cat," she remembered with a wince. "Let's go inside and I'll make you some hot cocoa and you can do whatever you need to do. I'll deal with this when we're finished."

Diego shook his head. "You go ahead and deal with this. It's probably better that you clean it up as quick as you can. I'll catch up with you later."

She glanced at the stocking waving in the chilly air and grimaced. "You're probably right. But I want to help you, too."

"I'll catch up with you later," Diego repeated, leaving before he could change his mind.

Later, when and where there were plenty of other people around. Diego didn't believe in fate or luck, but he wasn't going to spit in the face of a chance to sidestep disaster.

And the pretty blonde with the sexy underwear?

She had disaster written all over her. At least, disaster for his peace of mind, possibly his career, and definitely the fit of his jeans.

FOUR HOURS LATER, Diego's head pounded with tension. He poked at his temple with a stiff finger. His hands ached. In part from the cold weather—apparently a visiting cop in a small town was a suspicious character who had to stand on the porch for interviews. In part from spending the last four hours clenching his fists to keep from lashing out.

Standing outside the café, he debated getting a cup of coffee, then figured he needed to walk off the frustration instead of fueling it with caffeine.

He'd been stonewalled. No two ways about it.

And it was frustrating the hell out of him. You'd think he'd be used to it. He figured people slamming doors in his face, shooting at him and, on one memorable occasion, trying to run him over were all part of the job description. But this was different. These weren't criminals, they were nice, run-of-the-mill citizens. Who wouldn't talk to him.

Diego shoved his fists in the pockets of his jacket as two more of those nice, run-of-the-mill citizens crossed to the other side of the street when he passed. Like, what? He had out-of-towner cooties? Or maybe they thought he'd shoot them. Typical small-town close-mindedness, he sneered. The same kind he'd seen over and over as a kid.

And just like when he'd been a kid, he was stuck here until some official deemed him good enough to move on.

Diego gritted his teeth so hard, he hoped this Podunk town had a dentist. He was gonna need one before the end of the week.

How the hell was he supposed to get information if he

had to wear kid gloves? He wasn't a kid-glove kind of cop, dammit. He felt both blindfolded and hamstrung. There was no way he was going to make progress playing nice.

He kicked a rock out of his path. A woman on the opposite sidewalk gathered her kid close, as if he'd kick it next.

He was seriously starting to hate this town.

Except for the sexy pixie. For her, he had some solid nonhate feelings brewing. But like his tried-and-true methods of solving a case, she was off-limits. Because she didn't just play nice, she was nice.

He wondered how deep that layer of nice went. Was it a surface thing? Or was she nice through and through? He had a feeling—mostly brought on by his body's intense reaction to her—that there was something naughty going on beneath the surface.

The question was…how naughty?

"Naked before the third date" naughty?

Or "whipped-cream bikini" naughty?

He thought about the pair of tiny black silk panties he'd fondled twice now. His body stirred, hardening in salute to the memory. A woman who wore black silk with tiny red roses? She might be convinced to try on some whipped cream.

Grinning at the prospect, Diego was a heartbeat away from convincing himself that pursuing the sexy pixie wouldn't have any effect on his ability to solve this case. Or more important, to solve it by Kinnison's stupid rules.

"Detective."

Glancing over his shoulder at the greeting, Diego slowed his pace to a halt. Then, with a barely discernible sigh, he came to attention.

"Sir," Diego greeted when the older man reached his side. "I'd planned to find you this afternoon to discuss the case."

"Great minds, and all that," Mayor Applebaum said, gesturing for Diego to continue his walk. The older man took control of the direction, though, heading for the park. And, Diego noted as they passed a few more wary citizens, some semblance of privacy.

"So, how is your investigation going?" the mayor asked as they reached the grassy area.

Diego debated. Then, with his usual tact, he stated, "It's sucking. Sir."

Applebaum's lips twitched as he gave a slow, contemplative nod. He looked around as if the bench choices were of prime importance before settling himself on the one in the sunshine.

And waited.

Diego sighed. Realizing he had no choice, he dropped to the bench, too.

"I've had a few phone calls this morning, Detective."

Shit. He'd been on his best behavior. He hadn't intimidated a single person. So why were they whining?

"Sir?"

"People are a little put out that I'd bring an investigator in for what most see as a joke."

"Yep." Diego nodded. "I can understand their position." Applebaum didn't bother to hold back the grin this time.

"Still, it's my decision to make. I want this solved. The prank element doesn't bother me. But there is a meanness involved here, son. Oh, sure, a lot of folks think it's innocent enough. But for the ones with their unmentionables hanging in the diner window…? They aren't so dismissive."

Diego thought about Jade's face when she'd seen the mess made of her bedroom. Prank or not, the mayor was right. Mean—and malicious.

"The problem is," the mayor continued, pulling out a

pipe and tapping it against his knee but not lighting it, "you're an outsider. Whether embarrassed or dismissive, it's hard for people to talk to an outsider."

"You knew you'd be bringing in an outsider when you called Kinnison."

"Yep. I did."

The older man looked toward the center of the park, with its big white gazebo and prettily decorated Christmas tree. Then he gave Diego a big, friendly smile.

Diego felt as if he was looking down the barrel of a gun, not sure if it was loaded or not.

"So here's what I'm thinking. You want to get this case solved, go on home before the holidays and get on with your life."

All right, except for the holidays part.

"With the break-in and destruction at Jade's, the situation is escalating. So the sooner this case is solved, the better for my town."

And…?

"To accomplish that, I've come to the conclusion that you need a little help."

A little help. Diego shook his head. Apparently the good mayor didn't believe in pointing a weapon unless it was loaded.

"Not someone telling you how to do your job," Applebaum assured him. "Not someone like me who everyone will be on their best behavior with. That's not likely to help you much."

Diego narrowed his eyes. The old guy was smarter than he looked.

"What you need is an intermediary. Someone the townspeople like and respect. Someone who can put them at their ease, as well as give you insight into whether or not they're being truthful."

"I don't need people at ease," Diego said between clenched teeth. "Nor do I need someone to tell me something I've been trained to observe myself."

"'Course you don't." The mayor tapped the pipe against his knee again before bringing it to his mouth and making a show of lighting it. A couple puffs, and he gave Diego a stern look through the sweetly scented smoke. "But it'd make me feel a whole lot better."

Trapped and screwed over, all at the same time. Diego wondered if this was how prisoners felt when the doors of the cell slammed closed.

RESTLESS, JADE SLAMMED one book after the other into a stack, taking great satisfaction at the noise. She'd played on her favorite website for a while, putting outfit after virtual outfit together. Until she'd realized all the outfits were designed for seducing a very uninterested detective. Then playing stylist had lost its appeal.

What good was Santa if he sent her the perfect man for perfect sex, but that man wasn't into her? It was like wrapping a remote-control race car in bright, fancy paper and putting the biggest, brightest bow on top. And not including the remote.

Typical to her life, she supposed. She glanced around and sighed. Just like this job. The library was nice enough. One of the prettiest buildings in Diablo Glen. Solid oak graced not only the floors, but the gleaming rows of tall bookcases and a dozen cozy tables. The chairs were the kind a person could sink into for hours, and the art on the walls were originals. Shooting off four of the walls in the octagonal room were arched halls, each labeled with a hand-carved wooden sign.

It was rich and warm and welcoming.

And felt like a prison.

"My Humps" rang out, pulling Jade from her funk.

At least the prison came with phone privileges. She snickered as she answered her cell.

Ten minutes later, she tossed the phone back in her purse and stared at the pages of notes she'd made.

"Good news, dear?"

"I'm not sure." Frowning, Jade shrugged before glancing toward her mom. "It was the administrative office at the community college. They invited me to do a series of guest lectures next semester."

Opal clapped her hands together, beaming with pride as she wheeled toward her daughter. "Darling, that's wonderful."

"It'd only be six classes, not a full load," Jade said, trying to decide if she was excited or not. "I'd have to send a course description and syllabus for approval."

Was this a good thing? A part of her was doing handstands. But another part was settling in for a deep pout, since this was yet more evidence that she wasn't living in a big city, working as a stylist to the rich and famous.

"A description and syllabus shouldn't be difficult. Would you use the empowerment workshops you've already taught here, or come up with something new?"

"I'm not sure yet," Jade said, staring at, but not seeing, the counter.

She loved the workshops here, and it'd be fun to take the message wider. Empowerment Through Fashion. Know Yourself, Know Your Style. Tried-and-True: Wardrobe Staples and Attitude Standards. It was a good opportunity. A chance to really expand her workshops and reach a lot more people.

Possibly a whole new career direction.

But she already had enough issues feeling like a fraud here in her small hometown. Would a bunch of people want to pay good money—at a college, no less—to listen to a woman who wanted to be a fashion stylist, but wasn't empowered enough to go for the dream?

"I'll have to think about it," she finally said, her throat so tight it was hard to get out the words. "It's no biggie either way."

Opal gave her a look that said she clearly saw the flashing chicken sign over her daughter's head. But she let it pass. She'd been letting a lot of things pass lately, Jade realized. She frowned at her mother, noticing that she was not only wearing a new shade of lipstick, but one of her best day dresses that Opal usually saved for church. Before Jade could ask what was up, though, her mother gave her watch a pointed look.

"My shift is finished and I'm meeting…um, someone for lunch," Opal said quickly, an attractive wash of pink coloring her cheeks and making Jade frown. What was her mother up to?

"Marion is due in an hour to relieve you. You go home when she gets here, Jade. Don't let her guilt you into thinking that taking a couple of hours off this morning is something you have to make up for by staying late."

If it was anyone but Marion, Jade might have.

Before she could make a snarky remark, or her mother could offer up any more warnings, the doors opened.

"Home in an hour," Opal said quietly as she turned her scooter toward the door to leave. The quiet whir of the motor stopped short when she saw who'd come in. A quick glance back at her daughter showed she was struggling, but after a deep breath, she continued toward the exit.

"Thank you," she murmured to the man holding the heavy oak door wide.

Jade waited until the doors shut behind her mother before letting the excitement building in her tummy spiral through the rest of her body.

"Good afternoon, Detective Sandoval. What a pleasure. What brings you back my way so soon?" Her question was innocent. The low, husky, flirtatious tone was anything but. She leaned her forearms on the high counter, tilting her head to one side, liking the way the bright afternoon light streamed through the library windows, the watercolor effect of the stained glass surrounding him in an ethereal glow.

Maybe Santa hadn't done her wrong?

Then again, the good detective was standing at the steps by the door, not budging an inch closer. A gift she had to work for? Hmm, she considered. Well, for one that fine, she was willing to expend a little effort.

"I just spoke with the mayor," Diego said, not looking as if it'd been a fun conversation. Jade was surprised. Applebaum had a way about him that people usually enjoyed.

"Do tell?" she invited, figuring he wouldn't have mentioned it if there wasn't something in the conversation that pertained to her. The detective just wasn't the sharing type.

"He seems to think that the investigation would go smoother, faster, if I had an intermediary."

Eyes rounding, Jade shot her brows up. She pressed her lips together to keep from grinning. Her toes wiggled in her boots, but she managed to still them as well. Nope, no happy dancing. It might change his clearly teetering mind.

"Does he?" she said as soon as she was sure she wouldn't sound as though she was gloating. "What sort of intermediary?"

The look he shot her said he knew exactly what her toes were doing and he wasn't happy about it. Still, he moved the rest of the way into the room, stopping just a foot from the counter. Must be in appreciation for her attempted restraint.

"Oh, you know. Someone to introduce me around, lay the groundwork so people will talk to me," he said stiffly, throwing her words back at her. "Someone who can gauge whether people are telling me facts or fiction."

A giggle escaped before Jade could stop it. Her hand flew to her mouth, but it was too late. His frown turned into a scowl. But she saw the light in his dark eyes. Oh, yeah, that was amusement in those sexy depths. She was sure of it.

"I swear," she said, holding up one hand as if taking an oath, "I didn't call him. After seeing my lingerie take the outdoor tour, I forgot about it."

Which was pretty much the truth. Well, she'd mentioned it in passing to her mom, but only as a setup to the "coming home to see her panties dangling from the eaves" story.

"Fine. I'll take your help. But first we need to get a few things clear."

Before he could get to those things, though, a wince-inducing squeak filled the room.

They both turned to watch Mrs. Green push a book cart, the top shelf covered in brightly colored romance novels, most with half-dressed couples looking as if they were going to jump each other. Jade made a mental note of a couple of the positions, hoping she'd get a chance to try them out soon.

"I've got my books for the week, Jade. Can you check me out? Carrie will be here any minute now to pick me up." She squeaked the cart to the edge of the tall counter. Then, a little breathless, she peered up at Diego through her tiny round lenses. "Detective. Are you here looking for clues?"

"Just checking with Miss Carson for some background

information on a few things." He hesitated a second, then, with the same look the neighbor boys had worn when caught smashing pumpkins two months before, he helped the elderly woman shift her book selection from the cart to the counter.

Jade's heart turned to goo.

"Ah, good idea. Our Jade is a fount of information."

Mrs. Green reached across the counter to pat Jade's hand, then snapped her fingers. "Or, if that doesn't work, the mystery section is quite extensive. I suggest you look to Miss Marple for ideas."

Diego's hand froze, his expression baffled. Jade ran her tongue over her front teeth, hoping the threat of biting it would keep the grin at bay.

Who? he mouthed.

Jade tilted her head. Following her direction, Diego glanced to the left. A portrait of a woman in a large, ornate gold frame hung on the wall. The plaque beneath it said Agatha Christie.

His gaze shot back to Jade. She busied herself checking out the books to keep her hand from patting his cheek. He was such a big, bad, tough loner, but there was something about Diego that made her want to cuddle him close.

"Um, thanks," he said. "I'll keep that in mind."

There it was. That was why she wanted to cuddle him. Because for a big, bad, tough loner, he was just about the sweetest, most sensitive man she'd ever met.

"See that you do." Mrs. Green gave a sharp nod in emphasis, then took the bag Jade held out, huffing a little at the weight. "Thank you, dear."

Diego nodded goodbye. The look he gave Jade warned that she keep all comments to herself. Since most of the ones floating through her brain were sappy and sweet, she didn't figure she wanted to share anyway.

"About that help," he said, stepping aside for the elderly woman to pass. As she did, Jade watched Mrs. Green's eyes drop, then a wicked expression crossed her wrinkled face. She could have warned him. But what was the fun in that?

The little old lady stopped right behind him, hesitated for just a second to give Jade a questioning look. Then, with a shrug that said life's too short to hold back, she reached out one gnarled, age-freckled hand and patted Diego's ass.

His eyes widened in shock. His body stiffened as if he'd just been hit in the head with a big stick.

The frown he gave Jade was ferocious.

Then, looking horrified, he turned to watch the little old woman toddle her way across the polished wood floor, her bag of sexy books over her arm and a candy-cane-striped scarf trailing down her back.

"That did not just happen," he vowed.

"Oh, it happened, all right." Jade laughed so hard she snorted. At his arch look, she clamped her hand over her mouth and, eyes sparkling with glee, tried to pull herself together.

"Oh, man, the look on your face," she said, wiping her eyes.

"That old lady just patted my ass," he said, nonplussed.

"Well, it's a nice ass," Jade said agreeably. "Surely it's happened before."

"I live in a big city. I'm surrounded by hundreds of thousands of people every day. I crawl through the dregs, the desperate and the depraved. But I can't remember the last time someone patted my ass."

Biting her lip, Jade watched him closely. It was one thing for her to think he had a soft, cuddly center. But he was still pretty much an unknown. And he'd just been fondled by a woman three times his age. He wouldn't do anything crazy, would he? Like chase the old woman down and write her a citation for inappropriate handling of an officer of the law?

"Should I be flattered?"

Relief and something else, something she was too scared to put a name to, poured through her.

"You should be flattered, in the sense that you do have a mighty pattable tush," she told him, giving her brows a playfully suggestive wriggle.

"But?"

She snickered at his play on words. "But, she pats my tushie, too. So it's not personal. Well, it is, in that it's your butt she's touching. But she wasn't making a move so much as showing affection."

"Affection?"

"Sure. She's babysat almost everyone in Diablo Glen at one point or another. Diapered most of us. Mrs. Green pretty much sees everyone as a little kid."

"That's kinda weird."

"That," she assured him, "is typical of Diablo Glen."

"You're on the clock, Jade," a voice said, coming from the employee entrance. "You can talk to your boyfriend on your own time."

Jade sighed. She turned to face her future in-law. As usual, Beryl's fiancé's mom Marion looked as if she'd woken up on the wrong side of the bed. Her iron-gray hair showed recent signs of a kitchen-shear trim, highlighting the deep creases between her brows. That's what years in an empty bed did to a woman. Jade rubbed her own forehead, wondering how long it'd take for her own scowl lines to etch in that deep.

Marion had arrived in Diablo Glen ten years ago, a single mom whose husband had run off, leaving her to raise

Nice & Naughty

Neal alone. Since then, she'd bought a large chunk of the land on the west side of town, harangued her way into a position of power in the community and hooked her son up with the prettiest girl in Diablo Glen—although Jade might be a little biased there. Despite her ferocious demeanor, she wasn't all bad. She regularly donated lovely handmade ethnic crafts and clothing to the local sales and every Christmas brought a feast of tamales, enchiladas and homemade tortillas to the Christmas party. Jade figured she saved her softer side for the revolving door of relatives that often landed on her property at the edge of town.

"Marion Kroger, Detective Sandoval with the sheriff's department," Jade introduced in lieu of a greeting or correction. After all, she wouldn't mind him being her boyfriend. Or man toy. Whatever. "The detective is here regarding the Panty Thief crimes."

"Don't give that ugliness a clever name, Jade. It only glorifies the rude act."

"Right," she said with a slow nod. "Okay, then. The detective is here to ask a few questions in relation to the recent series of unfortunate events."

Before the other woman could call her out on the smart reply, Jade looked back at Diego. "Detective, this is Marion Kroger. She volunteers here at the library part-time, and she's the chairwoman of Diablo Glen's Friends of the Library group."

"Detective," Marion greeted stiffly after bending low to push her handbag to the very back corner under the desk. "Does the sheriff really think it necessary to assign an officer for just one crime? Especially one as frivolous as this seems to be?"

Frivolous? Jade thought of the mess in her bedroom. The torn books, the lingerie strewn everywhere. Of how hard it had been to sleep there, in the room that'd once been her haven. The creepy feeling of being invaded, of violation. That didn't even take into consideration the two thongs and red satin panties that were missing.

Those, she figured, would cost her a few months of teasing, a lecture from her mother and probably a few heavy-breathing phone calls after they were publicly displayed.

Unless Diego solved the case first. She wasn't sure which she wanted more. For him to catch the creep before her panties were draped over Joseph's head in the town-square manger. Or to keep him around long enough for her to have her way with him—a few dozen times.

"I'm sure when all is said and done, it'll be found that this whole thing is some holiday hoax," Marion continued dismissively, primly restacking the books Jade had already sorted on the counter.

"The burglaries are real," Diego stated. "And thanks to the recent vandalism and destruction of property, the case has been upgraded from petty theft to an aggravated misdemeanor."

"Destruction? Vandalism?" Hands so freckled with liver spots they looked tanned, paused. Kroger gave Diego a hard stare, then folded her fingers together. "I didn't realize the problem had escalated to that degree. If this keeps up, we'll need an entire fleet of policemen here to protect us. What are you doing about this, Detective?"

"That's what Ms. Carson and I were discussing. The mayor suggested she help me out."

"Then what are you still doing here?" Marion asked Jade, giving her a shooing motion with her fingers. She looked around, ducked her head beneath the counter, then straightened and pushed Jade's purse into her hands. "Go. Help the detective. Do whatever it takes to catch the nasty little thief."

Well, then. No guilt trip over a short workday, no bitching about the books that hadn't yet been sorted. Jade made a mental note to jot that down in her diary. It was a first, after all.

"Shall we?" she said to Diego, giving him a flirty look through her lashes. She'd be happy to give him a few other things, too, once they were in private.

The same spark of interest that'd made her tummy flutter earlier flashed in his eyes again before it was quickly banked.

He was such a challenge, clearly interested but just as obviously determined to resist the attraction.

Wouldn't it be fun to see which one of them won?

7

WHICH WOULD BE LESS PAINFUL? Bellied up to a rock? Or wedged between a hard place? Diego had his orders, from two bosses, no less. And both sets of orders sparkled like crystal. Solve the case, follow the rules and enlist Jade's help. Hello, rock.

When the crotchety old woman added a hiss to her glare, as if questioning why he was still breathing her air, he forced his feet to follow Jade toward the back of the library and what he was sure was a waiting hard place.

Clearly ignoring his concern about spending more time with her, he settled his gaze on the sweet rear view. Her shirt was too big and baggy, despite the cinched belt around the waist, to give a good look at her butt. But there was something hypnotic about the sway of her slender hips, the way those boots reached so high up her legs. His fingers itched to trace a path between the black suede and the full curves of her butt, draped under that crisp cotton.

Fantasizing now about which pair of panties he'd discover if he did, Diego barely noticed they'd left the building until the bright December sun smacked him in the face.

Blinking, he glanced around. A redwood pergola arched

over the slate patio. Dormant winter branches climbed the posts, empty flowerpots were dotted here and there between benches. At the far end, opposite the door, was a small play area and covered sandbox.

"So, His Honor, the mayor, would like me to help on this case. But what about you, Diego? What do you want from me?" she queried, her look as innocent as her tone was naughty. Echoing the naughty, she stepped closer.

Close enough that he could smell the sweet spice of her perfume. Could count the row of tiny red gemstones curving around her earlobe, getting smaller as they rose toward her temple. Close enough that all he'd have to do was breathe deep to feel her breasts against his chest.

A fit she might not mind checking out herself. She looked as if she wanted to lap him up in a saucer, her eyes as satisfied as her cat's. But there was something else in her gaze. Something hesitant, almost afraid. Like she wanted him, but was worried that he might want her, too.

Nothing said *I want you to take me now, but stay the hell away* like that kind of look. The latter lined up perfectly with the warning siren going off in his brain. But the finger triggering that siren wasn't his. It wasn't Kinnison's or even Applebaum's. It was his conscience. Rarely let out to play, it was screaming *Nice girl*. And guys like him should stay away from nice girls.

Diego wondered if this was how he was going to go. Not a nice, clean bullet through the head or something that'd look heroic written up in the newspaper. Nope, he was going to die of sexual frustration brought on by a conflict between his body's desperate cravings and those nagging voices in his head. The voices wouldn't be so bad if they were in line with his own finely tuned sense of right and wrong. Instead, he had tight-ass nagging boss voice and avuncular old mayor with a worrisome resemblance to a talking cricket in a top hat.

As always when he was conflicted, Diego fell back on intuition. And his intuition was telling him that Jade Carson was as sweet as she was gorgeous, would be as wild in bed as she was amusing out of it. And that she was trouble, through and through, for a guy who planned on cruising through life alone.

Chilled for some reason, he stepped back, putting some distance between him and Jade. Something flashed in her big green eyes. Hurt? It was gone so fast, he couldn't tell.

It shouldn't matter. He shouldn't care.

But all he could think about was finding a way to bring joy back to her eyes, to make her feel happy again. Hell, he had to bite his tongue to keep from asking her if she wanted to talk.

To talk?

If his dick wasn't hard enough to drill railroad spikes right now, he'd wonder if he was turning into a girl.

Clearly, Jade was a serious threat to his sanity.

Diego steeled himself with the reminder that he was a loner. A hard-ass who didn't do relationships that required more depth than a paper plate. Bad news to any woman who considered a future past rolling out of bed in the morning.

Good enough. All he had to do was ignore that flash of heat, that almost kiss, those unnamed emotions in her eyes. As long as he did, she would keep her distance. Good girls were predictable that way.

Satisfied, and yeah, maybe a little smug, he prepared to fill her in on how he wanted this town-liaison role to work out.

Before he could say anything, she closed that distance between them again. He froze.

"I made you uncomfortable, didn't I?" Her smile pure mischief, she reached out to give his upper arm a sympathetic pat.

"Don't be ridiculous." Nerves he hadn't realized he had exploded. Unfrozen, he took three steps back. Then another one just for good measure.

"You are uncomfortable. Nervous even." Her smile widened, delight dancing in her eyes. "It's not like I licked you or anything."

What the hell? Was she reading his mind and delighting in trying to blow all his preconceived perceptions to pieces? Diego could only shake his head. "You are one hell of a confusing woman. Did you know that?"

"Me?" She batted her lashes.

"It's not a good thing," he groused.

"Oh, but it is. You're so by-the-book, I'll bet you categorize, organize and file every single thing and person away in your mind. I like the idea of not fitting into a tidy little slot somewhere."

Diego frowned. "I'm not uptight."

"I didn't say you were."

"That description sounded pretty damn uptight to me."

"Was it wrong, though?" she teased.

Not sure if it was frustration over the unquenched thirst she inspired, or if it was ego demanding he show her just how un-uptight he was, Diego lost it. He actually heard his control snap like an overstretched rubber band.

He reached out and grabbed her by both arms, easily lifting her off her feet to pull her close again. She gasped. But she didn't look scared. She looked intrigued.

That was good enough for him.

"How uptight is this?" he growled just before his mouth took hers.

Jade's body melted against him, so slight, so soft. Her

arms rested on his shoulders for balance, her fingers lax. Her lips, sweet and yielding, didn't move.

Okay. So maybe he'd read her wrong. Or maybe this was how good girls kissed. Since she was his first, he didn't know.

She tasted delicious. Like warm honey with just a hint of something dangerously addictive. Needing one more sip before he let go of the fantasy, he ran the tip of his tongue slowly over her lower lip. Then he gave a gentle suck.

As if he'd turned a magical key, she went wild. Her fingers spasmed, then dug tight into his shoulders before sliding behind his neck to tangle in his hair and grip his head.

Her mouth opened, welcoming and eager. Diego dived into the deliciously warm depths, wanting to eat her up in fast, greedy gulps. Her tongue met his in an erotic dance. His breath sped up, his pulse raced. And his body hardened like steel. He needed more. Wanted it all.

His hands were still gripping her arms, though. His fingers ached to touch her. To feel her soft curves, to slide down the length of those gorgeous legs. To explore every hot, sexy inch of her body.

But he'd have to put her down to do that. And he wasn't sure he could force his fingers to release her. He'd never wanted anything, anyone, the way he wanted Jade right now. It was as if he'd suddenly discovered the most important, powerful elixir of life. Kissing Jade made him feel as though he could actually have happiness. Real, lasting happiness.

A bell rang out, faint but insistent.

Diego surfaced fast. As if someone had grabbed him by the scruff of the neck and yanked him out of the pool of magical elixir. He shifted, softening the kiss and tuning in to their surroundings again. Or, as Jade's tongue enticed his back into her mouth, trying to.

Why had he thought he should slow it down? He couldn't remember as the taste of her filled his senses again.

The phone chimed again, accompanied by a buzzing this time. Loud, grating and way too insistent.

"Shit."

Furious for losing control, and for being interrupted before he could lose more of it, Diego set Jade down with a thud. Ignoring her shell-shocked look, he stomped a safe two yards away.

"That's my cell phone. I have to take the call."

"Huh?"

His ego swelled almost as big as his dick at the sex-fogged confusion in her eyes.

The phone buzzed again. He glanced at the display.

Kinnison.

It was like getting kicked in the ass in an ice bath. And, he realized, exactly what he needed. A reminder to keep his hands, mouth—and any other body parts—away from temptation.

WATCHING DIEGO TALK on the phone, Jade's body trembled with the aftershocks of desire. All she could think of was how much she wanted Diego, covered in hot fudge and whipped cream. She'd never felt this way before. Anticipation, excitement, heat, they all tangled together.

It was too fast, though.

Wasn't it?

Her mind pointed out that sex, even fling sex with a passing hottie who fit every single one of her fantasy requirements, always had repercussions. Responsible women made sure they could handle the repercussions before they dived off the deep end. They thought through the consequences.

And they made sure they were dressed appropriately. And since all Jade's good lingerie was being washed— again—she was stuck in granny panties and a torn cotton mustard-yellow bra. Pretty much the unsexiest undies she owned.

There. Shaking her hands as if she could fling off the sexual tension, she gave a decisive nod. That should keep her from giving in to temptation.

Feeling like one of the teenage girls she often lectured, Jade tried to at least look calm. Sure, her stomach was dancing. Her pulse was racing. Maybe anticipation was doing questionable things to the bagel she'd had for breakfast. But she didn't have to look as if she was freaked out. Faking It with Fashion 101… Look good and people believe you *are* good. Or in this case, look confident and he wouldn't realize her toes were shaking.

While a part of her wondered when she'd become obsessed with sex, or at least sex with Diego, the rest of her—the parts that weren't racing, dancing or threatening to spew—tried to remember everything she knew about being strong and empowered. About taking charge and going after what she wanted.

Clueless that he was front and center in her obsessive mental debate, Diego ended his call and tucked his phone into his pocket. She watched him stride across the slate, legs long and lean in dark denim. Here he came, temptation in a leather jacket.

She tilted her chin high, pulled her shoulders back and pressed one hand against her stomach. Strong and steady, she was ready to face down temptation. How's that for empowered? she thought as she mentally patted herself on the back.

"We should get to work."

She frowned. What happened to temptation?

"Work?" She peered at his face. Closed, distant and almost chilly. Her gaze slid to the phone he was tucking into his pocket. Had someone died?

"Work. I need to solve this case and get back to my own life," he said.

If he'd sounded angry, or impatient, she'd have been able to dish it right back. But he simply sounded…gone.

The way he'd be as soon as he solved this silly Panty Thief case. Gone, back to his own life. His exciting world. His career and his dreams.

And Jade would be here.

Same life.

Same town.

Same unfulfilled existence.

Pressing her lips tight together to keep the sudden tears at bay, Jade rubbed her hands over her arms, wishing she'd thought to grab her jacket.

"You okay?" he asked, closing the distance for a brief second to sound concerned.

"I'm fine," she said, shrugging as if it'd knock the tension off her shoulders. "Just chilly. I have an extra coat inside, though."

"C'mon, then." He gestured toward the library door. "Get it so we can go talk to people. You said you'd be able to ease the way so they'd open up to me, right? Fill me in, gauge fact from fiction?"

"Sure thing," she murmured absently, stepping into the dimly lit back room and making her way to the employee break room where she kept a spare jacket.

Suddenly—and she didn't care how illogical the idea was—she was sure Diego was more than just a hot, sexy temptation for incredible sex. He was inspiration, and for more than kinky positions. Empowerment meant grabbing ahold of what you wanted, taking risks and learning new things.

She didn't know what she might learn from him, what he might spark in her. She just knew he represented freedom. Excitement. She might have to settle for a life without her fantasy career as a stylist, but here was a chance to have a few of her other fantasies.

The sexual ones.

She just had to figure out how to convince him to strip naked and start making those fantasies come true.

THREE HOURS LATER, she was still figuring.

"I think that's it," Diego decided as he flipped through his little police notebook. "We've talked to all the victims and their families, as well as everyone who discovered the stolen goods. Was that the entire population of Diablo Glen?"

"Well, a large part of it," Jade agreed, keeping step with him as he strode down the sidewalk of Main Street. "There are about two dozen people out of town for the holidays. Visiting family, vacations, that kind of thing. And there are a few families who live out on the edge of the city limits, but we'd have to drive to see them."

Nonplussed, he shook his head. "I can't believe you can get from one end of town to the other without needing car keys."

"We can't have spoken with everyone. What about all the rest? The ones you waved to in stores, the diner. Gathered at that big building on the edge of the park. All prettied up to look like it's made of candy? Was that the town hall?"

Jade smiled at his description. The town hall, heck, all the public buildings, looked great. She'd actually had fun watching his reaction, seeing the disdain slowly melt from building to building as he came to appreciate all the artistry in the thematic decorations.

"You talked to all the major players in the panty drama, and most of the minor ones," she assured him. "There are a lot of people who aren't even bystanders, though. You caught us at our busy season. Rebecca Lee's getting married the first week of the new year, so she's got a bunch of relatives visiting. A lot of the families have company in for the holidays, too. Our quaint small-town-Christmas thing holds major appeal for some people."

As much as she craved the big city, she couldn't imagine doing the holidays any other way. Looking intrigued, Diego stopped to read a flyer in the bookstore window that announced the Twelve Days of Books event, complete with gingerbread and hot cocoa.

"You get a lot of strangers through?" he asked, nodding to a Washington license plate as he tucked his notebook back in his pocket.

"Sure, some. Like I said, there are a lot of visitors for a small town this time of year. You met Marion Kroger in the library?" She waited until he nodded before continuing, "She's got at least a dozen or more people out at her place. She must have a huge family, because they cycle through at least three or four times a year."

"Any of them come into town?"

Jade shrugged.

"Probably. Every once in a while we get a few people I can't place. But not too often. That's not a stranger's car, for instance. That's Mrs. Green's grandson's, Eddy. He's studying engineering at Washington University."

For the first time since he'd taken that phone call outside the library, Diego looked directly at her. Jade shivered a little. It wasn't that she'd forgotten how intense his gaze was. Not really. But a few hours in his company without feeling it had a way of making a girl think she could handle it.

Silly girl.

"I need to go over my notes," he said, still studying her face as if he was weighing something.

"Ah, well, I guess playtime's over then." Despite her cheery smile and light words, Jade's shoulders sank. Sure, he'd spent the last few hours holding her at arm's length, as if afraid one touch, one look, would be all the invitation she needed to straddle his body and demand he finish that kiss. But she'd still had fun.

It'd been exciting to help out, and fascinating to watch him work. The way he led the discussions, asking questions in such roundabout ways she didn't think most people had a clue how much information they'd given him. Even she, who'd lived here all her life, had found out a few new tidbits today.

She'd also had some seriously delicious fudge, a hot toddy, three cookies and had gotten a new recipe for double-butter pound cake.

Even more exciting, she'd been asked to help two women find the perfect outfits for their Christmas parties, been recruited to do a styling workshop on dressing right for New Year's Eve and had been advised that she talked about sex too much.

Diego had choked on his cookie at the last one, she remembered with a grin.

Maybe she hadn't gotten any closer to him, as she'd hoped. And perhaps the adventurous, self-sufficient vibe he radiated hadn't rubbed off on her, as she'd wished. But it'd been a fun experience, and hey, an afternoon with a hot, sexy guy was never a bad thing.

Focus on the positive, she always told herself. Even if

it didn't include another taste of the most tempting mouth she'd ever felt against hers.

So, forcing her chin up and her smile wider, she tilted her head to one side and said, "This was fun. And even though it still seems like a pointless crime, I hope I was able to help." All that in a single breath. Not bad. She inhaled slowly, preparing to force the goodbye past her lips next. Before she could, he tilted his head toward the other end of the street.

"I need to make sure I've got all my facts straight. Let's go to the diner," he suggested. "I'll buy you a cup of coffee and you can make sure I didn't miss anything."

A date? He probably didn't see it that way. Still, Jade's tummy danced in anticipation. Then the clock in the tall spear of the town hall caught her eye.

"The diner's closed," she said.

"It's only four."

"Holiday hours," Jade said with a shrug, her mind racing with possibilities. Despite her nerves—she'd never asked a guy out before—she blurted out, "But I have coffee at my place. We can go back there. You wanted to see the crime scene again anyway, didn't you?"

There you go, a subtle invitation into her bedroom and one she could totally deny if he freaked.

And if he didn't? Well, she'd just have to strip naked before he saw her ugly underwear.

IT TOOK CAREFUL SKILL to walk that thin line between instincts, cravings and pure stupidity. Diego told himself his toes were still firmly balanced.

Of course, anytime he looked at Jade, took in her sexy bod and gorgeous smile, the balance teetered. So much for that myth about long poles adding stability.

Diego sighed, torn between tying things up and taking a break to get his brain straight.

After his useless round of interviews that morning, he'd figured this case was pure crap. After his much more insightful, informative and productive—thanks to Jade—round of interviews this afternoon, he was still sure this case was pure crap.

At least, intellectually he was sure.

But his gut was saying something different. Instinct screamed loud enough to drown out his desperate need to get out of this Podunk town and back to the faceless, nameless anonymity of a big city.

And Jade was the key.

She'd sparked something when she'd mentioned all the strangers in town. Now he needed to get more information from her, but without tipping her off. Until he figured out what it was his gut was sensing, he'd be keeping his instinct's tingles all to himself.

And, he warned his itching fingers, his hands. No touching the sexy blonde. No feeling the curve of her ass to see if it was as tight and smooth as it looked. No weighing the feel of her full breast against his palm to see how it fit.

His body hummed at the image. He shifted, trying to shake off the sensual spell the afternoon with Jade had cast over him.

The sooner he solved this case, the sooner he could get the hell out of here. Back to real life, to his shiny new promotion and yet another new start. The idea fell like a ball of lead in his belly, a dull and lonely ache. Too many Christmas cookies, he told himself.

To solve the case, he needed to toe Kinnison's line, which meant following Applebaum's directive to use Jade's help. Since Diego's own gut agreed, he figured that was three against one.

"Sure," Diego finally agreed, realizing he'd been standing there like a moonstruck idiot long enough. "Coffee and another look at the crime scene sound good."

And wasn't he the big brave cop, heading off to Temptation Central. But hey, he was armed. He could handle a tiny little blonde with a smart mouth. Just as long as she kept her lingerie hidden away.

8

DIEGO SAT in Jade's kitchen, staring across the table at the soft, furry features of Jade's cat, wondering what was wrong with the people in this town. Once they'd loosened up and quit seeing him as an outsider whose face needed to meet their closed door, they'd all had similar warnings to offer.

Watch out. Caution. Dire consequences.

And all because of this sweet kitty?

"Why is everyone so freaked about your cat?" he asked, glancing over from the lush, long-haired feline perched on the opposite chair toward Jade. "It's like they've all got different opinions on the correct color of lights to string from a house, whether a tree should be green, white, aluminum or fake, and who makes the best cookies. But the fact that the panty thefts are a joke and your cat is pure evil seem to hit a total consensus."

"Well, you have to admit, it's hard to take the thefts too seriously," she said over the sound of water running into a coffeepot. "And are they technically thefts if the panties are always returned?"

"They're usually being left in weird places, on display and used to mock their owners."

"*Mock* is a pretty harsh word." She pulled the coffee-maker away from the wall to pour in the water.

"There was a pair of black lace panties big enough for three toddlers to play in with the words *Do Me* on the ass hanging from the blow-up reindeer in front of the post office this morning," he reminded her. How was that a joke? Did this town have no sense of privacy? No secrets at all? Not even who wore what style underwear in what size? He'd always thought sizes were like their real weight and age to women, closely guarded secrets.

"I'm not saying it wasn't a little disturbing to find out that Mrs. Kostelec has the same panties that I do. But the whole thing seems more like a joke than a crime to me," Jade admitted, taking a bag of coffee beans from the fridge and pulling a grinder out of a drawer. Diego was busy reveling in the addictively rich scent of the grinding coffee, so it took a few extra seconds for her words to sink in.

"You're kidding, right?" he asked, not sure if he was amused or horrified. His gaze dropped to Jade's ass, covered way too much in that big black shirt. Did her panties have an invitation written in glitter, too? His mouth watered. Maybe there was something to be said for following directions.

"Nope, I really was disturbed," she confessed. After flicking the on switch, she glanced back. She frowned at his impatient look, then gave an edgy sort of shrug. "Look, I know it's serious, even if most people aren't taking it that way. I saw the mess in my bedroom. It was all I could do last night not to run over to my mother's instead of sleeping in my own bed."

The look on her face, nerves and just a hint of the fear he'd seen the day before when she'd walked into her bedroom, made him feel even worse.

"I know it's serious. But if I think about it too much,

I'm scared," she told him quietly. "It's easier to trust that you're going to catch this guy, that you're really good at what you do and to believe I don't need to worry."

He grimaced at the anxious look in her eyes. Wanting to make her feel better, he promised, "While I'm on the job, nobody's going to hurt you. Or your underwear. I promise."

What was wrong with him? He didn't do promises. But the way her face lit up made him feel pretty damn good. She gave him a smile that made him feel like a superhero, then followed it up with a teasing wink.

"So the rumors are true, hmm? I heard you're quite the hotshot." As she spoke, she stretched on tiptoe to get two large red mugs off the shelf overhead. Diego shifted as if to help her, then seeing her fingers hook the ceramic handles, he settled back in the chair to continue enjoying the view.

"I thought the rumor was that I was a crappy cop who was sent here as punishment." The idea of people thinking he sucked at his job and the reality of being sent to Podunk, Nowhere, both grated on his ego in equal measure.

"One of the many joys of small towns. We wear the same underwear styles and the gossip changes with the direction of the wind," she said, giving him a teasing look over her shoulder as she poured the freshly brewed coffee into the mugs. "Word that the mayor has been bragging about your arrest record and police skills is spreading fast. He really likes you."

A cozy sort of feeling warmed Diego's chest. He'd never looked for cozy before and suddenly it was oddly appealing. The mayor was a kick. A fun old guy with a great sense of the ridiculous, he was the easiest authority figure Diego had ever worked with. Which meant he'd better get over it. Things that appealed in his life? They always ended up short-term, if they even lasted that long.

"Probably just making his decision to bring someone

in look good," Diego said dismissively with an uncomfortable shrug.

The teasing smile shifted to contemplation as Jade studied his face. Finally, just as he was about to actually shuffle his feet, she handed him his coffee.

"Applebaum really isn't into the spin game. I mean, there's not much point in a town this size. I think that's how he's gotten reelected so often. People know he's telling the truth," she said before gesturing toward the room behind him. Diego glanced at the plush, curvy couch. Bright blue, it was diamond-tucked with at least a hundred buttons, glossy wood accents and curlicue legs. It should have said fussy discomfort, but he could picture Jade laid out there in a sassy, sexy invitation much too easily.

He looked over her shoulder toward the dining room table with its long bench-style seats. The hardwood looked as if it'd make for some uncomfortable sexy times, not in the slightest bit encouraging toward stripping Jade's clothes off one piece at a time to search for invitations.

"Why don't we take this into the dining room." He covered his inward cringe with a big smile. "I was hoping for some cookies, and the table means fewer crumbs, right?"

The smile she flashed was bright and happy, as if he'd just answered the secret question and was about to be awarded his prize. Diego's heart picked up a beat as his imagination flipped through all the prizes he'd like from her. Most involved bare skin and a few required feathers.

"I figured you'd be cookied-out after all the offers this afternoon. But just in case…" She gestured toward the living room again. He followed the wave of her hand. A tall tree, glistening in rich jewel decorations, was displayed in the window. In front of the couch was a low table that looked like a polished brass surfboard. On it were some magazines, a free-form glass bowl in brilliant shades of streaky blue, indigo and purple, and an old-fashioned holiday tin with a bright red lid. He glanced back at Jade in question.

"The cookies are already out," she said. Then, taking matters into her own hands, she skirted around him. Not touching, not even close to making inappropriate contact. But the glance she offered through her lashes was as naughty as if she'd pressed her breasts into his chest. His body reacted as if she had, too, his breath catching and his dick going hard.

"It's comfier in here. And besides, if we have cookies here, Persephone will leave us alone. If we eat in the dining room, or even sit in there, she's going to raise a ruckus."

Diego gave the cat a doubtful look. It looked harmless. "A ruckus?"

"Yes," Jade confirmed, sinking onto the couch as if the matter was all settled. When she curled her feet up to tuck them beneath her hip, he figured in her mind, it actually was. "In here, she'll jump on the couch, check us out, then curl into a ball under the tree and nap. If we were in the dining room, she'd weave between our feet meowing, angry that she can't get up on the bench or table to dismiss what we're doing."

Bowing to the inevitable, Diego crossed the room. A quick glance told him that the other seating choices weren't optimal. One was a round footstool, about four feet in diameter and covered in furry leopard print. The other looked like a prop from a fifties movie, with its angular shape and retro polka-dot fabric. Safe enough to sit in, but made for a pixie-size woman. Reluctantly—at least that's what he told himself—Diego sat on the couch with Jade. As far away from her as he could get. So far, their body heat didn't even mingle. So far, he couldn't reach out and trail his palm over the smooth line of her jaw, or comb his fingers through those silky strands.

Close enough, he figured, that if he kept a cookie in one hand and the cup of hot coffee in the other, he'd do just fine.

"Here," Jade instructed, pulling the red lid off the cookie tin to show a variety of holiday treats. "Cookies fresh from my mom's kitchen. And that shoe-shaped disk? That's a coaster. Just set your coffee there."

He glared at the bright red shoe with its glittery bow and glossy heel. A coaster. A sexy coaster. What better to lure him into temptation with.

Stop, he silently demanded. He was here to solve a case and get the hell back to his own life and his bright new promotion. Not to be led around by his dick and quite possibly hurt what was probably the nicest, sweetest, sexiest woman he'd ever met.

"Have a cookie and tell me more about yourself, Diego," she invited with a smile warm enough to melt the frosting off the holly cookie she'd chosen. She bit off a piece, the crispy cookie snapping. Her tongue, small and pink, slid over her lower lip, gathering the scattered sugar.

His mouth watered. She'd missed one glistening green crystal. It sparkled, tasty and tempting, inviting him to lick it off the corner of her mouth.

"How about we talk about the case instead." He didn't care if he sounded desperate. He knew damn well that the minute his coffee cup met that shoe coaster, he was in a whole lot of trouble.

JADE'S LOWER LIP trembled a little. She didn't want to talk about the case. She didn't want to think about some panty-stealing creep being in her house. In her underwear. She didn't want to consider what it meant that the crimes had gone from undetected thefts to someone breaking in and trashing her bedroom. Either the creep was escalating to meaner crimes—or he had it in for her, specifically.

Instead, she'd rather take comfort from the information her mother had passed on. Apparently, Opal had been chatting with the mayor, who'd filled her in on Diego's many crime-fighting talents. The good detective had quite a fan in Applebaum. Of course, rumor was that the mayor was in talks with two neighboring towns to create a dedicated police force so they didn't have to rely on the county sheriff any longer. He'd gone on and on about Diego's close rates, his ability to think outside the box and what sounded like an almost mythical talent when it came to reading people.

Diego was here to solve this case. And she had complete faith that he'd do so—and keep her safe while he was here. But the minute he nabbed the Panty Thief, he'd grab his duffel bag, swing one long, lean leg over that big beast of a motorcycle he'd driven into town on and roar right back out.

As if to prove her point, he dug one hand into the pocket of his leather jacket and, still holding his coffee as if it was a lifeline, pulled out the little notebook he'd used all day.

She figured she could pout that the sexiest man alive was only here for a tiny amount of time, barely enough for her to learn his loner ways and independent spirit. Or she could make the most of what little time there was before he left.

"So you'll be heading back home soon," she said before he could start flipping through his notes. "Just in time for the holidays and all that, right? Do you have special plans?"

As in, a woman to kiss under the mistletoe? A family hell-bent on setting him up with Ms. Perfect? A slew of lovers waiting to unwrap his…package?

"Special plans for what?"

"Celebrating, of course. Tree-trimming parties, naughty-gift exchanges, secret-Santa festivities. You know, plans."

He looked so baffled, she had to force herself not to scooch over and give him a hug. It was as if he'd never experienced Christmas. At least, not a fun, festive one. The kind with candy canes and homemade decorations. Carols and cookies by the tree.

The kind she took for granted. Jade glanced at the cookie tin, feelings of guilt and joy mingling. Diablo Glen might not be the fashion mecca of the world, but it was pretty awesome in so many other ways.

"I'm sorry," she said, giving in to the need to touch him by patting his thigh—and what a strong, hard thigh it was. "But I think I'm going to have to expose you to as much Christmas as I can while you're here in town. I'm pretty sure it's my moral obligation."

"You have a moral obligation to foist tinsel and sugar cookies on people?" He sounded horrified.

Jade grinned. "Okay, it's my holiday obligation. And it's more than just sugar cookies, you know. There's gingerbread, too."

"That's okay." He gave an adamant shake of his head.

"No, no," she said dismissively, waving her hand as if he'd protested out of some need to not put her out rather than dread. "I really want to show you the delights of the season, and you can say a lot of things about Diablo Glen, but you can't claim we don't know how to show Santa a good time."

"You should save the good time for him, then. I'm fine without it."

"Nope," Jade insisted, both amused and delighted at his baffled reaction. "We have wonderful seasonal celebrations every day in December, winding up with my mom's open house on the twenty-third. Tonight the grade school chorus is doing a musical of *How the Grinch Stole Christmas,* the O'Malley family are doing hayrides through town after sunset and the ladies' auxiliary kicks off their annual sugarfest fundraiser."

Maybe it was his look of baffled trepidation. Or maybe it was the need to show him a little holiday cheer. Or, more likely, it was a desire to spend as much time as possible with him before he roared off into the sunset.

Whatever it was, Jade was determined that for whatever time he was here, Diego was going to experience a Diablo Glen Christmas.

"You'll have fun," she insisted, offering him another cookie from the tin. She wanted to see if he actually could have fun. Did being a loner who only had to answer to oneself mean giving up the simple, easy pleasures?

"I'm not interested in fun." He didn't sound sure, though. His eyes, hooded and intense, dropped to her breasts. Jade's breath caught. Her heart skipped a beat before racing like crazy through her chest. Her nipples stiffened, pebbling tight against the red lace of her camisole. Nerves raced faster than her pulse. She wanted him like crazy. She'd give anything to taste him, to strip him naked with her teeth, then run her tongue over his bare skin.

Her fingers trembled. The shaking was accompanied by a rattling sound. Realizing she was still holding out the tin of cookies, she lifted it a little in question. His eyes met hers again.

"Christmas is my favorite time of year. The lights, the glitter. All the great presents," she babbled nervously. "You really should give all the celebrational fun a try."

"Maybe next year," he said, making it sound like maybe never. She wanted to push, but the look on his face, closed and distant, said *back off.* Figuring she'd done enough to promote the season—for now—she complied.

"You're up for a promotion," she said with a smile, shifting topics and choosing a stained-glass sugar cookie for something to do with her mouth besides irritate him. "Will you still live in Fresno when you get it?"

"I'll be transferred to San Francisco."

"Oh, fun," she exclaimed, not a little envious. "I love it there. I used to live in the Haight, in the cutest Painted Lady. It was one of those gorgeous Victorians all done up in bright colors and divided into four condos. Walking distance to the best boutiques and oh, man, the food."

"You lived in San Francisco?"

Jade frowned. Why did he sound so shocked? Did he think she couldn't fit into such an exciting, metro place? That she was so small-town she couldn't handle the culture and diversity and challenge of one of the most dynamic cities in the world?

"I lived there for two years while I went to school at the Art Institute. My degree is in fashion merchandising and management." She tried to smile, hoping it'd take some of the stiffness out of her words. If the narrow look he gave her was any indication, it didn't come close.

She waited for the inevitable questions on why she'd returned to Diablo Glen. Whether she hadn't been able to hack it or if she'd come running back like a homesick small-town girl. Or if she'd been so overwhelmed by the expenses and the pressures and the demands, she'd used the first excuse she could find to throw it all away and scurry back to mommy.

Jade puffed out a breath. Maybe she had a few issues.

"I'm confused," Diego said after a few seconds. "Aren't you a librarian?"

Well, that hadn't been on the list of neurotic questions

she'd been prepared to field. Feeling as though her skin had shrunk two sizes too tight, Jade wrinkled her nose.

"No. Absolutely not." Realizing she sounded as if he'd just accused her of skewering Santa with a metal nail file, she sucked in a breath and tried to tone it down. She really did love the library and respected the profession, so she tried to explain. "I mean, I work at the library, but that's not my vocation. I love clothes, love creating looks, but I don't have the imagination to be a designer. I *do* have a great eye for combining pieces that suit people, in bringing together a look, an outfit, a style."

Diego blinked a couple of times, as if he was trying to connect the dots, but a few too many were missing for him to make a solid picture.

"It was my dream, working in fashion." She tossed the uneaten cookie on the table with a sigh. "But family obligations, expectations, they got in the way. You know how it is, right?"

His eyes softer than she'd ever seen, he looked as if he was going to give her a comforting hug. Jade started to lean forward, more than ready to feel his arms around her. Then he shook his head.

"No. My only obligations are to the job."

"How do you avoid family ones?" she asked, wondering if she should take notes.

"No family. No obligations to avoid." His words were flat, his eyes cold.

"But…" Jade's words trailed off, her mind flailing about, searching for a way to put to words the millions of questions suddenly bombarding her mind.

"I have a mother, she's still alive. Somewhere," he said, his tone as distant and cold as the North Pole. He didn't drink his coffee to warm it up, though. Instead, he stared off at something only he could see over Jade's shoulder.

"She was a party girl, only dropped into my life once or twice before heading off to the next thrill. Dumped me in foster care, or with an uncle now and then."

Jade pressed her fingers to her mouth to hold back her protest.

"It's no big deal," he said, seeing the look on her face. "I did fine. And it's easier to focus on the job without those obligations you talked about."

Jade's heart melted in sympathy, tears threatening, hot and burning in her eyes. That poor little boy. No mother, no family, no love? How'd he survive? What incredible strength did he have inside that had placed him on this side of the badge instead of the other?

"You're not getting any sloppy sentimental ideas over there, are you?" he asked, his tone as light as possible for someone who sounded as if he had his nuts in a vise— emotionally speaking, of course.

"Me?" she asked with a cheery laugh. Blinking fast to ensure her eyes were clear and bright, she picked the cookie up again and nibbled. The sugar tasted like dirt, gritty and bland. "Sentimental? Unless you're talking vintage fashion or stop-motion Christmas cartoons, I'm never sentimental."

She shifted on the couch, making her once-over look like a teasing inspection, when she was actually looking deeper, as if she could actually see the emotional scars.

It was easier to kiss them better if she could see them first.

"Look, it's no big deal. Lots of people grow up in worse situations. I had food, shelter, all the fundamentals. I turned out fine."

Indeed he had. Which spoke more to his inner strength than the resilience of human nature.

"You're disillusioned," she observed quietly, her heart

weighing heavy in her chest as she traced a soft caress over the back of his hand for comfort.

He laughed, the sound surprised, not cynical. "Disillusioned? Nah. You have to have illusions for that, don't you? I never had any."

"What about being a cop? You had to have illusions of what that'd be. Is it what you expected?"

After a few seconds, he met her eyes again. The frustrated disappointment in his dark gaze made her feel as if she'd just kicked a sweet little puppy.

"Yeah, I guess I am disillusioned."

"Yet you do a job that requires that you believe in good," she marveled.

"Believe in good? Hardly. I deal in proof of the exact opposite." His bitter laugh wasn't an insult to her, she realized, her smile sliding into a frown. It was directed at himself.

"You believe in the power of justice. In right and wrong. And you believe, you must believe, that you can balance the two somehow," she said, her words soft, almost a whisper. As if saying it too loud would send him flying off her couch and out that door.

Still, she couldn't not say it. She spent most of her life keeping things in. Playing nice and not speaking out, worried about making others upset or uncomfortable. But unlike her family, with whom it would serve no purpose to share her dreams and frustrations, Diego needed to hear what she had to say.

Her fingers skimmed his wrist and forearm, muscled and tense. Hard. Like the rest of his body.

He needed to know what she felt.

She let her eyes travel from her fingers, milky white against his golden skin, up his deliciously muscled arm and broad shoulder to the curve of his chin. The soft, just-this-side-of-pretty fullness of his lower lip. The sharp line of his nose and—her breath caught as she met his gaze—the intensity of his dark eyes.

He should be told what she saw.

"You really are a hero, aren't you?"

He cringed. Beneath her fingers, his arm tensed. She figured he was mentally already halfway out the door.

"I like heroes," she murmured, risking his mental trip shifting into high gear and sending him running all the way out of town. She didn't care. She didn't know how he was key to her happiness, to her freedom. She just knew her gut believed it. Which meant she had to take the risk. Had to tell him her truth.

The horrified look in his eyes turned speculative. Hot. Sexy.

Jade slid her hand up his arm, sighing in appreciation as her palm skimmed the hard, round rock that were his biceps. She pressed her fingers to his chest. There, just between his heart and his shoulder. The heat of his skin through his T-shirt warmed her palm. Filled her with a desire strong enough to drown out the nerves clamoring through her body.

She stared into the rich depths of his eyes for a second, then let her gaze drop to his lips. Full, tempting lips. The hint of stubble. The small jagged scar above his mouth.

She wanted to taste them again. Needed to feel them against hers. He'd kissed her once and now it was an addiction. She had to know what else he could do. They'd done the hard-and-fast route. Could he do wild and intense? Was it in him to be slow and sweetly gentle?

Maybe it was time to grab on and enjoy finding out.

Hardly daring to breathe, Jade leaned forward. His eyes narrowed, a dangerous heat flaring in their hypnotic depths. Her stomach jittered.

Nerves racing with excitement, she shifted closer. Close enough for the tips of her breasts to brush his chest. Her nipples instantly stiffened. Desire, hot and molten, ran down to her core. The intensity of it made her dizzy.

Just a simple touch and she was teetering on the edge of an orgasm. God knew what she'd do if they actually got naked. Melt into a puddle all over his bare toes?

She narrowed her eyes. And him? He still had that same stare going on. How did she entice a man so sexy he probably had women throwing themselves at him every day? How did she satisfy a man whose expression she couldn't even read?

The only way to find out was to try.

Even if it scared her to pieces.

She wet her lips. Then, eyes locked on his, she leaned in and brushed her mouth over his jaw. Soft and unthreatening.

His body was rock hard. His expression didn't shift. But his eyes? They were flaming hot now, filled with a passion that excited, terrified, empowered her.

"I really, really do like heroes," she whispered again.

Then, just to see what they'd both do, she ran her tongue over his lower lip, sucking the soft, tender flesh into her mouth.

9

OH, BABY. He tasted so good. Delicious and decadent, with a hint of coffee and a sweet layer of powdered sugar. She wanted more. She needed as much as she could get. But she forced herself to pull back. Holding her breath, her stomach tumbling with nerves and excitement, she waited to see what he'd do. Kiss her back? Get up and leave? Both options were a little scary.

He gave her another one of those deep, soul-inspecting stares. Her heart raced and the nerves outdid the excitement, knotting themselves into a tangle. She resisted the urge to squirm.

"This is a mistake," he said, his voice a low, husky rumble.

"Do you always avoid mistakes?" Breathless and seductive, her words were both curious, and, well, yes, a little bit of a challenge. Because she didn't care if it was a mistake or not. She just wanted to do it again.

He didn't answer.

Instead, he kissed her.

Hot.

Intense.

Wet and wild.

Jade moaned against his lips as they slid, silky soft, over her mouth. His teeth nipped softly, so that she parted her lips to gasp. Then his tongue swept in, swirling deep. Sweet and hard at the same time. Deliciously sweet, and, holy cow, so temptingly hard.

She grabbed on to his shoulders to keep from melting all over him. His hands swept up her jeans-clad thighs, making a soft scraping sound against the crisp cotton of her shirt before settling on her waist. Her breasts grew heavy, aching as she waited to see if his hands would go a little higher. Just a little, please.

Instead, he gently pulled his mouth from hers and waited. Her nerves spun out of control. She didn't know what he was waiting for, nor could she tell if he was any-where near as affected by that kiss as she was.

"Wow," she breathed in a rush, unable to handle the lack of commentary any longer. "You really are good at that."

His lips twitched, but he stuck with the strong, sexy si-lence as he tightened his hands around her waist, then ef-fortlessly lifted her onto his lap. Jade giggled, excitement making her feel light-headed. Before she'd even settled—or had a chance to appreciate the hard length of his erec-tion against the back of her thigh—he took her mouth.

And drove her crazy. Tiny nibbling kisses. Big eating bites. His hands stayed at her waist, but his mouth wor-shipped her in a way that was sexier than anything Jade had ever felt in her life.

She wanted more.

She needed more.

She reached her fingers under the soft fabric of his shirt, intending to take more.

Diego had other plans, though. He shifted, his hand covering hers.

"We should stop," he groaned against her lips. Then,

proving he had way more willpower than she did, he released her mouth and moved back. Just enough to shift the intensity from high heat to medium simmer.

She closed her eyes and leaned her forehead against his chest, gratified to feel his harsh intake of breath and racing heart.

"Why?" She didn't want to stop. Not now, not yet. Not while the passion swirling through her senses was promising such a delicious and powerful result. But she kept her hands to herself. Because forcing her needs, her wants, on someone else? That just felt wrong.

"Because you're a nice girl and I'm not a nice guy. Because I'm leaving the second I solve this case. And because I have nothing to offer." His gaze dropped to her lips and heated. As if he was magnetically drawn, he leaned closer again. Then, forcing himself to stop, he tilted his head back to glare at the Christmas tree, taking in deep, controlled breaths.

Jade sighed.

He was right. He wasn't a nice guy. Which was one of the reasons he appealed to her so much. He was a guy who led the life he wanted, and was strong enough to accept and deal with the consequences but still go his own way.

And she wanted all that. Even if it was just for a few days, she wanted to experience that kind of inner strength. Even if it was secondhand.

"I think what you have to offer is mighty appealing," she told him. Even though it took all her nerve, she held his gaze as she pressed her palm into the hard planes of his chest, then let her fingers slide downward. Just to the rigid flatness of his belly. Her fingers itched to go lower. To encircle the stiff length of his erection pressing against her thighs.

Maybe he believed her, or maybe he was feeling the

same intense need she was. Either way, he gave a slow, contemplative nod. Excited anticipation raced through Jade's system.

"Just so you know, fraternizing with me might move you to Santa's naughty list," he warned, nuzzling his mouth against the sensitive curve of her throat.

"Naughty, hmm?"

"Babe, I'm as bad as they come." He leaned back. Just enough to give her an arch look. "And you'd be bad, too. If I got your clothes off, I predict you'd find yourself doing all kinds of naughty things. I expect you'd even teach me a thing or two, as well."

"Me?" she asked in her flirtiest tone.

"You've got some naughty inside," he promised, his tone as serious as the intense nod of assurance he offered.

He was so cute.

Her hands cupping the incredible breadth of his hard shoulders, Jade laughed in delight. She'd already accepted that he was gorgeous, sexy and dedicated. She considered it pretty awesome that his lips were magic and that his hands held the secrets to all physical pleasure. But now he was fun, too?

It was almost too much for a girl to handle.

At least, not without giving up a piece—and oh, please let it be a tiny piece that she could afford to lose—of her heart.

The cautious part of her mind—probably ruled by all that nice he'd mentioned—worried. What did she know about Diego?

Other than the fact that he was gorgeous and sweet, smart and funny. That he was a good, solid cop who believed in justice. That he'd had a horrible, lonely childhood and deserved to feel loved—even if it was only the physical kind of love.

Was she trying to talk herself out of sleeping with him?
she wondered. Or trying to justify stripping him naked,
slathering him in whipped cream and calling him dessert?

Confusion, and fear, overwhelmed the passion. She
wanted him, unquestionably. And she didn't know what
scared her more. Having him, and it not measuring up to
her expectations. Or having him and finding out it was
better than anything she'd ever imagined.

Both were terrifying, because both would hurt.

"I should refresh our coffee," she decided, jumping up
from the couch. It didn't count as running away if she
only went as far as the kitchen, right? "Did you want more
coffee?"

She grabbed his mug, sloshing liquid over her knuckles.
She was halfway across the room before she realized the
brew was still hot. She stopped so fast, it sloshed again.
She set the drink aside before it landed on her feet.

"What's the deal?" Diego asked, rising as well.

He stood so tall, so broad and strong. But not intimidating, she realized. As crazy as it sounded even to her,
he felt safe. He felt tempting. He felt like her once-in-a-
lifetime chance to be as naughty as he thought she could
be. To live her life for herself, her own way. To experience
living in the moment, on her own terms. Everything she
said she wanted but was too afraid to actually do.

Just like Diego.

"Jade?" he prompted. "What's wrong?"

She met his gaze, letting all her fears, her worries and
probably even her naked soul shine in her eyes. Licking
her lips, she gave a helpless shrug.

"I'm a little worried," she confessed. Before he could
ask what about, she used both hands to gesture toward him,
then waved one in the general direction of her bedroom. "I
want you. It's all I can think about. Getting naked, getting

wild, doing all those naughty things you mentioned, then hitting the internet to find a few dozen more to try out."

She took a second to breathe deeply and assess his reaction. Not easy, since he'd frozen. Probably afraid if he moved, she'd jump him. Which just showed how smart he was.

"But I'm not sure it's a good idea," she continued, figuring she might as well confess it all. If he was going to run screaming into the night, he might as well be well fueled. "I'm too smart to fall for you. You're temporary. You're not a relationship kind of guy. You're a loner who likes his life the way he's made it."

She paused, realizing that those were a lot of the reasons she was attracted to him. He was all that, smart and temporary. A loner who wasn't looking for more than she could give.

"You're right," he agreed slowly, a dark frown creasing his brow as he shoved his hands into his pockets and rocked back on his heels. The look he gave her was pure speculation. As if he knew her doubts went deeper, but knew the doubts she had about those doubts were huge enough that a simple push would send her over the edge. He just had to decide which edge he wanted her toppling over. "This spark, this heat between us? It's a bad idea. Better ignored."

Well, there you go. Jade set the coffee cup on a side table so she could cross her arms over her chest without tossing coffee all over the place. See, he agreed. The two of them, together, not a good thing.

"It'd feel good, though," she mused aloud, staring at the Christmas tree as if the right answer would suddenly appear beneath the green boughs, gift-wrapped in glitter and foil. "It'd be incredible. I've never been this attracted

to someone. It's like all my inhibitions packed their bags
and are ready to leave the minute you touch me."

Diego's groan pulled her out of her dreamy reverie. Jade
winced, then couldn't help but grin as he shoved both his
hands through his hair.

"You're killing me," he decided, his face a study in
frustration.

Because he wanted her that much, she realized. Not just
sex with any woman. Not just a notch, or something to
pass the time while he was stuck in town. He. Wanted. Her.

"I'd rather you taught me how to be as naughty as you
are," she confessed, her words rushing over the tops of
one another in her hurry to get them out. To hell with
fears. This was what she wanted, wasn't it? A chance to
live life to the fullest.

Well, there he was, ready to fill her up. Her breath stuck
somewhere between her chest and her throat, Jade waited.

Too bad she wasn't sure what, exactly, she hoped would
happen when the waiting was over.

HE'D BEEN RIGHT. She was trying to kill him. Diego stared
at the sexy little pixie, her blond hair swirling around her
shoulders like fairy floss. Those eyes were huge, and if
her words hadn't been enough to send him over the edge,
she'd added a cute little nibble of her bottom lip to the mix.

This was insane. He should walk out the door right
now, stay the hell away from Jade while he wrapped up
this case, then get out of town.

Instead, he took two steps forward, grabbed her by the
arms and lifted her onto her tiptoes to meet his kiss.

She gasped. Then, with desperate hands, she shoved
his jacket off his shoulders. Diego released his hold on
her waist just long enough to let the leather drop from
his hands.

His mouth devoured. Lips raced. Tongues danced. Her fingers clutched the back of his shirt. He couldn't get enough of her. Wanted more.

Needed more.

Diego shoved his hands through her hair, the soft strands wrapping around his fingers. He tilted her head back farther, holding her captive as he ravaged her mouth with the same edgy, desperate need he wanted to take her body.

"I want you," he confessed against her lips. "Now, desperately, I need you."

Too desperately. Diego struggled, using every ounce of willpower to keep his body in check. *Slow it down, buddy. Don't scare her. Definitely don't hurt her.*

"You want me?" Jade asked in a throaty voice. "Then take me."

Willpower disintegrated. Frantic animal passion took over. Barely aware of his moves, finesse and skill gone along with his mind, Diego could only feel. Only touch.

His hands skimmed up her tiny waist, curving over the delicious soft curves of her breasts. Already hard for him, her nipples pressed into his palms as if they were coming home.

He scraped his fingers over the pebbled tips, reveling in their getting even harder. Just like his dick.

"Lose it," he demanded against her mouth. "All these clothes have to go."

Her breath as shaky as his knees, Jade pushed against his shoulders until he released her. Then, her eyes glowing with slumberous pleasure, she tilted her head toward the hall. "My room?"

"Strip first."

Surprise joined the pleasure on her face, but only for

a second. Then she arched one brow and gave him a look of pure challenge.

Her eyes locked on his, Jade unbuckled the vivid red belt and let it drop to the floor with a light thud. Then, her fingers swift and easy, she unbuttoned the front of her oversize blouse. It only took a shrug of her shoulders to send it fluttering down over the belt.

His body tense enough to explode, he stared as she skimmed her fingers over her torso until they reached the lacy red hem of her camisole. Slowly, so slow he swore he was going to cry if she didn't get naked soon, she lifted the fabric. Higher, so he could see the smooth pale skin of her belly.

Diego groaned as the light glinted off her navel ring. Then Jade pulled the fabric higher, over her head, and tossed it aside. His gaze locked on the perfect curves of her breasts cradled in raspberry lace, he was barely aware that she'd pushed her jeans free of her waist until she kicked them aside.

He ate her up with his eyes. Her panties were cut high on the thighs, a narrow raspberry-colored panel of satin surrounded by ruffled lace.

"You are so sexy," he breathed.

"I think you're just obsessed with my lingerie," she teased.

Noting how the lace created a scallop design, dipping deep between her breasts, Diego couldn't deny that.

"You do have some incredible lingerie," he agreed. Then he flashed her a dare-you grin. "Maybe you can give me a little fashion show later. Take me on a tour of my obsession?"

"Maybe," she agreed, giggling softly. "Did you know that a woman's lingerie is more about her identity, her vision of herself, than it is about sex? What she wears under her clothes is like her secret self."

"You mean this sexy lingerie isn't all a show for the guys?" he teased.

"Oh, no. Guys are too easy. Lingerie is for women. To feel sexy about themselves, to prove to other women that they really are sexy. To make their secret self happy playing dress-up."

"Your secret self is the sexiest thing I've ever seen," Diego decided, tracing his finger along the edge of her bra. Dipping it lower, he rubbed her nipple with the back of his fingernail.

"I'm glad you like it," Jade murmured as she slipped her hands beneath his shirt. She gave a low moan when she pressed her palms to his abs. Diego grinned. He might not have lingerie, but thanks to no social life and an at-home gym, he had some pretty tight abs.

Then her hand slipped lower. Cupped his rock-hard erection through his jeans.

Diego's grin faded. So did his thoughts. All he had left was sensation. And that was being commanded by the hand on his control lever.

Her hand squeezed. Barely aware of the sound of lace ripping, Diego tore her bra away. He filled his hands with her soft flesh, his mouth with the rosy tip of her pebbled nipple.

She gasped, her hand clenching. Diego almost came right there in his jeans. Needing her now. Desperate to bury himself in her delicious warmth, he grabbed the edge of her panties and tugged. She gave a delighted shudder, her fingers working his snap and zipper with the same clumsy, desperate impatience he was feeling.

"I'll replace it," he promised, shoving the tattered satin aside.

"Naked," she demanded before he could reach the treasure his fingers sought. She gave up her quest to get his zipper past the rock-hard pressure of his dick. Instead, she scraped her fingernails lightly up his belly beneath his shirt. "Naked, now."

"I like a woman who knows what she wants," Diego said, his words as choppy as his breath. He forced himself to release her, stepping backward to tear his clothes off. He didn't take his eyes off her. Nude now, her body was a work of art. Petite, delicate, all sexy cream with berry-tipped breasts and a golden thatch of hair that beckoned him home.

Diego barely remembered to grab a condom from his jeans before he tossed them across the room.

Before they hit the ground, he had his hands on her again. His mouth took hers. His fingers slid down, dipping into the hot, wet delight between her thighs.

He wasn't going to last. He couldn't, he wanted her so badly. Sheathing himself now, before he lost the awareness to do so, Diego pulled her tighter against his body.

His hands curved down her hips, grasping the soft flesh of her butt and squeezing. Jade gave a mewling sound. Then, her arms wrapped tight around his shoulders, she gave a little leap and wrapped her legs around his waist.

Diego groaned, not sure whether to be thrilled with the new position or upset that the shift put her breasts out of reach of his mouth.

"That way," Jade instructed, tilting her head. He followed the tilt, noted the hallway, and, gripping her butt a little tighter so she wouldn't hit the floor, headed that way.

Walking became a new, delicious form of torture. Every

step slid the hard tip of his dick against her curls. Every step was a new lesson in sexual torture.

He barely got halfway down the hall.

"Can't make it," he declared, turning fast to press her body between his and the wall. Grabbing her feet, he angled her higher. Then plunged.

Jade cried out, her throat arched and her breath came in fast pants. Barely able to see through the haze of passion, Diego watched the flush climb her chest, up her throat, and coat her cheeks in a warm pink glow.

Her heels pressed against his butt, urging him to go deeper. To move faster. Her wish being his command, he did exactly that.

He plunged. She swirled. He pounded. She met him thrust for thrust. She might be little, but there was nothing fragile about the hellcat in his arms.

He shifted, just a little, to angle her higher. She gasped. Her back arched, bringing those yummy nipples back within tasting range. Unable—unwilling—to deny himself, Diego took one delicious morsel into his mouth and sucked.

Jade gave a keening sort of scream, her body so tense it felt as if she could snap in half. Then she ground herself against him, wet heat sucking him in deeper.

Ready to pass out, breathing heavily with no blood getting to his brain, Diego let go. He plunged, nailing her to the wall. Her fingernails dug into his shoulders. He plunged again. She cried out urgent pleas for him to go harder. Go faster.

He came.

Wave after wave after wave, the orgasm pounded out of him with an intensity he'd never felt before.

Barely aware, unable to stay upright, Diego slid to the floor. His arms wrapped tight around Jade, he took her right down with him.

IT MIGHT HAVE BEEN ten minutes, it might have been an hour. Jade didn't know how long it took for her to float back into her body.

So this was what love felt like. She shifted so her hips weren't pressed so tight against the cool wood floor. Her emotions had taken on a rosy glow that only added to the incredible sensations still trembling through her so-satisfied-she-was-exhausted body.

"It's too fast," she mumbled, trying to lure her heart back to the same side.

Silly heart, what did it know? This had to be sexual infatuation. Her body and mind were totally gaga over him, so her emotions were trying to join the club. Which was just crazy. She couldn't fall in love this quickly.

"You're thinking too hard," Diego muttered, his face still buried in her neck. Anchoring one hand on either side of her shoulders, he pressed himself into a push-up to get a look at her face. Not wanting to meet his eyes while all the crazy thoughts were still dancing through her head, she focused on the sculpted muscles of his biceps.

"You're so strong. So hard," she murmured, grazing her palm over his arm and purring in appreciation.

As distractions went, it worked pretty well.

"Hard, hmm?" He gave her a wickedly naughty grin just before he kissed her again. His mouth was ravenous. He'd just come with a power that had almost broken down her hallway wall. But she could feel him stirring back to life against her still-trembling thigh.

"Trying to prove something?" she teased.

"Let's find out."

His mouth trailed down her throat, kissing, nibbling. Delighting her with tiny shivers of pleasure.

Yeah, Jade sighed as she shifted her head to give him better access as he scraped his teeth over her collarbone.

She was in love with him. It was too fast. Too soon. Too complicated.

"Way, way too fast," she muttered just before her body arched in a shocked gasp of delight. He sucked her nipple into his mouth, swirling his tongue around the hard tip and sucking at the same time. Jade's thighs quivered.

Who cared about time, though? She'd known Eric for twelve years before they'd gotten engaged. Look how that had turned out. With her secretly grateful that he'd saved her from a life of mediocre sex.

"Did you say you wanted it fast?" he asked, his voice an erotic rumble against her belly.

Tunneling her fingers into his hair, Jade gave a helpless laugh. "I don't think I can go much faster."

He lifted his head, his eyes slumberous and heavy with fulfilled passion. Slowly, like watching a fire take spark, the wicked gleam grew, intensified.

Jade's own eyes widened. Her pulse tripped.

His fingers slid down her hip and over her still-trembling thigh.

"What are you doing?" she gasped.

"Seeing how fast you can go."

His whiskers scraped a delicious path over her belly as he slid lower. His fingers combed through her damp curls, parting her. Exposing her. Making her tremble.

"Go…? Where?" Here, there, anywhere. She'd go wherever he wanted, just as long as he kept doing these sweet things to her body. Then he shifted again, scraping her thighs with his jaw as he settled in to feast.

His tongue dipped, swirled, dipped again. Jade's gasps were pants now, her head thrown back in delight as the sensations pounded through her body at the speed of sound.

"Go over," he demanded, adding his fingers to the dance.

Unable to do anything else, Jade flew. Faster and faster, the sensations swirled. Deeper and more intense, the orgasm quaked through her. Her legs shook. Her heart pounded.

"Oh," she gasped, soaring along the crest of pleasure with a power she'd never felt in her life. "Oh, I love this."

Unaware of anything but what was going on inside her body, Jade tried to think. Tried to focus. But she couldn't. Like a storm-tossed ocean, she crashed. Wave upon wave, the orgasm just kept going.

Slowly, breathtakingly slowly, the waves smoothed, softened. As if she'd been drugged, her body sank into an exhausted state of barely-there awareness. She had a vague sense of Diego lifting her, carrying her to bed. When the cool pleasure of her own silk sheets slid against her back, she tried to surface.

But then he kissed her. And she dived under one more time.

10

"HELLO, SON."

Diego jumped. Actually jumped, like a strung-out meth fiend trying to lift a cop's wallet. Four days in this town and look at him. It was pathetic.

"Sir," he said, wiping his palms on his jeans and nodding to the mayor in greeting.

"You're here for the meeting?"

"I thought I'd take it in."

Diego glanced past the older man to the ornate arched opening to the town hall. For a small town, Diablo Glen was sure big on fancy architecture. It was also home to an extensive arts program that included music, dance and three gallery shows a year. It didn't boast its own police department or newspaper, but it was home to a famous online bakery. And it was peopled with a lot of characters, some a little more out there than others. Only one, though, was unforgettably sexy, overwhelmingly sweet and pretty much the biggest mistake of Diego's life.

"Thinking you'll find some clues during our discussion over what color to paint the park benches this spring and which band should play at the New Year's Eve Bash?"

Tension rippled across Diego's shoulder blades as he shrugged. Better to focus on his failure to close this case than on Jade, he figured. With that in mind, he followed the mayor up the wide steps, waiting while the other man unlocked the ornate doors.

"I figure it can't hurt. From what I've heard, pretty much everyone shows up for these things. Maybe I'll catch a break."

"Don't be down on yourself, Sandoval. You're doing everything right."

"If I was doing everything right, I'd have solved the case," Diego pointed out as he followed Applebaum into the cavernous foyer. His tone was matter-of-fact, but the look Applebaum gave him made it clear his frustration was coming through.

"Do you think all cases can be solved just like that?" Applebaum asked with a snap of his fingers. "Or is there a natural progression to investigating?"

"It depends. A case like this one, where the perp appears to have gone underground, it's harder," Diego admitted. At Applebaum's arch look, he shoved his hands in his pockets, rocked back on his heels and considered the bigger question. "But yeah, I think there's a natural progression. Except it's never the same from case to case. Each one has to be looked at individually, and treated as priority. Big or small, a good cop never gets lazy and follows a checklist."

Which was why Kinnison's rules and protocols drove him nuts, Diego realized. The guy was all about the checklist.

"I like how you think," Applebaum said slowly, with a look that made Diego want to squirm. It was as if the old guy was peering into his soul. What the hell he thought he'd find there was the big question, though.

Trying to shrug off the compliment, Diego looked around the room.

A large blue spruce decorated the corner, beribboned packages spilling out from under its boughs. It looked as if there were enough gifts for every family in town. What was that like, that sense of inclusion, of being a part of something that considered everyone so special, they all deserved presents? Diego could count on one hand the number of Christmas gifts he'd gotten in his entire life. It must be the effects of Diablo Glen's familial warmth and close-knit community that were making him suddenly wish his name was on one of those shiny boxes.

"Do you think this case is different, being small-town, than one you'd face in the city?" Applebaum asked, pulling him back into focus.

"Yeah, but not in the way you'd think," Diego said. "Crime is crime. Human nature doesn't change according to zip code. But in the city, I'd have other cases to work on while I was chipping away for a break. Here, I'm spinning my wheels, looking like a failure and, no offense, sir, bored to death."

Applebaum flicked a switch that lit the far rooms with a warm glow, then led the way into the main hall. Rows of chairs stood in neat lines, with cushioned benches along the walls. At the front of the room was a raised dais, ten chairs at the rear behind the polished mahogany podium. Directly behind the podium was yet another Christmas tree, this one decorated with cookies of all shapes and sizes.

"Then your problem isn't failure, son. It's that you don't have enough to do." Clearly a man of action, Applebaum gestured to the closet labeled Storage. "Go ahead and set up the refreshment tables, why don't you."

Diego squinted. He was kidding, right? Busy unlock-

ing more doors, then wheeling out sound equipment, the
old mayor didn't look back. Maybe he wasn't kidding.
Clueless as to how a refreshment table should be set up,
Diego squared his shoulders and dived into the supply
closet, hauling out three folding tables. He and the mayor
worked quickly, the companionable silence only broken
by the mayor's occasional instruction.

"So how did things go with Jade?" Applebaum asked
after a while. His expression hidden under the podium as
he hooked up the sound system, he sounded curious but
nothing more.

Large stainless-steel coffeepot in his arms, Diego froze.
Had Jade told someone about their night together? Not
even a night, he swiftly corrected. More like a few hours.
Hours of passion, power, sexual nirvana and an afterglow
of terror.

"Jade?" he asked with an inward cringe. Just how much
gossip did this small town have on tap?

She'd used the *L* word. Oh, sure, she hadn't said she
loved him, per se. But "love *this*" was close enough to
scare the crap out of him. So much that he'd been halfway
to the door under the guise of rescuing his leather jacket
from the sleeping cat when he'd glanced back. Lying,
naked and deliciously glowing, on the hall floor, Jade had
offered a sultry smile and he'd been lost. He hadn't been
able to resist scooping her up and carrying her into her
bedroom for one more bout of pleasure. But the minute
she'd fallen asleep, he'd sneaked out.

The only thing he was proud of was the fact that he'd
managed to keep the cat, who'd somehow decided he was
the next best thing to catnip, from following him out into
the decoration-filled world.

"I figured she'd open doors for you around town. Everyone loves her. And why wouldn't they? The girl is a

wonder," Applebaum continued, as if he hadn't noticed Diego's lack of response. "She stepped right up when her daddy died. Gave up her dreams, moved back to town to take care of her momma. Not that Opal needs taking care of, now. But Jade promised Chris, so that's what she did."

"Her dad died when she lived in San Francisco?" Diego confirmed. Skilled in the art of interviewing unwilling suspects, he knew how to make it sound as if he didn't care about the response.

"Yep. Moved back, got engaged, went to work at the library. That first year or so after Chris died, Opal was in a rough way. The MS kicked into high gear, and her grief was taking over." There was something in the mayor's voice that caught Diego's attention. A sadness, mingled with a lot of admiration. For Jade's mom? Interesting. Before Diego could wonder about it too much, Applebaum continued, "Jade? She kept Beryl in school, made it so Ruby could marry without guilt and guided her momma back to healthy living."

"Jade was engaged?" Yes, he knew Applebaum had said other words besides those. But the rest were just blah-blahblah in his head, unheard over the ringing of that announcement. "What happened?"

Applebaum peered around the podium, his arch stare making Diego hunch his shoulders. So much for his covert interview skills.

"Eric was her high-school beau. They'd split when she moved, but drifted back together when Jade came home. They were due to marry about four Christmas Eves ago. A week before the ceremony, Eric got cold feet. Apparently he couldn't handle the responsibility."

The responsibility of marrying a gorgeous, sexy woman who was as sweet as she was smart? One who had a body that wouldn't quit, a personality so fun it practically glittered and a talent with her tongue that had made him want to weep in gratitude.

"Was the guy an idiot?"

Applebaum gave an appreciative smile. "Idiot, careless ass, too weak to do the right thing. They're all the same in this case. I suppose he figured he did the right thing by taking total responsibility. He decided he wanted out of Diablo Glen, but Jade's ties meant she couldn't, or wouldn't, go."

Diego focused on settling the coffeepot onto the middle of the table, then instead of moving the table away from the wall to plug in the cord, chose to crouch underneath it instead. All he needed was a few seconds to process that info. A moment or two—without Applebaum's eagle eye on him—to accept that Jade was here for good. Not that he'd thought about asking her to leave. Or considered what it would be like if she happened to move back to San Francisco after he was transferred there. It wasn't as if he'd already come up with five or six different options for asking her out. Nope. That she and Diablo Glen were permanently attached didn't matter to him at all.

Teeth clenched so tight his jaw ached, he rose, flicked the switch to make sure the coffeepot was juiced. Then, blank, he stared at the white table until Applebaum cleared his throat.

"Maybe grab the other coffeepot, and the big trays on the storage shelf?" the older man suggested gently. "I'd appreciate it."

Get a grip, Diego warned himself. And the speculative look in the mayor's eye served as a solid warning. Asking meant caring about the answer. And he had way too many reasons not to care. So instead, he asked, "So what's the deal? Does Jade's history have something to do with my case?"

Applebaum's face was tough to read. The speculation

was still there, making Diego's shoulder blades itch. There was a weird, fatherly sort of benevolence in his eyes, and a shrewd tilt to his chin.

"Probably not. But it never hurts to have as many details about the people you're dealing with as possible."

Almost as confused by the paternal affection Applebaum treated him with as he was wondering about Jade, Diego decided that a mental-health break was mandatory.

"I'll be outside," he told the mayor. "Gotta check in with Kinnison, follow up on a few loose ends back in Fresno."

"Uh-huh."

Shoulders stiff, he took his time sauntering out of the room. No point in confirming that knowing look on the old man's face.

Forty minutes later, Diego deemed it safe enough to go back into the hall. He'd had enough time to check in with his boss, confirm that he'd be in court in January and give himself a nice long lecture on the need to live in the real world, how life in Podunk, Nowhere, was just fogging his brain and that sex was sex—not a golden ticket to the magical world of happiness.

Figuring he had himself lectured into shape, he stepped into the hall. And winced. It was like walking into the BART station when the train was pulling through. Crazy loud, he saw Applebaum hadn't been kidding when he said everyone came to these meetings.

This was it. His chance to get a solid lead and solve this damn case. Before he ran out of lecture material.

"Detective."

He returned the greeting with a nod. And the next one, and the ten after that. He turned down three offers to save him a seat, two plates of cookies and a chance to hold someone's baby.

Still shuddering at the last offer, he approached the refreshment table.

"Coffee, black," the woman behind the table said as she handed him a large mug. "And I saved you a slice of gingerbread. Fresh this afternoon and still warm."

Nonplussed, he stared at the plate and mug for a second before taking them. "How'd you know—"

"Doesn't take more than two visits before I figure out someone's tastes," Lorna said with a big laugh that made her round belly jiggle. "Since you've eaten in my diner every night for the last week, I figure I've got yours down pat."

Not sure if that was a good thing, Diego muttered his thanks.

"Not that I'm trying to run business away," she continued, talking as she laid cookies out on plates, her hands as dark as the chocolate filling. "But there are plenty of people who'd be happy to have you to dinner. To show appreciation, you know. And, of course, to pump you for information."

Figured. Nine out of ten people who talked to Diego wanted something. Information on their case, something to fuel their gossip, dirty little secrets, tips on skirting the law. Or sometimes it was simple—they just wanted him to sign off on their traffic ticket.

"Appreciation for what?"

"Those obnoxious panty thefts have stopped since you came to town." Before Diego could deny credit for that, she continued, "As for information, well, you're the hottest catch in town, Detective. The married women want to know your romantic history and if you'd like to date their daughters, nieces or cute neighbor. The single women are wondering a whole lot more."

His jaw dropped.

Before he could figure out how to process that image, someone jostled his elbow.

"Oops, sorry, Detective. Lorna, give me one of those snickerdoodles, please, before my boy gets here and tries to eat them all up."

Mind still reeling, he stared blankly at Marion Kroger. The librarian frowned back, then gestured to Lorna for more cookies. "Well, this can't be fun for you. I'll bet you want to get home to your family, start celebrating the holidays. Have you given up on finding the silly pranksters yet?"

Brow creased, he watched her take a plate, piled high with a dozen glistening cookies. "I'll be here until the case is solved," he said.

"Oh, dear," Lorna exclaimed. "Even through the holidays? Not that I don't admire a man doing his job, but this is the time for family. Can't you come back after the first of the year? I'm sure people will still have panties missing in January."

"Nope. No family, so no problem seeing the case through. I'll solve the case before January, no problem," Diego assured Lorna.

Marion and Lorna both stared. Then, dark color washing her cheeks, the diner owner cleared her throat. "So, Marion. I see you have more family visiting. A whole truckload, from the looks of it. Are they all here for the holidays? Or to help you harvest your Clementine crop?"

"Oh, a little of both," Marion said before eating two cookies in rapid succession. "I wish you'd share your recipe for these, Lorna. They're about the best in the world. Detective, have you tried one?"

His intuition was zinging, the tiny hairs on the back of his neck standing on end. Why? While his mind replayed

the last few minutes, he automatically accepted the prof-
fered cookie.

Before he could hone in on what'd flipped his intuition
switch, or even take a bite of the cookie, there was a loud
commotion by the door. Gasps and yells, the sound of
chairs banging together, skidding across the floor.

Diego ran toward the back of the hall. Jade, Beryl and
Neal all chased into the room after a streak of black fur.

Snorting, Diego took his alert system down a notch.
This town had a crazy idea of just what constituted an
emergency. His eyes locked on Jade, who resembled a
fashionable butterfly. She looked totally out of place in her
body-hugging sweater dress, the cherry-red knit hugging
her slight curves from shoulder to knee. Paired with knee-
high suede boots and a matching black vest, she looked
totally rock-star-does-Christmas. Except he didn't figure
too many rock stars entered a room crouched low to the
ground, trying to catch a cat.

"I've got her," Neal yelled, sprinting toward the raised
dais, leaping and damn near landing on the frantic feline.
He landed on his knees. The cat launched itself into the
tall Christmas tree, scurrying through the branches. As she
got higher, Diego could see something dangling from her
mouth. Eyes narrowed, he tried to make out what it was.

"Neal, be careful," Beryl pleaded breathlessly, bending
low to rest her elbows on her knees and pant.

Apparently his idea of careful was to grab for the cat,
who growled, gave a spine-shuddering howl and reached
one paw out to take a swipe at him.

"You…" Face screwed into an expression of anger, his
mouth tight with embarrassment, the younger man grabbed
again. He missed the cat, but got hold of whatever was in
her mouth. He yanked. Hissing, the cat yanked back. He

pulled harder, making the whole tree lean ominously as onlookers yelped and cried out warnings.

"Don't hurt her," Jade yelped. "Just let her calm down. Then I can coax her out of the tree."

"You get her out now," Marion Kroger demanded. "Those are real cookies hanging there. Food products. They can't come into contact with a dirty cat."

Diego slanted the woman an ironic look. "What? And after hanging a few weeks from a tree that spent most of its life outside, they're gonna be edible?"

"That's not the point," the librarian said gruffly, red washing over her cheeks as she glared at the cat, who was now mewling pathetically about a foot over Diego's head.

Neal pulled again, snagging the white fabric away from the cat. Her mouth now empty, she tried to take a bite out of his hand instead. Cussing, he shook a bough.

"Neal!" Jade yelled, shoving at him so he let go of the tree. He stumbled. His fingers caught the ribbon of a dangling gingerbread man and yanked the tree sideways so it tilted precariously. The cat hissed, giving him a slit-eyed growl that made the hair on the back of Diego's neck stand on end.

"Enough," he commanded. "Jade, calm down. I'll get your cat."

A cat that was now perched somewhere around the ten-foot mark in that tree. Diego looked around, then pulled the heavy podium forward. He couldn't get it close enough to the tree, though, because Neal was in the way.

"What're you doing?" the guy asked, scurrying out of the way at Diego's arch look. Diego didn't bother to answer.

"Be careful," Jade said. He smiled at her. A mistake, since she smiled back.

"Here, son," the mayor said, holding out a broom.

"He gonna swat the cat out of the tree?" Neal asked, laughing.

"Balance," Diego said, wondering if he'd been that stupid at twenty. Since Jade was looking as if she might shove him again, Diego figured he'd better get the cat fast, before he had to arrest her.

Great. Just what he needed before he did a balancing-act cat rescue in front of half the town. The vision of Jade, in handcuffs.

Naked.

JADE WATCHED, her hands clenched against her churning belly, as Diego effortlessly vaulted onto the tall podium. She should be too worried for Persephone to be turned on over the way his biceps flexed. Tell it to the tingles, she decided since she didn't seem to have any control over her body's reactions when it came to the sexy cop.

Two days of avoiding him hadn't impacted her reaction one bit. Nor had the endless lectures. The man might be off-limits and out of her league—although she could get used to a dozen orgasms a night pretty easily—but she still wanted him.

Good thing she lived in the "you don't always get what you want" world.

On the edge of the podium, teetering dangerously, Diego stretched his arm up toward Persephone. The cat gave him a long look. Then she let go of whatever she'd been hauling around in her mouth to issue the saddest, most pathetic meow Jade had ever heard out of her.

Sniffles and sad *awes* filled the room. Someone rubbed a supportive hand over Jade's shoulder. Recognizing her sister's touch, she reached up to take her hand.

"Be careful," she cautioned Diego again, this time in a whisper. As if thinking the same, the entire room had hushed. She didn't have to glance behind her to know they were all staring, breaths held, as if their tense waiting would keep Diego from falling.

As Diego stretched higher, Neal scurried forward to grab whatever Persephone had dropped.

"They're just doll panties," he said with a laugh, holding up a pair of tiny cotton drawers with lace trim. "Looks like the cat probably dragged them off one of the Victorian carolers in front of the church. Guess we didn't need a fancy city cop to figure out who the Panty Thief is."

There was a scattering of laughter, but it died quickly. Jade was too afraid for Persephone to spare a glare to toss at Neal. But her growl elicited another shoulder pat from her sister. Whether Beryl's gesture was to keep the growl from growing into a threat or in sympathy, Jade didn't much care. She'd deal with the smart-ass who'd scared her cat up the tree later.

The fancy city cop was now standing on top of the podium, stretched dangerously high with one hand anchored on the broom handle the mayor held for balance. The other was lifted overhead, holding a small piece of cookie as bait for the terrified feline.

"Let's try for some quiet, please," the mayor requested, sounding his usual calm, controlled self. But his knuckles were white on the broom, a furrow of concern creasing his brow.

As usual, his loyal constituents fell in line, quieting the roar to a sibilant whisper punctuated by the occasional comment or cough. Jade, standing at the base of the dais, could now hear Diego's murmured encouragement.

"Aren't you the pretty kitty," he said softly, his words not carrying beyond Jade, Applebaum and the cat. "Did that dumb guy chase you? Aren't you uncomfortable up there? Bet you are. Come on down here. I'll give you a cookie."

As he soothed her cat, Jade finally tore her terrified gaze away from the hissing fur ball to look at Diego. His face was tense, his body pure muscled control. She recognized his cop mode, but beneath it was actual concern. For her cat.

Jade pressed her hand to her belly, promising herself the sinking feeling there was worry. Nothing crazier than that. Diego Sandoval was inspiration, eye candy and entertainment. But that was it.

"This is stupid. Can't we start the meeting already? The cat will be there when we're through. Probably come down on her own if we get on with things, instead of standing around like a bunch of dorks watching some hotshot cop show off."

"Neal!" A loud smack accompanied the exclamation.

It could have been the sudden noise, or maybe Neal's obnoxious comments, but Persephone started. With a loud growl, she scurried even higher up the tree, now teetering precariously at the very top, her paws wrapped around the gold star. The bough, slender and green, bent sideways. Ornaments crashed to the floor in a loud, shattering clamor.

"See what you did."

"Smack him again, Beryl," Jade muttered as her sister's admonishment was echoed through the room.

"Just saying it's stupid," Neal said, sounding as if he was pouting. "The cat's safe. She climbs trees all the time. I figure she must be happy up there, surrounded by all those decorations and stuff."

Diego ignored it all. Hand still stretched so high Jade figured he must be getting a shoulder cramp, he continued to murmur sweet endearments.

Suddenly the cat jumped. With a loud, miserable-sounding moan, she launched herself from the star toward Diego. Jade ran forward. The mayor bobbled the broom. Gasps and warnings chorused around the room.

Other than letting go of the broom so he had both hands outstretched, Diego didn't move. Which meant he was right there, in bull's-eye position, when Persephone landed on his chest.

Jade's knees almost gave out. Tears sprang to her eyes, relief pouring through her in a hot wave. Babbles, laughter, cries of relief all rang out. Bodies surrounded Jade, pushing her backward, farther away from the dais, her cat and her hero. On tiptoe, she could see Diego take someone's hand to get down from the podium. He kept the cat curled tight against his shoulder, though.

It took Jade a solid five minutes to make her way through the admiring throng. As soon as she was close enough, Jade's gaze raced over Diego, looking for scratches or punctures. He didn't appear to have a single one. Frowning, she shifted her look to the cat. Purring, Persephone's eyes were slatted, her tail curled around Diego's forearm and her paws resting comfortably on his chest.

She was safe. Unharmed. And so, so smug.

A gurgle of laughter, part relief and only slightly hysterical, escaped. Diego's eyes met hers.

"Thank you," she said, easing between a few more people so she could run her hand over the cat's silky fur.

"It was nothing."

Nothing? Neal had chased her cat through the streets, up a tree and Diego had saved her. That was hardly nothing.

Her mouth trembled. Her lips parted, just a bit, as she sighed. Then, forgetting that they had an audience, she stood on tiptoe and pressed a kiss to his cheek.

"You really are my hero," she whispered.

"I'm not anyone's hero. Never have been, never will be." His words were stiff, uncomfortable.

Maybe it was her ego talking, but to Jade, he sounded as if that fact might cause him a little bit of regret. Not enough that he'd bothered to call, though. Not that she cared. That's how things were in the big city. Itches got scratched, needs got met. All it added up to was a really good time.

"Don't try to tell my cat that," was all she said, though. Then she added, "I'm pretty sure she thinks you're her hero, too. Big-tree rescue, keeping the mob contained and stopping them from chasing her. And didn't I see you feeding her cookies? She's going to be yours for life now."

Diego ducked his head, making a show of glaring at the cat. Jade's lips twitched. He looked so cute when he was embarrassed. Whether it was the hero reference, or because he'd shown her multiple glimpses of heaven two nights ago, then spent the last couple of days trying to avoid her. Given the size of Diablo Glen, she'd been impressed with his success.

She supposed she should have been hurt, too. What girl wanted to be avoided like an STD after a hot, sexy night with a gorgeous guy? But she'd seen the fear on his face after the first time they'd made love on her hallway floor. And she'd seen the intense desire that'd replaced it. If she were a loner, hell-bent on going her own way without commitments or ties, she'd have left before sunup and played the avoidance game, too.

So what if she'd felt a little rejected when she'd woken up alone. And if she'd rolled over to tightly hug the pillow he'd slept on, it'd just been for a second. Just long enough to remind herself that he was her motivation. A role model to study, to figure out how to emulate so she could find a way out, too. What would that say about her if the instant she found someone who embodied everything she'd been wishing she herself could be, she started wishing he would change?

A heavy heart and empty bed? No big deal, she assured herself. To prove it, she gave Diego a friendly smile.

His frown deepened.

"Your cat is a menace," he told her, handing over the purring bundle of soft fur. "Do you always bring her to town meetings?"

Gathering Persephone close, Jade buried her nose in the purring cat's fur for a second before giving her a fierce look. Despite cats' fabled ability to land on their feet, she'd been terrified that her beloved pet was going to end up a splat on the podium.

"I try not to let her out of the house from Thanksgiving to New Year's. I came straight from the library, but she was locked up safe and sound when I left this morning."

His frown shifted in an instant, going all cop.

"Someone was in your house? Let's go."

Still holding the cat close, Jade laid one hand on his forearm. He froze. Went rock-still. Was that a good thing or bad? Without permission, her gaze dropped to his jeans. Did her touch turn him rock solid everywhere?

"No," she finally said, after a quick squint in the murky light didn't tell her one way or another. "My aunt was in town and said she'd drop off some packages for me to wrap. She probably forgot to keep Persephone inside."

He nodded. He didn't relax, though. If anything, he tensed up even more. Because now it was just them, she realized as her stomach sank into the toes of her Frye boots. They weren't talking about the cat rescue, or the need for him to pull out his detective's badge.

Her breath stuck somewhere in her chest, Jade sucked in her lower lip and sighed.

," she said, her words low and husky. Quiet, be-
 f the crowd encircling them. Afraid he'd think they
w   a come-on, she cleared her throat and tried again. "I
mean, can we talk?"

He looked as if she'd asked him if he wanted to strip
naked and climb back up the Christmas tree while sing-
ing "Grandma Got Run Over by a Reindeer."

"About the case," she said. If cop mode was all she
could have from him, she'd take it. At least until he realized she wasn't trying to lure him into anything. Not a
relationship, not a commitment. Not even her bed. "Or,
you know, we can just sit and I'll protect you from all the
matchmaking mommas who are eyeing you right now."

His cringe was infinitesimal, but she knew she'd hit her
target when he cast a wary eye around the room.

"I'm not interested in matchmaking," he said loud
enough to make a couple of matrons frown. Then he met
her gaze, his dark eyes serious, with just a hint of regret.
"Or in being matched."

Jade's expression didn't change as she slowly nodded.
Message received.

"I'm not either. But we can be friends, can't we?" she
asked quietly. Her heart trembled in her throat as she stared
into his eyes, waiting for his response. Hoping it'd be positive. She might not get to keep him forever, or even for a
little while. But couldn't she have him for just a little longer? Maybe just until Christmas, since he was her Christmas wish.

Because no matter how much her heart whined, she
didn't expect him to change. She'd given up too many
dreams for other people's good that the idea of someone
giving up even a portion of theirs for her filled her with
dread. Not even if it meant that he'd suddenly realized he
was insanely wild about her, and declared his life incom-

plete unless she climbed on that Harley behind him to ride off into the sunset.

"Got a solid hold on your cat?" he asked.

Jade blinked in confusion, but checked her grip on Persephone. "Yes?"

"Let's go then."

"Go?"

"Go talk."

_11_

DIEGO STOOD in the doorway, waiting while Jade checked all the windows and doors in her house to make sure the cat's escape had been an aunt-related error and nothing else.

She'd invited him in, but as much as he hated looking like an idiot, he hadn't felt it smart to go farther than the entry. Not until they'd established a few things.

So there he stood, looking at anything and everything except his own personal crime scene, aka her couch. But not looking didn't stop the memories of how she'd looked, naked beneath him. Of how her skin had felt, silky soft and sleek under his hands. Of how she'd tasted, rich and tempting against his tongue. The sounds she'd made echoed through his mind like the sweetest song, one he was desperate to hear, again and again.

But as long as he didn't look at the couch, he'd be okay. Like looking into that snake-headed gal's eyes…avoid them and he wouldn't be turned to stone.

Trying not to feel like a wimp, Diego gratefully greeted Persephone as she padded out of the kitchen to wrap around his ankles.

"You doing better now?" he murmured.

She meowed and looked up expectantly.

For what? He'd done his good deed for the day. Unless she was about to splat against a hard surface again, this was as close as they were getting.

He crossed his arms and stared. She stared right back.

He wasn't about to be intimidated into submission by something that weighed less than ten pounds.

She stood on her back legs, leaning both front paws against his knee. Then, in evil-cat fashion, she rubbed the side of her face against his leg.

"Crap."

Glancing around to make sure Jade wasn't nearby, he held out his hands. The cat plopped back on her butt and glared.

"Best offer," he told her. "Take it or leave it."

With a graceful leap, she took it. He tried not to grin as she curled against his chest as she'd done earlier, purring like a freight train.

"Told ya you were her hero," Jade said.

Diego damn near tossed the rumbling cat across the room. He hadn't heard her come in.

Jade didn't smirk, though. Instead, she looked serious. Like a woman who wanted to have a talk. His gut tightened, but avoiding the couch was about as chicken as Diego would allow himself.

"I think she's still stressed from her tree adventure," he defended, handing Jade her cat, despite the feline's protest. "No reason to think I'm a hero for just doing my job."

Jade gave him a long look before bending down to set the cat on the floor with a quick scratch behind her ears.

"I suppose 'hero' is just a part of the job description for you," she commented as she straightened. The move shifted the knit fabric so it slid temptingly over her body, hugging her waist, curving along the sleek lines of her hips. "But Persephone and I aren't used to heroes, so we think it's pretty special."

He remembered what Applebaum had said about her fiancé bailing at the last minute. Compared to a loser like that, he could see why someone who did the right thing might seem heroic to her. Diego frowned. But that didn't make him one.

"Look, we need to talk."

"Hmm, I'm pretty sure I said that already." Her tone stayed serious, but her eyes danced with humor as she gave him an arch look.

He'd sneaked out of her bed like a creep, turning an incredible night of passion into a cheap one-night stand. He'd spent two days avoiding her and hadn't had the courtesy of even acknowledging what an ass he'd been. And she wasn't pissed? As he crossed his arms over his chest, his frown shifted into a glower. What the hell was she up to?

"Did you want to sit down?" she invited, waving a hand toward the living room. Diego's gaze inadvertently followed to land on the blue velvet couch. The soft, tempting blue velvet couch.

"No."

"You'd rather stand here, in the hallway?" She still sounded serious enough, but her lips were twitching now.

Why was she so easygoing? He'd spent enough time in Diablo Glen, talked to enough people and heard enough gossip to know that Jade Carson didn't have guys sliding in and out of her bed.

So why wasn't she more, well, girlie about it?

Unless she was relieved.

Diego's ego cringed.

"I'd rather say what I have to say," he told her quickly, needing to get back on track before he gave in to his ego's need to prove his worthiness. "After I'm through, we'll see what's what."

She bit her lip as if debating whether or not she wanted to hear him. He figured not. But like broccoli and exercise, it'd be good for her. And for him, he admitted with a sigh. He wasn't a fan of opening up and sharing. But he owed her.

"I need your help on this case," he admitted, figuring that was the best place to start. A factual appeal to her civic duty.

"Again, I'm pretty sure I've made that offer already." She stepped around him, close enough that the floral scent of her twisted through his senses. It wasn't perfume, he remembered. It was her shampoo. Soft, like roses at midnight, with just a hint of citrus. She didn't touch him, though. Just moved past and settled onto the bench next to the front door.

"You didn't want to sit," she explained, "but my feet are killing me. These boots weren't made for chasing a cat through town."

Diego just nodded. He didn't want to get distracted, afraid that the minute they shifted into comfortable, friendly chatter he'd forget why he'd agreed to talk.

"I need your help," he repeated. "But we need to establish some parameters."

"You want my help, and you want to make sure I agree to follow your rules before you let me give it?" she clarified, finally showing a crack in her friendly shell. Anger sparked, making her eyes flash like brilliant emeralds.

When she put it that way, his request sounded so arrogant. Then again, there was a good reason why he was a loner. He didn't do this talking crap very well.

"Look, I told you that I'm up for a promotion. Getting it means a lot to me," he explained, biting back the impatience and trying to sound reasonable. "But for that to happen I have to stick tight to regulations on this case. Sleeping with someone connected to the case falls in the category of flipping off the spirit of the regulations, even if it doesn't break the actual rules."

When her eyes rounded, he wondered if he'd gone too far. Maybe he should have sugarcoated his comments? But her complacent sweetness was digging at his ego.

"So sleeping with me was a bad career move? Is that why you sneaked off without even a goodbye? The reason you've avoided me the last two days? Because you're afraid of upsetting your boss?"

He winced. When she put it that way, it sounded pretty rotten. But, again, she didn't look hurt. Or pouty or upset or about to throw a tantrum. None of the typical female responses. He narrowed his eyes, suddenly more worried than he'd have been if she'd hefted a big-ole frying pan toward his head. Instead, she looked like a woman who'd just grabbed the gauntlet. Not good.

Like a clever cat stalking a wily mouse, Jade stood. The slow smile curving her lips was wicked. Wicked enough to make him forget she was a good girl. To forget he didn't do small towns, that he didn't do good girls and that he wouldn't be around long enough to get his fill of her, even if he forgot all the rest.

She took three steps forward, close enough for him to feel her body heat. With no input from his brain at all, his body leaned toward hers. He craved the feeling of her soft warmth again. The memory of her breasts crushed against his chest filled his mind. Sent the blood pounding through him to energize—and harden—his entire system. He craved the taste of her. He needed to touch her. He desperately wanted to strip her bare and worship every inch of her before driving the hard, throbbing length of himself into her waiting heat.

Diego tried to swallow, but his mouth was too dry. At that moment if his promotion sprouted wings and flew around his head screaming warnings, he'd have swatted it away.

Then, with that innate instinct some women had, Jade seemed to realize that he'd hit his breaking point.

And she used that exact moment to lean in just a little closer. So the flowery-citrus scent of her shampoo filled his senses. So close he could see the creamy perfection of her skin and know for sure that her lush black lashes were a gift from Mother Nature, not Maybeline.

So close he could reach out with one bite and eat her up if he wanted.

And man, oh, man, he wanted.

The look in her eyes warned him that she'd bite right back. And there'd be nothing sensual about her move.

"Look, hotshot," she said, tapping her silver-tipped red fingernail against his chest three times. "I've already taken the ride, so I can say firsthand that you're amazing in bed. The key to hearing angels sing, even."

His ego purred.

"But?"

Because he knew there was a *but* there. One that would probably make him look like an ass.

"But I don't have to chase a man to get him into my bed. Nor do I have to trick him or trap him or play some silly game to keep him there…." Her pause was a work of art, drawn out just long enough to make it clear who she thought had played the game. Then she tilted her head to the side, so her hair swept like a silken wave over her shoulder. "And I promise, if we end up naked together again, it'll be because you begged me."

This time when her gaze swept his body, it was as electrifying as if she'd skimmed her fingers over his hard, bare flesh. Despite the cool air, a trickle of sweat slid down Diego's spine.

"And if that happens," she continued, her tone as arch as the look she gave him, "I promise, I won't be as easy on you as I was last time."

He couldn't help but be impressed. He'd never been put so tidily in his place. Even as his brain flashed danger signals, his bruised ego demanded a chance to prove itself. His body was aching to let it have its way. Begging was looking pretty damn good.

He was insanely attracted to her big eyes and the appeal of her dimples. Her body was a gorgeous combination of curves and sleek lines. And those legs. His mouth watered just thinking about how they'd felt wrapped around his hips. Throw in her taste in underwear and she was just about the sexiest woman he'd ever met.

But he was pretty sure it was her smart-ass mouth and clever mind that attracted him the most.

A scary thing for a man who prided himself on the fact that the few relationships he'd ever had were emotionally distant and completely superficial.

"I'd beg for you," he said, putting it all out there because she deserved nothing less. "But that'd be a mistake. A big one. For both of us."

Her eyes flashed hot and excited at his vow to beg, then dimmed as she frowned.

"A mistake? We were pretty freaking awesome together." The crease in her brow deepened as she tilted her head to the side. "Weren't we?"

"Yeah. We were. But I'm short-term. As soon as I solve this case, I'm leaving," he reminded her. If nothing else, he had to know he'd been honest. He might not be able to give her hearts and flowers and forever. But he could give her honesty. Well, honesty and the most incredible sex she'd ever had. Except he shouldn't be thinking about the incredible sex, he reminded his hardening body. He shouldn't be angling to have it again and again and again.

But he was.

"You're going to do your best to solve the case as fast as possible. Which means you'd feel guilty, like you were doing a hit-and-run, if we kept getting naked together," she stated. No recriminations, no pouting. Just simple understanding. Diego swore, if he believed in love, he'd have fallen for her right then and there. The woman was incredible.

As if she'd read his thoughts and figured it was time to step up the game and show him a whole lot of you-ain't-seen-nothing-yet, Jade offered a slow, sexy smile.

"You really are a hero, aren't you?"

"I am not," he snapped, offended. Not offended enough to blunt his desire for her, though. Maybe if she insulted his manhood or disused Harleys, his hard-on would ebb.

"Sure you are. You're worried about me. You want me, but you need to do the right thing. So instead of begging like you'd like, you're going to push this—" she waved her fingers between their bodies, as if indicating invisible, yet potent, flames of desire "—away and pretend it's not flaming between us. Sort of like you sneaked out of my bed the other day."

He opened his mouth to deny sneaking, then snapped it shut and gave a bad-tempered shrug instead.

"You don't want a purely sexual relationship," he told her, even though he hoped he was wrong.

"Nope," she agreed. "I don't."

Diego nodded. See. He'd been right. It felt like getting

kicked in the nuts, then force-fed liver and onions. But hey, right was right, even if it felt like crap.

"But I wouldn't mind an honest, open sexual relationship with a gorgeous man," she mused out loud. Her words were light and easy. The look in her eyes was intense and searching. "A friendship, hanging out together, maybe a few dates. No promises, no regrets."

"A relationship?" he hazarded, not sure since he'd never really had one. Didn't they come with requirements, though? Like no guaranteed expiration date.

"A relationship," she agreed, biting her lip and looking afraid for a second. Then she took a deep breath, as if gathering her courage. And gave him a smile that sent every concern, every argument, clear out of his head.

"Just like that?" he asked, realizing that feeling in his chest was hope. Almost afraid to believe, he gently settled his fingers on the slender curve of her hips. She felt so good, he silently groaned, giving in to the need to pull her closer. To feel her body, warm and soft, against his.

"Just like that."

His eyes locked on hers, he slowly—so, so slowly—lowered his head to hers. A second before he could kiss her, she pulled back a tiny bit.

"Except for one thing," she said.

Just one? He could think of a million things he'd do, offer, promise, to have her.

"Anything," he promised, meaning it.

"Say please," she whispered against his lips, her eyes lit up with wicked glee. Then she ran her tongue, hot and wet, over his lower lip.

"Please," he groaned just before taking her mouth with desperate, biting kisses.

Begging, his mind intoned. It does a body good.

HOW COULD A FULLY CLOTHED, nonsexual encounter have
her just as hot and bothered as a totally naked, decadently
sensual exploration? Jade wondered. A week of hot, wild
sex should have blunted her need for Diego, shouldn't it?
Or at least put a dent in the clawing desperation to lick
his hard…muscles.

Sitting on her living room floor, carols playing softly
in the background as the tree lights flashed gentle colors,
Jade was surrounded by wrapping, ribbons and glitter.
All of which usually made her very happy. Dressing up
a package was almost as fun as dressing up a person. At
least, it usually was.

Today? She was so distracted, she'd wrapped Mayor
Applebaum's cherry pipe box in Valentine's paper with
a green bow before she'd realized what she was doing.

All she could think of was Diego. If she wasn't reveling in the incredibly erotic feel of the hard length of him
inside her, or of how good it felt to slide down his body,
curl her fingers into the scattering of hair across his chest
and hold on while he took her for another wild ride, she
was reliving it in her head.

She'd known when she'd invited him to continue their
sexual relationship that she'd been asking for trouble. Sexy
trouble, to be sure. But trouble all the same. But she'd figured it'd be worth it.

What she hadn't known—couldn't have expected—
was to find out she liked him. Just flat-out liked spending
time with him, talking to him, laughing together. They'd
spent the last few days becoming, well, friends. He'd decided to lull the Panty Thief into complacency while still
keeping a close eye on things. So they'd attended the high
school's performance of Scrooge and the kindergarten re-
cital of *The Nutcracker.* They'd gone to dinner, met Beryl
and Neal for coffee, run into her mother and the mayor at

the high school movie showing of *Grinch* and hit every boutique sale the senior ladies of Diablo Glen had to offer.

She'd loved every second of it.

And so, she suspected, had Diego.

And that was the scary thing.

"You're out of cat treats," he told her, coming into the living room. Having spent the past morning in Fresno testifying in court, he was dressed more formally than she'd seen him before. Black slacks and a black dress shirt gave him a dangerous air, especially when combined with the gun holstered at the back of his waist.

"A can of treats usually lasts her three months," Jade pointed out as she carefully measured a length of paper against a big box. "Someone has been spoiling her."

Diego's grin flashed as he settled into the wicker rocker.

"I don't have to spoil her. She likes me." As if to prove his point, the cat padded out of the kitchen, still licking what was probably treat crumbs off her whiskers. She jumped onto Diego's knee, sniffed at the cup of coffee in his hand, then curled into a purring ball in his lap.

He arched a brow and grinned. "See."

Despite her dismissive eye roll, Jade was touched.

"So what's the deal?" he asked all of a sudden. "Did someone post a sign claiming my lack of family? Suddenly, everyone's trying to mother me. Or offering fatherly advice. Or worse, wanting to be my big brother or little sister. It's the weirdest thing I've ever experienced."

"I think it's sweet," Jade said, tucking her heels under her hips and rocking from side to side to settle into the pillow before pulling a large box toward her. "You know, for a guy who was so dismissive of small towns when you got here a week and a half ago, you're sure fitting in well."

"Just acclimating to build trust and break the case," he said dismissively.

Not an easy thing to do, given that after Persephone had been caught with the doll panties six days ago, most everyone in town figured her for the Panty Thief. Except the mayor, who refused to consider the case closed and set Diego free. Since Diego didn't believe that, either—after all, how many cats trashed bedrooms?—he hadn't argued much.

But Jade knew he was frustrated.

"Is that why I saw you working on Marion Kroger's car the other day?" she asked, teasing him out of the bad mood she could see him teetering on.

"Her engine wouldn't start," he said, staring into his coffee cup instead of meeting her amused gaze. "She had a trunkful of groceries that would have gone bad if she'd waited for a tow truck."

"I heard you followed her home, just to make sure she was safe."

He squirmed. Big bad cop squirmed. Jade pressed her lips tight to keep from giggling.

"Nobody likes melted ice cream at Christmas," he muttered. Then he gave her a questioning look. "She's got a lot of property out there, though. I didn't realize how big her orchards were. How does she handle all that, with just her and Neal to work it?"

"It is big, isn't it? I don't know how she does it, but she's making great money. Enough that she offered to buy Neal and Beryl a house as a wedding gift."

"Here?"

Wouldn't that have been nice? Jade swallowed the bitterness that coated her throat. A house, here in Diablo Glen, would have set Jade free.

"No. Neal wants to head down south. I guess it's always been his dream to live somewhere warmer."

Diego gave her a long look. Leaning over to set his cup

on the table, he irritated the cat, who jumped off his lap. With a growl and a glare, Persephone stalked over to the tree and curled up there.

"Why aren't you chasing your own dreams?" he asked, his words short, verging on angry. As if her being stuck here was a problem for him somehow.

"I have a life here."

"Not the one you want."

Jade focused all her attention on getting the bright red ribbon tugged and pulled so all the loops were even. It was hard to see them through the teary haze in her eyes, though.

"It's the life I've built, though," she finally said when she was sure her expression was serene. Meeting his dark, troubled gaze, she smiled. "Hey, I'm doing great. I have a secure job that, thanks to my grandmother leaving me this cottage, pays well enough to keep me in designer shoes. I have a wonderful family close by. A growing reputation as an It Stylist on the internet, thanks to Polypore. I'm even teaching a class at the college after the first of the year."

Deciding the bow was good enough, she snipped the ribbon at an angle, then tugged the ends into place before clapping her hands together to indicate a job well done.

"It sounds like a pretty good life to me," she insisted.

"But is it the life you want to be leading?" Without being asked, he hefted the now-decorated box and carried it to the tree, then grabbed another and set it in front of her to wrap.

Could he be any more perfect? He knew her needs, met them, without her saying a word. Just being with him made her happier than she'd ever imagined feeling. Her heart ached at the idea of what life would be like when he left. And he was worried that she wasn't leading the life she wanted?

Jade's smile hurt, but she didn't let it slip. Why should she? He cared enough to be angry for her. The least she could do was fake it enough to soothe that anger.

"Diego, sometimes it doesn't matter how good you are, how nice. Santa just can't bring you what you want." Which was why it was better to just not ask. It hurt less that way. "Unless you want to be miserable, it's smarter to figure out how to turn that lump of coal in your stocking into a diamond."

Or at least a chunk of prettily cut glass.

"I think it's crap."

Jade laughed.

"Seriously. You should be in San Francisco. Los Angeles. Hell, New York." He didn't sound very enthusiastic about that last one, though. "Somewhere that you could shine."

"I'm shiny enough here. Shinier, in fact, since I don't have much competition." Jade ran the strings of the gift tag through her fingers, twisting and untwisting the ends until the twine frayed. Finally, she gave a little shrug and met his angry gaze. "I can't leave. I thought I might, someday. But I can't."

He leaned forward, his shoulders hunched as if preparing to argue. Then he paused and looked closer at her face. Jade tensed. She hated confrontations. Someone's feelings always got hurt. And it didn't seem to matter if it was hers or the other person's, either way she felt horrible.

As usual, though, Diego surprised her. Instead of pushing the topic, all he said was, "Sometimes you need to put yourself first, Jade. People who love you? They'll understand."

Jade twirled the silver curling ribbon around her finger,

then unwired it again. He was right. They would understand. But if she left to chase her dreams, someone else would have to give up theirs.

"And sometimes you learn to be grateful for the little things. Love means understanding why someone needs to leave, and letting them do it," she said, looking up to stare into the hypnotic depths of his eyes and baring her soul. "And every once in a while, it means being okay with giving up the dream so the people you love can have theirs."

If that wasn't enough to make a girl want to haul on the Grinch costume, she didn't know what was. Because her heart felt three times too big for her chest. He made her want more. Made her wish she could just grab on and demand more.

From her life.

From herself.

And from him.

12

DIEGO FONDLY REMEMBERED a time, not so long ago, when he'd known what to expect from life. People sucked, he could only count on himself and black clouds were the norm.

Ah, those were the good old days.

Now? Here in Diablo Glen?

Friendly residents acted as if he was one of their own, trying to include him in all sorts of cheerful holiday happenings. He'd lost his pen the other day and five people offered theirs. The last time he'd stepped into the diner, two customers had offered to buy his coffee. And despite the chilly December weather, it seemed like sunshine was the rule of the day.

It was freaky.

Freakier still was that he was starting to like it. Sort of. Or, he admitted as he dismounted his Harley, maybe that had something to do with Jade. What was with her? It was as if she was coated with some invisible magnetic substance. No matter how much he told himself to pull away, he couldn't. She was sexy. She was sweet. She was fun and clever and smart.

She was the woman he hadn't realized he'd been dreaming of. And now that he'd found her? Letting her go was going to be worse than being kicked out of every foster home he'd lived in, worse than watching his mother's back as she left him yet again. Because unlike the people who'd bounced in and out of his childhood, Jade was the real deal.

He was walking a tightrope already with his feelings. Her sweetness, her sass and her lingerie had all hooked him good. But the explosive power between them in bed had reached inside, to a place he hadn't even realized was there, and grabbed hold. He was terrified that if he wasn't careful, the minute he slid inside her again, he'd grab hold and never let her go. Drag her to San Francisco with him, promising her anything to get her to go.

Because she was so deeply rooted in this little town, taking her with him would require handcuffs, his sidearm and enough Christmas cookies to put her into a sugar coma.

And she'd still come back.

Shoulders hunched against that depressing reality, and not sure what to expect from Applebaum's summons, Diego stepped through the diner door. He looked around in surprise. A quick head-count estimate put the room at over thirty people. What? Every family in town had a body here for lunch? And what did it say about him that he recognized all of them?

Except the Hispanic couple in the far booth, he realized, narrowing his gaze and trying to place them. Definitely not from around here. He wondered if their car had broken down. They had the look of people who'd traveled a long way by foot.

"Hey, Detective," Carly greeted, a menu in one hand, her tray in the other. The pretty little redhead looked as if she should be in home ec. class instead of working tables. But Diego knew she was a mother of two, and if rumor was right, would have another stocking on the mantel next year. "The mayor's waiting for you at the back table."

The back table meant walking through the diner-filled sea of staring patrons. But unlike most places he was used to walking through, the stares weren't angry or hostile. They weren't coldly assessing. They were welcoming, most with cheerful greetings and a couple of friendly waves. Some were a little too friendly. He subtly shifted away from the table full of lunching moms all staring at his jeans as if their eyes were measuring tapes.

"The mayor's having the lunch special," Carly offered over her shoulder. "I can bring you the same. Or Lorna's got some of that corned beef you like. She'd be happy to make you a Reuben. Just let me know."

Debating, Diego glanced at the menu board. A one-pound meat-stuffed Asiago roll with a side of frings? Maybe he should find out who was next-in-charge in case Applebaum had a heart attack from eating that sucker.

"The Rueben sounds good," he decided.

They reached the booth set to the far back of the diner, at least five empty tables away from anyone else. Before he'd settled his butt on the soft fabric, Carly was back with a cup of coffee.

"You've got a strange town here," Diego said after the waitress had left to fill their order. "A whole bunch of people got their underwear stolen, the thief is still at large, and they don't seem to care."

"The thefts have stopped," Applebaum pointed out.

"The thief hasn't been."

"And that's bothering you?"

Diego looked at the older man as if he'd lost a few

marbles. "Of course it is. I'm a cop. I was hauled here to solve a crime."

Applebaum sipped his coffee, watching Diego over the edge with narrowed eyes. "You're pissed."

"I didn't say that."

"Okay. Frustrated, irritated, stymied." He took another sip, but before Diego could find that tact he'd been warned he'd need, the mayor continued. "You're trying to figure out why I won't just cut you loose, since the crime—such as it is—seems to have hit a dead end."

"Your side job as a fortune-teller must come in handy come election time," Diego said, wondering why he wasn't more irritated. Everything the old man said was true. He should be stressed and anxious, furious to get done with this and get on with his promotion, his move and his life.

Except getting on with any of that started with saying goodbye to Jade. Diego stared into the murky liquid of his cup and sighed. Life had been better when he hadn't cared. It'd hurt less, and he was pretty sure his spine had been stronger.

"Why are you keeping me here?" he finally asked. Both to avoid the other points, and because he was actually curious.

Applebaum gave a low hum, then gestured with his cup.

"You see a lot of the ugly side of life in your line of work."

In his work. In his life. Same difference.

Something to remember. Definitely not the kind of life he should be wishing Jade wanted to check out.

"I guess I do. Crime's usually committed by ugly people."

"I guess it'd be hard to shift views, then. To see the good in people. See the possibilities and understand the motivation behind the foibles."

Diego had never had a guiding figure in his life. No dad to pass down wisdom. No counselor to motivate and inspire. So it was weird to suddenly find himself looking up to an older man, wishing he could embody some of the guy's wisdom. Wanting, just a little, to ask for advice.

Stupid. Applebaum was practically a stranger. One Diego would be saying goodbye to as soon as possible.

Diego cleared his throat, his gaze dropping to the smooth varnish on the wooden table. Time to change the subject.

"I have to say that you have a disturbing lack of perverts in this town," he said after a second. And he was truly bothered by that. Dirty old men, degenerates and moralless lowlifes were his stock-in-trade. But if there were any in Diablo Glen, they hid it well. Not just well enough to slide past his radar, but so well that they'd fooled the entire town.

"We have our share of characters. But most people looking for that kind of thrill have to go outside town to find dirt and kink. Still…" The mayor paused, giving Diego a long, searching look. Resisting the urge to squirm, Diego consciously cleared his mind of any and all kinky thoughts as they related to Jade. Which took him a couple of seconds.

"Still," the mayor continued, "we are seeing crime rise. Unlike the last decade, when more people moved away than were born here. Now the town is growing. Young families, kids who couldn't find jobs—or those thrills—in the city stay here, plus a few relatives who are looking for a nice place to retire."

Diego had watched enough baseball to recognize a windup. He wasn't sure where it was going, though. So he leaned back in the cushioned seat, waiting for the pitch.

"The neighboring towns are seeing the same thing. Between us, Barkerville and Middleton, we've seen our populations grow by a quarter in the last two years. There's no sign of that slowing down." Applebaum paused to take a deep, appreciative gulp of coffee, staring at Diego the whole time. Looking for what? "Given that, we're strongly considering not renewing our contract with the county for protection and starting our own police department instead."

Kerthud. His heart gave one strong slam against his chest. Possibilities swirled. None had anything to do with his personal career goals or ambitions. All had to do with what he was feeling for Jade. How had this happened? After a week and a half together, he was thinking about a future? Wondering how to mesh his job and her commitment to her hometown?

He had to force himself not to leap from the booth and race right out of town.

Just to prove he could.

"Me? I'm getting older. Not so old I can't take good care of Diablo Glen. But I'm starting to think there's more to life than the job," Applebaum mused aloud, staring out the window for a second. Then, as if snapping out of a reverie, he gave Diego an unreadable look. "I might be shifting a little of my focus, and I could use someone here in town that I can count on."

Someone was keeping secrets, Diego realized with a narrow look of his own. And keeping them damn well, since they hadn't surfaced on the town gossip wires. Curiosity, once only inspired by crime, flared in Diego's mind. What was the good mayor up to? Or should that be who?

"We just finished up the nail-down-the-details stages, me and the other two mayors," Applebaum said quickly, as if realizing he'd let on too much. "We're ready to start considering who we want as the chief of police. I think we'd be interested in chatting with you, boy."

As far as distractions went, that was aces.

Chatting. Diego resisted the urge to run his finger around the collar of his T-shirt to feel for noose fibers.

He was saved from responding by the waitress, who carried a tray much too huge for two sandwiches. The smile he gave her was so grateful, she blinked a couple of times before turning a soft shade of pink.

Then she swung the tray off her shoulder. Diego stared in shock. His sandwich was flat as a pancake compared to the mayor's.

"Is that a serving platter?" he asked as the waitress set the oval dish in front of Applebaum.

"That, my boy, is a delight to the senses." While the waitress unloaded her tray and refilled their coffee, Applebaum waxed poetic about his lunch choice. A strategic master, the mayor had cast out the bait. Now he was patiently waiting to see if Diego bit. And scarfing down the world's largest sandwich at the same time. The old guy was good at multitasking.

He'd be a good man to work for, Diego mused.

Shit. Appetite gone, Diego had to force himself to lift his tiny-looking sandwich to his mouth.

He might as well admit it. As much as he wanted to solve this case, snag his promotion and get the hell out of this tiny claustrophobic town... He didn't want to leave Jade.

"JADE?"

Jade set lacy cookies on a white doily, carefully widening the circle of sweet treats as if one millimeter of difference from one to the next would ruin her mother's annual holiday open house.

Since the gift-wrapping discussion two days before, she'd been avoiding Diego. In part because she felt as if he'd turned on her. No longer the sexiest adventure she'd ever had, he'd become a reminder of everything she didn't have. Which would soon include him and his incredible body, dammit.

"Jade?"

Why was he still here? She slammed the empty plastic container on the counter with the others, then grabbed a full one to start setting out fudge. Why didn't he call the case done, like everyone else had, and go? Just go.

What'd started out as a fun way to experience freedom and a little fun now felt like a prison. A tempting, orgasm-inducing prison.

It was enough to make a girl want to cry. Or—Jade shifted to ease the discomfort the waistband of her jeans were causing as they dug into her side—cause her to eat way too much chocolate.

"Jade!"

She jumped, and the fudge flew from her fingers to stick against her mother's kitchen wall with a dull thud. Jade's chocolate-covered fingers were halfway to her heart before she remembered she was wearing white.

"What?" she exclaimed breathlessly. "Why are you two yelling at me?"

Ruby and Beryl exchanged looks, with the eldest sister shaking her head and the youngest frowning with irritation.

"I've been calling your name for the last two minutes," Ruby said as she wiped her hands on a tea towel before stepping around the island toward Jade. "What's wrong?"

"Nothing."

Ruby arched both brows before tucking the towel into the waistband of her clearly not-too-tight skirt. For the first time, Jade wondered if her sister's perfect size three was due to regular married sex and a non-Diablo Glen zip code.

"Something is wrong," Ruby insisted. Then, ever the big sister, she shifted her gaze to Beryl, who was arranging cheese on a tray and wearing her own frown. "With both of you. What's the deal? I've been toting the good-humor banner all by myself this morning. Why are you two such grumps?"

"We're not grumps," Jade said in chorus with Beryl. She shared a smile with her younger sister, then realized that Ruby might be right. At least, as far as Beryl was concerned. The younger girl had dark circles under eyes that looked a little swollen. "Beryl? What's up?"

"Just like you said. Nothing."

Using Ruby's tea towel, Jade wiped the chocolate off her fingers, then off the wall. And debated. She knew her problem—kissing a dream goodbye combined with sexual frustration. But Beryl looked, well, sad. But the sisterly law of fairness said that if she wanted to prod her sibling, she had to offer up her own woes in exchange.

"See," Jade said as she turned to face Ruby, all the pieces of the fudge cleaned up. "We're fine."

Ruby split her irritated look between the two of them, then gave a jerk of her shoulder. "Fine? Be pouty and grumpy. See if I care."

"Since you're bossy, pouty and grumpy were the only T-shirts left," Jade quipped as she returned to arranging candy on her mother's favorite two-tiered Waterford server.

"Good thing they fit so well, then," Ruby groused. She glared at her sisters for a couple more seconds, as if her angry frown could scare confessions out of them. Then she threw both hands in the air and returned to the turkey she'd been slicing.

Adding peppermint fudge to the chocolate, Jade forced her expression to stay cheerful. She wasn't surprised that it actually hurt her face.

Not nearly as good at faking happy—why should she be, when Jade was the big faker in the family?—Beryl sniffled.

"Okay, that's enough," Ruby snapped. "I want to know what the hell is going on. You'd better just tell me now because I won't quit nagging until you do. You aren't ruining Mom's party with these crappy moods."

"Beryl, what's wrong?" Jade asked, setting the finished candy dish on the counter before moving to her little sister's side. "Sweetie, you're so unhappy."

All it took was an arm around her slender shoulders to turn Beryl into a crying puddle of mush. She clutched her sister, making Jade wince as her fingers dug into the delicate crochet of her knee-length vest.

"Neal and I had a fight," she sobbed into Jade's neck. "That's all we do lately. Fight."

"What are you arguing about?"

"He wants to move away. He's obsessed with going south, somewhere by San Diego or El Centro. His mom hates me—she must because she won't let me come out to their house. He is snappy and moody all the time—" she paused to suck in a breath, then before either of her sisters could say anything, she finished in a sob "—and I think he's cheating on me."

Jade blinked a few times, trying to process the laundry list of fighting topics. She gave their older sister a questioning look. Engaged couples fought all the time, didn't they? Well, she and Eric hadn't, but she didn't think they were the stellar example of a successfully engaged couple. Not when marriage was the final test, at least. So she didn't know. Were these normal reasons? Ruby's frown said this was something to worry about, though.

Her stomach tumbled at the concern on her sister's face. She pulled Beryl into a tighter hug.

"Why do you have to move away?" Ruby asked, tackling the easiest issue first as she rubbed Beryl's knee. "You love Diablo Glen. Both of you have family here, there are jobs and the real estate is more reasonable here than in most of California."

"He wants somewhere else. South, closer to Mexico. I still have a semester left of college and I kinda wanted to stay here for a while. Just, you know, to give it a chance before trying something else."

For one second—admittedly a bitter-tasting second—Jade wondered what it was like to have that sort of freedom. To only worry about what you wanted to do, where you wanted to be. Then, like dirty laundry and ugly shoes, she hid the thought away where she didn't have to see it, think about it or admit to having it.

"There's nothing wrong with staying here when you're through with school. Just for a while, to try it out," Ruby said.

"If you want to stay, tell him," Jade suggested. "You're building a life together, which means you get equal say. Don't give up what you want without a fight."

There it went, Jade's mental fraud meter, dinging out of control again. She really needed to live the life she preached one of these days.

"What if he says no?"

"Then maybe he isn't the guy for you," Jade said gently, giving her sister's hand a sympathetic squeeze. "But if he loves you, he's going to listen. He's going to understand why you want to stay here."

"Do you really think so?" Beryl asked with a flutter of wet lashes.

"Of course, sweetie," Ruby assured, giving her a tight hug.

"Heck, if you were staying for a while, you could have my place while you decided," Jade muttered. Her eyes rounded when, at her sisters' stares, she realized she'd said that aloud.

"Where would you live?" Ruby asked.

"Somewhere. Maybe somewhere else, you know." Jade shrugged. Excitement spun in circles in her tummy at the idea of time, even just a little bit, to spread her wings again. Only this time, instead of seeing herself clubbing and making her fashion mark in a big city, she was cuddled up on a couch looking out a window at the cityscape, Diego's arms holding her close.

Pain, sharp and jagged, cut through her. Since when had he replaced her dream of happiness? And how stupid was she to have not stopped her heart before it got this close to danger.

"What's the deal?" Beryl pulled back to get a better look at her sister's face. "Is it that sexy cop? Is he why you'd give up your house?"

"I wouldn't give anything up for a man," Jade exclaimed. Well, anything besides her heart, her panties, her body, her dreams. All that minor stuff.

"You love your house," Beryl said, shaking her head. "I couldn't take it."

Knowing Beryl would guilt herself into moving out of town rather than take the cottage and inconvenience her, Jade rushed to say, "Maybe I could try something else. You know, somewhere else."

As soon as the words were out she bit her lip, as if she should pull them back in.

Ruby exchanged a long look with Beryl this time. Both sisters settled their butts more firmly in their chairs, as if gearing up for battle. Both folded their hands together on the tabletop and, damn them, both gave Jade identical knowing looks.

"You want to leave." Ruby made it a statement, not a question. "Why haven't you said something before?"

Tracing an invisible design on the hardwood with her fingertip, Jade stared at the table instead of answering.

"She did say something about checking into jobs in San Francisco. Wasn't it last spring that you mentioned it?" her little sister asked.

Jade's shoulder twitched.

"And then I got engaged and said I was moving out of town," Beryl realized.

"And you figured you had to stay for good. Be here to take care of Mom," Ruby realized.

"You both had other stuff going on," Jade said, trying to make it sound as if it didn't really matter one way or the other.

"Saint Jade, always sacrificing." Ruby sighed, her tone somewhere between exasperated and angry.

"You both have lives outside town," Jade defended, irritated that her, yes, sacrifice was so unappreciated. "You've got a job and a life and Berry's got school and a future to build. I had, what? An underpaid internship and a ton of student loans. It makes sense for me to stay here." Sweet girl that she was, Beryl nodded. Ruby just rolled her eyes.

"Do you think Mom would want you giving up your dreams? Because, what?" she asked, the exasperation gone and anger taking full hold. "You have to babysit her?"

"I'm not babysitting," Jade snapped. Then, leaning forward so far her butt left the chair, she glared at her sister. "And don't you dare say anything to her."

Ruby shifted, too, so their glares were nose-to-nose. Before she could respond, though, the doorbell chimed. As one, the sisters winced and glanced at the cookie-shaped clock above the stove.

"Guests." With one last shake of her head, Ruby rose and gave Jade a narrow look. "We're not through with this."

"She's mad at herself," Beryl pointed out quietly as Ruby swept from the room. "You know Ruby. If someone's going to score the major sacrifice points, she wants it to be her." Jade's laugh was weak. So were her knees, because she knew damn well Ruby would follow through with her threat. They'd be having that talk, and as far as confrontations went, Jade figured it was going to be an ugly one.

"But just so you know, as soon as she's through with the sacrifice lecture, I want all the details on you and the hottie cop," Beryl said. It was clear from her tone that she knew she was adding punishment on top of punishment. It was just as clear from her smile that she was enjoying the idea.

Jade almost growled.

"Darlings," Opal said as she wheeled into the kitchen, her bright red scooter decorated with holly and pine boughs, her face so bright and cheerful she looked like a three-wheeled Christmas decoration. "People are arriving and you've spent enough time in the kitchen. Now, join me so we can celebrate the holidays."

Grateful for an excuse to run away, even if just for a few hours, from the box of worms they'd opened, Jade leaped to her feet and gathered as much food as she could hold to carry it into the dining room.

The Carson Family Open House was in its twentieth year, and the girls all knew the drill. Greet everyone and make sure they had food. Socialize with everyone and make sure they had more food. Keep everyone chatting with everyone else, and, again, make sure they had food. Opal Carson had a moral objection to anyone leaving her party anything less than stuffed till they groaned.

The sisters went their separate ways, and for once Jade was grateful for her mom's divide-and-conquer hostessing rule. She was kept busy enough to avoid even looking at her sisters. But there weren't enough people in all Diablo Glen to keep her from glancing toward the door every few minutes, hoping Diego would walk through. She'd invited him. Opal had invited him. She'd even heard the mayor invite him. Two hours into the party, she glanced at her watch. Shouldn't he be here by now?

"Did you hear the latest?" Mrs. Green asked, stubbornly standing with her crackers and cheese instead of sitting comfortably. "Applebaum got the go-ahead on the local police department. He and his crony mayors really did it."

"I'd heard that rumor." Almost a dozen people at the party alone had mentioned it. It was gossip, yes, but Jade knew most had said it as encouragement. Her seeing Diego was hardly a secret and they were all trying to make her feel better, as if there was a chance he'd stay. She knew better, though.

"Your pretty detective should take the job. He'd be good at it. He's got that strong, silent thing going on, like Clint Eastwood. But he's got a sweet side. Everyone likes him. More important, they respect him."

"He's fitting in really well," Jade agreed. Her face hurt from keeping the smile in place. It was like Eric's desertion all over again, only this time everyone was offering pre-emptive support. They were doing it to show they cared, but she really wished they'd stop reminding her of what she didn't—couldn't—have.

"I'd like it if he stayed around," the woman decided in her creaky voice. She inspected a pepper cracker from all sides before scooping up some cheese dip and giving Jade a wink. "He's got a nice butt. Strong, but pattable. That's what you want in a man."

Strong, but pattable? Jade's stiff smile melted into a delighted laugh.

"You're a treasure, Mrs. Green." She hugged the elderly woman carefully, so glad to have this kind of support. These kind of people in her life.

"Jade, we're running low on snickerdoodles," Ruby said quietly, offering Mrs. Green a friendly smile. "I've got to get more ice from the garage. Could you check the cookie trays?"

Jade gave the front door a hopeful glance, then deflated. She'd clearly used up all her holiday wishes, because it wasn't Diego who came in, but Neal and Marion.

She looked around for Beryl, sure her sister would greet them. But Beryl stayed in the corner, talking to a group of her girlfriends and their families. Brows arched, a little irked that she was now on greeting duty and a quest for snickerdoodles, Jade hurried to the door.

"Happy holidays," she said, her words as cheery as her smile was fake. Marion had been getting more and more irksome lately, and now that Neal had upset Beryl, Jade's mind was compiling lists of reasons why he was a jerk. "I'm glad you could make it. Let me take your coats."

"Your cat isn't here, is it?" Neal asked, looking around nervously. "I swear, it's got it in for me. All that growling and hissing and stuff."

"She's home, locked up safe and sound," Jade assured him as she draped his denim jacket over her arm.

"I'm surprised they haven't done something about her," Marion said, sliding out of her coat. Jade's brows rose as she took the rich, buttery-soft leather. The quilted design was gorgeous. Brand new, too. Oranges must be paying well this year.

"Who are 'they' and why should anything be done about my cat?" Jade asked as she turned to take their jackets to the small room designated as coat check.

"She's a menace. Neal already proved she's the problem behind the stolen underwear. Maybe they should put her down or something," Marion said contemplatively. "Isn't that what they do with dogs who've gone bad?"

Frozen in place by that horrible image, Jade's jaw clenched almost as tightly as her fists. "Persephone hasn't done anything wrong."

"She's caused stress and drama all through town," Marion countered.

Jade wanted to point out that Marion had done plenty of that herself. But the woman was a guest in her mother's house. Which meant it was time to get away before Jade said something her mother would make her regret.

"Help yourselves to the buffet," she snapped.

Forgetting the snickerdoodles, Jade tossed their jackets on the bench, not bothering to hang them up. Not even the gorgeous leather, which spoke to how angry she was. Needing air, needing space, she bypassed the kitchen and headed for the backyard. Blinded by anger, she made it all the way across the wraparound porch that encircled the house before she stopped short.

What the hell?

She blinked.

Then, ignoring her party makeup, she rubbed her eyes and blinked again.

"Mom?" she breathed.

There, seated at the old picnic table with her mother, was the mayor. His graying hair gleamed in the winter sunshine. She couldn't see his expression, though. Because his face was plastered up against her mother's.

Her mom? And Mayor Applebaum?

Since when? And how? And, oh, God, why?

Baffled, too freaked to even want any of those questions answered, Jade hurried around the porch toward the side, then the front of the house. *Home* was all she could think. There were snickerdoodles there. She'd bring them back after she'd sifted through the emotional hurricane of the last ten minutes. She figured it was a good sign when she reached the front of the porch undetected. Then her eyes landed on the eight-foot-tall blow-up Santa globe on the lawn.

She dropped to her butt on the top step and dug her fingers into her scalp, then lifted her head again.

Yep. Those were her panties, a bright red thong with glittery accents. In true holiday fashion, they were draped over the white fluffy ball of Santa's hat. Too high for her to reach. But in clear view, like a naughty beacon, for all to see.

Just when she thought the day couldn't suck any more, it proved her wrong.

13

DIEGO PULLED UP in front of the Carson house and dismounted the Harley. He squinted at Santa, then shifted his gaze to Jade. Then looked back at Santa.

"Those are yours?" he confirmed.

Jade cast a quick glance at the houseful of people, including, he imagined, her entire family. Then, with a wince, she nodded. "Can you get them without anybody noticing?"

"Sure." Diego reached into his pocket and pulled out his handy-dandy multipurpose knife. Before he could flip the blade, Jade rushed forward with a gasp and grabbed his arm.

"You can't stab Santa."

He grinned at the horrified look in her big green eyes. Unable to help himself, he leaned down and brushed a soft kiss over her open lips. She tasted like cinnamon. And now she looked shocked instead of horrified. Mission accomplished.

"Don't you trust me?" he asked, only half teasing.

Her eyes still a little foggy with desire, she shifted her gaze from his face to the jolly elf, then back again. Then she glanced over his shoulder at her mother's house.

"Just be fast." Her hand lingering on his arm for a second, smoothing over his bare wrist in the softest of caresses, she finally stepped back. "And quiet, too. He's likely to go out with a bang."

Diego grinned. Then, walking around her, he grabbed a low branch of the mulberry tree and cut off a long twig. One eye on the house, he reached up, snagged the thong on the end of the wood and flipped it into his hand.

"Quiet enough?"

"Perfect," she said, giving him a thumbs-up. Then she held her hand out for the panties. Diego, still inspecting her face, shook his head and tucked them into his pocket.

"You're upset," he observed.

"My panties were on Santa's head."

He noted the shadows in her eyes and the tension in her shoulders. His gaze slid to the house, full of people and obligations and expectations.

"Let's go," he said. Then, despite his vow to keep a physical distance, he wrapped his arm around her slender shoulders to guide her away from the house.

"I…"

"You should listen to me." He glanced at her feet. As expected, she wore skyscraper heels. White booties, they went just past her ankles to show off scrunched socks that glittered with silver threads. Skinny white jeans hugged her legs all the way to her hips, where her silky blouse was cinched with a wide silver belt. Fluttering ruffled sleeves and a vest that flowed from shoulder to knee completed the festive winter look.

"You up for a ride on my bike?"

Staring at him so hard, so deeply, he wondered if she'd delved into the secrets of his soul, Jade finally nodded. "Sure. A ride, a walk, whatever you'd like."

Diego almost groaned as a visual of all the things he'd

like flashed through his mind, most involving her naked, and one terrifyingly including old age, holding hands and scary commitments.

He handed her his helmet, watching to make sure she buckled up properly before swinging his leg over the seat. Then, even though he only planned on going a block or so, he took off his jacket and handed it to her.

"It gets cold on the bike," he muttered sheepishly.

"You are such a hero." Her smile was a little wobbly, but she pulled the black leather jacket on.

"C'mon," he instructed. Before his good sense took over and he changed his mind.

After one last guilty look toward the house, she complied.

How she balanced in those boots was a mystery, but she swung her leg over the seat, then slid close behind him. He wondered if she'd be willing to try it again, naked except for the footwear.

"Hold tight."

He kicked the bike to life, waited until her grip on his belly felt solid, and with her knees pressing into the sides of his hips, he roared off.

She waited until they got to the end of the block before letting out a whoop of delight. Diego laughed, feeling freer, happier than he ever remembered. Since most of the town was at the Carson open house, the streets were empty as he cruised around. He actually felt the tension draining out of her as Jade leaned into his back, her face resting against his shoulder blade. Not ready to end it, he took a side road out of town.

Opening the throttle, he roared away from Diablo Glen. The space between houses widened, serene green fields and orchards blurring as they flew by. When he came to a fork, he slowed. It was so tempting to keep going. But running wasn't going to solve anything.

As he turned back, the orange orchard in the distance caught his eye. He narrowed his gaze. The shadows of a dozen or more people moved between trees. Harvesting? Wasn't this a weird time to do that?

"Whose place is that?" he yelled over the engine rumble.

He almost regretted asking when Jade lifted her head off his shoulder. A chill shivered through him at the loss of her warmth.

"That's the Kroger property. I guess Marion's family is helping harvest this year. I don't know why she didn't bring them to the party, though. That's kind of rude."

She tensed up again, all the way back to the fingers digging into his abs. Brilliant detective that he was, Diego figured Marion had played a part in Jade's afternoon stress. Let it go, he decided. With one last glance at the orchard, he shifted into gear, waited for her arms to tighten again, then took off without asking any of the questions running through his mind. Five minutes later, he pulled up in front of her cottage. He smiled at the deep sigh she gave before she unwrapped her arms from his body.

"That was great," she said as she found her balance on the sidewalk next to him and took the helmet off. She ran her fingers through her hair, the pale blond glistening in the sunlight. "Thanks for the ride."

He took the helmet, debating whether to hook it to the seat or put it on and get the hell out of here.

"You're freezing," she realized, rubbing her hands over his arms. The warmth of her palms, the friction of her touch, sent a shot of desire right through his body. Diego shifted uncomfortably on the bike seat. Harleys weren't made for horny times. "Come inside. I'll warm you up."

He went rock-hard, making straddling the leather seat torture. His fingers tightened on the helmet straps.

"Hot cocoa? Maybe some gingerbread?" she tempted.

He should go. The more distance between him and Jade, the easier it would be when he left town. His detective's intuition was humming, the answer to the case buzzing just out of reach. He just needed a little time to mull it over. Distraction-free time.

"I have homemade whipped cream. It's great on warm gingerbread."

He swung off the bike and followed her up the steps like a lovesick puppy.

Freaking pathetic.

"I left my purse at my mom's," she said when they reached the door. Before he could offer to break in, she hurried back down the steps and around the side of the house. A few seconds later, she was back, key in hand.

"Who knows you stash a key?" he asked, frowning.

Opening the door carefully to make sure the cat didn't escape, she shrugged. She bent down, giving him a sweet rear view, and scooped Persephone up, then let the door swing wide to welcome Diego in.

The cat gave a long meow, leaped from Jade's arms into his. Diego laughed as he was hit in the face by silky fur. He met Jade's eyes over the purring mass. Her face was lit brighter than her Christmas tree. Every cliché of day's-end comfort, from a cool drink to a cute puppy with slippers clenched in its teeth, filled Diego's mind. None could hold a candle to feeling welcomed, feeling wanted, for the first time in his life.

JADE WISHED she could read minds. She'd give anything to know what was going on in Diego's head. He looked sad, confused and sexy all at the same time. The sexy she was getting used to. But big, bad, hotshot detective rarely showed any emotions, so the sad and confused worried her.

"Do you want whipped cream on your cocoa as well as your gingerbread?" was all she said, though.

"Sure." He gave her a long look, then smiled. "Whipped cream sounds good."

He followed her into the kitchen, where she started the coffee and pulled out a pan of gingerbread from the fridge. She set it in the oven on low to warm, then wordlessly gathered the makings of whipped cream.

Getting nervous at his continued silence, she took off his jacket so she didn't get anything on it. He tossed it over the back of a chair, then set the cat on the floor and took a seat.

"I heard you were at the Caroling in the Park this morning," she said, pouring cream into the freezer bowl she usually used to make ice cream. She added some sugar, a little vanilla and a splash of rum. "Did you have a good time?"

"Sure. It's a nice park. From what people were saying, you hold a lot of events there."

"Next to the town hall, it's the most popular gathering place." Over the sound of the hand mixer, she said, "You should see it in the spring. Flowers cover the gazebo, the barbecues pop up and picnics are the norm. The ladies' auxiliary funded new playground equipment last year, too. The swings are fabulous."

"I don't think I've ever been on a swing," he mused aloud, his attention on the cat, who was staring intently at his jacket.

"Never?" Too shocked to pay attention, Jade splattered not-yet-whipped cream all over the counter. With a grimace, she went back to aiming the mixer with one hand while wiping the mess with a towel in the other. Still, she eyed Diego. "I didn't realize it was possible to grow up without playing on a swing."

"Most of my trips to a park involve narcs, stakeouts or arrests." His words were offhand, his focus still on the cat, who was now growling at his jacket, swatting the pocket with her paw.

"You didn't have a lot of trips to the playground as a child?"

'I bounced around a lot as a kid. Foster homes, mostly in areas where playing in the park meant risking your life. Every once in a while, I'd be tossed back to my uncle. He lived in a Podunk town that wasn't big on strange kids." Diego's smile flashed.

If that wasn't a good reason to hate and avoid small towns, Jade didn't know what was.

She gave an obligatory smile, even as her heart broke a little. She'd thought it was so exciting, being a loner and not having to answer to anyone. But that meant not having anyone, too. *Loner* and *lonely* were the same, she realized. She wished she could wrap her arms around Diego and hug him close, so he felt loved, and never alone again.

Before she could figure out what to do with that realization, Persephone lunged with a hissing yowl onto Diego's jacket. Jade flipped the switch and tossed the mixer on the counter, running across the room to yank her cat's claws from the nice leather.

"I'm so sorry," she gasped, pulling back in shock when Persephone aimed a hiss her way. "I don't know what her problem is. She adores you."

A frown creasing his brow, Diego crouched down, holding out one hand. Eyes narrowed, the angry feline backed away. Jade gaped. The cat worshipped him. Why was she acting so crazy? Diego didn't seem offended, though. He was calm. Mellow, even.

The way he had when the cat was stuck up a tree, he murmured quiet nonsense talk. This time it didn't soothe or calm her, though. Instead, Persephone's paws shot out, snagging his jacket again. She hissed. Moving slowly, cautiously, Diego slipped his fingers into the pocket. He pulled out the pair of panties he'd stashed there after rescuing them from Santa's head.

The cat hissed again, gave an ugly growl and leaped at them. Snatching them out of his hand with her teeth, she flew from the room.

"Holy cow," Jade breathed. "She's never been like that before."

Diego didn't respond. He stared intently at the doorway through which the cat, and her bounty, had disappeared. Jade recognized his cop look, distant and considering.

"Diego?" she asked quietly, not sure what was going on.

After another second, he pulled his gaze back to her and offered a quick smile. "Well, that was fun. So, is the whipped cream ready?"

Jade studied his face, then looked toward the door. She didn't know what had just happened, but she could feel the air change. Feel his intensity level ratchet up.

"What's the difference between real whipped cream and that stuff in a tub?" he asked.

As distractions went, it was blatant and obvious. Jade debated for another second, then decided he was too much a cop to tell her anything he didn't want to.

"The difference? Mostly flavor."

"Yeah? I don't think I've ever had it before."

"So many things you haven't done," Jade teased. Then, wanting to lighten the mood, she scooped up a fingerful of the rich whipped cream and offered it to him. Dark eyes intent on hers, Diego hesitated. Since he was a smart man with a finely honed instinct for anything sexual, she knew that he knew exactly what she really wanted to offer, and it wasn't just rum-infused sugary goodness.

She held her breath. As soon as his mouth wrapped around her finger, though, the breath whooshed out. His lips were as soft as his tongue was hot.

Oh, God, it felt good. He slid his tongue along her finger, then sucked softly. Wet heat gathered between her thighs, making her want to squirm. His eyes locked on hers, he slowly, so deliciously slowly, released her. He didn't lean back, though. Instead, he gestured with his chin to the bowl.

"More."

Her eyes locked on his, Jade scooped up more whipped cream. But instead of lifting it to his mouth, she wiped it on her lower lip in invitation.

His eyes gleaming with passion, he leaned forward. His gaze held hers as he swiped his tongue over her lip.

"Mmm," he murmured. Then, as if he couldn't get enough, he sucked her lip into his mouth, nibbling gently.

Jade almost whimpered when he pulled away. "So…" she said slowly, smoothing her hands down his shoulders and over the warm expanse of his chest.

"So?"

She wet her lips, then met his eyes. She knew she probably looked nervous. Or maybe a little freaked out. But she also knew he had the power to see past that. To the desire. The passion. The intense need she had for him.

"Do you want to see more of my lingerie?" she blurted in a breathless rush. Asking for anything for herself was hard enough, but asking when they both knew it was a bad idea? Oh, man.

Diego's smile was slow, wicked and totally hot. The worry in her body melted away, along with most of her thoughts, all of her resistance and every objection she'd ever had. His hands tightened on her hips, pulling her closer, brushing against her.

The long, hard bulge in his jeans pressed against her belly. Jade's knees turned to Jell-O. Desire spiraled, tight and tempting, tightening her nipples and making her pulse race.

Her fingers dug into his chest. Not out of desire this time, but purely from a desperate attempt to keep from oozing into a lusty puddle on his feet.

"Can I ask one little favor?"

"Anything," she promised breathlessly.

"Will you wear those boots with your lingerie?"

NEVER ONE TO WAKE EASILY, Diego slowly worked his way out of the depths of sleep. His brain sputtered to a start. Then, like a beeping answering machine overflowing with urgent messages, he tuned in to his body.

It was wide-awake and horny.

With good reason. He sighed, reveling in the delighted exhaustion that only intense sex could bring.

He'd known she had a deep, intense sensual streak. A woman didn't wear the kind of lingerie she did and not enjoy sex.

And having tasted her before, he'd known the sex between them would be awesome. But last night? Diego threw his arm over his eyes to block the dim light that could only be the morning sun. Last night—and those boots—had been mind-boggling. His awareness might only be registering in the single digits, but he was 100 percent sure of two things.

That Jade was incredible.

And the two of them, together? Freaking awesome.

And nothing said good-morning better than a warm, sleepy round of freaking awesome.

"Mmm," he mumbled, not opening his eyes as he reached out to haul Jade—and her sleepy, sexy warmth—much closer. He wanted to feel her naked flesh sliding beneath his again. To taste her as her cries of ecstasy filled the room.

Blinking groggily, his eyes automatically locked on Jade.

She was still fast asleep and wrapped in a very thin, very smooth sheet. Not as smooth as her skin, he decided as he skimmed his hand down her back, taking the fabric down as he went.

"Wake-up time," he murmured with a wicked grin. What a sight. Her hair surrounding her like strands of sunlight, Jade's face was buried in the ice-blue satin of her pillow. Which left him with the tempting view of her bare back. And, he noted as his body leaped ahead to fully awake, the sweet curves of her just-as-bare butt.

She had a tattoo. Right there where the curve of her butt sloped toward her spine, just above the left cheek. A tiny purple-and-gold butterfly, flying free from a vivid green cocoon. He lightly traced his index finger over the cocoon, noting that the artist had made the threads look like bars.

Is that how Jade saw herself? Trapped as she tried to change? There, at the edge of his consciousness, was her declaration of love. He'd tried to ignore it the night before. He tried to keep on ignoring it now. No point in desperately latching on to something that wasn't real. That couldn't be real. Better to focus on what he could depend on.

Like how delicious Jade was.

Giving in to his body's demand, he shifted down to press a kiss on the butterfly. Safe flight, he wished her with a grin. Because he intended to make it a wild one.

He slid his hand over the gentle slope of her butt, sliding between her thighs with whisper-soft fingers.

She stirred. Mumbled something, then burrowed her face deeper in the pillow. The move angled her leg just a little. Just enough for his hand to find easy entry.

Diego's fingers tangled in the warm curls. Slid over the soft bud. Burrowed slowly, ever so slowly, into the welcoming depths.

She gave a low, mewling sort of noise into the pillow, her hips pressing against his questing fingers.

Diego shifted lower, nibbling a line of kisses up the firm, smooth skin where her thigh met her butt. Her perfect, butterfly-decorated butt. His fingers swirled, dipped, slid in and out. Her body, awakening much faster than she did, grew slick, wet. Welcoming.

His mouth watered. His dick, already rock-hard, pulsed against the silk sheet. With his unoccupied hand, he gently pressed her thighs apart, giving himself more access. And a better view as his fingers danced along the glistening pink flesh.

"Oh, my." Jade awoke with a throaty moan. He glanced up to see her grab the pillow, silk clenched tight in her hands. Her body trembled. Her thighs tensed.

He blew, his breath hot on her quivering flesh.

And sent her over the edge.

Her cries of delight filled his ears. Warmed his heart. And made his body ache.

Throbbing with desperation now, he grabbed a condom from the pile she kept next to the bed. Then he slid up her body, reveling in her moan of approval. Poised above her, he shifted his hand under her hips to raise her higher to meet his thrust.

He slid into the hot, slick heat of her with a groan.

Her moan was muffled by the pillow, her butt tight against his hips as she undulated, swirled. Tempted.

Diego almost lost it right then and there.

Carefully, slowly, he slid in and out of her tight flesh.

"Mmm," she moaned, her sigh long and welcoming.

He moved faster.

"Oh, Diego," she panted. Over, and over, and over. Her breath came in gasps now. Her words in pants. Her thighs quivered under his fingers.

Diego plunged harder.

Deeper.

She cried out.

Her body arched, stiff and shaking, against his.

He pressed deeper.

Swirled his hips.

Through slitted eyes, he saw her fingers clench the sheets, yanking the fabric toward her as if to keep herself from flying away as she cried out one more time.

It was probably the most erotic thing he'd ever seen.

Diego pulled back, his body so tight, so desperate for relief, that he had black spots dancing in front of his eyes.

He plunged.

She gave a mewling sound of satisfaction.

He groaned, then plunged again. Once. Twice.

Then he exploded. Stars echoed his release, flashing bright and intense behind his eyes.

His heart pounding so loud it sounded like a machine gun ricocheting through his head, Diego collapsed. Careful not to crush her, he slid to his side, pulling Jade's still-trembling body against his.

She was incredible.

Responsive. Enticing. Delicious.

She was everything he'd never known he wanted in a woman.

And everything his heart now swore it couldn't survive without.

As he tried to find his breath, and his sanity, Diego reveled in the warm softness of Jade's still-trembling curves. He'd figure it out, he promised himself. Once the blood returned to his brain, he'd find a way to solve this mess his heart had made.

Suddenly there was a loud crash. Adrenaline surging, his body flew into a protective arch over hers. He made sure she was tucked safe under him even as his hand automatically flew to the small of his back. His naked back, since his gun was tucked in a drawer across the room.

Shattering glass exploded with a staccato tinkling. Something rough scraped wood, slid through glass. The cat gave an angry yowl, as if it'd been hit.

"Sophie!" Jade cried.

"Don't move!" Holding her tight, Diego waited. Jade wasn't having any of that, though. She struggled beneath him, trying to see past his body.

"Persephone."

As if she'd conjured the feline, as soon as the words left her mouth, four feet stabbed Diego in the back. He winced, but managed to hold back his manly yelp.

"She's fine," he muttered, cringing as the animal scampered for the safety of Jade's arms. Since that put the furry mass smack-dab between them, he figured—safe or not—it was time to move.

Slowly, his senses on full alert, he rolled off Jade, still careful to keep his body between her and the window.

"Shit."

"Oh, my…" She gave a horrified gasp against his back. "Why…"

She couldn't finish the sentences, clearly overcome by the sight of her window splattered in a million pieces across her bedroom. There, in the middle of shards and splintered wood, was a brick with the word BITCH written in fat black marker.

Diego wanted to hit something. Or, his gaze shot to the now-empty window frame, someone.

Swinging his feet off the bed, he'd just reached for his jeans when Jade grabbed his arm. "Be careful," she cautioned.

He shot her an amused look. "I don't think the brick is loaded."

"Of broken glass, silly. Watch your feet and shake out your clothes before you put them on."

He didn't know when—or if—he'd last been called silly. Or why it made him want to grin. Maybe it was Jade, her hair snarled like sunshine around her head, the terrified cat cuddled close to her chest. Her naked chest.

Wishing he could switch places with the yet-again growling and hissing cat, he gave his jeans a quick shake before pulling them on. The glass pattern swept clear under the bed, so he shook out his boots, then yanked them on, too.

Careful not to step on glass and damage the floor further, he walked over to examine the brick. Spying a piece of white fabric on the floor, he grabbed it to lift the object. Part of her curtain, he realized, keeping his face stoic, clear. No point upsetting her by letting her see the fury that was pounding through him.

Nope. He'd save that for the asshole who did this.

"You know who it was," Jade said, her eyes wide as she stared at his face. What? Could she really see into his soul? And why didn't that bother him more?

Diego just shrugged, though. He was on the job now, and he could see the end of the case as clearly as he could see her pretty face.

His entire career, his goal was to close the case as fast as possible. For the first time, he hated finding the answer.

"Are you going to arrest someone now?" she asked, set-

ting the cat on the bed, then wrapping a sheet tight around
her body. Diego looked around, then opened the closet to
find a pair of hard-soled slippers to hand her.

"I have to go through channels. Talk to Applebaum,
confirm a couple of things."

His jaw clenched. And deal with the fact that it was
time to go.

MISERY WASHED OVER Jade with the same power as the orgasms that had pounded through her the night before. He
was leaving. Sure, he had those channels to go through,
the cop steps to take. But he was leaving.

She wanted to cry.

"Is it a bother, having to take those extra steps?" More
important, did they take a lot of extra time? She hoped so.

"The trials of a guest cop," he said with a dismissive
shrug.

She almost asked if he'd decided about the job offer.
But that meant a) letting on that she knew about the offer.
And b) pressuring him to make a decision not only about
the job, but about them.

The idea of asking him, of hearing his answer, scared
the hell out of her. Jade clutched the sheet between her fingers, wishing she was brave enough to ask. Strong enough
to tell him that she wanted him to stay. But if he stayed,
it'd be for her.

"I'll be right back. Gonna get the vacuum."

She opened her mouth to call him back. Then snapped
it shut again when a wave of hot black terror washed over
her at the prospect of confronting both her emotions and
his decision. She couldn't leave. Not without hurting her
family. And herself, she realized. She was a part of this
town. Seeing it through his eyes had shown her that.

The only drawback to living in Diablo Glen was not having a career she loved. Well, a career, and Diego.

Even if she found the nerve to ask him to stay, she knew he'd choose to go. A guy didn't grow up exposed to the ugly side of small towns, then want to live in one.

Back, vacuum in one hand, grocery bag and paper towel in the other, he lifted the brick without touching it and settled it into the bag. Then, setting it aside, he stood with the vacuum cord in hand. He didn't plug it in, though.

"Applebaum mentioned a local job," he said finally, tonelessly. As if he had no opinion. As if he was filling her in on something he knew she already knew, and figured he should do the polite thing and mention it. "A cop deal, here in town. You probably heard about it."

Jade nodded. She swallowed hard, wishing she were brave enough, strong enough, to ask him to sacrifice for her. That he give up his big promotion and transfer, and stay here. To risk hearing that he didn't care enough to want to.

Besides, she'd already used him enough.

For excitement and great sex, sure.

But she'd hoped through him she'd find the answer to making her dreams come true.

Turned out, he was the answer.

But she couldn't ask him to give his up to make her happy.

"I did. But is that the kind of thing you'd want to do?" she heard herself saying as if from far, far away. "Be tied down to a small town? It'd probably be pretty boring compared to what you're used to. There aren't any promotions or juicy cases to solve around here. And who knows how long it'd take for another panty-thief caper to ensue."

She tried to smile at that last part, but her face felt stiff.

Painful. Almost as painful as the little pieces of her heart breaking away as she realized this was it.

He'd solved the case, so he was leaving.

She was too afraid to ask him not to.

And equally afraid of what would happen if he actually stayed.

14

A CHILLY DECEMBER AFTERNOON probably wasn't the best time to sit in the park. Still, Diego had needed time and space to think. He slumped on the bench and glared at the swings. What had he expected? For Jade to be excited when he'd mentioned the job here? To want him to stay? He'd barely got the words out before she'd rejected the idea. Clearly, he'd served his purpose, rocked the sex and had shown her a good time. But faced with the possibility of having him around on a long-term basis? She wasn't much interested.

Story of his life.

"There you are."

Frowning because he hadn't heard the approach, Diego inclined his head to Applebaum. "How'd you figure on finding me here?"

"Just followed the trail of bread crumbs. Or, you know, asked a few people if they'd seen you about."

The older man settled onto the bench and pulled out his pipe. Diego's glance slid to the no-smoking sign. Was he going to have to bust the mayor? Kinnison would love that.

But Applebaum didn't light the pipe. He just passed it from hand to hand. And waited.

The man would have made one hell of a torturer. He'd just sit there like a benevolent grandpa, waiting for his prisoner to blurt out everything and anything.

It was a trick Diego liked to use himself. Except for the grandpa part, of course. Still, it shouldn't work on him.

A few more minutes of forcing himself not to look toward Jade's house, not even to see if Persephone was still watching from the window, and Diego shifted. He stretched his shoulders. Cracked his neck. Ground his teeth. And finally, he sighed and gave in.

"The thefts never made sense," he said quietly, dropping his voice even though nobody was close enough to hear. "The nature of it suggests a sexual focus. There aren't too many other ways to regard the theft of women's underwear."

"Unless the thief is a closet cross-dresser too afraid to actually buy his own," Applebaum mused aloud, his attention focused on buffing the gleaming wood of his pipe.

Diego snorted. Then he slanted the other man a curious look. "And would there be suspects if that were the case?"

"There would. But given the sizes of underwear stolen, and the fact that I looked into this particular resident myself to make sure he really is in Florida visiting his daughter, I think we can rule that out."

"I'm oddly comforted to know you do have perverts," Diego murmured. Too bad it added another weight on the stay-in-Diablo-Glen side of the scale. Unable to resist a peek, he glanced toward Jade's. His lips twitched. Persephone had plastered herself, lengthwise, up the window as if she was trying to reach the ceiling.

Applebaum followed his gaze, smiling around the pipe now clenched between his teeth.

"You're on to something?"

Diego shrugged. "I know who did it. I just don't have that last puzzle piece. It feels big, though."

"The motivation for stealing panties is big?"

Diego laughed at the sarcasm in the older man's voice. Then he shook his head. "Like I said, it was set up to look sexually motivated. But it isn't. That's what threw me."

"You think you know what that missing piece is, don't you?"

Diego nodded.

"But?"

Diego almost blurted out all the reasons he didn't want to close the case.

That he'd grown attached to the town.

When he made this arrest, people were going to get hurt. People he'd come to care about.

An arrest meant saying goodbye.

And he was in love with Jade.

"No buts. I need to go over a few things with you first, though."

"Give me ten minutes to take care of a few details. I'll meet you at my office."

Without another word, no questions, no recriminations, no nagging insistence to share information, Applebaum sauntered away.

Leaving Diego alone, trying to find the courage to take the scariest leap of his life.

The leap of faith to believe that the feelings he had for Jade were not only real, but that they had a chance of lasting in the real world.

JADE ATTACKED THE STACKS in the far back corner of the library with a vengeance. As if eradicating every speck of dust on books that nobody ever checked out would clear her head, settle her stomach and help her figure out what the hell to do with herself now.

How sad was she. Little Ms. Empowerment, emotionally cowering behind dusty books. Because she wasn't brave enough to risk hurting anyone. Not herself. And definitely not anyone else. Not when it really mattered.

Maybe she should get a new tattoo. FRAUD in big fat letters.

"Hiding?"

"Working." Shoulders stiff, she didn't look at her sister. Just kept on dusting.

"C'mon out to the lobby."

"I said I'm working, Ruby."

"Beryl's out front. She's a mess."

Pulled out of her pout, Jade tossed the duster on the cart, wiped her hands on a cloth and faced her older sister. Barefaced, wearing a ratty sweatshirt and jeans, Ruby looked stressed. But Ruby never looked stressed.

"What happened?" It had to be bad if she brought it to the library instead of waiting to deal with it at home, especially since their mother only put in a few hours doing paperwork on Sundays.

"She broke up with Neal."

"Oh." Jade tried to sort through the dozens of emotions to settle on a reaction. Relief was most prominent. And, she figured, the least welcome.

"Exactly."

The look on Ruby's face made it clear she wasn't on the Neal bandwagon either. Why hadn't Jade known that? Was she such a total wimp that she didn't even tell—or ask—the people she loved things just because she worried they'd have a different opinion?

She was finding out so much about herself this weekend. And other than her newly discovered ability to straddle a guy while wearing five-inch heels, none of the rest was very admirable.

"C'mon, Jade," Ruby prodded. "And remember, this is going to be hard for her. But be careful, because I don't know if it's a real breakup or just a tiff."

"I know how to be supportive," Jade snapped.

Together, they wove through the tall bookcases and display racks toward the lobby. As Ruby continued to whisper instructions on how to be a good sister, Jade pulled on her most sympathetic face. At the same time, she shoved her real opinion of Neal—quite likely colored by her feelings about his mother—into a dark corner of her mind.

The lobby was empty. Silent and dim.

The office door was closed, blinds pulled.

"How anticlimactic."

Ruby's lips twitched. "So we wait to be sympathetic and helpful."

Jade shrugged. It wasn't as if she had anywhere to go.

"I brought your purse. You left it at Mom's when you bailed on the party yesterday," Ruby said as they both stared at the closed office door. "Where'd you go? Rebecca Lee was looking everywhere for you. Then someone mentioned that they saw you leave with the hottie cop, so we figured you'd found other entertainment."

"What'd Rebecca want?" Jade didn't feel like justifying her departure. Sharing Marion's rudeness wouldn't help support Beryl, and outing their mother's make-out session was just, well, weird.

"I think she wanted you to do a styling party for Cathy's wedding. She's treating the bride and her sisters, as well as five of their friends, to a weekend in the city. She wanted to know what you'd charge to go along, help the bride choose the perfect trousseau and outfit the wedding party for all the bridal events. You know, rehearsal dinner, luncheons, bridesmaids' tea."

"That sounds really...cool," she decided. Cathy Lee and her sisters were pretty girls, all a little on the heavy side. They'd be so fun to style, to show them how to dress to make themselves feel great and look fabulous.

"I heard her talking to people about it at the party," Ruby continued. "It's a really hot idea. By the time they'd finished sandwiches and moved on to dessert, at least three other people were talking about contacting you. A couple more wanted to know prices so they could put you on their Christmas list."

Jade laughed in surprise. "Me? On a wish list? That's so wild."

"Is it something you'd be interested in?"

Jade leaned against the countertop and considered. It was a fun concept. Something she'd be good at and would enjoy. The trick would be finding the right clothes, since she didn't have a store or designer affiliation. But all that would take was a day or so of preshopping, maybe making a few new contacts and checking out store websites ahead of time.

If it actually made money, and the teaching took off, she could quit the library. Build up her contacts, put together a few styling events, maybe expand her online presence. She could actually call herself a stylist by occupation.

Excitement stirred.

Wouldn't that be too freaking awesome?

"I think it's definitely something I'd like to try," she finally said, trying to temper her excitement.

"What about wanting to leave? Wouldn't you rather focus on that?" Ruby asked quietly. "If you want to, we'll help. Berry and I were talking last night. We didn't realize how much we'd put on you here, or how trapped you might feel."

Trapped.

Jade looked at the closed office door and sighed. Was she trapped? Or was she just afraid? The possibility of building a career as a stylist here was so exciting. The cost of living was much lower than in a big city, especially since her house was paid for. She had support, friends and a solid foundation in Diablo Glen.

All she needed was a career she loved.

And Diego.

She pressed a shaky hand against her churning stomach. Could she ask him to stay? Ask someone to put her wants, her needs, ahead of their own dreams?

What if he resented it, as she had?

What if he didn't care enough to even give the idea a try and find out if he resented it?

She laid her head on the cool desk and sighed.

What if she was such a big wuss, she scared herself out of reaching for both her dream, and her dream man. The dream seemed to be finding its way back to her, whether she'd earned it or not.

The man, though? Once he roared out of town, she was sure he was gone for good.

"Are you okay?" Ruby asked, her hand warm and supportive as she rubbed Jade's shoulder. "You don't have to decide now, you know. We are here for you. And Mom will be, too. Although she's been acting a little funny lately. Have you noticed?"

Jade suddenly remembered the first shock yesterday, before seeing her thong flying from Santa's head.

The mayor. Kissing her mother.

Kissing.

She winced. Then, with a sigh, relaxed. Mayor Applebaum was a good guy. And Mom had been alone for a long time now. She deserved to be happy, to have a little fun. The question was, would Ruby and Beryl agree?

Before Jade could decide whether or not to share what she'd seen, the door opened. They both looked toward the front of the library. And winced.

"Damn," Ruby whispered.

Marion strode in with a rain cloud of a scowl, looking like the Grinch before he'd found his heart.

Jade grimaced. "I forgot she was coming in today."

"This is going to be ugly," Ruby predicted, setting her feet more firmly into the floor, as if preparing to go to battle to defend her little sister.

A good thing, too, because just as Marion was stomping her way down the steps toward Jade, the office door opened and out came Beryl and their mother.

"You," Marion barked, whirling to glare at the youngest Carson.

Before she could follow that up, the door opened again. Jade stepped forward, prepared to throw herself at the feet of whoever it was.

Diego.

Would she ever get used to how gorgeous he was?

Her heart thumped, then took off at the speed of sound. She'd rather throw herself on something besides his feet, but she'd take what she could get. And given that her mother was right there, and the mayor at Diego's shoulder, that was probably for the best.

"Gentlemen," she greeted in a bright tone. "What brings you in today? Can I interest you in a holiday book?"

"Actually, we're here to let you know we arrested the Panty Thief," Diego said.

"What? Who?" everyone asked at once.

"Neal Kroger," he said quietly. Instead of looking at

Jade, he stared at Neal's mother. Jade ripped her gaze from her sister's face, pale with shock, to look at Marion. The older woman looked furious. As if she wanted to leap across the room and tear a chunk out of Diego's flesh.

It was kind of scary.

"How dare you. What right do you have to come into our town and make such a baseless, ridiculous accusation?"

Diego didn't say a word. He just pulled out his badge and held it in front of her, offering up proof of where his rights came from.

"Why?" Jade asked her quietly. "What'd any of those women do to him? What was the point of stealing underwear?"

"Distraction," Diego said with a shrug. Then he gave her a small smile, just a little wicked around the edges. "He got the idea from your cat, by the way."

"That damn cat," Marion snarled. "This is all ridiculous. That cat's the one who stole the underwear. You caught it in the act, remember."

"Marion," the mayor said quietly, as if trying to get her to slow down and think before her next idiotic accusation. Since Jade was still smarting at the suggestion the older woman had made the previous day to put the cat down, she hoped Marion kept on babbling and digging her own grave.

"You have nothing on my son," the woman said, her furious tone echoed in the fist she shook at Diego. "Nothing, you hear me?"

"Actually, we have enough proof that the D.A. is doing backflips," Diego interrupted. "Right down to the brick he threw because he blamed Jade for Beryl dumping him. As to why? It was all a distraction."

Clueless, Jade shook her head. Everyone else looked

just as confused. Everyone except the mayor, who looked resigned. And Marion, who just looked pissed.

Despite all the drama, the confusion, the fury on Marion's face, all Jade could think about was one thing.

Diego was making an arrest.

He was done here.

Her lower lip trembled. They were done now.

HIS BODY TENSE, Diego questioned his sanity. What had he been thinking, taking this route? He should have waited, got her when she came home. But he'd wanted to do this here, in front of Jade and her family. He'd wanted to make sure they had closure.

And yes, he'd wanted to show off a little. He figured seeing him do his job would either convince her that his being top cop in Diablo Glen was a great idea. Or it'd show them both that she couldn't handle his job. Either way, he had to know.

"This is all your fault," Marion Kroger spat at Beryl, glaring at the younger woman as if she'd like to take a go at her face. "First you broke my son's heart, now you're getting your sister's fancy city boyfriend to cause trouble for our family. I'll sue you, and your family, for libel. For slander. For pain and suffering."

Diego rolled his eyes.

"Mrs. Kroger, you might want to chill down. Quit bitching at Beryl," he said. "It's not her fault your son was an ass."

Okay, so that last part had been inappropriate. But it'd scored him a lot of points with the Carson women, if their grins were anything to go by. And a man making a major career move had to play to his future.

The old lady gave an outraged gasp. When it didn't elicit

the sympathy she wanted, she gave a huff and slammed her arms over her chest.

"Rudeness is not acceptable. I'll be contacting your superior, young man."

"I'm sure he's been expecting a call or two," Diego said with a shrug. "You might not want to waste yours complaining about me, though. Better to use it to call your lawyer."

Her stance shifted from irate to nervous with the twitch of her pudgy fingers.

Diego slanted a glance at the mayor. His eyes sad, Applebaum gave a resolute nod of the head.

"Marion Kroger, you're under arrest." Diego followed the announcement with the charges, then the so-familiar-he-chanted-it-in-his-sleep Miranda. He wasn't positive she heard him, though, because she was yelling at Beryl, who was now hiding behind Ruby. Jade and Opal flanked the other women, making a united front of anger.

And he thought being a cop in a small town would have been so easy it'd be a bore? Despite the gravity of the situation, a grin escaped. To cover it, and to yank control back before this turned into a catfight, Diego stuck two fingers between his lips and whistled.

As one, the five women turned to stare at him, their faces painted with varying degrees of offended.

It was Applebaum who grinned this time.

"Excuse me," Diego said formally. "But I'm trying to make an arrest here."

"I thought you said Neal was stealing all those undies," Beryl said, her tone equal parts shock and horror.

"He was. He's also been arrested for assault and destruction of property."

"He's the one who threw the brick through my window?" Jade asked.

When her mom and sisters started peppering her with
questions, Diego lifted his hand again. He didn't even get
his fingers to his lips this time, though, before they qui-
eted to hissing whispers.

"Yeah. Minor charges, compared to his mother's, but
he's definitely going to do time."

Marion Kroger hadn't paid any attention to the charges
because she'd been too busy playing drama queen, but this
got her attention. Her face stiff, her gaze shifted from Diego's to the mayor's and back. Gauging what they knew,
probably. Wondering how strong the charges might be.

"I'm innocent of any wrongdoing," she claimed.

"Human trafficking, harboring and hiring illegals, tax
evasion are the initial charges," Diego told her. The gasps
and whispers around the room echoed to emphasize the
accusations.

The Kroger woman stared, stone-faced for a few seconds. Debating denial, Diego figured. It'd be harder to cop
a plea deal if she confessed.

"I didn't do anything wrong." Her gaze shot from person to person, searching for something. Sympathy probably. When she didn't find it, she dropped her chin and
gave a sniffle. "What makes you think you can get away
with this?"

"It's pretty easy when we found proof at your house.
A dozen illegal aliens you were hiding, and exploiting in
your orchards. Transit records and bookkeeping ledgers
recording the funds you were paid as part of the underground trafficking movement." Diego shrugged. "Sounds
like you did plenty wrong to me."

"How dare you? Do you know who I am? What I do for
this town?" The mayor shifted, just one foot to the other.
But it was enough to put a cork in that line of outrage. She
sucked in another breath.

Diego held up one hand for her to stop before she could get going again.

He'd had enough. They had the truth, it was time to end this. Besides, he had much more important things to do now. Like plan his life with Jade. He inclined his head toward the entrance. The mayor nodded, walked over and unlocked the heavy doors. When they swung open, the two immigration officers he'd contacted were standing there, ready to haul her off.

"It was the pressure," Kroger babbled as soon as she saw the uniforms. Her eyes widened, her face drooped. She gave a huge sigh and did everything but toss her wrist over her forehead. "The overwhelming emotional and mental pressure. It was so hard, raising a child alone. The expenses of keeping the orchard up, of surviving in this economy. I wasn't thinking clearly."

Diego gave an impressed nod. "That's pretty good. I don't think it'll get you an insanity plea. But it's a good foundation for emotional distress. You might want to work on the tears, though. It took Immigration Services seventeen evidence boxes and a bus to haul everything and everyone off your property. A little more drama might help balance that out."

Sandwiched between the two officers, the older woman glared. When one took her arm, she smacked him. "You keep your hands to yourself. Applebaum," she demanded, "you'd better come along. I want protection against police brutality."

"Not a problem." The mayor gave Diego a nod, letting him know he'd handle her from here. After giving Jade's mom's shoulder a quick squeeze, he followed Kroger and her escorts out the door.

The room was silent for a solid minute after their exit. Diego waited.

Suddenly the women exploded. Questions, horror, exclamations. They flew faster than Santa's reindeer, ricocheting off the vaulted ceiling and bouncing from mother to daughter to sister.

There it was.

He leaned against the tall desk until they got past the initial shock. Jade got there first. Stepping away from the chattering horde, she gave him an intense, indecipherable look. He'd faced down junkies with loaded guns, but had the feeling she could hurt him a lot worse.

"Mom, can you take over my shift?" she said quietly.

The chatter stopped. Her sisters both gave him an appraising look while her mother focused exclusively on Jade. Apparently satisfied with what she saw on her daughter's face, Opal nodded.

Glancing his way, her eyes filled with too many emotions for him to read, Jade held out her hand and quietly asked, "Can we go for a walk? I need to talk with you."

This was it. His chance to convince her that she wanted him to stay around. To make her see that they had a future together. One she wanted to experience.

And if words didn't work, he still had his handcuffs.

15

JADE WAS GRATEFUL for the silence as they walked together into the park. She wished she could use it to gather her thoughts, to formulate how she was going to convince him to stay. But everything sounded stupid in her mind.

The gazebo lights were shining already, red and green glowing brightly against the white wood. She bypassed the Christmas display, heading for the playground instead.

"Swing?" she asked Diego as they reached the large metal structure. She waited until he sat, then took the swing next to his, sitting the opposite way so they faced each other.

And tried to find the perfect words to make her dreams come true.

"Wow. Big arrest" was all she could come up with, though. Jade wrinkled her nose. Talk about lame openings.

"You don't seem shocked."

"I'm not shocked," she mused out loud, smiling when he gave her a confused look. "I mean, I wouldn't have expected anything like this from the Krogers. Marion's always been such a stickler for her reputation, so focused on advancing her standing in the community. I wouldn't have thought she'd risk that."

434   Nice & Naughty

"That's hardly a glowing character testimonial."

Jade grimaced. She didn't know which was worse. Harboring what she'd thought was an unjustified, unreasonable dislike for someone. Or being clueless that someone in her life was despicable enough to deal in human trafficking.

"You're right, it's not. I guess that's why I'm not shocked. There's always been something about her, and Neal, too, that bothered me. But I didn't know what it was. I mean, on the surface, they were nice people."

"Surfaces are deceptive."

"You saw through it, though," she said. "What was it that clued you in?"

"A lot of little things that when put together just added up. And one odd thing that really stood out."

"Like?" She really wanted to know how he'd figured it out. She'd lived in the same town as the Kroger family since she was a little girl. Her sister had almost married into the family. And other than a nagging something in the back of her head—which she'd easily ignored—she'd been clueless.

"Like Persephone."

"My cat?" Shocked, she glanced toward her house, a few yards away past the trees and hedges. "How?"

"She hated Neal. Not that she was overly friendly with anyone, but him? She growled, yowled and spit whenever he was around."

Confused, Jade nodded, but said, "But that's not exclusive to him. You saw it yourself. She did the same thing yesterday over my rescued underwear..."

Her words trailed off, her mouth forming an *oh*.

"I knew dogs could track things, find things through scent, but I didn't realize cats could."

"I didn't, either," he said. "But she reacted the same

way over your thong, and over that brick that was tossed through your window."

"So you arrested Neal?"

"So I used arresting Neal as an excuse to get onto their property and have a closer look."

"Because?"

He hesitated, then saying it quickly, like taking bad medicine, he said, "Intuition."

She wasn't sure what fascinated her more. That he believed in something so esoteric. Or how adorable his sheepish expression was.

"If I'd followed procedure, like my captain prefers, I'd have busted Neal and the case would be closed. But I knew there was something else going on. He'd hatched the panty thefts as a distraction because they had a busload of illegals coming in. But instead of moving them on out within a few days, Mrs. Kroger apparently saw a chance to bring in her harvest and not pay for labor."

"But if you'd followed procedure and arrested Neal here in town, you wouldn't have had anything to justify going out to the Kroger property," she confirmed.

"And by arresting him there, I had enough probable cause to call in Immigration." He grimaced. "Kinnison's still likely to bitch though."

"Will he mess up your promotion?" As much as she wanted him to stay, Jade didn't want it that way.

"Nah. I reported to Applebaum while on this job. He okayed the bust." Diego gave a wicked grin. "He gets credit for it, too. That's gonna piss Kinnison off even more."

"Probably not as much as it will losing such a talented detective to a big promotion," she said, reaching over to lay her hand on his knee. She pulled back after a second, though, needing to keep her wits about her for this next part.

"It's easy to see why you got the promotion. San Francisco will be lucky to have you on their force."

She watched his face, desperate to see a hint, any little bit of encouragement, to continue. He was in cop mode, though. Inscrutable and unreadable.

She swallowed hard before forcing the words past the lump of terror lodged in her throat. "Of course, Diablo Glen would be luckier to have you stay here."

His stoic expression flickered. Narrowing his eyes, he shifted backward on the swing to better see her face.

"I know you've got a lot to look forward to in San Francisco. It's a big promotion and a much more exciting place to fight crime than Diablo Glen." She bit her lip. Then, unable to hold back the words, unable to even imagine life without him, she blurted, "But I wish you'd stay here. Applebaum wants you to head up the new police department. Everyone's talking about it. And they all want you, too."

"What?"

Why did he sound surprised?

"Everyone loves you," she told him, stating the obvious. "At least, everyone I've heard mention the subject. They're all hoping you'll take the position."

She gave him a naughty smile, then added, "Of course, some of the ladies are hoping you'll take it because they think you add a sexy vibe to the view around town."

He pulled a face. Then he gave her another searching look. "What about you?"

She couldn't read his voice. Couldn't tell what he wanted to hear. So she had to go with what she had—the truth.

"I want you to stay. You'd be wonderful at the job. You're good for the town, and I think the town would be good for you." At his arch look, she put it all out there, reaching over to take his fingers in hers. "I want you to stay, for us. To see if we can make this work."

He didn't say anything. Jade's stomach pitched into her toes, but she continued anyway. "I have a lot more shoes. Boots. Sandals. The variety of lingerie and footwear combinations are endless."

His eyes turned to liquid heat and he gave a low hum of approval. Then he shifted, reaching over to lift her out of her swing and onto his lap.

Jade laughed in delight, wrapping her arms around his shoulders.

"If I hadn't already accepted the job, the shoe offer would have done it for me," Diego said with a laugh. Beneath the humor, though, his words held an emotion she couldn't read. Jade shifted, needing to see his face. In his eyes, she saw a joy that was almost childlike. So pure, so happy, it brought tears to her eyes.

"I was going to take it, move here and chase after you until you gave in," he told her. "I figured it'd take a few months, maybe some bribes, but I'd wear you down eventually."

"I can't believe you're really going to stay." Delighted, and feeling freer than she ever had, Jade snuggled deeper into his arms.

Strong, warm and so tight she didn't think he'd ever let her go.

Good.

His mouth took hers in a kiss so sweet, so gentle, her heart wept in delight. The feelings that poured through her, through them, were stronger than anything Jade had ever felt. Or ever dreamed of feeling. He was amazing. And he made her feel amazing.

"My hero," she whispered when he lifted his mouth. Needing a second, she buried her face in his throat, letting his scent fill her, empower her. She really, really did love him.

"What kind of bribes?" she asked when he released her mouth.

"I took the job on a probationary basis. Six months. I figured I'd have convinced you that you were crazy about me by then, and I could give you the option of us staying here." He pulled back so he could see her face, his eyes so intent they made Jade nervous. "Or, if it's what you wanted, I'd find a way to set things up here so you, so we, could move to San Francisco. Or Los Angeles, New York, anywhere you wanted."

Her heart turned into a puddle of gooey joy. Jade couldn't stop smiling. He was giving them a chance. A shot at a future together. Here, there, anywhere that made them happiest.

"Are you sure about this?" she asked. "You're giving up a promotion, aren't you?"

"I'm not giving up anything. I'm getting everything."

Diego reached out, his finger tracing the line of her jaw. Then, his eyes intent on hers, he leaned forward to brush his lips over hers in a soft promise of a kiss.

"Don't worry," he whispered.

Just like that, all Jade's fears melted away.

Right here, waiting patiently, was her every dream come true.

Jade giggled, the emotions exploding through her with the excitement of glitter and confetti. She threw her arms around Diego's neck.

"I love you," she declared happily.

"I've never had anyone love me. Never had anyone want me to stay around. You make me feel amazing." He pulled back, just enough to see her face. His eyes intent, his expression as serious as she'd ever seen it, he said, "I didn't believe it existed, to be honest. But you've made me believe that love is real. That I deserve it, and can give it. I love you, Jade. I never knew anything could feel this good."

"And it's only going to get better," she vowed, her words a promise to them both.

* * * * *

Under Wraps

JOANNE ROCK

While working on her master's degree in English literature, **Joanne Rock** took a break to write a romance novel and quickly realised a good book requires as much time as a master's programme itself. She became obsessed with writing the best romance possible, and sixty-some novels later, she hopes readers have enjoyed all the 'almost there' attempts. Today, Joanne is a frequent workshop speaker and writing instructor at regional and national writer conferences. She credits much of her success to the generosity of her fellow writers, who are always willing to share insights on the process. More importantly, she credits her readers with their kind notes and warm encouragement over the years for her joy in the writing journey.

For the beautifully talented Winnie Griggs, who calls and checks in on me, who cheers me on, who always makes me feel like a success! Thank you for many years of friendship and wise advice.

Prologue

NORMALLY, THE LAST PLACE Jake Brennan would want to be the week before Christmas was sitting on a stakeout.

He'd promised his mom he'd come home for the holidays this year, a pledge, which made him a liar three years running. Instead, he sat in his SUV across the street from a suspect's business in downtown Miami, where neon palmetto trees made a tropical substitute for white lights in the snow back in Illinois.

But when the stakeout involved Marnie Wainwright, there were perks involved. Enough perks that Jake didn't mind watching the storefront for her business, Lose Yourself, from inside his vehicle on a Friday night. It didn't matter that the rest of the world went to holiday parties right now. He had Marnie for entertainment, and two months of surveillance on the entrepreneur behind Lose Yourself had taught him that was more than enough.

His hand hovered over the screen of his BlackBerry where an internet connection allowed him access to the camera he'd installed in her place eight weeks ago. Soft holiday music and Marnie's warm, sexy laugh greeted his ears even before the picture on the video feed came into focus.

Thanks to the wonders of technology, he could sit two car lengths up the street and still see exactly what went on inside her high-end adventure company that specialized in exotic fantasy escapes.

And as long as Marnie was there, he always got an eyeful.

"If you'll just give me your credit card, you can pay the balance on the trip and I'll mail you a detailed itinerary next week," she was currently saying to an attractive middle-aged couple in front of her desk.

Marnie had a pen tucked in the swoop of cinnamon-colored hair piled at the back of her head. He knew from hours of watching her that she sometimes stuck as many as three pens back there at a time, occasionally losing all writing implements to her hairdo. His camera was hidden inside a bookcase he'd built for her two months back, when he'd posed as a carpenter and helped remodel the front office. The carpentry skills, a long-ago gift from his dad, had been fun to brush off after his years in the military and the Miami P.D., and they'd certainly come in handy for concealing the surveillance camera at Marnie's business.

At that time, she'd been a prime suspect in a white-collar crime at Premiere Properties, her former employer. Vincent Galway, the CEO of Premiere, had fired her right after discovering embezzlement that had cost the company $2.5 million.

Vincent only had very circumstantial evidence pointing to Marnie. The missing funds had been funneled through her department, and there had been a rise in client complaints about double billing. Coupled with her frequent overtime, easy access to the accounts and constant work outside the office, Vincent had let her go for superficial reasons—easy enough to do since Florida was an "at-will" state for employee termination. Then, with Marnie out of the company and none the wiser as to why, Vince had asked Jake to quietly investigate a few key remaining employees and to keep his eye on Marnie, too. While Jake hadn't found the missing money yet, he had leads.

Today, he had the distinct pleasure of taking Marnie off the list of primary suspects thanks to the ridiculously stripped-down lifestyle she'd led for the past two months. Marnie had demonstrated obvious financial hardship while funds continued to disappear from Premiere's accounts. But Jake couldn't even share with her since she'd never known she was a suspect. Still, Jake thought of today as a damn happy occasion because clearing Marnie meant he could do more than just watch her from afar.

His eyes locked on her luscious curves as she came out from behind the desk to shake hands with her clients. Yes, the time approached when he could return to her life—as the carpenter she hadn't seen in two months—and ask her out. He could remove the surveillance equipment easily enough if she left the front office for even a minute.

There'd been a definite attraction between them when he'd first met her, an attraction he would have never acted on while she remained a suspect. But now, the path was clear to explore the fireworks he'd felt when he'd been in her office building that bookcase for her. If anything, he admired her all the more after watching her pull her life together in the wake of losing a job and getting dumped by the waste of space she'd been dating up until she'd been terminated. Marnie had defied the odds and opened her own business in a crap economy, using her travel smarts to her advantage in the new gig.

Smart. Sexy. And she'd be all alone inside in another minute once her customers left. Would he knock on the door as soon as they were gone? Or, knowing that she was prone to stripping off a few layers of clothes as soon as she flipped the Closed sign on her storefront, would he tune in to the BlackBerry a few minutes longer?

Heat crawled up his back at the thought. The need to be honorable warred with the urge to look his fill.

As she ushered her clients to the door, Jake figured he'd split the difference. He'd only watch for a minute and then he'd flip off the feed.

And this time, he wouldn't settle for just fantasizing about Marnie. He'd follow it up with a house call, because damn it, he wanted to see the show in person one of these days.

Yes, a very Merry Christmas to him....

1

A DETAIL-ORIENTED, TYPE A personality, Marnie Wainwright took all necessary precautions. So she checked and double-checked the lock on the street-level door to her business. She closed all the blinds. She flipped the sign on Lose Yourself from Open to Closed.

Only then, in the privacy of the small storefront where she'd converted the back offices into a living space, did she pump her fist in victory and break out her best Michael Jackson move.

"Yesss!" She shouted her triumph, letting down her hair with one hand and switching the satellite radio tuner to dance grooves with the other.

Two months of hard work at Lose Yourself had paid off with her biggest profit yet now that she'd booked an African safari followed up by a beach getaway to Seychelles for a wealthy local couple. Two months of nonstop trolling for clients. Sixty-one days of researching unique trip ideas to appeal to an increasingly competitive travel market full of selective buyers who could easily book online. But her idea to pitch one-of-a-kind fantasy escapes was working.

"How do you like me now?" She sang a tune of her own

making, rump-shaking her way into the back to retrieve a bottle of champagne she'd been saving from the days when her paycheck had been fat and the perks of working in promotions for a luxury global resort conglomerate, Premiere Properties, had been numerous.

She hadn't salvaged much financially from that time, thanks to the bad investments she'd foolishly let her financial adviser boyfriend oversee. Little did she know then that he'd been even more clueless than he'd been charming, losing her hard-earned money almost as soon as she'd entrusted it to him. She'd been royally ticked off about that, but that had only been the prelude to *him* dumping *her*. On Facebook, no less. Apparently he hadn't been interested in her once she lost her cushy benefits at Premiere. At least she understood Alec's reasons. She never had figured out why Premiere had let her go or how her department had been losing as much money as her boss had claimed. But while getting laid off had hurt, it hadn't broken her.

Tonight's sale proved as much. She'd taken her travel smarts from all those years crisscrossing the globe for Premiere and used them to match up adventure seekers with just the right unique escape to suit them, whether that meant a spa trip to Bali or backpacking around the Indus Valley. The inspiration for Lose Yourself had come from her need to do just that. Since she hadn't been able to take a vacation from her own problems, she enjoyed helping other people to do so.

Ditching her suit in a celebratory striptease for the benefit of a life-size cutout of a Hawaiian guy offering a lei to her, she tugged on a long black silk robe for her private after-party. The Hawaiian dude had been a promotional item from a hotel and not quite in keeping with the upscale, personalized appeal of Lose Yourself. But he was cute company in the copier room that doubled as a galley kitchen until she got on her feet enough to afford a real house again.

"Cheers to me!" She raised the proverbial roof with one hand while she twisted off the wire restraint from the champagne cork with the other.

Pop!

The happy sound of that cork flying across the room pleased her as much as the taste of the bubbly would. It had been so long since she'd had reason to celebrate anything. About the only other victory that came close was curing herself of the need to throw darts at the ex-boyfriend who'd helped her lose a job and her savings. She used to regularly wing a silver-tipped missile at a photograph taped to the dartboard she kept on an office wall, but she'd torched that picture a month ago in an effort to take ownership of her mistakes.

She'd almost taken a cute guy's head off with one of those darts a couple of months ago, she recalled. Handsome contractor Jake Brennan had been handcrafting a display case for her storefront and had unwittingly opened a door into one of her tiny arrows. It hadn't been her finest moment. Although Jake Brennan himself had been very fine indeed. Memories of his strong arms coated with a light sheen of sweat and sawdust as he'd sculpted the wood into shape had returned to her often ever since.

Pouring the top-shelf champagne into substandard stemware, Marnie lifted one side of her robe like a chacha girl before testing out a high kick. A little champagne sloshed out of the cheap glass, but the bubbles felt like an electric kiss sliding down her arm as she lifted the glass in a toast.

No doubt it had been thoughts of Jake Brennan that had her thinking of electric kisses.

"To me!" she cheered, then took a drink.

Rinnng! A call on her cell phone interrupted her celebration and she scrambled to grab it just in case it was a potential client. Seeing her former colleague's name on caller ID didn't mean it was a casual call. She'd been pitching her fantasy adventures to all her overworked, overstressed friends these past two months.

"Hello, Sarah." Marnie turned the music down just enough to hear her friend on the other end of the phone.

"Hi, Marnie." Sarah Anders's voice was low, her tone oddly serious next to Marnie's good mood. "Have a minute?"

"Sure." Marnie sashayed her way toward the display case the sexy contractor had built, still dancing as she savored the taste of her drink on her tongue. "I'm just having a little toast to rich world travelers who aren't afraid to take a chance on a new business."

"You made another sale?" Sarah asked.

"An African safari. Not exactly the most original trip, but it's long and involved and will keep me in business well into the New Year. Between that and a little holiday escape I booked for a couple who wanted to check out an ice hotel in Quebec City, I've had my best week yet."

"That's great." Sarah's voice didn't match the words.

"What's wrong?" Feeling the groove vibrate the floor through her bare feet, Marnie set her glass on one of the shelves of the bookcase.

"I just wondered if you'd heard any rumors about misappropriation of funds or big losses at Premiere Properties before you left."

"Embezzlement?" Marnie told herself she shouldn't

care what happened over at Premiere Properties after she'd been terminated six months ago for bogus reasons. Her boss, Vince Galway, had told her some B.S. about cutting back on promotions, but the company spent money hand over fist to promote its luxury resorts. Still, she had to admit she was curious. "What makes you think that?"

"Nothing concrete." Sarah sighed, a world of stress in one eloquent huff of air over the mouthpiece. "But there's been a guy asking questions this week. He's been discreet enough, saying he's part of some forensic accounting team that Vince hired to double-check the books, but I think something's up."

For the first time in six months, Marnie almost felt lucky to have lost the job she loved at Premiere. Her business was taking off, and she didn't have any worries about corporate scams or office politics.

"I'll keep an ear out since I still do business with a lot of Premiere's hotels." In fact, Marnie had sent more than one client to the properties she used to promote. Although she didn't think it had been fair that she'd been axed with no warning, she still recognized Premiere ran first-class resorts.

"Thanks, Marnie. I'd appreciate any word."

Disconnecting the call, Marnie cranked the tunes back up, ready to get back into celebrating her successes. She'd dealt with enough crap these past six months to know that she damn well needed to toast the good stuff when it came along since life didn't give you happy days like this all that often.

Standing in front of the custom-made bookcase that displayed miniature buildings, crafts and other souvenirs from destinations all over the world, she placed her palms where Jake Brennan's broad hands had once been and ran her fingertips over a smooth edge. He'd done a beautiful job on the piece and he'd done it for a song, all things considered. She'd really needed that financial break since she'd been trying to get the doors open for her business on a budget.

Between the memories of the man, the champagne and the swish of silk around her bare legs, she experienced a rush of longing. Jake had been big-time attractive. Too bad she hadn't been in a better place emotionally when they'd met or she might have invited him to stick around after the job was done. Maybe asked him out for a drink.

Or—in her wilder fantasies—simply peeled off all her clothes and plastered herself to that gorgeous body of his.

Walking her fingers across a shelf, Marnie blew a kiss to a model of the Egyptian sphinx on one side of the case and winked at a tiny replica of Michelangelo's David. She had to freshen her flirting skills sometime, didn't she? One day, she'd get back out in the dating world again.

Retrieving her champagne glass, she knocked over an iron Statue of Liberty nearby. As she moved to straighten it, she noticed a smear on the back of the case—a dark spot that didn't belong. Unwilling to suffer a smudge in an otherwise perfect display, she reached past the travel guides and mementos meant to entice her clients.

But the spot felt smooth as glass—different than the rest of the wooden cabinet.

"That's odd." Shoving aside a few more famous buildings for a better look, Marnie peered into a small circle of smoky glass.

Her champagne flute fell from her fingers and shattered on the floor. The electric thrill pulsing through her over her good payday fizzled to nothing, even though the bass from an old club tune still pumped through the speakers.

Because at the center of that smoky glass rested a tiny camera lens. Someone had been watching her.

And given the way the gadgetry had been so perfectly incorporated into her custom-built cabinet, she only had one guess as to who that might be. After what she'd gone through with her ex-boyfriend, the next guy who crossed her would be wise to run for cover.

And right now, it looked like that man was none other than her sexy contractor.

Jake Brennan.

MUSIC PULSED FROM INSIDE the Lose Yourself storefront fa-cade until it sounded more like a raucous bar than a ritzy travel agency specializing in exotic adventures. If Jake Brennan hadn't known Marnie so well, he might have turned around and come back another day, thinking she had company.

But weeks' worth of video surveillance on her fledgling business had not only taken her off his primary suspect list in a major white-collar crime. It had also taught Jake that Marnie liked to dance. And damn, but her shimmy-shake routine while stripping off her jacket and blouse hadn't disappointed.

He would have closed his eyes if she'd ditched more than that. Honestly, he would have. But he'd wanted to be sure she was alone before he went to the door. Could he help it if she had a habit of peeling off work clothes in favor of a silk lounging robe the second she shut her door for the day?

Rapping on the door through the hole in the middle of a fat green holiday wreath, he grinned at the memory of old surveillance footage and the brief, two-minute snip-pet he'd allowed himself back in the car—just enough to see her whip off the clothes and grab the champagne. He'd made sure to only point the cameras toward her work space for legal reasons, even though she'd had plans to live in the back offices. That had eased his conscience somewhat since he hated the idea of spying on anyone who was innocent—especially in their most private moments. But at the time he'd installed the camera he now sought to remove, Jake had very good reason to think she was anything but innocent.

Inside Lose Yourself, the volume of the music decreased. The quiet of the business district on a Friday night surrounded him and he couldn't help a rush of anticipation at seeing Marnie now that he'd all but cleared her.

"Who is it?" came her voice, sweetly familiar to him after scanning hours of video for evidence in his case.

Yes, he'd gotten to know Marnie Wainwright so damn well that just hearing her voice had him salivating like Pavlov's dog. And that happened even though he'd forced himself to shut off the video feed on those few occasions where she'd started to strip off a little more than a stranger had the right to see.

"It's Jake Brennan," he called through the door. "I did some work on your office a couple of months ago and I think I might have left one of my tools behind."

He knew she'd remember him from his brief stint working there. He'd given her a steal on his labor, mostly because his work was entirely self-serving.

Plus, she'd eyeballed him enough that day to make him think she hadn't been oblivious to his presence in her office. If it hadn't been for his suspicions of her back then, he would have asked her out.

Now that he was going to retrieve the surveillance equipment and declare this part of his case finished, Jake looked forward to seeing her again without his work as a barrier.

Inside, he could hear her slide a dead bolt and flip one other lock open. He could picture it perfectly since he knew the inside of that office like the back of his hand from watching Marnie run her business day in and day out. Other than the brief view he'd allowed himself in the car, however, he hadn't reviewed any tapes in a while. Not since his case had led him in another direction.

Slowly, the door creaked open.

A whisper of black silk fluttered through the crack. She'd left the final latch on the door—a long hook like the kind used on hotel rooms—so she could see into the street without leaving herself vulnerable.

Recognizing the black silk as the calf-length, sexy number she liked to wear around the place before bed, he swallowed hard, knowing damn well she wasn't wearing much else.

"Sorry to bother you so late—"

The expression on her face froze him in his shoes. Pursed lips, a clamped-tight jaw and gray eyes staring daggers at him all suggested he'd interrupted something. Had she been arguing with someone on the phone? Protective instincts flared to life.

"Is everything okay in there?" He stepped closer, trying to look past her into the familiar office interior that he'd seen often enough on his surveillance tapes. Framed prints of the Egyptian pyramids hung next to a map of London highlighting historic pubs.

"Everything is fine." She spoke the words oddly, like a marionette where the mouth's movement didn't quite match up with the sounds. "Especially now that you're here."

"I don't get it." He didn't like the brittle set of her shoulders or the flushed color in her cheeks. Was she not feeling well?

Before he could ask, she raised a silver-tipped dart that he remembered well from an earlier meeting.

"You're just in time for target practice while we wait for the cops to arrive."

"What?"

His confusion only lasted until she arced back her arm and let the missile fly, aiming for his eye.

Oh, shit.

Belatedly, he realized her assortment of symptoms pointed to stone-cold fury. All directed at him.

Luckily she was so angry, that her release point was late and the dart clattered harmlessly to the concrete pavement at his feet.

"How could you?" she yelled through the narrow opening. Disappearing for a moment, she returned with a whole handful of darts. "You pervert!"

The darts started flying in earnest now and he took cover against the door.

Ace detective work told him she'd found his hidden camera.

"Marnie?" He tried leaning into her line of sight between rounds of incoming fire. "Did you really call the cops?"

That was going to be a nightmare. He had as many enemies on the force as he had friends. With his luck, one of the former would answer the call and gladly lock his ass up for the night until he could straighten away the paperwork.

"Of course." Another dart.

He ducked.

"You can wait with me while the local police bring you a pair of handcuffs and an orange jumpsuit." A painted pink stone that he happened to know was her paperweight came hurtling through the opening now, joining the darts on the pavement.

He heard the stomp of furious footsteps away from the door. Leaning into the vacated space, he used the time to make his case.

"Marnie, wait." He pulled out his wallet and tossed it inside her storefront where it skidded across the gray commercial carpet and thudded against her ankle. "There's my ID. I'm a licensed private investigator."

She slowed her battle with the buttons on the desk phone. Apparently, she'd been making more calls. To a friend or neighbor? Backup to be sure he stuck around long enough for his own arrest?

"If that's true, that sounds only marginally less smarmy than being a complete and total perv." She cradled the phone against her shoulder and started punching buttons again, this time with slow deliberation.

"Premiere Properties didn't terminate you because they couldn't fund your department. They terminated you because of a major embezzlement scam that originated in your sector of the company. You were a prime suspect."

She shook her head. Confused. Shocked. He'd seen that expression on people's faces when he'd worked in homicide and he'd had to face grieving family members to question them. Hell, he still saw that expression as a P.I. when a wife learned her husband had been cheating. He didn't take jobs like that often, but sometimes he could be persuaded. Having been on the clueless end of an unfaithful relationship made him empathize.

Marnie's face mirrored that kind of disillusionment now.

"Who are you?" She seemed to see him for the first

time that night, her brows furrowed in concentration as if she could guess his motives if she stared hard enough.

Relieved, he pointed to her feet.

"My ID is right there. Just hang up the phone long enough to let me talk to you."

With a jerky nod, she replaced the receiver and retrieved his wallet. Seeing his Florida private investigator's license inside, she met his gaze again.

"I didn't really call the cops yet. I only just found that camera a minute before you arrived."

Thank God. He didn't want to deal with that drama tonight.

"I'm going to collect the darts out here," he told her, scooping up the littered sidewalk. "If you want to meet me somewhere you'll feel safe, we can talk."

By the time he straightened, she was already back at the partially opened door. The stiff set to her shoulders had vanished.

Her caramel-colored hair slid loose from a messy twist on one side, the freed strands grazing her shoulder where her satin robe drooped enough to show she wore a black cotton tank top underneath it. Her gray eyes locked on his, searching his face for answers.

"I don't want to go anywhere. Not when my thoughts are so scattered and my head is spinning like this." Over her shoulder, he could see the mess in her office. It looked as if she'd cleared everything off the display case he'd built, probably searching for other cameras. "I'm suddenly very, very tired."

Without warning, she closed the door in his face and he thought she'd ended the conversation. Then, he heard the safety latch unhook and she reopened the door, silently inviting him inside.

"Are you sure you're okay with this?" He didn't like the idea of setting foot in there if she thought for a second he could still be some random lecher taking video for fun.

She nodded. "A real perv would have put the camera in the bedroom or over the shower, not pointing at where I do business. Besides, a colleague from Premiere called tonight and mentioned something about rumors of a financial loss. I know you're not making it up about possible embezzlement. Are you the guy Vince hired to ask discreet questions around the office?"

He nodded.

"Then you might as well come in." Her words lacked the red-hot fury of the flying darts, but there was a new level of iciness that didn't feel like a big improvement.

Accepting the grudging invitation, he stepped inside the storefront and closed the door behind him.

"I'll just set these down." He piled the darts on her desk, an elegant antique piece out of place with the rest of the utilitarian furniture. Kind of like her. Her silk bathrobe probably cost as much as the old beater she drove to work lately.

Marnie Wainwright had fallen on some hard times, but he admired her grit in not letting them get the best of her.

"I refuse to apologize for the darts." She produced an open bottle of champagne along with two glasses, then dropped onto the love seat in her office's waiting area. "Even if you were conducting an investigation, a hidden camera is still a disturbing way to go about obtaining information."

But legal for an investigation of this magnitude, as long as the device wasn't inside her private residence. He took the chair at a right angle to her, observing the way she recovered herself. Her fingers shook with the leftover churning of emotions as she handed him a glass of bubbly. He hated that his investigation had freaked her out. Hated that she'd found the damn camera in the first place. He'd been banking on hitting on her, not having her glare at him as if he were evil incarnate.

"Granted. But it was also the fastest way of proving your innocence. If my client had gone to the cops, you could have been stuck trying to clear your name from inside a cell, since the evidence they had on you was pretty damning." He set the glass she'd given him on the coffee table.

She seemed to think that one over as she poured her own glass and held the cool drink against her forehead like a compress.

"Why didn't they go the police?" she asked softly, her hands shaking just a little as she lowered the flute and took a sip.

He tried not to envy the glass for its chance to press against her lips. She was dealing with a crisis, after all. But he'd been battling an attraction to this woman ever since the week he'd built the custom-made cabinet to house his spy equipment. He couldn't help subtly ogle a bit now that he was finally free to act on that attraction. Her dark robe slipped away from her calf enough to reveal the delineation of the long, lean muscle in her leg. A gold toe ring winked from her bare foot, a small row of pearls catching the light as she shifted.

Jake had a sudden vision of that long, bare leg in his hands, his body planted between her thighs. And wouldn't that fantasy be helpful in explaining why he'd been spying on her? Cursing the wayward thoughts, he forced himself to talk about the case.

"The CEO of Premiere doesn't trust the local police

ever since they misplaced key evidence that would have convicted some crooks involved in his last company."

The case still pissed off Jake, too, even though it had been two years ago.

"Brennan. You were the investigator on that crime." She snapped her fingers in recognition. "I thought your name sounded familiar when we met. I did a little research on it because I worked for Premiere when they hired Vincent Galway to take over as CEO."

Great. Jake didn't want to be associated with an investigation that screamed police corruption. He'd left the force because a couple of the cops appeared to be flunkies for some bigwigs who didn't want that particular corporate fraud case prosecuted. To keep his eyes off Marnie's legs, he diverted his attention to a nearby painting of the Anasazi cliff dwellings, decorated for the holidays with a few balsam sprigs on the top of the frame.

"I quit when the system screwed over Vince. He talked to the cops and the Feds to try to throw some light on dirty dealings in his last company, and he was the one with mud on his face after the evidence was misplaced." Jake swiped the champagne glass off the table. "But I know Vince from way back. He served in Vietnam with my dad. Because Vince trusts me, he hired my services to help him wade through the embezzlement scandal that could have hurt his company if news about it leaked."

Marnie swirled her glass and watched the bubbles chase each other.

"So you got onto the work crew when I had the office overhauled and you installed a camera." Her bathrobe slipped off her knee, unveiling bare skin for as far as the wandering eye could see up her leg.

A slice of creamy thigh proved too much competition for the picture of the damn cliff dwellings. His gaze tracked up her skin as he calculated how quickly he could have her naked...

"Yes." His throat went dry. "It was a fast way to either clear you or confirm your guilt, and it's a tool the cops rarely use because—"

"—because it's highly unethical and borderline illegal?"

"Because it takes a lot of reviews to obtain permission for it." He'd be damned if he'd let her call his honor into question. "Technology is saving a lot of manpower hours at your local cop shop, so I can guarantee you it's not illegal when there is just cause—for me, or for them."

"But I've been cleared of any wrongdoing, thanks to having my life put under a microscope?"

"You're no longer a prime suspect." He watched her retuck the bathrobe around her legs, possibly feeling the heat of his stare despite his best effort to rein himself in. "In fact, I was hoping to remove the equipment tonight."

Right before he hit on her. He planned to get very close to Marnie Wainwright in the near future. Now? Who knew how long it would take for him to rebuild some trust?

"You thought you'd just saunter in here tonight after I hadn't seen you in two months?" The precariously lopsided twist in her hair finally gave up the ghost, spilling caramel-colored strands and spitting out a pencil that had been holding it all together.

"I figured you wouldn't want to have that equipment running any longer than necessary," he told her reasonably as he retrieved the fallen pencil and placed it on the coffee table.

"Of course not, but since I didn't know I'd been under surveillance for the past two months, might I inquire why you thought I'd even let you in?"

Animal attraction.

But he knew better than to say as much.

"I figured I'd look into a fantasy escape." Heavy on the fantasy. God knew, she'd been occupying enough of his lately.

The woman had compromised his investigation every time she sashayed past that surveillance camera, her confident feminine strut one hell of a distraction.

"At this hour?" Her gaze narrowed. Suspicion mounted.

And with damn good reason.

He hadn't even come close to laying his cards on the table with her yet.

"I work late." He shrugged, not sure what else to offer in his defense. "Do you want me to take the equipment now?"

"No." She leaned forward on the love seat, invading his personal space in a way that would have been damn pleasant if she hadn't fixed him with a stony glare. "I know how to take a sledgehammer to the cabinet, but thanks anyway. Right now, I'm more interested in two things."

"Shoot." He breathed in the warm, spicy scent of an exotic perfume he wouldn't have noticed if they hadn't been this close.

"First, you didn't say I was cleared of suspicion. You carefully distinguished that I'm no longer a prime suspect. Care to explain what that means?"

Her silk-covered knee was only inches from his. One bare foot sat so close to his loafers that he'd have to be careful of her toes if he stood. The nails had been manicured with glittery white polish except for the big toe on each foot, which featured a carefully painted holly berry leaf.

Lifting his gaze to meet hers, he wondered if he was the only one fantasizing about peeling off her robe.

"It means that there's an outside chance you could still be a conspirator, but we don't think that's likely and we are one hundred percent sure you are not the primary force behind the embezzlement."

"How reassuring." She tucked a strand of hair behind one ear, frowning as she seemed to consider the implications of that.

"You said you were interested in two things?" He saw the dartboard behind the love seat no longer contained a picture of her ex-boyfriend, something he hadn't known from the video feeds since his camera didn't give him enough of a wide angle on the room.

Good for her for not caring anymore. Jake's investigations had dug up more than a little dirt on him.

"Right." She fixed him with her gaze. "I'd also like to know just how much of me you've seen with that camera lens of yours."

2

MARNIE HAD HER ANSWER in a nanosecond.

The heat that flared in the private investigator's eyes practically singed her skin before he said one word.

Hell, he didn't have to say a word.

"Oh, my God." She buried her face in her hands to escape Jake's gaze. Or maybe to hide from the answering heat inside her that she had no business feeling for a man who had spied on her.

Damn him.

"Please believe it was never my intent to see more than the business transactions." He had that cool, authority-figure voice down pat and she wondered how she ever could have believed he was a carpenter, let alone a good guy.

Jake Brennan had *dangerous* tattooed all over his big, imposing bod, a wedge of powerful muscle that looked fit to take care of business in a back alley. The brooding, hot expression in his eyes communicated something altogether inappropriate, as if he knew exactly what she looked like naked and had devoted a fair amount of thought to seeing her that way again.

Was she reading into that enigmatic look of his? Maybe. But his presence made her twitch in her seat.

"But you did see more than business transactions," she snapped, frazzled by sexual thoughts. She lifted her head and quickly realized she'd sat far too near to him for this little tête-à-tête.

His knee was so close she could feel the warmth of him through the thin silk of her robe. He sat forward in his seat, his sculpted shoulders leaning toward her as if he debated offering comfort. A worn gray Henley shirt stretched over the taut muscles of his arms, the sleeves shoved up to his elbows past a heavy silver watch that rested on one wrist. Wavy dark hair brushed his collar; his jaw was bristly with a five-o'clock shadow.

She wondered what it would feel like against her skin. And damn it, why did she care? It had to be because she'd spent the past weeks thinking about Jake the Carpenter in a romantic way, building him up to be someone he wasn't based purely on attractiveness. A stupid habit, that. Hadn't she been burned oh so recently by a guy who was all flash and no substance?

Although comparing Alec to Jake was sort of like weighing a cheap copy of a famous painting against the original. One was nice to look at. The other took your breath away it was so freaking magnificent.

"When I installed the camera, I had no idea you would make yourself so comfortable in your office space. How many people work in their pajamas? Um, legally, anyway."

He said it without a trace of a smile, but she could swear she saw a glint of amusement in his flinty gaze.

Defensiveness steeled her spine.

"I thought I was alone so I refuse to be embarrassed." Could she help it if she'd gotten in the habit of peeling off a layer as soon as she flipped the Closed sign on the business?

It had been a damn difficult year between losing her job, losing her savings due to her ex's crappy financial management and finding out the ex himself was the kind of superficial jerk who only cared about her worth as his personal sugar moma.

Oh, and that was all before she found out she'd also been under suspicion for embezzlement.

"You definitely don't have any reason to be embarrassed." He cracked a smile that time—the barest hint of a grin that revealed an unexpected dimple. "I thought your dance moves were great."

In different circumstances, she would have been totally charmed.

But flirting with the P.I. who'd surely seen her mostly naked and who, by the way, hadn't fully crossed her off his suspect list didn't strike her as a particularly wise move.

"Thanks. But on that note, maybe I should let you take the camera and get back to your investigation." She stood, feeling awkward and too aware of him.

"I appreciate that." He stood, too, topping her by several inches and filling her vision with more than his fair share of studliness. "I'd hate to lose expensive equipment to a sledgehammer."

He didn't move, however. At least not right away.

Her heartbeat quickened.

"Jake." Saying his name aloud felt foreign and familiar at the same time. She'd thought about him often enough since their first meeting.

Strange that all the while he'd been feeding her daydreams, she might have been playing a role in his, too. The thought stirred desire so palpable it made her breath catch.

"Yes?" He'd been waiting. Watching.

Still not moving.

"Who else has seen those surveillance tapes?" She had to know. Because while she might be able to write off Jake's eyes following her in her most private moments, she didn't think she could handle knowing her former employer had been reviewing the footage.

"No one but me has seen the actual footage. I just pulled off a few stills to show some of your transactions in progress. I would never compromise your privacy any more than absolutely necessary."

She nodded, believing him.

"Thank you for that, at least." Warmth swirled through her, although why she should feel so comforted that he would keep her amateur stripteases to himself, she wasn't quite sure. "Do you need any tools to remove the camera? I have a screwdriver somewhere."

Turning, she moved to retrieve it.

"Marnie, wait." His hand clamped lightly around her shoulder and she froze. Not that he was holding her in place. Far from it. She could have easily kept on walking.

But it was the first time that he'd touched her for real and not just in passing—or in fantasies. The contact made her mouth turn dry and her legs felt a little shaky.

"What is it?" Her words were breathless.

She hoped he would interpret that as nervousness from finding out she'd been suspected of a major felony and under surveillance all in one evening. And honestly, that was part of it.

His hand slid away now that he had her attention, but the memory of it continued to warm her shoulder like a phantom touch.

"Would you consider answering a few questions about your work with Premiere Properties?"

"Of course." She resisted the urge to fan herself. Obviously, if she was so desperate for male companionship that she would continue to think about someone who had spied on her in an, er, romantic way, she needed to get out more often.

"I've eliminated a lot of people." He reached into the back pocket of his jeans and emerged with a paper. "My focus has narrowed to people involved with this place."

He handed her the folded sticky note with a half-dozen luxury resorts listed, along with highly placed individuals within those properties. Although a handful of names were still legible, only one resort wasn't crossed out.

"The Marquis." She knew the property well. "You've got your work cut out for you."

Returning the paper to him, she took a step back in every way possible. He might as well have indicated a nest of rattlesnakes.

"Why do you say that?" He frowned, looking at the paper again.

"You haven't done much homework for a guy who's been on the case for two months, have you?" She thought about pouring herself another sip or two of champagne, then figured she'd be better off just finding the damn screwdriver so he could take his camera and go.

She slid out from behind the coffee table to hunt through her desk.

"On the contrary, I've worked my ass off. White-collar crimes like this can be filtered through so many different accounts electronically that it makes it damn difficult to trace." He followed her to the desk, sidestepping a few items on the floor from when she'd cleared the shelves in a frightened fury. "After hiring a forensic accountant, I spent most of my time investigating you since, on first look, the money appeared to have been leaking wherever you traveled last year."

Her frantic culling through pens and paperclips paused.

"You think someone wanted it to *look* like I was responsible?" A new fear gripped her, superceding her outrage at being secretly videotaped.

"Yes. And when you opened this business, I wondered if you'd just found a new way to skim money from the same properties you worked with at Premiere since you continued to book trips to a lot of the same resorts."

"Because they're great destinations and I know them inside and out."

"Including the Marquis?"

Slamming the door shut with her knee, she rubbed her temple where a stress headache wanted to take root.

"No. That one isn't really—" Sighing, she began again. "It's a unique place. Well off the beaten path just outside of scenic Saratoga, New York. Strictly for adults."

"It didn't come up in my early searches, but I just figured it was one of those high-end places that doesn't advertise."

"It is." Just thinking about the things she'd seen there the last time she visited made heat crawl up her cheeks and take up residence. "Technically, Premiere doesn't own it, but they are a partner of the eccentric owner and they take care of the food service and a few other basics. It's a complicated relationship and it's important that it remains under the radar since the guests are guaranteed a highly—" she cleared her throat "—sensual experience."

Was it just her, or was sex coming to mind way too much during this conversation? While she'd like to believe it was just the buzz of good champagne in her veins that made her feel so pleasurably warm inside, she knew it had more to do with Jake Brennan being in the room with her. He would make any woman take notice.

"Sounds like the perfect place to hide an embezzlement crime." His jaw flexed, and she could almost see the wheels turning in his head, fitting this new piece of evidence into the puzzle.

"Actually, precious little is hidden in the rooms of the Marquis." She studiously avoided looking at him while thinking about what went on in that private resort. Her eyes locked on the screwdriver in a silver cup holder on her desk. "Here."

She passed him the tool and eased past him to clear a path to the bookcase so he could take his equipment—and his questions—and go.

He took the screwdriver, following more slowly.

"It also sounds like the perfect place to lose yourself."

"Excuse me?" She pulled the belt tighter on her bathrobe.

No matter that she wore a tank top and comfy pair of girly boxer shorts underneath it. The more layers the better during a conversation about a sex-drenched playground with a droolworthy stud who'd not only seen her mostly naked, but seemed to enjoy the view.

Ah, who was she kidding? She was enjoying checking him out just as much. Too bad he had already pulled a fast one on her or she might have considered acting on the sizzling connection between them.

"I want to avail myself of your services through Lose Yourself. I need you to book me a trip to this place as soon as possible."

The image that presented—Jake Brennan stalking the

secret lairs of the sexually adventurous—gave her heart palpitations. And, oddly, inspired a ridiculous surge of jealousy for all the women who would dole out their best tricks to attract his notice.

"No." She folded her arms. Shook her head. "You don't want to go there. There's a strict policy about hidden cameras anyway. Definitely not your kind of place."

"Don't you want to find out who tried to pin about ten different federal crimes on you?"

"Yes, but—"

"Good. That's why you're going with me."

3

"FORGET IT."

Marnie wrenched the screwdriver out of his hand and turned toward the display case that held his camera as if to remove it by herself.

"I need you there." He slid his arm between her and the bookcase to stop her. The fact that his knuckles brushed against her flat stomach and his shoulder rubbed along hers was a pleasurable bonus.

"Don't be ridiculous." She stepped back, her face flushed and her pulse twitching visibly at the base of her throat.

Agitated because of his touch? Or his proposition?

He couldn't deny a bit of agitation of his own at the thought of spending time with her at some trumped-up luxury love shack. While he'd had every intention of getting close to her sooner or later, he hadn't intended for the circumstances to be quite so intense.

But then, he hadn't considered what an asset she'd be in an investigation at a hyperexclusive resort. She knew the place. And if the real embezzler had set Marnie up to take the fall for the crime, she might be able to finger the enemy faster than he could on his own.

"You said it yourself." Sliding the screwdriver from her grip, he set it aside, not needing it to free his surveillance equipment. "You visited dozens of properties all over the globe for Premiere, so you know these resorts well. You've been to the Marquis and you've dealt with the people who work there. Why let the trail turn even colder while I waste time trying to get the lay of the land when you know the place inside and out?"

She gaped at him as if he'd just suggested she sign on for a suicide mission. Was the thought of spending a few days with him that bad? He forced his attention to the camera equipment as he extracted a tiny wireless transmitter.

"Even if I wanted to do that—and I don't—I can't just take off at the drop of a hat. I have a business to run." She held out her hand to take the transmitter from him while he pried out the camera itself.

"Everyone deserves a getaway," he parroted back her business's pitch line, knowing he was onto something. He had to convince her to do this—and not just because he wanted to get to know her better. Her input could be the key. "Besides, maybe you can't afford *not* to go."

Straightening, he tucked the small camera in his back pocket, then took the transmitter from her and did the same.

"What do you mean?" Frowning and distracted, she didn't seem to notice when he put his hands on her shoulders to turn her around so they could converse somewhere besides the narrow space in front of the shelves.

How easy would it be to slide his hands lower, to graze her chest just above the rise of her breasts? The fragrance of her temptress perfume wafted along his senses as he guided her toward the desk.

With more than a little regret, he released her.

For now.

"Someone went to considerable effort to make it appear as though you were behind a highly lucrative crime. That suggests you've got an enemy you don't know about. What if this enemy raises the stakes next time?"

Her gray eyes searched his and he could see the moment she wondered if he could be the guilty party.

"Here." He took out his cell phone. "Vincent is on speed dial. Call your old boss at Premiere Properties and check out my story. He can tell you how seriously he's taking this investigation."

And although it stung a little to see how fast she reached for the phone and dialed, Jake knew the line separating the criminals from the cops—or P.I.'s—could be razor-thin sometimes. He'd left the force just because there was too much crossover in his opinion. He could hardly blame her if she found it difficult to know who to trust.

Still, he didn't care for the lack of color in her face by the time she disconnected her call and handed him the phone in silence.

"You okay?" He didn't want to crowd her when she'd had one hell of a night, but she sure looked as if she could use a shoulder.

"You're right. He says 2.5 million dollars is missing. That's a lot of money." Her bleak tone was a far cry from her normal Friday-after-five voice. Usually she spent a good hour belting out tunes along with her radio.

And while he regretted bursting her bubble of ignorant bliss, she was better off knowing the truth. He had to consider her safety.

"Someone's taking great pains not to get caught. That raises the chances they could resort to violence if they think we're on his or her trail."

This would have been a whole lot simpler if he hadn't investigated her. Hadn't lied to her and spied on her. If none of that had happened, he'd be dusting off seduction skills he hadn't used in too damn long. Instead, he needed to tread carefully to convince Marnie to help him nab Vincent Galway's embezzler. But it was the least he could do after all the ways Vince had been screwed by the justice system. Jake had always hated that one of the most honorable guys he knew—after his own dad—had had his integrity questioned. His life put under a microscope because he'd tried to do the right thing.

And yeah, he couldn't deny an unexpected need to protect Marnie. His case had taken on a new slant after talking to her and he wanted to be sure the embezzler didn't try something more drastic to point suspicion her way.

"I agree that it would be in my best interest to figure out who this person is before he targets me all over again." Marnie stalked toward her work computer and sat down at the screen. At first, she simply squeezed her temples, as if she wanted to rub out all the worries in her head. Then, she peered up at him with new determination in her eyes. "Since I have this bastard to thank for putting me under suspicion and exposing me to a stranger, it would be worth the time off if I could help put him behind bars."

Surprise, surprise.

She was going to agree to this without a fight. But she didn't look happy about it. Figuring it would be in poor form to break out the victory dance while she was so clearly upset, he concentrated on all the plans he needed to make for this new strategy to work.

Jake watched her click through some keys to pull up a web page for a genteel-looking inn with wide white columns and a long veranda. Four stone chimneys dotted the roof. It could have been out of *Gone with the Wind* except for the fact that the place was surrounded by snow and decked with holiday evergreens. A cobalt-colored front door was the only feature of the building that didn't fit with the classic Georgian architecture.

"You'll get us into the Marquis?"

"Damn straight," she muttered, clicking a code into the system that activated a reservation form he assumed wasn't available to the general public. The photo of the Marquis didn't even have a sign out front, though a caption under the photo gave an address in upstate New York. "I've gone through hell the past six months because of this. I had to move out of my house and into a room in the back of the business to protect my credit after I lost my job. My savings. All this time, I thought I'd done something wrong to make Vince question my capabilities, when in fact I just had an enemy I didn't know about. An enemy who made me look like a criminal."

He heard the hurt in her voice. Felt for her situation.

"Can you be ready to leave tomorrow?"

"Are you kidding?" She turned frosty eyes on him. "Someone wants me behind bars. And whoever it is, I have that person to thank for losing a great job at the worst possible time. So I can have my car gassed up and ready to head north in an hour."

Surprised at her new level of commitment to the plan, he wondered if she had any idea how close they'd have to be throughout this trip.

"Are you sure you don't want to wait for a flight out in the morning?"

"Tomorrow is a Saturday. We'll be lucky to find an afternoon flight, let alone something in the morning." She went back to her computer keys and started filling out information for the exclusive resort. "Besides, I won't be able to get any sleep with this hanging over my head."

Twenty-plus hours on the road with Marnie? His agenda shifted to accommodate the prospect.

"Fine, but you need to give an assumed name for check-in purposes, just in case the embezzler is someone who works on-site. We can pick up a wig or something on the way up."

She nodded, lips pursed in a tight line.

"Plus, I want to take my SUV and we can spot each other in the driver's seat so we can go straight through the night and into the day tomorrow." Before she could protest, he added, "I've got four-wheel drive and it looks like we'll need it where we're going."

"Fair enough." She frowned as she paused her typing. "You can fill me in on how you think it's going to be any safer for me there than here since—assuming you're correct about where the embezzlement originated—we'll be walking right into enemy terrain."

"Easy." He dug his keys out of his pocket. "You'll be in disguise and hidden away in the room as much as possible. More important, you'll be with me."

She bit her lip but kept right on with the data entry thing, flipping to a new screen.

"And don't forget," he reminded her as he headed for the door. "We'll need to stick together both for appearance's sake and for safety purposes, so—only one room."

At last, her typing fingers slowed. Stopped. He hadn't expected to get that one past her.

"Is your client springing for the expense of this trip?" she asked, her eyes narrowing shrewdly.

"Yes. But while I'm sure he could afford two rooms—"

"That's not necessary." She went back to the keyboard, a golden brown lock of her hair sliding off her shoulder to frame her cheek. "I'll get one room, but it's going to be the biggest damn suite in the place. Vincent Galway and Premiere Properties owe me that much."

IT WASN'T EXACTLY the kind of fantasy escape she tried to sell to her upscale clientele.

Even reclining in the leather passenger seat of Jake's full-size SUV, Marnie didn't think a twenty-five-hour car ride counted as decadent and indulgent. But at least— twelve hours into it—they were making excellent headway. Jake had shaved off some serious time overnight by tearing through Georgia and the Carolinas like a bat out of hell. Easy to do when traffic was so light. No one wanted to head north in the winter, except for a few die-hard skiers.

"You don't think you could sleep if you leaned back the rest of the way?" Jake peered over at her from the driver's side, his shades hiding his eyes now that the morning sun was well over the horizon.

He'd turned out to be a decent travel companion. He'd stocked up on bottled water prior to the trip and kept her cup holder stocked. Periodically, he pointed out rest areas and asked if she wanted to stop. Best of all, he'd given her control of the radio stations. Considering he had spied on her and played her for a fool by pretending he was a cute contractor instead of a dangerously deceptive P.I., Jake was turning out to be an okay guy.

She would have felt more comfortable around him, however, if she wasn't still highly attracted.

"I can't sleep when I'm wound up," she told him finally.
"Doesn't matter if I've got the world's best accommodations and total silence. If I'm upset, nothing short of an
animal tranquilizer would help me close my eyes."

"That explains a few late-night dart-throwing sessions."
He changed lanes to avoid a semitruck trying to merge
into traffic.

All around them, the lush greenery had faded, leaving
them in a brown and gray barren part of the country. No
snow yet, but the temperature had dropped a good twenty-
five degrees.

"You know, I don't think it's fair that you've got all
kinds of inside dirt on me and I don't know much of anything about you."

Maybe her attraction would lessen as she got to know
him better. Real life had a way of dousing the best fantasies. Besides, talking about his world would keep her
from picturing him watching her dance around her office
in her skivvies at midnight when she realized she'd left
some notes out front that she wanted to work on.

The thought of him keeping tabs on her all that time
sent a fresh wave of awareness through her. She so could
not let herself start thinking he was an okay guy, damn
it. She needed to help him with his investigation—find
out who wanted to frame her—and get back to rebuild-
ing her life.

"You want the life story?" He drummed his fingers on
the steering wheel with a staccato beat that smacked of
impatience.

Too bad. She was only too happy to turn the tables

on him. Let him see how it felt to be the one under the microscope.

"A few highlights would be nice."

"I'm a Midwestern farm boy turned Marine. I liked it a little too well. After my last tour was up, I figured I'd put the skills to use and became a cop."

The life story was decidedly condensed.

"What brought you to Miami?" It seemed more appropriate than asking him how many women he'd spied on while they undressed.

"More varied and interesting crime."

"Oh." She wasn't quite sure what that said about his psyche, but she could respect the desire to utilize his skills.

"I'm good at my job. Rather, I *was* good at the job before I quit the force. At the time I figured I might as well challenge myself." He downshifted for construction work ahead and then tapped the windshield lightly; on the other side, snow had begun to fall. "And you can't beat the weather."

"Tell me about it. I have a coat from my trips to ski destinations, but since I usually scheduled those in the off season, I've hardly ever worn it." She shifted uncomfortably in her seat as the topic of wardrobes came up. "The resort we're headed to has extensive shopping facilities if you need anything, by the way. We'll have to buy some clothes for the parties."

Up ahead, traffic condensed into three lanes as they left Washington, D.C., in the distance. The snow was falling faster and Jake switched on the wipers.

"I brought a suit," he assured her, clicking a button for the defrosters. "I should be fine."

"Actually—" She adjusted a fleece blanket on her lap that he'd brought in case either of them wanted to sleep on the way. But even if she could have talked herself into sleeping, she was a little afraid that the man was so much on her mind she might end up moaning his name during a sexy dream or something equally embarrassing. Between Jake and their unconventional destination, she was having a hard time keeping her thoughts on the straight and narrow. "This resort caters to a very particular clientele. The name Marquis is a nod to the underground gentlemen's clubs that served British aristocrats in the latter half of the nineteenth century. Guests are expected to uphold the fantasy element of the experience, so we'll have no choice but to dress like the natives."

He cut a quick glance her way, eyes full of skepticism.

"I hope you're messing with me."

"I wholeheartedly wish that I was," she answered, envisioning herself stuck in layers of petticoats with a bustle and corset.

"What kind of hotel imposes a dress code?"

"First of all, this is not your normal hotel. It's a privately owned club—more like an elegant country house that offers exclusive invitations. Second, the period costumes aren't mandatory. But if we don't play the game, it would be like wandering around a nudist colony in a tux. You don't want to stick out at the resort if you're there to question people and track down information."

"I'm not wearing a sissy-boy collar up to my chin with a two-mile necktie."

"I'm pretty sure it's called a cravat." And it would be a far cry from the blue dress shirt he wore with a worn-in white T-shirt underneath.

Though she was pretty sure he would look as mouthwatering in one as the other. Her gaze darted over his broad shoulders. Everything about him broadcast power. Strength. Hotness.

"Whatever."

"The good news is that I recall a lot of functions that call for masks of one sort or another. That will help me mingle more since there will be very little chance of being recognized that way."

In the pocket of her trench coat, her cell phone vibrated with an incoming message. Checking it, she saw a note from the management at their destination.

"It's a confirmation for our reservation. They want us to know that we'll miss the main seating for dinner and that they'll serve us in our room." She scrolled down the screen, not ready to think about sharing a bedroom with the man in the driver's seat. The suite contained a queen-size bed plus a trundle; apparently pullout sofas weren't period-accurate for their furnishings. The trundle thing had always struck her as amusing since they so obviously weren't meant for people bringing kids to the hotel. Apparently a trundle was the Marquis's comfortable answer to a threesome sleeping arrangement.

But in their case, it meant Jake would be sleeping only a few feet away from her, even in the biggest room available.

How awkward would that be to go from throwing darts at him to bedding down with him in a thirty-hour span? A quick shiver chased down her spine.

"Sounds good. I won't be ready to face a bunch of role-playing swingers the moment we step into the place anyhow."

"Although—" her thumb hovered over the scroll key on her phone "—we are invited to the evening entertainment that starts at eleven."

"Should I be afraid to ask?" He cruised past signs for Baltimore as the snow coated the landscape.

A few cars with Christmas trees tied to their roofs passed, the sight a little surreal during this conversation about private sex clubs and role-playing naughty aristocrats.

"Apparently it's a vignette called The French Maid." Jamming the phone into an open compartment on the door of the SUV, Marnie didn't want to think about it anymore, let alone discuss the nature of the club with Jake.

"You've been there before. What are the entertainments like?"

"I—" Her cheeks heated at an old memory. "I don't consider myself overly uptight, but I couldn't sit through the only one I ever started to watch."

"You're blushing?" He sounded far too amused.

"How would you possibly know that if your eyes were on the road?" The air in the SUV's interior felt warm and heavy—too intimate by half.

She shoved the blanket from her lap and tossed it in the backseat.

"Details, please."

Retrieving her bottle of water from the cup holder, she took a long swig, partially to delay. Partially to cool off.

"It was that good?" he prodded, all too aware of her discomfort.

"No. I don't know." It would be important to prepare for their stay, to steel herself against whatever wayward thoughts the place inspired. "It was more elegant than I imagined it would be. More of a peep show exhibition than anything overt."

"You ran because it was a turn-on."

"I didn't run. I left because it felt icky to share a steamy moment with a room full of strangers."

"How was it any different than watching a movie at the theater?"

She pointed toward the sign for 95 North where the interstate divided.

"There's more anonymity in a theater somehow with the chairs all facing one direction. Plus, that's a movie. This had real live people acting it out in front of us and the show was nowhere near PG-13. The entertainment at the Marquis felt more…communal."

Now Jake reached for his water bottle and chugged it faster than she had.

"Maybe this isn't the best topic for someone who needs to drive for ten more hours, after all." He replaced the water and cracked the window.

Had she been aware of him before? Now she could practically feel the warmth of his exhalations across the console between them.

"You asked," she reminded him.

"And with good reason. The more I know about this place, the better." He tugged at the collar of his dress shirt even though the neck was open. "But for now, maybe we shouldn't dwell on the gratuitous nudity."

"I never said anything about nudity."

"And you see where my mind went anyhow? Moving on." He cleared his throat and straightened a pant leg at the knee. "Did you bring anyone to that show with you? A work colleague, friend, boyfriend?"

"As a rule, I don't mix business with pleasure and I always traveled alone in my work for Premiere."

"You should make a list of everyone you remember from that last trip—anyone from management to waitstaff who stands out in your memory, anyone you came in contact with who worked there."

"Okay." Grabbing her phone, she slid open the keypad to type some notes.

"I'll have you email it to my office and we'll run some background checks to see if anything unusual comes up."

"We should do that before we arrive. Did I mention there's no wireless on-site? Or phones, either. Well, you can have a phone, but if they see you with one in any of the common rooms, they hold it until your departure date. You have to agree to that in a waiver when you check in."

"For a luxury resort, it's damn restrictive, isn't it? Although I'm sure that's what makes it all the easier to commit a crime from a place like that. Less eyes watching your every move."

"On the contrary, there are eyes everywhere. They're just more focused on erogenous zones than technology."

He slid another sideways glance at her and she felt it shiver over her skin as surely as if he'd touched her.

"I'm beginning to think the surroundings are going to prove a hell of a distraction."

No. The biggest distraction would be Jake himself—but she didn't want to put that into words when she needed to be building barriers against him instead of demolishing them.

"As long as we focus on finding a crook, we'll be fine." Some anonymous scumbag had cost her a lucrative living and tried to have her jailed for a crime she hadn't committed. The sooner she found out who, the easier she'd sleep.

"Or…" He rubbed a hand over his jaw like a man in deep thought. "Instead of ignoring the obvious, we could act on it."

She blinked, not sure she'd understood.

"Excuse me?"

"Part of the problem is not knowing how we're going to deal with the inevitable sexual chemistry once we're bumping up against each other day and night in a small space." He got into the left lane and slowed down as an exit approached.

"I think it's imperative we ignore that in a working relationship." She hadn't been kidding about not mixing business with pleasure.

"It'd be easier to ignore if we confronted the chemistry, tested the wattage and found out it was just some idle urge, wouldn't it?" Getting off the exit, he darted into a coffee shop parking lot.

Next thing she knew, the SUV was in Park and Jake Brennan had his seat belt off. He reached over to pop hers open with a click, as well.

When his knuckles grazed her hip, she knew this wasn't a routine java run. He'd pulled the car over with a clear purpose that he communicated through a hot perusal of her body, from thighs to hips, belly to breasts.

"That's a ludicrous idea." Mostly because she had the feeling that "testing" any chemistry would uncover a wellspring so hot it would take days to tamp it back down.

"Is it?" He reached across the console to smooth a strand of her hair behind one ear, inciting a path of gooseflesh up her arm directly underneath his hand.

The words *hell yes* never made it to her lips, even though she darted her tongue along them to prime the path for the utterance.

His eyes followed the movement like a tracking device, his pupils dilating so that his green eyes turned almost completely dark. Her heart hammered against her chest. Her brain trotted out every misplaced fantasy she'd ever had about Jake since first laying eyes on him that day he'd built her cabinet.

Each of those sexy daydreams came back to her now, conspiring against all her best intentions.

Just one kiss.

The thought crossed her mind long enough to propel her forward a scant inch—past the point of no return.

4

Two months' worth of waiting for Marnie paid off.

Big-time.

He knew the moment she'd consented to the kiss and he sealed the deal an instant later, capturing her mouth with his for that first experimental taste. The bubble gum scent of her lips and the subtle hint of a surrendering sigh drew him closer. He wrapped an arm around her back, anchoring her to him.

Hands coming to rest on his shoulders, she twisted her fingers in the fabric, her nails scraping lightly over the pressed cotton. He'd waited so damn long to feel that sensation of her arching against him. How many times had he watched her in his surveillance footage, only to war with his conscience about wanting her? Now, her lips slid sweetly over his, her whole body melting into his like hot butter.

The gearshift pressing in his side didn't matter. Nor did the water bottles rolling on the floor as he knocked things off the console. Marnie's breathy hum sang in his ears like a victory tune.

If only he could have a little more of her…

He hooked a finger in the V of her trench coat and tugged her nearer. She responded by wrapping her arms around his neck, ratcheting up the heat. The soft swell of her breasts grazed his chest and his blood surged south so fast he could have taken her then and there.

If it had been dark outside, he would have been able to pull her onto his lap without anyone around them being the wiser. But in the middle of a parking lot in broad daylight?

Damn it.

He broke away from her with a truckload of regret, his breathing harsh. Her eyes opened slowly as she seemed to process the break in the action. Her pupils were dilated, her lips slightly open as if awaiting another kiss. Finally, her fingers unfurled from his shirt, freeing him.

"Bad idea." She pronounced the verdict even as her cheeks remained flushed and she ran her tongue over her lips as if to seek a final taste of him.

"The kiss wasn't to your satisfaction?" He swiped his thumb along her jaw, unable to release her totally.

"You know perfectly well that's not the problem." She slid away from him, settling back into her own seat until his hand fell away. "Testing the chemistry was the bad idea since all we did was prove how combustible it could be if we touched each other."

Frowning, she tightened the belt on her trench coat and tucked the lapels closer together. Did she think a frail cloth barrier could stifle the sensations that surely raced over her skin the same way they sizzled along his?

The hell of it was, all she accomplished by cinching that belt was to accentuate show-stopping curves he wanted to thoroughly explore.

"Wrong." His fingers itched to undress her since he

knew better than anyone how much she liked to wear silky slips under her buttoned-up business attire.

Not that it would help his cause to remind her of that particular fact.

"Excuse me?" She glared at him across the console, her golden brown hair trapped in the collar of her coat until she flipped it free with a flick of her wrist. "Have you forgotten we need to work together this week? Don't you think this kind of distraction complicates a working relationship?"

"Maybe. But that doesn't make the kiss a bad idea." He put the car into Reverse, trying to turn his focus toward getting them safely to their destination as quickly as possible. He sure hoped he could shave some time off the twelve hours his maps suggested it would take. "It's always better to know what you're dealing with than to wait and wonder."

"And now we know." She didn't sound too happy about the fact. "We're not only stuck in a hedonistic sensual haven together, we're also susceptible to sexual temptation. Don't you think that's a problem when we need to concentrate on finding a thief before he bankrupts your client or me, or both of us?"

When she put it that way, it did sound like a problem.

"Nothing will interfere with my job," he assured her. "I guarantee you that much." He owed Vincent Galway a quick resolution to this mess.

Without the handful of investigative jobs from Premiere during the year since he'd left the force—and the contacts Vince had shared to help land Jake some lucrative work—Jake would have never grown his thriving business so quickly.

"Good." She settled into the corner of her seat farthest

from him and closed her eyes as if she would finally sleep. Or at least, pretend to. "Then we're agreed we'll never let that happen again."

Never?

That was a long time in Jake's book and he didn't plan to agree or disagree. As far as he was concerned, strong sensual chemistry would lend their cover more authenticity.

And after one electric taste of Marnie Wainwright, Jake knew there wasn't a chance in hell they'd resist the lure of that attraction for long.

"NAMES, PLEASE?"

The request was issued by the sleek and incredibly sexy brunette behind the desk of the Marquis that night.

Marnie half hid behind Jake as they checked into the resort to ensure no one recognized her. She had never seen this woman who greeted them before, though, not unusual since the Marquis didn't employ many regular staff members, preferring to run the place more like an ashram than a business. Guests who lingered there for more than a week took turns as greeters and hosts, welcoming other guests. Guests could even sign up for waitstaff and housekeeping duties, jobs that frequently filled role-playing fantasies. No doubt tonight's greeter was a hotel guest looking to meet new people if she'd volunteered for desk duty.

With that in mind, Marnie didn't worry quite so much about being recognized. Besides, she'd purchased temporary hair color when they hit the New York border and was now a redhead. She'd also braided a plait around the crown of her head so that she fit in with the historically themed Marquis. A small, cosmetic change, but it gave her a very different look.

"Jack and Marie Barnes," Jake lied, signing the old-fashioned register with fake names while the hostess ran a credit card.

Marnie had been interested to see if the transaction would work, but Jake had assured her that the card was tied to a false business that could not be traced back to him.

Apparently, no one knew their way around the law quite as well as an ex-cop.

"Welcome, Jack and Marie. I'm Lianna." The dark-haired siren handed Jake a room card imprinted with a photo of an old-fashioned iron key. "Is this your first time with us at the Marquis?"

The woman looked as if she could have walked right out of a late nineteenth-century painting. Everything from her loosely upswept curls to her pink gown fit in with the elegant surroundings. Exotic Persian carpets in an array of patterns dotted the highly polished wooden floors. Wrought-iron sconces hung at regular intervals along the walls of the reception parlor, the flames flickering with the regularity of gas fixtures. Softly worn tapestries depicting maidens in varying states of undress were the only indication that the Marquis might not be your average historic hotel.

The sensual works on the walls made for an interesting contrast with the holiday decor. Every inch of the place was decked in greenery and holly berries. Evergreen boughs had been struck through the spindles on the wide main staircase as they entered. Bowls of fruit with gold ornaments dotted tables and stands.

"We've never been here before," Jake told the woman, taking the key. "It's my understanding we can have dinner brought to our suite?"

"If you wish, but we encourage all our guests to become acquainted with the layout of the rooms and the other residents as soon as possible to make the most of every moment here." Lianna came out from behind the secretary desk that served as guest reception, her bustled pink skirts swishing softly with her movements. "Ideally, your first night under our roof should give you a taste of all the delights to come."

She paused so close to them that Marnie could smell the woman's perfume. Her long, dark lashes fell to half-mast as she sent a look of blatant invitation in a glance that darted from Marnie to Jake and back again.

Marnie had known she and Jake would face temptations at the Marquis—from each other as well as from third-party invitations. She just hadn't expected them to start arriving so damn quickly. Possessiveness made her thread her arm through Jake's, even though she had no idea if Lianna was flirting with him or her.

"I'm sure the meal will taste just as delightful in our room as it does in the dining hall." Marnie tugged on Jake's elbow, away from the bombshell in pink satin.

"Lianna." Jake remained in place. "We'd like to observe some of the evening's activities without joining anyone else. Is that possible?"

Lianna's dark eyes lit with approval.

"We welcome voyeurs, of course." She turned back to her desk and, bending forward over it to search for something, she presented them with a close-up view of her ruffle-swathed rump and a hint of seamed stocking.

Marnie suddenly hoped the woman proved guilty of the crimes they were investigating so that Marnie could see the flirtatious temptress behind bars.

Jake wrapped his arm around her, at least, assuring Marnie he hadn't forgotten she was alive. Not that she wanted to embark on some torrid affair with the P.I. herself. But somehow it would have bothered her to have him ogle another woman while he pretended to be her husband.

At least, she wished that was the only reason for the surge of jealousy.

"Here you go." Lianna turned around in triumph, holding another key card in her hand. This one had a picture of a wooden door with a cutout slit, sort of like the flip-open slots used in a prison to serve a confined inmate his meals. "Just slip this key into any of the peepholes that look like this around the hotel."

She tapped the card to indicate the image of the wooden slot.

Marnie recalled seeing those slots around the Marquis the one other time she'd visited in her promotional efforts for Premiere Properties, but she hadn't had the slightest notion of their purpose. Consensual voyeurism was one thing. Being spied on unaware was something totally different. Had she been watched on her last trip here without ever being the wiser?

"Do any of the private rooms have peepholes that we won't know about?" Marnie was horrified to think some unseen guest might be able to spy on her and Jake in their suite.

The thought reminded her all over again that Jake had watched her for two months without her knowledge. She couldn't help another surge of anger at his violation of her privacy.

"Of course not." Lianna leaned closer to give Marnie's arm a reassuring squeeze as if they were close friends. "The only guests who have ones in their rooms request it specifically at check-in."

"Exhibitionists," Jake clarified, pocketing the key.

"A voyeur's best friend," Lianna added with a wink. She settled her hand on her hip in a pose worthy of Mae West, her curves displayed at a suggestive, pinup girl angle. "Let me know if there's anything else either of you need. I'll be at the desk all night."

"Thank you." With a nod, Jake turned away from her and tucked Marnie under his arm to lead her through the hotel.

Ducking her head, she allowed Jake to guide her toward an antique-looking elevator with the old-fashioned gold gate that pulled across the doors. They had agreed in advance to let Jake be the public face of their couple since there was a chance Marnie could be recognized even in disguise.

"We can take the elevator to our room on the third floor." Marnie knew she should be exhausted, even though she'd slept a little on the trip. Still, adrenaline coursed through her after the run-in with Lianna and being inundated by talk of voyeurs and images of half-naked women on the larger-than-life tapestries. She'd seen those same wall hangings the last time she'd visited, but somehow they packed more punch with Jake standing next to her. Her senses seemed to have become hyperacute ever since that kiss in the SUV on the way up here.

Now she wondered how she could have ever visited this place without thinking about sex every second.

"No." Jake kept walking past the elevator. "Let's see the clothing store first. We're going to want to get straight to work tomorrow and apparently we'll need the right duds."

They passed a woman—clearly a guest—dressed in a red velvet maid's uniform with a Santa hat and stilettos. The volunteer worker pushed her cart full of scented soaps and complimentary bottles of edible massage oil as if it were all in a day's work, but her eyes cut to Jake with even more obvious intent than Lianna had shown.

Marnie had seen enough. Her senses couldn't take another moment of nonstop sensual bombardment.

"I can't do this." She lowered her voice until the maid disappeared around the end of the hall where a seventeen-foot-high Christmas tree welcomed visitors.

"What do you mean, you can't do this?" He turned to face her in the now-deserted corridor. Only a few sconces lit the long stretch of hallway. Somewhere nearby, she could hear hints of chamber music and laughter. A party of some sort, or dinner perhaps.

Jake's green eyes narrowed, all his attention on her, his arm still wrapped about her waist. He let go of the rolling suitcase behind him.

"I think I'm just overwhelmed. It's been such a long couple of days. I went from a normal life to finding a hidden camera and then starting on this thousand-mile... odyssey to seek vindication."

With a dark look, he covered her mouth with his hand.

"Not here."

The feel of his fingers on her lips sent a surge of longing through her. She had the strangest impulse to flick her tongue along the inside of his palm but she forced herself to be sensible.

Of course, he was right. She was just overtired and muddleheaded. Someone could be listening. Or watching. Hadn't they just discovered there were peepholes for private spying everywhere? But she was so keyed-up she couldn't think straight.

She wanted to tell him that she needed to find their room and get her bearings, but before he released her, a door sprang open about ten yards away. Light and sound spilled into the corridor from a large gathering where the string music originated. A young blonde in a white linen gown raced from the room, laughing and trailing blue ribbons from a silk scrap of lace she hugged to her chest. With a squeal, she lifted her long skirt with her other hand, picking up her pace to run past Marnie and Jake. Seconds behind her, two men emerged from the same door. With broad, muscular shoulders housed in matching dinner jackets, the guys resembled one another in every aspect from their long, dark hair to otherworldly tawny eyes that could only come from colored contacts. The twins set off in pursuit of the blonde, though the one who trailed a step behind his brother bumped Marnie as he passed.

"Excuse me." He halted immediately. Tawny cat's-eyes sought hers as he reached to straighten her. "So very sorry."

He bowed over her hand and kissed it, eliciting a low, possessive growl from Jake.

"Move. On." Jake leaned toward the other man without ever releasing Marnie's waist.

Nodding serenely, the other man let go of Marnie's hand and jogged in the direction where the other two had gone.

"Come on." Jake pulled her away from the open door and back toward the elevator.

And while Marnie's hormones remained stirred by her private eye companion and not the he-man twin playing dress-up with his eyewear, she appreciated that the incident had caused Jake to feel the same jealousy that Lianna had inspired in her. The possessiveness in his voice and in his grip stirred a warmth low in her belly.

"It is not as fun when the shoe is on the other foot, is

it?" She tipped her head onto Jake's shoulder, seeking comfort from a source she couldn't afford to resist any longer.

They needed to present a united front while they were in this place full of potential land mines.

"No one else touches you while we're here." He punched the elevator button and the doors opened to reveal a silk settee resting in front of an Indian-printed length of gold fabric.

A thrill ran through her that she had no business feeling as he ushered her in. How could she be so turned-on by a guy who'd investigated her and spied on her for weeks without her knowing? A guy she needed to work with? She tried to work up a surge of anger and failed. She was too tired. Overwhelmed.

And still turned-on in spite of everything.

Her pulse spiked at his obvious interest.

"Does that exclusivity work both ways?"

"Would you like that?" He turned her toward him while the lift took them up two floors. "Would you like knowing you're the only woman who touches me this week?"

She knew he asked her so much more than what the surface question revealed. Mostly—did she want him as much as he wanted her?

And while she hadn't been prepared to take that plunge before, now that she'd experienced the way this place was going to get under their skin, she needed to be a little more realistic.

"Yes. I want to be the only one." She couldn't deny how much she wanted that assurance of exclusivity when it came to Jake.

Her blood stirred at the thought of the kiss he'd given her.

No matter how awkwardly their relationship had been

forged—her on one end of a camera lens and him on the other—she couldn't deny that he'd peopled her fantasies even before then.

The elevator door chimed but they remained still a long moment before Jake reached to open the outer gate on their floor. The scent of spicy incense from a nearby censer wafted toward them while her heartbeat sped faster.

She'd just committed to far more than an investigation this week.

<u>5</u>

WOULD SHE REMEMBER what she'd said the night before?

Jake watched Marnie sleep the next morning from his spot in an armchair a few feet away. Pale northern sunlight filtered through drapes on the French doors to dot her face and shoulders while the sheet wound around her midsection and thigh like a snake.

She'd slept fitfully most of the night. He knew because he was highly aware of this woman at every moment. Being with her almost nonstop for the past forty hours had given him new insights about her that he hadn't been able to glean through his surveillance of her.

For one thing, she was in constant motion. He'd known she had an energetic personality from her penchant for dancing around the office and belting out rap tunes for her own entertainment. But he hadn't realized that part of that was because she was tightly wound and driven to succeed. She had a tough time sitting still and letting life happen. Even in sleep, she waged battles, taking on Egyptian cotton until she had it in a choke hold.

His gaze dipped to where the creamy fabric pulled her yellow nightshirt up over a heart-shaped bottom. She wore pink panties covered in tiny hearts and he didn't stand a chance of pulling his eyes away.

Which accounted for his need to keep his ass firmly planted in the armchair. Once he lay anywhere on that bed with her—trundle or otherwise—there would be no turning back.

As it was, he'd been plagued by erotic dreams every time he slept for more than ten minutes at a stretch. Every last one of them had starred Marnie—sometimes with her natural caramel-colored hair, sometimes as a redhead. Dressed in black silk, a trench coat or nothing at all. He didn't have a clue how he'd move forward with this investigation until he had her. The wanting was going to kill him.

"You're still watching me, aren't you?" Marnie's sleep-husky voice acted like a caress down his spine.

She hadn't moved a muscle for a long moment, which perhaps should have tipped him off to her wakeful state.

"At least I've gone from spying on you to looking out for you." He reached for a crystal carafe of orange juice a maid had brought in on a breakfast tray half an hour before.

Pouring her a glass, he tried like hell to rein in his thoughts.

"Is that what you call it?" Marnie yanked up the down comforter she'd kicked to the bottom of the bed hours ago and covered everything from the neck down. "Looking out for me?"

"Hey, I'm not the one who chose to sleep without pants." He leaned forward enough to hand her the glass and something the maid called a crumpet, but that he felt sure was a doughnut. "You damn near blistered my eyeballs."

She took both the offerings and settled back against the carved headboard of the four-poster bed to eat.

"Will you get a load of this place?" She peered around their suite with appreciative eyes and he didn't know if she'd changed the subject to distract him or because she was genuinely impressed. "I stayed in a smaller room last time and the decor in here is completely different. My last room was a nod to ancient Rome with lots of baskets of grapes and silk cushions on the floor. There were even complimentary togas instead of bathrobes. To me, that's the mark of a really interesting property, when the rooms are all unique."

He hadn't taken much note of the suite beyond the extravagant gilt mirrors dotting the walls and even on the ceiling. Somehow the heavy carved frames featuring intertwined Celtic designs made all the mirrors feel a little more upscale.

"Guess I'm not much of a world traveler. As long as there is good water pressure, I'm content." He would rather study the way her newly red hair slid out of the braid she'd fastened it in last night.

She'd accomplished the whole dye job in the bathroom of a fast-food restaurant, the operation as quick and efficient as any superspy would have managed. No wonder the woman had recovered from a job loss by opening her own business seemingly days later. She was a detail person—a planner who took charge and got things done.

"Spoken like a man. I would have thought you'd have at least been curious about the carved positions from the *Kama Sutra* around all the mirrors."

"Kama Sutra?" He couldn't help but look at those damn mirror frames again. And sure enough, they weren't deco-

rated with Celtic symbols at all, but intertwined couples. Threesomes. Moresomes. "Is that one even possible?"

He stood to take a closer look at a pretzel-twister of a position on the mirror closest to him.

"Doesn't it make you wonder where they got all this stuff? Pervy Antiques R Us?" She turned a brass alarm clock toward her and seemed surprised at the time. "So what's on tap for today? Shadowing suspects? Setting up a stakeout?"

"Hardly." He passed her another pastry but she nixed it. "I stayed up late last night to contact my office and run some preliminary workups on names from the guest book. It turns out most of the guest names are aliases, just like ours."

"How did you get a copy of the guest book?" She frowned and set aside the empty juice glass.

"I took a picture of it with my phone while Lianna ran the credit card."

"Lianna." Marnie's lower lip curled in evident disapproval. "Could that woman have wriggled her butt any more for your benefit?"

Jake grinned. "It didn't compete with the show you gave me before you pulled the blanket up."

Tugging a pillow from behind her back, she hurled it across the bed to hit him, but he deflected it easily so that it landed onto the floor.

"You can't blame me for honoring our agreement." His cell phone vibrated with an incoming text message.

"What agreement?"

"We're not going to let anyone else touch us besides each other this week, remember?" He didn't move any closer, but he could feel the spark of awareness arc across the bed between them. Oh, yeah, he liked that. "Which I interpret to mean that I won't be demonstrating interest in anyone else, either."

"I—" She nodded. "I remember. This place has a way of rousing emotions."

He suppressed another grin. It aroused something, that was for damn sure. And since he'd known that he'd wanted Marnie for months, he was grateful that a little competition for his attention had made her realize maybe she wasn't as immune to him as she'd like after all.

"I'll check my messages while you shower." He'd already taken a cold one around 3:00 a.m. after a vivid-as-hell dream. Though the cold water hadn't helped much when he saw the big claw-foot tub built for two, surrounded by showerheads at convenient angles for maximizing the feel-good effect. "Then we can secure some clothes downstairs and check out the lay of the land. The sooner we get to work, the sooner we figure out who could have moved the Premiere Properties money around and tried to frame you in the process."

Although it was going to be a challenge since he'd be picturing Marnie in that shower the whole time.

"Right." She nodded, causing more hair to slide out of the braid circling her head. Rising from the bed, she tugged the blanket off with her to throw around her shoulders like a robe. "Let the charade begin."

WAVING OFF THE dressing-room attendants later that morning, Marnie had found four semiauthentic late nineteenth-century gowns to wear during her stay at the Marquis. Well, they were probably authentic for late nineteenth-century prostitutes. The low necklines warred with the major push-up effect of the foundation garments, making her breasts the objects of continually opposing forces.

Successfully picking out the clothes was no easy feat, considering all she had on her mind between the unsettling attraction for her P.I. roommate and the uneasy news he'd received from his Miami office this morning.

Then again, picking out the dresses themselves was a cakewalk next to picking out all the assorted undergarments she needed. And while she would have liked to have blown off that portion of the shopping spree, the underwear of yesteryear served important functions for making the clothes fall properly. It wasn't as simple as substituting a cotton bra for an elaborate corset. The gowns needed the straps and hooks, the stays and the wiring provided by the foundation pieces in order to stay up. Of course, they came complete with openings in the most interesting places. Ease of access was apparently a high priority in clothing provided by the hotel's boutique.

Now, Marnie checked out her reflection in the full-length dressing-room mirror, ensuring her bustle had been properly pinned and her dress covered the corset around the low bodice and down the back. The boutique didn't just sell period costume—they specialized in the most scandalous of historical dress so that Marnie's gown gave way to a surprise lace-up inset that plunged to the top of her bottom. If she'd been sporting a tramp stamp back there, it would be perfectly framed by white muslin.

"Marie." Jake's voice called to her through the thin pink taffeta curtain separating their dressing rooms.

They'd been given the couples' fitting room in a far corner of the establishment, providing them privacy from the staff with a locked door while separated from each other only by the diaphanous piece of fabric. Despite the supposed privacy from the outside world, however, she noticed he called her by her assumed name.

"Yes, Jack?" She responded in kind, hoping she could remember to use the alias today as they began their investigation of the property.

"Are you ready?" He sounded tense. Irritated.

She wasn't sure if it was because of the news he'd received this morning that all five employees Marnie remembered from her last trip here two years ago were no longer working on the property, or if he was simply frustrated about the elaborate menswear he needed to wear if he had any hope of "blending in."

Marnie took a deep breath, remembering the glimpses she had stolen through the curtain while he tried on his clothes. She'd told herself not to look, knowing he'd be even more tempting without a shirt. Or pants. It turned out he was a boxers man. She'd gotten a peek at blue plaid shorts before she'd forced herself to turn around.

"Yes, I—"

No sooner had she answered then he wrenched the curtain open.

He stood in the other half of the dressing area looking as if he could have set sail on the *Titanic* with the upper crust, although she knew the clothes dated from about forty years before then. Still, the long charcoal cutaway coat revealed slim-cut pants that showed off strong, muscular thighs and narrow hips. A starched white shirt with tiny crystal fastenings didn't begin to take away from the broad masculine appeal of his chest. The half-tied cravat loose around his neck made him look like—what did they call it back in the day?

A rake.

Yes, he looked as roguish as Rhett Butler right before he carried Scarlett up to bed to prove sex was best left to men who knew their way around a woman.

Her pulse rate spiked. Fluttered wildly.

"I didn't spend this much time dressing when I wore a flak jacket and enough combat equipment to take out a city block." He tugged impatiently at the tie. "I'm going to burn this when the week is up."

"I think it's…" Gorgeous. Delectable. Enough to make her weak-kneed. "…nice." She stepped closer, her jeweled, high-heeled satin slippers surprisingly comfortable.

Untwining the knot he'd made, she slid the silk free to try again, the feel of delicate material an appealing contrast to the hot, tense body beneath it.

"You have to admit it's excessive." His eyes took on a dangerous gleam as he looked at her. "Although when I look at what you're wearing, I begin to see the appeal."

His gaze tracked downward in a long, thorough sweep of her body. She wasn't immune to the words or the low, confidential voice in which they were uttered. Her skin heated in response.

"Thank you." Lifting her arms to wrap the silk around his neck again, she couldn't help but notice the way the movement raised her breasts to rub tantalizingly against the stiff confinement of the corset.

Apparently, he noticed, too, since his gaze dipped to the swell of cleavage at the neckline of her white muslin day dress.

"Wow." His second compliment struck her as even more eloquent than the first since his breath sounded more labored.

She eased back, satisfied with the new knot she'd tied around his neck.

"You look good, too," she acknowledged, her fingers itching to slide between the crystal buttons on his shirt to test the warmth of the skin beneath. "I think that's the lure of so much clothing. It makes you all the more aware of your body, and the restrictiveness adds a layer of difficulty to touching or fulfilling any…urges."

Sure a miniskirt could be sexy. But sometimes keeping the body under wraps created an eagerness and delayed gratification that only heightened awareness. It was a theory she'd developed while watching *The Tudors*.

"Interesting." He ran a fingertip over a silk rosette on one shoulder of her dress before following a line of pale blue piping along the top of the neck. "But I like thinking about you half-naked in the sheets this morning, too."

His finger hovered over the plump curve of one breast, his touch almost straying onto her bare skin, but not quite. Her breath caught at the gossamer-light contact, a pang of desire bolting straight to her womb.

"Shouldn't we—" She knew they had something else they should do but it was difficult just now to recall what. Hypnotized by his green eyes turning darker by the second, she never finished the thought.

"In a minute." He dropped his hand to span her waist, steadying her as he bent to kiss that tingling patch of skin a mere inch from her aching nipple.

Tongue darting along the cup of the corset, Jake tasted a path that made her knees weak. She might have twisted an ankle in her jeweled heels as she fell into him, but he held her upright against the hard length of his body.

A moan slipped free from her throat, the sound a wordless plea for more when she had no business making such a demand. Still, sensations ran through her at light speed, her thoughts swimming. The hypnotic swirl of his tongue along her flesh sent an answering thrill to her most private places.

Debating how to ease off her dress, she rolled her hips

and shoulders in the hope some fabric would fall away. But the motion only heightened the sweet torment of her situation since it brought her in delicious contact with the hot, hard length of his arousal.

Knock, knock.

A rap at the door startled her, halting her hungry hip shimmy. Jake peered up at her from where he'd started to peel down the corset with his teeth.

"Can I get you anything?" A woman's voice drifted through the door that separated the couples' dressing area from the rest of the store.

"No." Jake's tone brooked no argument.

Yet the female dressing-room attendant pressed on.

"We have some very sultry pieces for private moments." Her breathless voice suggested the woman was intimately acquainted with just such encounters. "Or not-so-private moments."

Her rich laughter on the other side of the door made Marnie wonder if their dressing room might be one of the places where outsiders could peek in.

Apparently, Jake had the same idea since he returned her dress firmly to her shoulder and eased back a step. Not until that moment did she notice the complimentary basket of condoms on a table nearby. She'd seen the grooming items lined up under a pewter lamp and had thought the hairspray and scented antiseptic hand sanitizers were thoughtful additions to the dressing area. But apparently, other couples had gotten even more carried away while trying on clothes.

"Come on." His breathing was as ragged as hers and she found herself wondering when they'd be able to continue this moment in private. "We'll pay for these things and have them sent upstairs while we check out the place."

She nodded her assent, since she hadn't fully recovered her capacity for speech. While she'd felt a draw toward Jake from the moment he'd switched on his jigsaw to craft her display cabinet with an artisan's skill and a laborer's muscle. But he'd become so much more in the past two days. More complicated. More appealing. And far more apt to lead her straight into danger, no matter what he said about keeping her safe.

With her heart pounding wildly and her senses still reeling from his kisses, she trusted him to protect her from the rest of the world. But who would protect her heart from him?

6

LIANNA CLOSSON DUCKED behind a wall of drawers containing silk hosiery and naughty underthings as Jack and Marie Barnes emerged from the couples' dressing room. She could practically taste the pheromones rolling off the two of them as Jack pulled the beautiful redhead through the store. Their flushed cheeks and tousled hair suggested they'd had some fun in the dressing room—the kind of fun Lianna wouldn't have minded indulging in herself if her new romantic interest had arrived at the resort this week like he was supposed to.

Dang it.

Not attracting so much as a second glance from either of them, she toyed with the crystal knobs on the tall cabinet full of exotic undergarments and wished her lover would show up at the Marquis soon.

Well, her soon-to-be lover.

Lianna had met Alex McMahon at the Marquis a year ago, back when they'd each been involved with other people—Lianna with her husband, who'd introduced her to a swinging, couple-swapping existence that had seemed fun until he dumped her for his best friend's wife. Alex had been a guest at the Marquis with a girlfriend who hadn't worked out for him, either, and he'd contacted Lianna out of the blue a month ago. They'd gotten better acquainted online until he'd asked her to meet him here.

And while Lianna looked forward to reigniting a love life for herself, she wasn't in a hurry to have her heart broken again. As fun as it might be to play sexy games with friends and strangers, she had new respect for protecting the deeper ties that bound a couple together.

Tugging open a drawer marked Holiday, Lianna discovered a wealth of seamed stockings, each set bearing different embroidered or studded icons around the ankle. She pulled out a white pair with red poinsettias to wear for tonight's entertainment.

She wanted to look special for Alex if he finally showed up. He'd made excuses about getting caught in a snowstorm the past two days, but if he didn't appear tonight, Lianna planned to keep an eye out for other entertainment. After all, Alex hadn't made her any promises. What if he was a total player?

He might be charming, but she wouldn't wait around for him forever. Besides, the fact that he wanted her to keep an eye on any new visitors to the Marquis had made her wary of his intentions.

Was he a swinger like her ex?

The thought had her worried as she paid a trim little blonde dressed as a courtesan for the stockings. No way would Lianna tread down that path again. But why else would Alex be interested in new hotel guests unless he was on the lookout for potential playthings?

She'd quizzed him about it on the phone the night before when he'd expressed such interest in the newcomers from Miami. He'd tried to reassure her, saying he was only cu-

rious because he used to live in Miami. As if he thought
he'd know Jack and Marie Barnes—surely not their real
names—from a city with half a million people? He'd asked
her to find out more to feed his "curiosity."

Well, she could tell him quite honestly that the new
couple only had eyes for each other. The sight of them
together filled Lianna with envy since her ex had never
looked at her that way. Perversely, she'd flirted lightly
with the couple, half hoping they'd ignore her and prove
that love and loyalty existed within a passionate romance.

She'd been oddly gratified when they'd done just that.

So if Alex McMahon didn't bother to show tonight—
and if he was only interested in having her scope out fresh
prospects for him—Lianna would cut her losses. All the
books she'd read on divorce counseled not to get involved
with anyone before the one-year mark anyhow, and she'd
only just reached that. Maybe she'd jumped into something too fast with Alex.

If he wanted to spy on Jack and Marie, he'd have to
come to the Marquis to do it himself because that wasn't
her style.

For her part, she planned to keep her eyes open for the
kind of chemistry that pinged between the couple. She'd
settled for a relationship based on shared interests last
time. That had resulted in a lukewarm marriage that sent
her husband out looking for adventure.

So when she got involved again, she wouldn't settle
for anything less than, hot, sexy, all-consuming passion.

SETTLING INTO A LOVE SEAT across from a floor-to-ceiling
window that looked out on the property's grounds, Jake
kept Marnie close to his side. They'd explored the hotel
this morning after the incident in the dressing room,

attempting to get acquainted with the place before it became crowded in the evening. Now, they watched out the window as a party of five braved the falling snow to enter a horse-drawn carriage complete with sleigh bells and fur blankets.

A driver in his mid-twenties wore a top hat with a sprig of holly at the band, and he peered back into the sleigh full of women with open eagerness. Did the kid really stand a chance with five women?

Jake was just damn glad to have a chance with this one. But he wanted to keep her under wraps here as much as possible, which meant he needed to get her back to their suite now that more guests were waking up.

"We should get back to the room." He checked his watch, thinking he should be able to get another update from his office regarding patrons of the Marquis over the past year.

If the embezzler had targeted Marnie to take the fall for the crime purposely, chances were good he was keeping tabs on her. Would he—or she—know by now that the scheme to frame her hadn't worked? Would the embezzler take enough interest in Marnie as to know she'd closed up her shop in Miami and had left town?

"Don't you think we should divide and conquer to cover more ground first?" Marnie kept her voice low and had gotten in the habit of leaning close to him to speak so that if they were observed, it looked as if she was whispering lusty suggestions in his ear.

He had the feeling she did it simply because she was a detail person who didn't overlook the small stuff. But he liked to think she got a charge out of being next to him. God knew he enjoyed the soft huff of her breath on his skin, the brush of her shoulder against his as she moved in close. It was all he could do not to press her down to the bench and see how fast he could unfasten all those clothes she was wearing. No matter how many ties, bows and buttons between them, he knew he'd set a land speed record getting her naked and hot underneath him.

"I don't want anyone to recognize you," he spoke softly in return, her neck within tempting reach of his mouth.

Memories of what had happened in the dressing room had never been far from his mind this morning. Every now and then, he'd catch a hint of her exotic floral scent and he'd be transported right back to that moment behind the curtain, tugging off her gown with his teeth like a damn ravenous beast.

"I bought a mask, remember?" From her drawstring purse, she withdrew the white scrap of satin. The fabric had been decorated with green sequins patterned to look like pine boughs.

She wrapped the pliable satin about her eyes and tied the white ribbons behind her hair. And wow, she was a knockout with the red hair spilling onto her shoulders, her plump lips the only feature of her face that remained visible.

"If I was looking for you," he confided, letting his breath warm the skin around her collarbone, "I would know that mouth anywhere."

The lips in question parted slightly. She licked the top one.

"Lucky for me, no one else is going to take such an interest."

"That's lucky for *them,* actually, because if I caught anyone checking out your mouth, I'd have to hurt them." He'd seen plenty of men notice her already, even though the resort was fairly quiet at this time of day. She had a natural confidence that drew the eye, a way of moving through the world that said she knew what she was doing. Maybe traveling the globe for her job had given her that ease.

"Violence will attract far more attention than any facial feature, so let's hope you can behave." She nuzzled his cheek as another couple walked by them, effectively hiding from view while driving Jake out of his ever-loving mind.

A lock of silky red hair slipped forward, teasing along his jaw. He struggled with the urge to plunge both hands into the auburn strands, to hold her still for a kiss that wouldn't stop until tomorrow....

Focus, damn it.

He needed to think about his investigation and not personal pleasure. His first responsibility was to protect her from whoever had made her a target.

"Maybe we can find some of the rooms with secret viewing." He passed her the security card bearing a picture of a peephole. "As long as we don't mingle, we can circulate a little while longer. I'd like to meet whoever runs the place on a day-to-day basis."

Something that had been tough to do with a resort run like a private club. Everyone he'd talked to so far—from a doorman to a waiter—was working in order to accumulate points that would help them to book rooms in the future. Marnie had explained that most of the guests volunteered for the jobs, but he'd thought they were just enjoying the fantasy of being a maid or a lusty waiter. But apparently the Marquis had a whole elaborate system in place to fill the gaps in the staff by offering guests incentives to work extra hours.

Jake had to hand it to the operation. It was a clever piece of business.

"That's very admirable of you to work so hard. Doesn't the atmosphere ever distract you?" Marnie nodded meaningfully to a white marble statue on a nearby end table.

The piece hadn't caught his eye before since the style was more impressionistic than realistic. But now that she'd pointed it out, the lines became clear. Like carvings he'd once seen in an historic Indian temple, the statue featured a woman lying on her back with knees parted to accommodate a man's shoulders. Clearly, his mouth was aligned with her sex.

And oh man, he'd like to think Marnie had pointed out that piece for a reason. He couldn't imagine anywhere he'd rather be than in their suite re-creating that moment for her. A growl rumbled up the back of his throat, and he had to fist his hands to keep them off her.

"Hell, yes, it's a distraction." But then, you couldn't look anywhere in this place without seeing something erotic.

And unlike some girlie magazine, this stuff was subtle. It crept up on you and settled into your consciousness before you could think about changing the mental channel.

Taking her hand, he pulled Marnie to her feet. She stood willingly enough, but he noticed she spared a small, backward glance for the statue on the end table.

And didn't that just torch his focus in a heartbeat? Bad enough to conduct an investigation while being tormented with carnal temptation on all sides. But it was even worse trying to think about the case knowing the woman beside him was every bit as turned-on.

"I'm losing my mind here." He had to touch her soon or he'd jump out of his skin. "Go back to the room and I'll meet you there in an hour. I need to check around for any accessible hotel computers where the embezzlement could have originated, but after that…"

He couldn't begin to articulate what he needed. The urge was deep and primal. He didn't just want to touch her. He wanted to possess her.

Thankfully, she spared him the effort of translating his need into words fit for her ears.

Nodding, she gripped her key to her chest. "Hurry."

BACK IN THE SUITE, Marnie fought off the sexual edginess by flipping through a few electronic documents that Jake had sent to her phone after receiving an update from his office. They hadn't been apart for long—forty-nine minutes, according to the clock on the nightstand—but every moment away from him only stirred a hunger she couldn't deny any longer.

She'd never felt sexual chemistry like this. It was so strong, so palpable, she didn't know what to do about it. Did other people feel like this about sex? Whoa, had she been missing out for her whole adult life?

Fanning herself, she tried to concentrate on the notes from Jake. He'd sent her a list of visitors to the Marquis in the past year, even though they'd already established that most of the names would be fake. Still, Jake had asked her to look at it since most people didn't vary the names much. Just like Jake and Marnie became Jack and Marie, apparently most people using an alias chose something close to their real names.

She tucked her toes beneath a blanket as she lounged in an oversize club chair. The moment Jake had left, she'd ditched the restrictive gown she'd been wearing along with the underskirts that made the train puff up. She'd kept the corset on, unwilling to have to wrestle with it again before dinner. But at least this way, her dress would remain wrinkle-free. She didn't know exactly how things would go with Jake when he returned, but she had the feeling clothes would only get in the way.

Fifty minutes.

With her finger hovering on the wheel to advance the screen, Marnie surreptitiously listened for footsteps in the hall. Her heartbeat danced a crazy rhythm in her chest. Odd how even the blood in her veins wanted Jake. It was elemental. Undeniable. The kiss he'd given her in the dressing room that morning had ripped away any illusion she had of keeping him at arm's length during their stay here.

In a space of time, Jake had become more than a hot contractor who'd flirted with her or an intrusive P.I. who filmed her without her knowledge. She could easily be in jail right now if it hadn't been for his determination to find out the truth of Premiere's missing money. Her ex-boss had assured her of as much in their brief phone conversation before she left Miami.

His fierce intelligence and sense of justice had made him invaluable to Vince Galway—a man Marnie respected. And his smoldering sensuality—well, that flat out left her breathless.

Forcing herself to finish combing through the documents now saved on her phone, Marnie clicked to the next screen, where her eyes alighted on a surprise name.

Alex McMahon.

She read it twice, knowing it wasn't her ex's name, but seeing a similarity between that and Alec Mason.

Double-checking the date of his visit, she saw that it had been a year ago, during the time that they'd been dating. And that Alex McMahon had checked in with a woman who'd shared his last name. Of course, it was entirely possible that Alex McMahon hadn't been married to Tracy McMahon. Plenty of dating couples signed hotel registers as married just for kicks.

Besides, Alec had been a crappy manager of money but that didn't necessarily make him a cheater, did it?

Her mind racing, she clicked out of that screen and opened the calendar function on her phone. As a true type A, Marnie could call up her activities electronically for every day of her life going back five years.

More if she consulted a paper file back home.

And while yes, that made her nerdy as all hell, it had proven useful a few times. Like now. When the calendar for last December showed that she'd been on the road during the time in question. Specifically, she'd been evaluating promo angles for a restored villa in Tuscany. Which meant that—while she'd assumed Alec had been back in Miami—he could have been anywhere in the world and as long as he'd called from his cell phone, she wouldn't have known the difference.

A knock at the door interrupted that troubling realization.

"Room service," a masculine voice announced, reminding her she'd ordered hot tea to help shake off the cold of December in upstate New York.

"Coming!" she called, dropping the phone and blanket to slide into a white spa robe provided by the Marquis.

Hurrying across the hardwood floor covered with a smattering of rich Oriental carpets, she unlocked the door to admit a waiter with a silver tea cart followed by a sexy brunette in a maid's costume complete with little apron.

Lianna.

Did the woman work at every conceivable job on the

property? Marnie stood back to admit them, and as they passed her with the tea, she realized that Lianna had found a new man to capture her attention since all her focus was on the young waiter. Not just any waiter, either. The guy setting up the tea tray by the fireplace was one half of the tawny-eyed twins who'd brushed past her in the corridor downstairs the night before. Instead of his dress attire, he wore tight breeches with—wow—everything readily displayed. His tunic was half-buttoned as if he'd just rolled out of bed or as if he were inviting the touch of every stray woman who passed.

"Would you like me to pour it for you?" the behemoth asked, his muscles testing the strength of those close-fitting pants and his voice taking on the tone of bedroom confidences.

Lianna all but drooled as she posed invitingly against the cart, her eyes glued to her cohort's bicep, visible through the thin linen tunic.

"Yes, please." Marnie waved him along to expedite the process. She wanted the pair of them out of her room before they got busy on her love seat.

Still, the guy took his time arranging the china teacup, lighting a single white taper and adjusting a pink poinsettia bloom in a pewter holder on the tray. Lianna watched every move in rapt fascination, it seemed, until she suddenly turned to catch Marnie staring at her.

The other woman smiled warmly, making Marnie feel small inside for thinking cranky thoughts about her. Beautiful women couldn't help being beautiful.

"Do you come here often?" Marnie kicked herself as soon as she brought out the well-worn barroom conversation staple. But it had occurred to her that if Lianna volunteered for so many jobs at the Marquis she must have seen a lot around the resort. Maybe it wouldn't hurt to cultivate her goodwill.

"It's my third time here," Lianna admitted. "It's fun to play dress-up, isn't it? Although I notice you seem to have lost your dress."

Lianna winked and the tawny-eyed waiter grinned. Marnie reminded herself that they weren't trying to be obnoxious because most people visited this hotel for just this kind of thing.

Hence the trundle bed.

Clearing her throat, she took a step back from the odd dynamics of the moment.

"The bustle and I weren't getting along," she confided. Then, forging ahead to firm up the new contact, she continued, "It's my first time here, actually. If you have time tomorrow, I'd be interested to find out all the inside scoop on the best things to do here."

It was another loaded comment, and both Lianna and Golden Eyes laughed.

"Um." Marnie tried again. "Beyond the obvious."

"Sure," Lianna agreed easily, crooking her finger toward her friend and leading him toward the door. "I'm up early. Meet you at noon for breakfast?"

That was early? Apparently that was the prevailing sentiment around the resort since it had been so quiet today before midafternoon.

"Sure. Sounds good." Marnie didn't know what she'd ask the woman, but while Jake conducted the supersleuthing, Marnie could at least offer up one skill to the mix. She knew how to listen. And sometimes women observed things that men never noticed.

As the two of them opened the door to leave, Jake stood in the entrance, key in hand as if he'd been about to enter.

He took one look at who'd been visiting and Marnie was pretty sure he flexed his muscles in predatory display. There was some silent message passed between the men, of that much she was certain. Lianna had to haul her friend away by the undone laces on his tunic to break the staring contest.

As the door closed behind them, leaving Jake facing Marnie in a robe and corset and nothing more, she could feel the awareness in the room simmer.

"Hi," she said needlessly, wanting only to break the silence.

Jake dropped his key and yanked off his jacket, letting both fall to the floor while he stalked closer. Green eyes fixing her in his sights, he tore off the neckwear he hated and wrenched open the top fastening of his crisp white shirt.

Her heartbeat tripped before it picked up speed. She sensed her fight-or-flight moment at hand. She would need to get out of his path right now if she didn't want this.

Him.

Licking her lips since her mouth had gone dry, she kept her feet rooted to the spot.

She wanted whatever he had in mind.

7

HEAT ROARED THROUGH HIM like a furnace, the atmosphere in the room growing taut with need.

"This place is making me crazy." Jake stopped himself a hairbreadth from Marnie to give her fair warning of his mood.

His intent to have her naked in the next ten seconds.

"Me, too," she admitted. Breathless.

"When I first saw them in here—"

"Nothing happened," she said quickly.

"I know." Of course he knew. "But this place messes with your head until all you think about—all the time—"

He gave her an extra second to let it sink in, his hands flexing at his sides from the effort to hold back. He needn't have bothered though, because she launched herself at him.

Thank You, God.

Relief and desire damn near took out his knees, but he held strong for her, his arms full of soft, warm woman. The clean scent of her skin and hair teased his senses. Gathering her close, he held her tight, her soft curves encased in too much stiff lace beneath her thick white robe. He lifted her higher, sliding his arms under her thighs so she had no choice but to wrap her legs around his waist.

Oh, yeah. She followed him willingly. Eagerly. Soft, urgent sounds hummed in the back of her throat as he maneuvered her right where he wanted her, the hot core of her positioned over his erection, their bodies separated by too many clothes. That connection soothed the hunger in him enough to slow things down just a little, to appreciate her the way she deserved to be. The moment was so damn charged, and he didn't want to miss out on a second of pleasure because they were so damn hungry for this.

She pressed urgent kisses along his jaw and down his neck as he held her. He took deep breaths, willing his heart rate to slow down, his body to put her needs first. Then, slowly, he lifted his hands to explore the soft skin between the tops of her stockings and the bottom of the corset. She was soft. More silky than the fabric of her expensive underthings.

He forced his eyes open, to see her and savor her. Her gray eyes were at half-mast, lashes fluttering as he touched her. Behind her, the silver tea cart glinted in the firelight, steam wafting up from the brewing pot.

"You had clothes on when I left you last time," he observed, tracing a pattern along the back of her bare thigh. "You can't blame me for wondering when I come back to find you mostly undressed and entertaining guests."

"My dress was highly uncomfortable." She worked the fastenings on his shirt, as nimble dispensing of his clothes as she was with her own. "So you can imagine how fast I ditched it after you left the room."

His shirt slid to the floor. Her cool hands raked down

his chest, his muscles twitching in the wake of her touch. He'd wanted this for so long.

"And I didn't even get it on tape." He could only imagine how much he would have enjoyed that show. "Was there any dancing involved, like when you closed up your shop on Friday night?"

"You enjoy your job a little too well." She gave his shoulder a gentle bite in retaliation, her teeth scraping lightly along his skin. "All that time, I thought you were concerned with protecting my privacy."

He flicked open one garter behind her thigh and then the other. She shivered. He couldn't wait to see what else would elicit that response.

"Guess I'm more concerned with protecting it from anyone else *besides* me." Lowering her to the floor in front of the fireplace, he nudged the black robe off her shoulders and his breath caught at the sight she made.

Firelight warmed her skin to spun gold next to the ivory-white corset. The rigid stays in the garment made her look like a naughty fifties pinup queen with no waist to speak of and breasts at eye-popping proportions. The curve of her hips was exaggerated in the back by a knot of gathered lace that helped the bustled gown sit high when she was dressed. At her legs, her stockings sagged a little in back where he'd unfastened them, but the fronts remained hooked. The white straps framed the juncture of her thighs, right where he wanted to be.

"Intimidated?" she asked, cocking a hip to the side, a hand at her waist.

"By you?" He grinned at the thought. "It seems to me like I have you completely at my mercy right now."

And he really, really liked the thought of that. They weren't leaving this room for a long time.

"Not by me. By this contraption I'm wearing." She gestured to the corset. "I'll bet you have no clue how to spring me loose."

"I think I'll manage." He reached for the remaining garter straps and plucked them free, eliciting another shiver from her. "Besides, if I touch you just right—" he stroked a knuckle up the inside of her thigh for emphasis "—you might melt right out of it."

The soft sound she made in the back of her throat pleased him to no end. Her hands found his waist. Fingers spanning his sides, she glided a light touch up his chest, her hips swaying closer as if she danced to a song only she could hear.

"Promises, promises," she whispered over his chest as she bent to kiss him there.

She was as sexy and sensual in real life as she'd appeared in hours of secret surveillance. And right now, she seemed as keyed-up and ready for this as him.

"Never let it be said I don't deliver." Stripping off his shirt, he tossed it on the ground behind her. Then, scooping her off her feet, he laid her on the rug in front of the hearth, carefully spreading the shirt out beneath her.

He stayed on his feet long enough to remove his pants and retrieve a condom. Marnie watched his every move, lifting one leg to slide off her stocking with all the finesse of a showgirl. When she had it free, she wound the silk around her wrists and extended her bound hands to him.

"Want to take me into custody?"

He carefully raised her arms over her head and held them there while he stretched over her.

"Not yet, but there's no telling what might happen if I find a strange man in our room again." He slid a hand down her back where a row of endless hooks kept her delectable body captive. One by one, he began easing them free.

"He only poured my tea," she assured him, wrapping her bare leg around his and massaging the back of his calf with the ball of her foot.

"I don't care about the tea." He loosened the corset enough to expose the plump swell of her breasts and he flicked his tongue over one taut nipple. Then, leaving the remaining hooks for the moment, he palmed the warmth between her thighs. "As long as you leave the cream and honey for me."

Her body quivered as soon as he touched her. Impatiently, he brushed aside her panties and sought the slick center of her. Circling the tight core with his finger, he mirrored the movement with his tongue along her nipple. Her breath grew short, her back arching under him as she sought more.

Drawing hard, he took the tight peak deep in his mouth as he slid two fingers inside her. She bucked and cried out, her release coming fast. The spasms went on and on as he coaxed out every sweet response.

Freeing her wrists from the slippery stocking bondage, she looped her arms about his neck and whispered a new demand.

"Come inside me."

Marnie willed Jake to comply with her request, her whole body crying out for his. She'd never peaked so fast or so easily, but then she'd been on fire for this man for days. The steamy atmosphere of the Marquis had only made it worse.

He stared down into her eyes, his strong features cast in stark shadows from the fire. The red light illuminated his sculpted muscles in deep bronze, every sinew visible as he positioned himself between her legs.

Tracing the outline of his hard flesh with her hands, she absorbed his heat and his strength as he rolled on a condom. The aftershocks from her release intensified as he entered her, sending her hips into motion as she rode them out. Jake stilled, splaying one hand on her waist to hold her in place.

When he moved again, it was to roll her on top of him. With both his hands now free, he unfastened the last of the hooks on her confining corset and slid it off. Then, taking her hips in his hands, he guided her where he wanted, pulling her close as he thrust deep inside.

The slow, satisfying rhythm made her rain kisses all over his chest and his face, the bliss of being with him so overwhelming she didn't know what to do with it all. Too soon, the steady, delicious dance built a new ache inside her; she could hardly stand the discipline of each measured thrust. Seizing his shoulders, she arched back to take her pleasure in her own hands and give her hips unrestricted access to every inch of him.

He called her name as she spiraled over the edge of the abyss again, her heart galloping wildly as the moment had its way with her. Jake wrapped his arms around her, anchoring her tight to him, and amid the haze of her own release she could feel his pulse through her, too.

Collapsing on him in a boneless heap, she couldn't catch her breath for long moments afterward. When she finally became aware of herself again, she realized he'd shifted her to lie beside him on his shirt, his arm tucked beneath her ear like a warm, muscular pillow.

He was more than a skilled lover. He was a thoughtful, considerate man. A watchful partner who would protect her no matter what. She saw all that clearly now as he came into focus for her.

He watched her just as closely, his eyes missing nothing, and she wondered what he saw. A strong woman who took her fate in her own hands by traveling to the other end of the country with a stranger for the sake of justice?

Or a woman who simply needed to lose herself, just like the name of her start-up company suggested?

She wasn't certain herself. And for a woman who'd always been so sure of herself, a woman who'd carefully marked out every path she would take so there would be no missed turns, that rattled her almost as much as having an unknown enemy lurking in the shadows.

The thought reminded her of the discovery she'd made before her tea arrived.

"Jake?"

"You look worried." He rubbed a finger over her forehead, making her realize she'd had her eyebrows scrunched together. "You aren't allowed to have any regrets about what just happened."

She relaxed against him. With nothing but the fire to light the room as dusk fell, the moon outside illuminated a few snowflakes swirling against the French doors nearby. The aroma of the ginger tea she hadn't touched mingled with the scent of burning wood.

"I don't. I've known that was bound to happen since you kissed me in the car on the way up here." She'd also told herself she wouldn't let it happen, but that had been before she'd experienced the full impact of the man and the Marquis. "I just hope it doesn't make working together awkward."

"It can't be more tense than it was to start with." He threaded his fingers through her hair and stroked the strands away from her face. "If anything, maybe this will make the rest of the week more productive now that we're not so preoccupied all the time."

This would make them *not* preoccupied? She was already thinking about when they'd be together again.

For that matter, her planner personality wanted to know what would happen to them when they returned to Miami. Would they return to being strangers and write this trip off as an intense getaway where emotions had flared out of control, never to be repeated?

Would her private investigator walk away from her as easily as the contractor had two months ago?

She hated not knowing.

Sensing the moment had come to protect herself from just such possibilities she retreated first, pulling a crocheted afghan off a footstool and wrapping it around her naked body.

"Actually, now that we're not preoccupied—" she used his term to show him she could be as easy with this as him "—I should tell you that I spotted an interesting name on the Marquis guest list for last year."

"Someone you know?" He tensed, instantly alert, and she half regretted bringing this up now.

Part of her had been hoping for a more romantic end to their time together.

"Not necessarily. But there was an Alex McMahon here last year and—"

"Sounds a lot like Alec Mason."

"That's what I was thinking."

He rolled to his side, still naked and amazing looking in the firelight in front of the hearth. He didn't need tight breeches or any other costume to make him completely mouthwatering.

"I looked into him early on in the investigation." He frowned. "I didn't think he could have pulled this off at the time, based on his lack of access to the Premiere accounts, but that was before I knew the crime involved a lot of cyber decoys..."

He trailed off as he jumped to his feet to retrieve a laptop. She watched the flex of muscles in his thighs as he walked and wished she could feel him against her all over again.

"You investigated Alec?" She felt adrift suddenly, both because Jake had bolted so fast after telling her they wouldn't be preoccupied now that they'd—essentially—gotten the sex impulses out of their system, and because she was at such a major disadvantage in a relationship where he knew far more about her than she knew about him.

"He made a few investments for you," Jake explained, not even sparing her a glance as he fired up the computer and connected it to his phone for internet access since the hotel didn't have wireless. "That gave him a certain financial savvy. And I knew you ended things acrimoniously based on the fact that you nearly took my eye out in an attempt to throw darts at a picture of his face."

"But you cleared him." Marnie tried not to let it sting that Jake had reverted to his supersleuthing. That was, of course, why they were here. "So you must have had some evidence to toss him aside as a suspect. When you cleared me, you needed video proof."

"You were a far more likely candidate for this. You're smarter, for one thing." Jake slid on a pair of boxers and a T-shirt before bringing the laptop back near the fireplace.

Near her.

Her heart beat faster, and for once, it wasn't simply because of his proximity. New worries crawled up her spine as she began to grasp the implications of Alec's possible guilt. She gripped the afghan tighter to her chest to ward off a sudden chill.

"Alec is a Princeton graduate," she reminded Jake. Not that she wanted to defend her ex-boyfriend, per se. But she wanted Jake to know she hadn't chosen a total loser.

"Actually, he lied about that." Jake flipped his screen around for her to see, showing her a brief background sheet on Alec Mason. "He doesn't have a criminal background, but it looks like he's bluffed his way into most of his jobs with padded résumés."

Marnie scanned the highlights of Alec's career as Jake spoke, trying to absorb the fact that her ex had betrayed her on even more levels. The ground shifted under her feet, and this time it didn't have anything to do with Jake or Alec. Instead, she simply felt like the world's biggest fool for trusting men in the first place.

"I used to think it was a good quality to see the best in people." How many times had she counseled friends to look on the bright side? How often had she told herself that life's obstacles were merely road signs to take a new and more exciting path? "I had no idea it made me so—"

She couldn't decide on any one word that would describe how she felt right now. Alec's face grinned at her almost as if he knew he could take her heart for a ride and get away with it.

"Hey." Jake set the laptop aside as he reached for her. Putting an arm around her waist, he pulled her close. "It is a good quality to see the best in people. I tend to see the worst, and I can tell you that has bitten me in the ass more times than I can count."

Her eyes burned, but she refused to feel sorry for herself.

"At least no one ever takes you for a sucker." That was the word she'd been looking for. She'd been a total sucker where Alec had been concerned. "You've never been taken in by someone who wants to use you."

"No. But I've been roped in by ideas and institutions, believing in the police force or the military only to be disillusioned when there's corruption." He planted a kiss on her hair, a gentle comfort that twined around her heart in spite of the dark cloud that had settled on her mood. "If everybody chose to see the downside of those places, they wouldn't be half as effective as they are."

"I just need to have more realistic expectations." Starting right now. Instead of baring her soul along with her body, she should be retreating. Building boundaries and erecting defenses so she didn't get sucked into thinking her time with Jake meant anything more than...sex.

Standing, she knew it would be safer for her heart not to accept comforting kisses from this man, who had a cynical side a mile wide.

Jake stared up at her in the firelight. The room had turned fully dark otherwise.

"I'll just finish up here and then we can figure out a game plan for dinner." He grabbed the laptop again, appearing to focus on the task at hand.

Just like she needed to.

"Good." Wrapping the afghan more securely around herself, she headed for the shower to wash away the tantalizing scent of him that clung to her skin. "The sooner we can find out who's trying to frame me the better."

Finding out who did it—and sending his or her ass to jail—would be her first chance to prove she wasn't the sucker they'd taken her for.

8

ALEX WOULD BE FURIOUS if he showed up now.

Lianna thought as much, but could not find the will to push Rico away since his hands were finally on her. She'd noticed him in the dining hall the night before. Had flirted with him when Alex—once again—hadn't bothered to show up for their rendezvous. She knew now that Alex must be a player. Maybe he got off on the idea that a woman was waiting for him at a sexy hotel. Well, not anymore. She'd captured another man's attention. A man who seemed so vivid, real and sexy that she had trouble recalling what Alex McMahon even looked like.

No more waiting around for a man who shared her interests. She would follow her passions.

"You kiss like an angel." Rico came up for air long enough to whisper soft words in her ear.

He was a sight to see as he hovered over her, his dark Latin looks and tawny eyes enough to make her melt. But he also listened when she spoke. Made eye contact instead of lingering over her breasts the way men on the prowl did.

The warmth of his caress on her hip soothed the bite of the hardware poking into her back as she leaned against a huge apothecary cabinet tucked into an alcove down a quiet little corridor outside the billiard room. She'd played Rico for a kiss to be administered wherever the winner chose, and while she'd heard some of those games had turned wild in a hurry when other guests played, Rico's request after winning had been for a traditional lip-lock.

Lianna hadn't decided if that was because he was a gentleman, or if he knew his persuasive powers of kissing would win him whatever he wanted in the long run. But was she really ready for more with a man she'd only just met?

Cold feet shouldn't happen when the rest of her body burned so hot, but there it was. She felt nervous. Vulnerable.

For a lawyer with a reputation as a shark in the courtroom, the feelings were uncomfortable.

"I shouldn't have played that game with you," she blurted loud enough that her raging hormones would hear her over the rush of her heartbeat.

Edging back a fraction, she gazed up at him by the flickering flame of a gaslight sconce on the wall to her right.

He loomed over her, broad-chested and infinitely appealing in his servant's tunic and breeches that revealed a—um—great deal of manhood. It was difficult to gauge his expression through the colored contacts he wore that made him indistinguishable from his brother. Apparently the two of them enjoyed being totally identical when they came here. Lianna had learned that, under the contacts, Raul's eyes were brown and Rico's were blue.

"You regret a kiss?" He frowned, his hands disappearing from her body even though his hips remained a mere inch from hers. "From the way you followed me around today, I had every reason to believe—"

"I know." She didn't want to think about the way she'd flung herself at him. Or flirted shamelessly with any number of guys since showing up here. "The kiss was great. It's just that I had told someone I'd meet them here and when he didn't show tonight, I figured I deserved to have fun anyway."

Rico's hips closed that last inch, his hands returning to her waist.

"You do," he agreed. "And I'll bet I can make you forget all about him by morning."

The rush of longing came at her so hard she had to swallow the urge to rub up against him like a cat and forget all about her niggling conscience.

In the background, she could hear a woman's shriek of laugher emanating from the billiard room and wondered if the stakes had gone up in the gaming area. Usually they waited to play games for articles of clothing until after dinner had been served, but some folks got rowdy early. It wasn't uncommon to spot a man coming from the hall minus garments that he'd lost in a game.

Or a woman as she streaked by in a corset. Or less.

"But I'm on the rebound from a divorce." Lianna had no idea what had come over her to pour her heart out to the hottest guy she'd ever been fortunate enough to kiss. But there it was. Apparently she wasn't too jaded for an attack of scruples. "So I can't trust my emotions so well where men are concerned. And for that matter, my ex cheated on me at the end of the marriage. I hate to do to someone else what he did to me, even if I don't know this guy that I planned to meet here very well."

Rico blinked, his long lashes sweeping low to fan over

his burnished bronze skin as the light from the flickering sconce cast stark shadows on his strong features. In the narrow alcove, he blocked her view of all else besides him.

"Lianna." His thumb smoothed a gently teasing caress along the bottom of her corset where it rested on her hip. With a little pressure, he could have slid it underneath that seam, even though her gown still would have been in the way. There was something endlessly tantalizing about a man navigating his way through that many layers to unveil you.

"Hmm?" She tried not to sway with the hypnotic power of his touch. She had noble intentions for once, damn it.

"Most everyone here is on a rebound of some sort or another." Perhaps he spied her confusion because he explained himself. "How many people would come to places like this just for the hookups? A few. But the Marquis packs the rooms every week because most of the guests need a complete escape. Here, you can forget about your job that's going poorly or your ex who cheated, or a wife who didn't want any part of a noisy, cantankerous clan of six brothers and decided she'd rather go out for groceries and never come back."

"There are six of you?" The mind reeled at the vision of so many studly males in one family.

"Who said I was talking about me?" He winked and something about the gesture made her realize he was the more outgoing of the twins—the one who liked to party. The hell-raiser. "It was Raul's wife who took off, but yes, I have five brothers. My point is that there is nothing wrong with getting caught up in the moment when you are not married. This man who did not show up to meet you does not have any right to claim you."

Persuasive fingers trailed lightly over her hip, the heat

of his touch penetrating the rose-colored taffeta and two layers of underskirts. He'd taken such care to ease her conscience. If he was so considerate of her needs now, what might he be like in bed when her needs would be more obvious and far easier to address?

A little breathless gasp robbed her of speech for a moment. Purposely, she leaned more heavily into the apothecary cabinet behind her, allowing the hardware of the drawers to poke against her uncomfortably and remind her that she couldn't just slide into his arms for the night.

"In theory, I agree," she admitted. "But in practice, I'll feel better if I send him a note and let him know my intentions before we, er, kiss again."

"I have a phone," Rico admitted softly, leaning close to nip her ear with a gentle bite. "You can call him from my room."

"Doesn't that seem a bit wicked?" Her eyelids fell to half-mast as she swayed against him.

"It's Christmastime, Lianna. And you've been a very, very good girl." Rico rubbed a path up her ribs to the underside of her breast as he kissed her neck. "Don't deny yourself the reward you deserve."

She felt her resolve slipping along with her red velvet maid's uniform that borrowed liberally from the wardrobes of Mrs. Claus and a Victoria's Secret catalog. The low-cut, fur-lined bodice inched down until it barely covered her breasts. Her nipples peaked against the fluffy white trim of her outfit.

"I wasn't *always* a good girl," she confessed, wanton heat swirling along her skin as he tugged the costume down a fraction of an inch more, exposing her to his waiting tongue.

Desire pooled in her womb as he drew one stiff peak

into his mouth and flicked it again and again. By the time he relinquished her breast and tugged her dress back up to cover her, she was such a trembling mass of nerve endings, she couldn't have denied him if she tried.

"I bet I'll enjoy hearing about the times you were naughty just as much as the times you were nice," he assured her in a low growl. "But you're going to have to sit on my lap the whole time."

He palmed her bottom in his hands and gave each cheek a little spank. He caught her squeal of surprise in a kiss, silencing her as he passed her his cell phone.

Fully, deliciously committed to the plan, Lianna tucked the phone into her cuff and told herself everything would be all right. Rico was a once-in-a-lifetime man, and she deserved this night.

Alex had proven his lack of loyalty by ignoring her this week, showing more interest in having her spy on Jack and Marie than in coming up here to be with her himself.

For all she cared, the three of them could play their voyeur games without her. If Alex ever showed tonight, he could watch the redhead all by himself.

JAKE WATCHED MARNIE from across the dining area, her green bustle twitching restlessly with every move of her hips as she walked toward the card parlor for the evening's entertainment.

The mood in the dining area had been raucous and bawdy, with guests flirting and dancing between courses. Now, as the tables were cleared away, some people lingered by the bar area to be close to the musicians, who were dressed like holiday court jesters in red and green velvet jackets. Other guests moved toward the billiards lounge and card room to wait for the evening entertainment. Jake and Marnie had agreed to split up after the evening meal, hoping to find out more about the staff behind the scenes at the Marquis. The embezzlement of 2.5 million dollars had originated on a Marquis computer; of that much his people were certain. So as long as Marnie wore her mask around the hotel, he didn't mind her searching out leads on where staff offices were located and who had access to them. For his part, he would do the same. But all the while he wove his way toward the library, he brooded over missing signs that Alec Mason might be more deeply involved in this mess.

"Looking for company?" a petite blonde in a vampy black dress asked him as he passed her in an archway between rooms.

Her gown was floor-length, but the insets down the sides were lace-up panels with nothing underneath, so you could see about an inch-and-a-half swath of naked flesh from knee to breast on either side of her.

"No." The word came out sharper than he'd intended for a guy who needed to schmooze if he ever wanted answers. "Actually," he said, changing tactics midstream, "do you know where I go to sign up for work here? Is there an office or do I just go to the front desk?"

"What kind of work are you looking for?" she asked, tossing her hair over one shoulder and angling a hip closer as she looked him up and down. "I've got a few jobs you'd be perfect for."

How could he ever check out this place when flirtatious women put themselves in his path at every opportunity? His case came first, and his carnal thoughts were all for Marnie.

And even worse than this woman flirting with him

was the fact that guys would swarm Marnie the second he wasn't attached to her side. Like right now in the card room.

"Sorry, I don't hire out to individuals, but thanks anyway."

The vampy blonde crossed her arms over her chest and glared at him.

"I'll keep that in mind when you end up as my waiter or my manservant tomorrow. Because the second you take on work for the Marquis, I will find you and make you do just what I want." With another toss of her stick-straight hair, she stalked off on sky-high heels, full of dominatrix attitude.

Who were these people? Jake had seen some strip joints in his day and a few sleazy cathouses when he'd been stationed overseas, but he'd never run into an operation like this one. It had to be tough to keep it from turning into an all-out orgy on any given night, which would definitely make the place lose a lot of its character. But the people who stayed here seemed hip to the game—to push the boundaries of public displays without sliding into vulgarity.

In the billiards room, Jake saw a waiter serving drinks and figured he'd ask the guy where the offices were. Until he got closer and realized it wasn't just any waiter but the behemoth pretty boy who'd hit on Marnie earlier.

He'd just decided to get his information elsewhere when the guy turned around and saw him, his expression surprisingly blank considering they'd had a standoff just a couple of hours ago.

"Dude, I know that look and I can guarantee you've got me confused with my brother," the guy said, easing past him with a tray full of empty glasses.

Jake did not appreciate the brush-off.

"Does that angle work on everyone? The old 'I didn't do it and it must have been someone else' bit?"

He kept step with the waiter, figuring that if nothing else, he'd follow him wherever he was going until he located the offices for the Marquis.

"No. Usually we just end up making twice as many enemies. But whatever Rico did to piss you off, just keep in mind he's my twin, not my responsibility." The guy hardly noticed an exotic-looking brunette dressed in a gown that—no lie—appeared to made entirely of whipped cream. "So no need to follow me, okay? I'm Raul, and you've got the wrong brother. I'm mostly here under duress anyway, so I don't need trouble."

Something about Raul's obliviousness to the whipped cream woman gave authenticity to his claims. Jake had a feeling that Rico's head would have been on a swivel if that walking dessert had just passed him.

"I'll take it up with your brother, then. But yes, I'm following you because I need to know where the offices for this place are located and shaking a straight answer out of this crowd is like pulling teeth."

Raul grinned. "It's an affliction I call sex on the brain." He nodded toward a back wall behind a fifteen-foot-high Christmas tree. "This way."

Peace made with the guy, Jake appreciated the heads-up. He'd checked out most of the hotel on his own earlier that day, but he'd only succeeded in locating kitchens, storage and laundry rooms—no real base for operations. He'd begun to think the administrative area must be somewhere well hidden, a fact that would really limit computer access for his suspect.

Tonight, he wouldn't give up searching until he'd found

the offices he sought and checked out the computers. His sixth sense had been itching all day that whoever was trying to frame Marnie could show up here at any time now—especially with an Alex McMahon on an old guest list. If Jake had overlooked something in the guy's past—some connection to this case he hadn't seen the first time—he didn't want Marnie to pay for that mistake.

The sooner he retrieved the necessary intelligence, the sooner he could pack up their stuff and get Marnie out of harm's way for good.

THE ATMOSPHERE IN THE card room made Marnie uncomfortable.

Still wearing her mask to protect her identity from anyone who might recognize her, she stuck to the outskirts of the room to avoid attention from the drunken revelers playing what amounted to strip poker in the center of the room. The game involved six players in varying states of undress while a crowd of onlookers obstructed her view of most of the table. Apparently the chips they used were not worth money but sexual favors, with the winner claiming whatever he or she wished from the players who'd lost.

Partially hidden behind an old-fashioned cigar store Indian, Marnie decided she would leave long before that moment arrived. The mood here was far more sexually aggressive than the vibe she'd felt earlier in the hotel. But before she departed, she hoped to catch a better glimpse of one of the men who observed the game. There was something familiar about his face and if only she could see him better, she felt as if she might be able to identify him. Did she know him? Or was he simply employed by the Marquis and she'd seen him here the last time she visited the property?

Ducking out from behind the carved wooden figure, she scanned the faces again, trying to see over a tall woman wearing an elaborate headpiece that made her look more like a Vegas showgirl than a nineteenth-century actress.

Before she could find the man in the crowd, however, two hands clamped over her mouth while two strong arms wrapped around her waist.

Panic coursed through her. She screamed behind the tight hold on her mouth, but any sound was lost in the laughter around the poker table. Without attracting any attention whatsoever, two tuxedoed men wearing black eye masks hauled her sideways into an opening in the wall where a bookcase hid a paneled door.

"Mmph!" she cried behind one hard hand, kicking at her captors' legs as they dragged her into the darkened space no bigger than a closet and then shut the paneled door behind them, locking the three of them in the dark.

"Damn, she's feisty," muttered one of the men, a smelly, stocky man whose strong cologne mingled with even stronger scents of alcohol and tobacco. "Are you sure this is the right girl?"

Her blood chilled as she wondered who they were and what they wanted with her. Were these the men who'd tried to frame her? She squinted in the darkness to try to make them out.

Just then, the one who'd been holding her—a shorter man built like a bull—released her mouth.

Whatever his answer was, the words were lost in her scream for help.

Over and over she screamed until one of the men struck a match and lit a sconce behind her head. The two of them had lifted their masks to sit on their sweaty foreheads, and they stared at her as if she'd grown horns and a tail right before their eyes.

"What the hell?" one of them asked, scratching his chest as he watched her with a worried frown.

They were no longer restraining her, but they'd locked her in here with them and she could not see the way out, even though she knew where the door should be. Her eyes could not make out any kind of knob or handle at all.

"She's wearing a mask," the other one observed. "Aren't you playing the game?"

Their conversation sounded far away because her ears were ringing from the panic alarms clanging relentlessly in her head. She fought to catch her breath while her unanswered cries for help seemed to echo eerily in the unmoving air of the closet.

"What game?" she asked finally, guessing the hidden space had been soundproofed since she couldn't hear anything from the card room she knew rested on just the other side of the wall.

The short man leaned closer and she arched away from his groping hand. Still, he succeeded in ripping off her white silk eye mask.

"The masquerade," the tall man answered, pulling a yellowed sheet of old-fashioned parchment from a pocket of his trousers. "Our clue said the next wench would be wearing a white mask with poinsettias."

He waved the silk in his hand like a pennant won in battle before making a lunge toward her.

Leaping backward out of his grip, she banged into a wall behind her. Nowhere to run.

"I assure you, I am not the next wench." She gave them a moment to let the words sink in since the two of them appeared to have imbibed early and often. She prayed they were just drunk and not complete bastards. "It is a simple coincidence that I'm wearing this mask, because I didn't sign up for any masquerade game."

Her heart rate slowed by a tiny fraction as the men who'd jumped her seemed to weigh that newsflash. She hoped they would do the right thing and release her. Heaven knew, it seemed like a good sign they weren't restraining her. But plastered, sexed-up males couldn't be trusted to behave like gentlemen. They exchanged inscrutable glances now, and her fear factor spiked again.

What if they were too lazy to go find the woman who wanted to play this awful game of theirs?

In the wake of that worry came a dull thumping on the other side of the paneled door.

"Marie! Marie, are you okay?" a faint feminine voice called to her in time with the knocking.

Hope surged through her.

"That's me." She moved toward the door, shoving past the manhandling creeps who'd grabbed her. "My friends are looking for me."

She could not imagine who would know she was in here, in fact, but the voice could have been shouting for Penelope, and she would have pretended it was her dearest and most protective friend in the world.

"But we're playing a game," the taller, more sloshed man explained patiently. He appeared confused and more than a little dismayed at the prospect of her leaving.

Marnie started banging on the door in response to whoever was on the other side.

"I'm in here!" she shouted for all she was worth. "Help!"

Swearing, the shorter, smarter man appeared to understand the potential consequences of holding a woman against her will as he moved away from her and toward a button now visible on the far wall. Jabbing at the small device with one chubby finger, he must have tripped the hidden door. All of the sudden, light spilled into the tiny closet.

There, centered in front of the door, stood Lianna with a worried frown.

"Marie!" she cried, wrapping Marnie in a hug that felt really, really welcome right now. "Are you okay?"

Marnie became aware of many faces swarming around behind Lianna. It seemed the whole card room, including the half-naked players who'd been involved in strip poker, had circled around the bookcase to find out what was happening behind the hidden wall.

As her eyes met their curious gazes, she realized she no longer wore her mask. Anyone here might recognize her. Anyone here could be the one who'd tried to set her up.

Ducking her forehead onto Lianna's shoulder, she kept an arm locked around the other woman's waist.

"I'm okay. I just want to go back to my room," she whispered, wishing Jake was there. "I—don't want to be alone yet."

She'd said it mostly so Lianna would walk with her and help keep her at least partially hidden from the room full of prying eyes. But it was probably truer than she'd first realized, since her knees were still shaking from being grabbed and dragged out of sight faster than she could blink.

"Of course," Lianna murmured soothingly, tucking Marnie close with one arm while she cleared a path with the other. "Coming through! Make way! Coming through, for crying out loud. Give the woman some room."

Shoving her way through the crowd, Lianna blocked like a lineman while Marnie hurried along half a step back.

"How did you know I was in there?" Marnie asked once they'd cleared the thick of the crowd.

Closing in on the elevators, Lianna loosened her hold.

"I've been—" She seemed to hesitate and Marnie couldn't imagine why. Unless, of course, the other woman felt bad about flirting shamelessly with Jake the night before.

"You're my new hero," Marnie assured her. "I really appreciate you knocking when you did because those guys really had me scared."

She shivered again, thinking about what could have happened.

"Usually the girls who sign up for the masquerade games like that sort of thing," Lianna murmured distractedly, peering around the main foyer of the resort as if she were looking for someone. "They really ought to have a sign near the masks in the costume shop so people don't pick them up without knowing what they mean around here."

"No kidding," Marnie agreed, her whole body buzzing with the adrenaline letdown.

Damn it, where was Jake? More than anything right now, she wanted to feel his arms around her.

She moved to hit the button to call the elevator and realized Lianna was staring at her with an inscrutable expression. Despite the red sexpot gown falling artfully off one shoulder and the sprig of holly leaves tucked in her dark hair, she had a shrewd intelligence in her gaze.

"Although," she began slowly, "why else would anyone purchase a mask?"

The question contained a note of assessment that made Marnie a bit uneasy.

"For fun." She shrugged off the question. "The masks are beautiful."

"Or some people wear masks to stay hidden," Lianna mused. "But that would mean they know they're being watched."

Did Lianna know something about her purpose here? Could she know who was trying to frame her?

Confused and more than a little worried, Marnie didn't want to step into the elevator cabin with Lianna, even though the lift had arrived and the doors had swooshed open in silence.

Lianna took a step closer to her.

"Did you know someone has been watching you?" she asked, her voice low.

Threatening?

Marnie clenched her fists. She'd been ready to take on two full-grown men if they touched her tonight. There was no doubt in her mind she'd do some serious damage to the woman in front of her now.

"Marie," a familiar voice called to her from the other end of the hall.

Both women turned to see Jake jogging toward them in his dinner clothes, the formal attire an enticing contrast to his raw masculinity. Marnie's knees went weak with gratitude and relief.

"Thank God," she murmured, not knowing who to trust and feeling as if she'd been ripped raw tonight.

"Don't go anywhere near her," he warned, though at first Marnie wasn't sure which one of them he was speaking to.

As he stopped short between them, though, he grabbed her by the arm and pulled her away. Turning to Lianna, he spoke through gritted teeth.

"You've got some explaining to do."

She shook her head so hard the holly berry sprig that had been perched in her hair fell to the carpeted floor of the main foyer.

"I didn't do anything," she protested, her voice sounding panicked.

But, oddly, she didn't sound all that surprised by the accusation.

"I don't understand." Marnie squeezed Jake's arm, feeling a strange twinge of empathy for the other woman, who, after all, had just saved her from possibly being assaulted.

"She's the one who's been moving money around." Releasing Marnie's arm, he pulled a sheaf of papers that looked like computer spreadsheets from his jacket pocket. "She's the one who breached the Premiere accounts and tried to frame you."

9

"You can't be serious." Marnie bit her lip as she looked from Jake to Lianna and back again. "I'd never even met Lianna until yesterday."

Jake kept his eyes on Lianna, who'd turned pale but hadn't run. The elevator doors closed again, leaving the three of them together on the main floor.

"Well, Lianna?" he prodded, evidence in hand thanks to the hotel's computer database.

"I don't know what you're talking about." She shook her head, as if she could make the accusations go away.

"But you just said something about me being watched." Marnie lowered her voice as a young couple came through the resort's front doors into the foyer.

Sensing the need for privacy, Jake pushed the button for the elevator again.

"You're coming with us until we get to the bottom of this," he warned, knowing he'd never get away with that kind of intimidation as a cop. But as a P.I. operating out of state? He figured the rules were open for interpretation. Especially if it meant keeping Marnie safe.

"In the interest of privacy, perhaps that would be best."

Lifting her chin, Lianna was the first one to step inside the elevator when it arrived again.

Jake knew a seasoned criminal would have never gotten into the elevator with him. He also knew that whoever had tried to frame Marnie had laid too much groundwork to pull off this crime to make mistakes now. So between this small tip-off and the fact that Lianna Closson was willing to face his accusations, he had a pretty good idea she wasn't the one who'd engineered the 2.5-million-dollar swindle.

But her vaguely guilty behavior told him she knew something, and he would damn well find out what.

Bringing her for questioning to the suite he shared with Marnie, he held the elevator door for the women as they arrived at their floor. Unlocking the door to the room, he tried to process Lianna's behavior while Marnie spoke quietly in his ear, insisting that Lianna had saved her from—

"What?" He stopped cold inside the door to their accommodations as Marnie's words finally penetrated the high-speed swirl of thoughts in his head. "Someone grabbed you?"

He tensed everywhere, already furious with himself for letting her out of the room. Out of his sight. Quickly, she recounted the ordeal along with Lianna's role in saving her.

"I will find them," he assured her. *And gut them,* he assured himself. "You're certain you're unharmed?"

His eyes roamed over every inch of her, looking for bruises on her arms or any signs of her dress being askew. The whole time he took his inventory, he had to swallow back fury by the gallon.

He flipped on more lights in the suite as he maneuvered her under the chandelier in the living area so he could examine her better.

Throughout it all, Lianna paced nearby. And though she appeared worried, she didn't have the shifty look of a woman who was about to run. Despite the rumpled and well-used tissue in one hand, she seemed resigned to get to the bottom of this.

"I'm fine," Marnie began, then stopped herself. "Actually, I'm still a little shaken up."

As if to prove the point, she held up a hand to the light. He could see her fingers tremble before she tucked them back into the folds of her dress.

This time, he swallowed back curses along with his anger. She didn't need to hear it.

"I'm sorry I wasn't there." Hauling her into his arms, he held her. Absorbed the quivers vibrating through her. "Have a seat, okay?"

He shoved aside some needlepoint pillows in keeping with the elegant Victorian-style room, clearing a place for her. Lianna pulled a small lap blanket off the back of a chair near the fireplace and put it around Marnie's shoulders.

And while that move won the other woman some points, it wouldn't let her off the hook if she'd had anything to do with his case.

Turning to her, he gestured for her to take a seat on a nearby ottoman.

"How did you know she was in that room?" He'd get to the other stuff in a minute. Right now, he wanted to find out everything he could about the men who'd grabbed Marnie.

"I was in the gaming area waiting to—that is, I had a phone call to make before I could meet Rico tonight." She peered over at the grandfather clock near the entryway. "Another guy stood me up this week and I wanted to tell him that I was going to see someone else before I, you know, started hanging out with him."

"How noble of you," Jake remarked. "So you're in the gaming room and you saw the men grab Marnie?"

"Marnie?" Her brow furrowed.

"Marie," he clarified.

"Oh." Her expression cleared; she was probably used to fake names being used by the guests of the Marquis. "No, I didn't see them take her or I would have reacted faster. But I noticed her in the room one moment and when I looked for her the next moment, she was gone. And I just had a bad feeling about it since the whole place was so rowdy tonight."

"You were looking for me?" Marnie asked, leaning forward on the sofa.

She seemed steadier now, though Jake noticed she hadn't taken her hands off him since they'd returned to the room.

"I—" Lianna shifted on the ottoman, her velvet dress pooling around her high heels. "I'd been keeping an eye on you because I knew it was your first time here and this place can be a trip for newbies."

Marnie appeared satisfied with the answer, but Jake sensed more to that story. Still, he left it alone for the moment in his rush to confront her with what he'd discovered earlier.

"Can you explain these?" He tossed the sheaf of computer printouts on the table and let her leaf through the spreadsheets, which showed her guest user account for the Marquis had been used to access the Premiere Properties account.

"I don't even know what they are, so I'm sure I'm the last person who could explain—" Frowning, she ran her finger over the lists of numbers dates and accounts. "Wait. This is my user information and pass code for the resort's guest volunteer system. I use this to sign up for work around the hotel."

Marnie moved to sit beside Lianna. Whatever dislike Marnie might have had for Lianna at one time seemed to have vanished when the woman rescued her tonight. Was that part of Lianna's plan? Had she sought to gain Marnie's trust? Jake tried not to think the worst of Lianna, but his tendency to see those darker motivations were what had made him a good cop, and a good P.I. now.

"It looks like her user name masqueraded as mine to hack into the Premiere Properties accounts." Marnie saw the implications immediately as she read over the sheets. Straightening, she gave Lianna a level look. "These papers suggest you used your access to the Marquis computers to frame me."

"Frame you?" She shook her head, uncomprehending or doing a damn good job of looking clueless. "For what? I don't even use a computer when I come here because there's no access. I have to sign up for jobs before I arrive or else use the main computer downstairs, which I only did once and—"

"You brought your phone with you," Jake pointed out, knowing she could connect through that if she wanted. "You said you were going to call that guy who stood you up."

"Everyone smuggles in a phone here," she argued, her voice rising to a higher pitch as she became noticeably agitated. "That doesn't mean I brought a computer."

"You could have internet access on the phone." Jake watched as the woman's eyes darted around the room, her pulse thrumming visibly in her neck. She was hiding something and she was scared.

"Are you a cop?" She looked back and forth between him and Marnie. "I want to know what this is about. You have no right to keep me here."

Jake held up his hands, waiting for her to break. "No one is holding you here."

Marnie, unaccustomed to interrogation, didn't wait for the breakdown.

"You've been everywhere I've turned since I got here," she told Lianna, still hugging the dark wool lap blanket around her shoulders. "As much as I appreciate you helping me get out of that hidden room tonight, I don't believe you were keeping an eye on me just because I'm new to the Marquis."

At first, Jake feared the comment would distract Lianna from her fears and delay a confession of whatever she knew. But then she pulled one of the needlepoint pillows into her lap and hugged it to her like a security blanket.

Shoulders tense, she seemed to collect herself.

"Look, I haven't done anything wrong. If I've been close to you the past two days it's because this guy I was supposed to meet here—the one who stood me up—wanted to know about any new people who checked in this week." She shrugged as if that was no big deal. "The Marquis is all about meeting new people, right? So I figured he just wanted to find out if there were any exciting strangers to, um, have fun with."

She had Jake's full attention now. And he had a damn good idea where the story was going. This was the missing piece.

"Right. You thought your boyfriend was on the lookout

for new playthings, and being fairly liberal-minded yourself, that didn't bother you in the least."

Lianna frowned. "First of all, Alex is not my boyfriend.
Second, I wouldn't say—"

"Who?" Marnie interjected, her gray eyes locked on
Lianna's face. "Who did you say is not your boyfriend?"

"Alex," Lianna repeated clearly. "Alex McMahon. He's
just some guy I met here last year. He got in touch with
me after my divorce and wanted to see me this week—"
Lianna stopped in mid-sentence. "Are you okay?"

Marnie folded her arms more tightly around herself. Her
lips moved though no words came out for a long moment.

"Alex McMahon," she finally repeated.

It was a name Jake wasn't surprised to hear. A name
that his investigation kept coming back to. But at least now,
he had a solid connection to a guy with a lot more criminal smarts than Jake had given him credit for.

"We need to know everything about this guy," Jake explained. "I'm a private investigator and I think he could
be a threat to you as well as Marnie."

He passed the woman his Florida P.I. license, even
though it wasn't worth all that much in a different state.
Chances were good she wouldn't know that.

Lianna looked over the license while Jake studied Marnie. Some color had returned to her cheeks by now, but her
lips were drawn tight as her mouth flattened with worry.

"Okay," Lianna said, situating herself more comfortably on the seat now that she didn't seem to fear getting
in trouble. "For starters, Alex was very interested in your
arrival. He asked me to follow you."

Two hours later, Marnie had her bags packed.

She'd offered no protest when Jake announced they

had enough evidence in his case to vacate the Marquis. Between Lianna's lead about Alec Mason—who she recognized from the photograph in Jake's online files—and the paper trail Jake had obtained from the hotel's database, he had enough to turn over to the police and ensure Marnie wouldn't be a suspect. And while she was relieved beyond words about that, she was even more glad to leave the hotel because of the uneasiness that had settled over her ever since those men had grabbed her. Although she'd stopped shaking long ago, she still felt a chill deep in her bones that no amount of layers had taken away.

Now, she tossed her bag in the back of the SUV, her leather boots crunching in the snow as the exhaust warmed her legs. White Christmas candles glowed in every window of the resort, imbuing the place with a magical allure in spite of the scary night she'd had.

"I don't want to leave," Lianna protested a few yards away as Jake hustled her out a side entrance.

They weren't running out on the bill since the place had their credit cards, but they weren't exactly following checkout procedures. Jake had thought it safest to leave as fast as possible without anyone in the resort being any wiser. That way if Alec came looking for them—and Jake felt certain he would—they would buy themselves a little time.

"Do you really want to be there when your boyfriend shows up now that you know what a rat bastard he is?" Jake asked her as they got closer to Marnie.

He carried his bag and a dark plum leather suitcase that must belong to Lianna.

The other woman hadn't even bothered to change into street clothes yet, her red velvet gown visible between the gap in her long winter coat as she walked.

"He's not my boyfriend," Lianna reminded Jake. "Remember? I haven't seen him in person in a year."

Marnie didn't want to think about the fact that Alec had been at the Marquis with another woman while flirting with Lianna *and* pretending to have a relationship with her back in Miami.

She hopped up front in the passenger seat while the other two settled in. Marnie watched Jake as he came around the SUV, a fresh snowfall dotting his shoulders and lingering in his dark hair.

He'd certainly worked quickly and efficiently here, flushing out evidence against Alec faster than she'd envisioned. But while she was grateful to him for finding out who wanted to frame her, she couldn't help but regret their time together was coming to an end quicker than she'd imagined.

While her rational side told her maybe it was best that they part before she fell for him—a possibility that felt all too real even after knowing him a short while—her heart longed for just a few more days.

A few more toe-curling nights.

"All set?" he asked as he fastened his seat belt.

Not by a long shot.

"Yes." Marnie nodded, trying to ignore the lump in her throat. "But where are we going?"

She knew Jake wanted to keep her and Lianna safe. But she didn't know what keeping them safe involved.

"We can go to my house," Lianna offered, leaning forward from the backseat. "I live just north of here."

"No." Jake put the vehicle in gear and pulled out onto the access road in the same direction they'd come from. "He'll know where you live. Don't you get it? He tried to ruin Marnie financially and then frame her to boot. You have no idea what he's capable of."

When Lianna remained silent, Marnie mulled over the fact that Alec had turned out so much worse than even she'd pictured. And she'd spent a lot of time winging darts at his mug.

"Why do you think he wanted to implicate me in his crime?" Marnie stared out into the snow rushing at the windshield as Jake's tires spun around a wide turn. "I don't understand why he had so much ill will against me. It's one thing to fleece me out of my savings, but it seems sort of excessive to make it look like I stole millions."

In fact, she was royally pissed off, and not just at Alec, either. How could she have dated someone so manipulative and heartless?

"One of the best ways to get away with a crime is to make it look like someone else did it." Jake said it so matter-of-factly that she realized he'd probably seen scenarios like this a hundred times in his line of work.

As far as he was concerned, she was just another gullible mark. And man, that knowledge didn't settle well.

"I'm going to sue his butt ten ways to Sunday," she muttered, out of sorts and angry with herself.

"I'll represent you," offered Lianna. She popped up from the backseat, a business card in hand.

Reading it, Marnie saw she'd used her real name at the Marquis. Lianna Closson, Attorney At Law.

"You're a lawyer?" She turned around in her seat to see the sexpot in the Mrs. Claus-Gone-Wild dress.

"Defense against medical malpractice mostly, but I've been thinking about taking on some flashier clients to make ends meet in this economy. And I'm no longer using Wells by the way." She tucked a silver card case back into her purse. "You can be my first flashy client. And we'll whip the pants off this guy in court. Because while I may not always get my man in my personal life, I can guarantee you I'm a shark in court."

She smiled and Marnie had to laugh, seeing Lianna in a whole new light.

"Somehow, I can picture that."

Jake turned the wheel hard all of the sudden.

"Hold on," he warned as they ducked in between some trees and he switched off his headlights. "Someone's following us."

10

Taking his 9 mm from the glove compartment just in case, Jake sat in the darkness as snow piled on the windshield.

Inside the SUV, he could hear the women breathing as they all waited. Watched.

After a long minute, the car that had been following them finally approached, the headlights cutting a dim swath through the snowy trees. Maybe it was nothing—just someone else who'd checked out late. But Jake's sixth sense twitched something fierce.

Then the car's headlights spun wildly, the car careened out of control on the snowy road and it landed—hissing steam—in a ravine nearby.

"Oh, no!" Marnie peered over at him, worried.

Crap.

Did he dare play Good Samaritan? What if the person in the other car had followed them on purpose? On the other hand, how could he *not* check when someone could be seriously injured in the other vehicle? At these temperatures, they could freeze to death in a hurry.

"I'm going out." Jake met Marnie's gaze in the dim interior lit only by moonlight. He checked the rearview mirror. "Lock the doors and do not leave the vehicle for any reason. I'll be back."

He clenched his hands tight around the gun and the steering wheel to resist the temptation to kiss her, touch her, reassure her. Then, levering the door open, he braced himself against the blast of cold air.

"Hey!" a man's voice shouted in the distance, echoing through ice-laden trees.

Alec Mason?

One of the men who'd grabbed Marnie earlier?

Both possibilities made him grip the 9 mm tighter as he dodged toward a frosty tree for cover. He moved silently through the soft cushion of snow that stifled sounds.

"Lianna?" the man shouted again, the voice closer this time. "Is that you?"

Jake pressed his spine to the tree, frozen bark rough against the back of his head, trying to see into the whiteout before the guy was on him. Who the hell would be looking for Lianna? Could she be working with Alec Mason after all?

Had he left Marnie locked inside the SUV with a dangerous criminal? He spun to check the vehicle.

From inside the cab nearby, Jake could hear scuffling noises. What the hell?

The rear door of Jake's SUV popped open just as he made out a shape jogging through the trees.

"Rico?" Lianna's high-pitched voice blurted into the night. Her white coat blended with the falling flakes as she leaped from the vehicle. She took big, awkward steps through the snow. "Rico, I'm here!"

A tall figure emerged from the shadows. Garbed in a long man's dress coat and leather riding boots that could have only been purchased at the Marquis's exclusive boutique, the guy who'd pissed Jake off on more than one occasion burst through the tree line. This was the twin he didn't like—Raul's brother, Rico, who'd eyed Marnie one too many times.

"Easy there, bud. She's not alone." Jake stepped forward enough to be seen. He didn't raise his weapon, but he didn't ease his grip in case anyone else came out of the woods. Then again, his fingers were pretty much frozen in place. "Is anyone with you? Were you followed?"

"No." Rico seemed to assess the situation, looking from the women in the vehicle to Jake. "Is that a gun? What the hell is going on here?"

"Were you following me?" Jake took another step forward.

He needed to find out who'd been behind them on the road before he relaxed his stance.

Rico lifted his hands about waist high.

"Take it easy, dude. I came after Lianna when I saw her leaving the Marquis. I couldn't tell who she was with and I wanted to make sure she was okay." He leaned sideways to see past Jake. "Is everything all right, Lianna?"

"I'm fine," she called back. "For crying out loud, can't you put the gun away, Jake?"

"Was anyone else with you in the car?" Jake pressed, unwilling to relax his guard until he was damn certain no harm would come to Marnie.

Hearing that she'd been manhandled tonight had awoken dark protective instincts that still had him on edge.

"No. I tried picking up speed when I couldn't see your taillights anymore, but then I started fishtailing and— boom. I live in Southern California. We don't get weather like this."

He studied the guy, weighing his words. In the end, he

trusted his gut. Raul had been a stand-up guy helping him out earlier. Could his brother be that different? Besides, Jake had solid evidence implicating Alec Mason, and he had no reason to believe Rico was involved in his case.

Finally, Jake slid the safety back into place on the weapon and tucked it inside his jacket.

"You can ride with us." He motioned the guy toward the rear door where Lianna still peeked out into the snow. "But we're not going back to the Marquis."

The other guy nodded, but he kept a wary eye on Jake.

"Sure thing. My brother can retrieve the car in the morning." He moved toward the SUV and Lianna, whose arms were already outstretched. "I just hope someone clues me in on why we're on the run with a handgun in the middle of the night."

Jake figured he'd leave that up to Lianna. He wasn't in the mood to talk considering all that had happened tonight. He would be on the phone to the cops as soon as he got Marnie somewhere safe.

Stepping up into the driver's seat, he punched in the request for lodging on the GPS and steered the vehicle back onto the main road. The faster he got checked in and handed off the dirty work to the authorities, the quicker he'd have Marnie all to himself. And with a hunger driven by that edginess that had gnawed at him all day long, that moment couldn't come soon enough.

"THERE IT IS." Lianna pointed out a blaze of red and green Christmas lights from the backseat.

Marnie smiled at the sight, her mood more relaxed now that they'd left the Marquis behind. It had taken almost an hour to drive twenty-five miles in the wretched weather, but they'd found the bed-and-breakfast. Or at least according to Lianna's pointing finger they had.

Marnie had the sense that Lianna was not a woman accustomed to the backseat. A moment later, the GPS confirmed they'd arrived at their destination, the All Tucked Inn.

It was hardly the Marquis—no elegant candles in the windows or stately chimneys at regular intervals. The All Tucked Inn was more of a country farmhouse that had spawned as many additions as it had survived generations. The original building looked to be a large white clapboard affair in the Federal style, but the add-ons were an assortment of oddities that had a collective charm. Draped with evergreens at every window and red and green miniature lights around all the porch posts, the bed-and-breakfast gave the impression of being a safe hideaway from embezzlers—and overzealous sexual thrill seekers.

Pulling into a parking space to one side of the door, Jake switched off the lights while everyone piled out of the SUV. Marnie noticed he hadn't said much in the car ride, letting Lianna and Marnie do the talking as they filled in Rico on Alex McMahon aka Alec Mason. Even now, as Jake carried in their bags, his jaw remained set like granite.

Marnie liked Rico well enough. He couldn't take his eyes off Lianna. And for her part, the formerly flirtatious Lianna seemed utterly smitten. There was a definite connection there that went beyond the obvious. They cared about each other.

Or maybe that was just her optimistic side talking. Jake probably saw something totally different when he looked at the couple.

She wanted to say something to break the tension as they walked in silence toward the inn, but before she could, an older woman with long silver hair tied in a festive red bow met them at the door.

"Welcome!" She held the door wide, making room for the four of them as they trooped inside. "I felt so bad for you being out in this weather. I worried ever since you called for your reservations an hour ago. I'm so glad you made it safe and sound."

The interior of the farmhouse glowed with holiday warmth. A fire crackled in a huge stone hearth while two sleeping black Labs slept on a braid rug in front of it. A tall fir tree packed with ornaments loomed in the far corner of the room. White lights twinkled above piles of brightly wrapped presents. Clearly, their hostess had lots of loved ones in her life. A family. Children and grandchildren. Seeing all those cheery decorations reminded Marnie that she would be the only one of her siblings at Christmas dinner without a significant other, let alone a spouse and kids. As much as she loved her family, there was a certain loneliness in being surrounded by so many couples. Even her friends were pairing off at an alarming rate. In the past months, two of them had found The One— the guy they wanted to spend their lives with.

The thought sent Marnie's eyes toward Jake. Would he want to be with her tonight, or would he be all about the investigation? The need to be with him warmed her blood, melting the chill she'd carried in from outside.

Fifteen minutes later, rooms were assigned, keys were distributed and Marnie found herself in a back wing of the house with Jake. Jake had liked that he could see three sides of the property from their room. Apparently, former cops appreciated a wide range view. He'd asked that Li-anna and Rico take the rooms nearby so he could hear if there were any disturbances.

For their part, Rico and his lady lawyer seemed oddly polite with one another—a real switch from all the overt flirting they'd done earlier in the week. Marnie wondered what the night would bring for them behind closed doors. She knew the confusion that came when you didn't know where you stood with a guy.

Like her. Now.

She unpacked the bulky gowns she'd bought at the Marquis and shoved them in an antique, painted wardrobe just so they would be out of the way. The room could have been an advertisement for shabby chic, the vintage cabbage rose wallpaper broken up by big, airy windows dressed with white lace curtains. Sturdy farmhouse furniture kept the room from feeling too precious, the oversize bed and stuffed chairs swathed in simple, crisp white fabrics. As a nod to the holiday season, a pewter urn of fresh spruce boughs stood tall in one corner, a handful of wooden ornaments dangling off some branches.

While she found her nightgown and switched on the gas fireplace, Jake used the inn's wireless connection to email his evidence to the local cop shop. He balanced a phone in one hand while he hovered over his laptop perched on the pullout stand of an old-fashioned secretary desk. He'd shoved aside the wooden rolling chair with his foot, all restless energy and intensity.

She had the feeling she was seeing the most authentic version of him, a man she wasn't entirely sure she'd understood before now. When they first met that day he'd handcrafted molding around her furniture to make the cheap stuff look like beautiful pieces, he'd flirted with her quietly—a nice, normal guy.

Then, she'd peeled away that laid-back veneer when she'd discovered he was a P.I. who'd been watching her.

Later, his urgent kiss in the car and his unrestrained love-making in the hotel had shown her a man of deep passions.

Now, seeing him work at the job he was so clearly meant for, she began to understand who he was underneath all that—someone intensely driven in his quest for justice. Someone who wasn't afraid to walk away from a job—or a woman?—if they didn't conform to his high standards.

The realization made her wonder how they'd ever ended up together in the first place. What did he see in someone who'd been under suspicion for a felony?

As he finished his call and turned toward her, she felt as if she'd been caught staring. Clutching her flowered bag of shampoo and toothpaste, she nodded toward the bathroom off to one side of the homey accommodations.

"I was going to shower." She backpedaled toward the bathroom, her socks gliding over a section of the varnished hardwood that wasn't covered by a throw rug. She felt awkward around him tonight, unsure what it meant that they were sharing a room. "What did the police say?"

He stripped off his coat, cueing her into the fact that he'd done nothing else since he'd walked in the room other than take care of business. Apparently she was the only one thinking about peeling his clothes off.

"They whined about jurisdiction until they received my files. Once they saw how much I've got on Alec, they started paying more attention."

"But since we don't know where he is—"

"They'll get a warrant and post his picture, but they can't make an arrest until they know where he is. He could be out of the country or back in Florida." He stalked closer, his blue-and-white Oxford button-down back in place now that he'd ditched the clothes from the Marquis. A worn gray T-shirt lurked underneath.

"Or he could be on his way to the resort, like he told Lianna." Marnie's heart beat faster, but only because of Jake's proximity. She didn't worry about Alec when she was with Jake.

He might have spied on her without her knowledge, but he'd also made sure her name was cleared. His sense of right and wrong had demanded it. And she really, really liked that about him.

"Alec won't touch you." Jake plucked her bag of shampoo and toiletries from her hand. "I promised you that no one else would touch you but me, and I broke that vow when those bastards grabbed you tonight."

Anger blazed in his eyes, but his hand was gentle when he slid his fingers beneath her hair along the back of her neck.

"I think the promise was that we wouldn't let other people touch us," she clarified, remembering well those words they'd spoken that first night at the Marquis when she'd been exhausted and acting on pure instinct.

She'd wanted him then for reasons she hadn't fully understood. She wanted him more now, even knowing he could stride out of her life without a backward glance once they returned to Miami.

"Semantics." He stood so close that she had to look up to meet his eyes. "I let you down tonight and I'm so damn sorry I didn't protect you."

Green eyes probed hers, asking for forgiveness she would have never guessed he needed. And, oh God, she wanted to give him that and so much more.

"Jake, I never would have sat quietly in our suite at the Marquis while you did all the investigating. So if you think it's your fault for not locking me up in the room, I can assure you I only would have left to contribute to your case in any way possible. Remember, it was my good name and reputation on the line." She smoothed a hand over the unrelenting wall of his chest where his heart thudded a steady beat. "I didn't ride shotgun with you for over twenty hours on the way up here so that you could put me in the backseat once we arrived."

He tucked both hands under her hair, his thumbs remaining on her cheeks to skim small circles on her skin. She could catch hints of his aftershave when she leaned close enough, and the spicy scent lured her nearer with vivid memories of the last time they'd been wrapped around each other.

"But I never would have involved you if I had thought there was any real danger." He shook his head, brows furrowed together in worry. "Embezzlement is a white-collar crime. The chance of violence is—"

"It wasn't Alec we had to worry about." She tipped her forehead toward his neck, absorbing the warmth of his skin. "I didn't know the guests of the Marquis could turn so aggressive, and since it's my job to be very well acquainted with all the properties I recommend to my clients, I assure you I won't advise anyone else to stay there."

"I'll call Vincent and make him aware of that, too." Jake rubbed his cheek over hers, the light abrasion of his stubble sending a sweet thrill of longing through her. "He needs to know that place is a lawsuit waiting to happen so he can disassociate with it before someone gets hurt."

His arms banded around her tighter as he spoke, his hands sliding down her back to span her waist. Her hips.

"I was just about to take a shower so I could wash away the feel of strange hands on me," she confessed, shuddering at the memory of being grabbed. Shoved. Held against her will. "Maybe you could help."

She hoped it didn't sound like a desperate come-on. But she needed him. Wanted him. Knowing that her last relationship had been a lie from the start had made her feel more than a little empty inside. And all the in-your-face holiday reminders urged her to take what happiness she could now.

He edged back from her enough to see her face, and perhaps to gauge her expression for himself.

"I'd like that," he said finally, picking up her bag and untwining himself from her enough to lead her toward the shower.

Marnie thanked her lucky stars.

Once inside the bathroom, he leaned over the tub to crank the hot water on high. Then, setting her bag down on the edge of the vanity, he pulled her into his arms. Kissed her.

Marnie had a vague impression of clean white tile everywhere and a crisp linen shower curtain surrounding a huge claw-foot tub, but after that, her senses were only attuned to the man and the moment. Jake's mouth covered hers, molding her against him to fit just the way he wanted. She seemed to melt everywhere, her knees going boneless and her insides swirling hot and liquid.

He filled her senses, obliterating everything but him and a vague sense of heat from steam filling the room. His tongue stroked hers with seductive skill, reminding her subtly of all the sensual tricks he could perform.

A moan reverberated deep in her throat and he answered it by sliding his hands under her T-shirt and skimming the cotton up and off.

"I fantasized about you in the shower at the Marquis," he admitted between kisses rained along her exposed collarbone. "I wanted to point all those showerheads at you." He palmed the cup of her corset where it pushed up one breast.

She'd been in too much of a hurry when they left the Marquis to change out of all the complicated underwear, settling for exchanging the gown for jeans and a T-shirt.

"I fantasized about you in the shower, too." It was impossible not to have sexy imaginings under the powerful water pressure at the Marquis, where the spray nozzles were strategically positioned to hit the erogenous zones. "Except I thought about focusing all that jet power here."

She palmed the hard length of him through his jeans, stroking upward while he sucked in a gasp between clenched teeth.

"But after the day you had, I'm going to make sure tonight is all about you." He turned her around so that he stood behind her, his one arm still wrapped around her waist. "Look."

Blinking her eyes open, she saw their reflection in a mirror above the double vanity. Any moment, steam would cover the image since it crawled up the glass already. But for the moment, she saw herself with flushed cheeks and eyes dark with desire, her red hair tousled and clinging to Jake's shirt. His muscular arm dwarfed her, the thick bicep making her look small and delicate against him while his tanned hand roamed the white satin corset.

"This is what I will remember from tonight." In a million years, she would not forget the sight of herself, wanton and all but writhing against Jake.

"You look so good. I can't wait for a taste." He unhooked the first few fastenings on the corset and bent to place a kiss on her back. In the meantime, the steam covered up their reflection in the mirror.

All at once, he wrenched apart the sides of the corset, undoing the hooks in one move.

"Come on." He tugged the garment down, unfastening the garters holding her stockings as he went. Soon, all she wore was a pair of pearl-gray lace bikini panties—something of her own underneath the layer of under things she'd bought at the Marquis.

She trembled everywhere as Jake hooked a finger in the lace and dragged the panties down her thighs. He didn't pause except for a single kiss on her stomach, right beside her navel. Toes curling against the tile floor, she didn't protest when he lifted her off her feet and stood her in the tub.

He shielded her from the water, taking the handheld sprayer off the hook to shoot down into the tub before he peeled off his wet shirt. When he reached for his belt, however, she couldn't simply watch any longer.

"Let me." Nudging his hands aside, she worked the buckle herself. "I want to taste you."

Jake couldn't have refused her on a good day. But tonight? After the scare she'd had back at the Marquis? He would have let her string him up by his toes if she wanted.

And this was so much better.

Her skin felt softer than silk against him, a sleek, gliding warmth that peeled his clothes away until he was bareass naked and rock-hard in her hands. Leaving a condom on the sink, he stepped into the tub with her.

Steam drifted up from the water around her so she looked like a slow-motion beauty shot in some film, her red hair curling around her neck with the heat. Her lips perfectly matched the tight peaks of her breasts, the deep pink flesh puckered and ready for his kiss.

Except then she was down on her knees in front of him. Kissing. Licking. Savoring every inch of him with a slow thoroughness that made his blood rush and all his muscles clench.

He longed to hold back, to let her take the lead in every way. But his release pounded in the base of his shaft already, coaxed on by the feel of her fingernails scraping lightly up his thighs.

"Marnie." He stroked her hair, blocking out everything from the day but this. Her.

A slick trick of her tongue all but did him in, and he had to pull back. When she blinked up at him, she moved as if to kiss him again, and he had to hold himself away for a second to pull it together.

"I want to be inside you when I finish." He dropped to his knees with her in the hot water rising slowly up the sides of the deep tub. "I want to be everywhere at once."

In fact, it seemed imperative to make her feel good all over. To erase every fear and unpleasant sensation and replace it with pleasure. Wrapping her in his arms, he bent his head to her breast.

"Like here." He flicked his tongue along her creamy flesh as he cupped her. "I've been thinking about doing this ever since I kissed you here in the dressing room yesterday."

Taking his time, he lingered over his feast, scarcely coming up for air until she whimpered and dragged his hand down her body, almost to the water level. Right to the juncture of her thighs.

He drew back enough to take in the full-body flush of her skin, the parted lips and half-closed eyes.

"You're so beautiful right now." He anchored her waist with one arm while he sifted through the damp curls that shielded her sex. "When I first saw you take off your dress at closing time in one of those surveillance videos, I imagined you just like this. Passionate. Demanding."

He'd fantasized about her all the time after that. Not because she'd been wearing the sexiest black-and-red bra imaginable, or because she possessed curves any man would love to touch. No, he'd been fascinated by her uninhibited dance and her obvious joy in life.

That was sexy as hell.

"Really?" She opened her eyes fully, the gray flecked with gold as she arched her back and rubbed against him like a cat. "Then touch me. Now."

By the time he stroked along her silky center, she was so ready for him that she cried out at the contact, her body convulsing in a heated shudder. He throbbed to be inside her, the need to take her so sharp that he couldn't possibly play around in the tub just for the sensual thrill of it. The time for playing had come and gone, leaving them both on fire and shaking.

He leaned away just long enough to retrieve the condom and roll it on. Then, leaning her against the back of the tub, he stretched over her. Hips immersed in the water, he edged her thighs wide to make room for him. When he slid inside her, she cradled his jaw in her palm, wet fingers trailing down his cheek as their gazes locked.

He'd never felt so connected to a woman. Not during sex. Not ever. There was a fire in her eyes that called to him. Challenged him. Made him want to join her in all those unrestrained dances of hers.

Jake responded by thrusting deep. He touched every part of her, possessing her for however long she would have him.

Her eyes slid closed and he focused on the building pleasure, the keen tension already so taut he thought he'd snap with it. Heat flooded his back as water swirled around his legs and sloshed over the sides of the tub.

Marnie's fingers clenched the porcelain rim to hold herself up. He thrust over and over, finding a rhythm that tightened the knot inside him to until it became sweetly excruciating. Her feet wrapped around the backs of his calves, holding him in place. She cried out as her release hit her, racking her body with shudders.

He followed an instant afterward, unable to hold back another second. Their shouts mingled as seamlessly as their bodies, the sound echoing through the tile bathroom and off the churning water as they moved.

Long minutes later, when he stopped seeing stars, Jake heard the sound of running water and remembered why they were there in the first place. Toeing off the nozzle, he shifted so that Marnie lay beside him in the bath. He would take care of her. Watch over her every second until they returned to Miami.

He couldn't risk her being hurt again, something that awakened a dark realization. Would she *ever* be safe with a guy like him? He'd been so certain when they first met that he would have made a move on her if she hadn't been a suspect. He'd wanted her badly. But now that he'd spent time with her, he recognized she wasn't the kind of woman he normally dated. She might seem easygoing and fun-loving on the outside with her impromptu stripteases and dancing around her office while belting out her favorite songs. Beneath that, however, she was as intense and passionate as him.

She could mean so much more to him than anyone ever had before. Which was exactly why he needed to be careful not to get any more caught up in her world. He didn't want her hurt, and that meant he had to protect her—from himself, from the dark world that he moved in and from anything else that might threaten the most warm-hearted woman he'd ever met.

11

AN HOUR AFTER they arrived at the All Tucked Inn, Lianna still couldn't stop shivering.

She hid it well enough, she thought, keeping her coat on while she unpacked her clothes, then trading it in for a soft chenille lap blanket while she prowled around the room she would share with Rico. But the chill that had set in back at the Marquis wouldn't go away.

If anything, she'd only gotten more nervous on the ride here, seeing the connection that shimmered between Marnie and Jake. It was obvious they had strong feelings for each other and it had made Lianna wish she could step back in time for a do-over with Rico. She'd thrown herself at him shamelessly, treating him like any other guy at the Marquis who only went to the resort to practice their seduction skills. But she didn't want a relationship like that with Rico. He was more than just a fantasy man. He'd come after her when he thought she was in trouble. Surely that meant he must care despite the superficial way they'd related to each other at the start?

Peering over at him now as he shoved around a few

logs in a cast-iron woodstove, she felt a fresh wave of nervousness.

"I'm glad you followed me," she told him, still surprised that he'd come after her in a snowstorm.

"Yes? You've been so quiet since we arrived, I was beginning to wonder." He set down the poker on the hearth and watched her thoughtfully.

Maybe she hadn't hidden her worries as well as she'd hoped.

"I'm just shaken up, I guess." It felt strange to admit the weakness. To talk about something that mattered with a man she'd once viewed as simply another player—like her. Or at least, like she used to be. She wasn't so sure she wanted to play the games going on at the Marquis anymore. "I'm a lawyer. I defend those accused of crimes. I'm not used to being on the receiving end of accusations. Having Jack—I mean, Jake—think that I could be a criminal…"

She trailed off, still processing the emotions of the night. She felt like she'd been on a roller coaster with all the highs and lows, beginning with Rico's kisses in the hallway outside the dining room and ending with taking to the road to elude a devious liar who'd fooled her from the beginning.

Rico rose and crossed the floor. As he drew near, she clutched the chenille throw tighter, not sure what she wanted from him just yet. Being with him here felt different than at the Marquis. She felt more naked here— under the layer of nubby chenille—than she ever had at the Marquis in her revealing costumes.

"This Alec Mason is a heartless bastard to incriminate the people he gets close to. But you are not the only one he deceived. How long did Marnie say that she knew him before she discovered his true character?" A trace of his accent came through the words as he touched her shoulders, warming her through the soft fabric of the throw.

"They dated for months, apparently." Lianna had been too upset to recall all the details of Marnie's story, which she'd shared with Lianna and Rico in the car on the way over. Normally, she had a clever mind for remembering nuances of information, an asset in her work as an attorney. But apparently all bets were off when she was the one under the microscope.

"And Marnie is a smart, successful businesswoman, right?" His fingers drifted up her arm and landed on her cheek, gently encouraging her gaze. "So that tells you that Alec is a skilled liar."

She noticed that he had removed the contacts that made him indistinguishable from his twin. Sea-blue eyes replaced the predatory tawny gaze. Another layer stripped away between them.

"Con artist, more like it." She sifted through her troubled feelings and tried to define what upset her most. "But I guess we are all playing games when we visit the Marquis. How can we trust what anyone says, when all of us are purposely pretending the whole time?"

"The idea behind the Marquis is a good one, but some people take it too far. In theory, it is nice to throw off the conventions of everyday society and play games for a few days. But we all have to be careful not to take the fantasy too far."

"Like the scumbags who grabbed Marnie."

"Yes. Or like Alec, who uses the anonymity of the place to slip into one character after another. Who knows how many other women he has taken advantage of in this way?"

The thought made Lianna want to jump into the nearest tub and scrub away every vestige of the place.

"I'm glad we're here now," she admitted, not sure how to proceed. How to tell him she wanted a do-over. "I don't know if I'll ever have fun playing those kinds of reckless games again."

"Maybe it isn't reckless when you stick to playing with someone...special." Rico trailed his fingers down the side of her neck and back up again, landing in the half-fallen mass of her hair that drooped just above her shoulder.

"What do you mean?" Her heartbeat sped up and she hoped she hadn't misunderstood.

Could he want a do-over with her, too?

"I mean, maybe we don't need sexy games to entertain us when we've found something better." His fingers did wicked things to the back of her scalp, massaging lightly as he reeled her closer. "Something deeper and far more compelling."

By now, her heart just about jumped out of her chest. There could be no mistaking those words. She wanted that—something better. Deeper. More compelling. Rico was all of those things.

Her skin humming pleasurably while her heart warmed with new hope, Lianna let herself be drawn in by the magnetism of the man and the moment. She wanted nothing more than him.

"I would like that more than you can imagine."

At her acquiescence, he unfastened two pins and her thick hair tumbled down, releasing the fruity scent of her salon shampoo. Since she always wore her hair up at the Marquis, she already felt she had one foot in reality.

"I'm so glad, Lianna." He traced a lock with the back of his knuckle, following it down her shoulder. "When I heard you left the resort tonight, I realized you were the only reason I wanted to be there."

His fingers sifted through her hair to graze the skin beneath, inciting the sweetest possible shiver.

"The Marquis has been like a summer camp vacation from my real life for the past two years. I love the waltzing and the glamorous gowns." Most of all, she loved the kisses in the hallway she'd shared with Rico.

He grinned with wicked knowing as he trailed a knuckle down her chest to the top of her cleavage.

"You have an open-ended invitation to indulge in those things with me." He wrapped an arm around her waist, pulling her hips close to his. With his other hand, he wove their fingers together, positioning them for an impromptu dance. "Waltzing is a specialty of mine."

He whirled her around, the quick spin making her skirts billow and sending a breeze around her ankles. At the same time the cool air drifted around her legs, the heat of his body pinned against hers shot a wave of erotic longing through her. There was no mistaking his interest in her.

For a moment, she could not speak. Sensations came alive, chasing away her anxieties with the reminder that her vacation was not over yet.

"You know what they say about men who can dance." Easily, she followed his lead around the smooth planked floor. He was a strong partner, guiding her without dominating her. Yet she knew she could give over the reins completely and he would still take them where they needed to go.

"My father is a steelworker," Rico confided, never missing a step. "I will refrain from sharing with you what he thinks about men who can dance."

The self-deprecating smile surprised her, along with the

insight into his family life. She felt a surprising surge of protectiveness toward this man, who dwarfed her in size.

"The wisdom among women is that men who can dance are good in bed." Her cheeks heated just a little, which was strange for a woman who had flirted so shamelessly all week. It must be another by-product of being away from the resort. She wasn't just another anonymous guest here.

Rico wasn't just another man.

"Ah." His sea-blue eyes darkened as he watched her in the firelight. "This I would be happy to prove to you in no uncertain terms. But only when you're ready."

The unspoken half of his message burned in his eyes. *Are you sure you're ready?*

He pulled her hand over his heart, folding it inside his palm. Silently, he waited for her direction.

"A few hours ago, back at the Marquis, I would have vaulted into your arms and ripped off your clothes with that kind of prompting." She wondered if she used her vacations at the Marquis to ratchet up the heat in her romantic encounters so that she wouldn't feel the emptiness inside her afterward. So she wouldn't dwell on the fact that she was missing out on a whole lot more intimacy than physical joining alone could provide.

"And now?" He massaged her fingers, one by one, working them from the base to the tip until he kissed each in turn. The last one he lingered over, flicking his tongue over her knuckle in an electric stroke while she watched.

Hypnotized.

"What would you like to do instead, Lianna?" he prompted her, since her brain has shut down.

Her only thought was for his mouth and how it felt over her skin.

As he watched her, she could almost feel that languid,

fiery stroke in other places on her body. Her breath caught. Held. Fire licked over her skin. Erotic images of her entwined with him rolled, slow-motion style, through her brain.

"I don't want to make another mistake. And I think that place messes with my judgment."

She'd nearly rendezvoused with Alec, for crying out loud. Apparently when she let down her guard to flirt and have fun, all her lawyerly instincts went out the window.

Rico took a step back, though he kept hold of her hands.

"Look at me," he commanded, even though her eyes had been tracking him every second. "You said yourself that coming here exposes us, right? No more hiding behind costumes and parlor games."

She nodded, reminded by his aquamarine gaze that he had made an effort to peel away the pretense. "But you went to the Marquis to have fun. To play."

"Right. I figured a few days up here would help Raul forget about his runaway wife, and I planned on having a good time as a reward for being a stand-up brother. But maybe I found someone who interests me on a whole different level. Someone who could mean a hell of a lot more to me than a vacation distraction. Why would I say no to that?"

In that moment, with his brow furrowed and his shoulders tense, Lianna realized it was the first time he hadn't sounded at all like her fantasy Latin lover. Another hint that she could see beyond the exterior to the person beneath.

And wow, did his words ever make her feel special. More than that, she believed them.

Mind made up, she took a deep breath.

"Did I mention how great it was of you to follow me

after I left the Marquis?" She splayed a hand on his chest, eager to feel the warmth and strength there. To return to that place of hot, lingering kisses and tantalizing touches.

"If what was between us was just a game to me, I would have opted for brandy by the fireplace rather than freeze my ass off in the snow to follow you." He twined his finger around a strand of her dark hair and used the end like a paintbrush to tickle along her bare shoulder. "So you can be sure there's nowhere I'd rather be right now than here with you."

Tingles skittered along her skin where he teased her. But when he trailed lower, following the line of her breastbone down into the valley of her cleavage, the humming sensation gathered and concentrated. Vibrated all the right places as thoroughly as any sex toy, when all he did was play with her hair.

"I'm right where I want to be, too," she said, her voice breathless. Excited. When his knuckle grazed the side of her breast in his quest to unfasten the front laces of her red velvet gown, she shuddered with pleasure. "I don't know what you're doing to me, but—wow."

"I'm seducing you," he whispered in her ear, relinquishing the lock of her hair to untwine laces in earnest. "Is it working?"

"That would be affirmative." Her knees turned liquid as he peeled away fabric, exposing the candy cane–striped corset beneath.

He whistled softly.

"You're the gift that keeps on giving, aren't you?"

"I like dressing up." Especially for Rico, since he rewarded her efforts with gratifying looks.

And a new urgency in his hands as he sought clasps and hooks to free her.

"I damn well like seeing you this way, too. But right now, I've only got eyes for what's beneath."

Which was just fine with her. She couldn't wait to feel his hands on her bare skin.

Arching up on her toes, she wrapped her arms around his neck, silently giving herself over to him. To whatever he wanted.

He groaned with approval as she pressed her breasts to his chest, her hips cradling his erection.

"Kiss me," he demanded, bending close to brush his mouth over hers.

She'd known that he was a great kisser from those stolen moments in the alcove outside the Marquis's dining hall. But the contact then had been skill and persuasion, restrained heat and tantalizing potential. Now, the bold sweep of his tongue was all about passion and possession, a seductive mirror of the mating they both wanted.

But even that wasn't nearly enough when she was ready to crawl out of her skin to be with him. Her hands were shaking and awkward as she shoved off his jacket and freed a few buttons on his shirt.

Rico made far better progress on her corset, flicking open the fastenings that held her stockings in place. The brush of silk sliding down her legs teased a fresh wave of want along her thighs, the contact too gentle for what she wanted.

He backed her against a closet door near the fireplace, his weight pinning her there.

"Another night, I will give you the fantasy," Rico promised, his breathing as unsteady as hers while he raked away the last restraints on her corset and sent the garment sliding to the floor. "Tonight, we strip it all away."

Lianna remembered how easily he fell into a role from

their time playing servants together at the Marquis. She had no doubt there would be sexy games in their future.

"Yes." She reached between their bodies to palm the hard ridge she wanted inside her. "The more stripping, the better."

He dispatched her panties on cue, dragging the imported silk down as he dropped to his knees in front of her.

Um...if this was his idea of delaying her fantasies, she couldn't imagine what fulfilling them might look like.

Then he spread her thighs to make room for himself and kissed the pulsing center of her. She would have fallen if not for the door behind her and Rico's hands bracing her legs where he wanted them. Liquid heat pooled inside her, gathering, swelling. Her fingers trailed helplessly along his shoulders as each stroke of his tongue propelled her higher.

When the release hit her, the pleasure swept through her so fast and so hard she twisted mindlessly against the door. Wave after wave of lush sweetness had her calling out his name, her fingers twisting in his dark, silky hair.

She'd only just barely come back to reality when he lifted her in his arms and carried her to the couch. Aftershocks still hummed through her when he sheathed himself with a condom. He loomed over her, gloriously naked. Deliciously hungry for her.

She reached out to him, trailing her fingers down the chiseled muscles of his chest. Down to the rigid length of his arousal. He sucked in a breath between his teeth as he followed her down to the couch, bracing his weight on one arm.

He came inside her slowly, allowing her to get used to him as he moved deeper. Deeper. He parted her thighs farther before he claimed her completely. His chest met her breasts. His teeth nipped her ear.

And then he started to move. The hot glide of his body inside hers sent ribbons of pleasure through her, making her shiver in delight. She ran her hands through his dark hair and over his broad shoulders, wanting to touch him everywhere. He treated her like a woman he wanted to take care of. A woman he wanted to please.

And *oooh,* did he please her. No man had ever tried to give her just what she wanted before. Just what she needed.

Rico anticipated her every desire. The thought sent her hurtling over the edge as surely as the drive of his hips into hers. She clutched him close, holding on tight as her release rocked her whole body.

He came with her, surging impossibly deep. She wrapped her legs around his waist, holding him right where she wanted him, her ankles locked.

There were no barriers. No masks. No games. Just a gorgeous, generous lover who made her feel special. Blissed-out. Sexy.

As she lay beneath him in the firelight, trying to catch her breath, Lianna knew another woman might have been simply counting her blessings in the wake of incredible sex. But she had never been particularly lucky in life, and fairy tales didn't happen to her.

So she squeezed Rico tight and soaked up the scent of his aftershave, hoping she'd remember this moment forever. Because her lawyer instincts were up and running again, and they told her that anything this good couldn't last for long. A smooth-talking criminal had tried to frame her as surely as he'd tried to frame Marnie.

And she didn't doubt for a second that Alec Mason would be back when she least expected it.

12

MARNIE COULDN'T SLEEP.

After her trip to the bathtub with Jake, he'd carried her back to bed and held her while she dozed off. But she'd become immediately alert when Jake moved away from her; it seemed he had no intention of sleeping himself while Alec was still on the loose and possibly looking for them.

He'd only gone to work on his laptop in a chair a few feet away from the bed, but just knowing that he wouldn't relax made her restless. Worried.

Well, that coupled with the sensation that the closer she got to Jake, the further he slipped away from her. She felt herself falling for him—knew she wanted more from him. Yet he retreated each time they touched, no matter how earth-shattering the sex was or how much he shared with her in bed. The thought of returning to Miami only to get dumped scared her. But the optimist in her told her he was a man worth fighting for. So she would try to walk that line between getting closer to him and not totally losing her heart to him.

Finally, she snagged her own laptop and cracked it

open, figuring she'd at least catch up with her friends or check her work email.

"Am I keeping you awake?" Jake asked, peering at her over the blue glow of the electronic screen in front of him.

"The idea that you think you shouldn't sleep is what's keeping me awake, if that makes sense." After firing up the machine, she waited for it to boot up. "It makes me nervous to think there's a possibility—well, actually, I don't know what there's a possibility of at this point. I thought we agreed Alec was more of a white-collar criminal."

Or had that just been what she wanted to believe?

"As the stakes get higher, people stop thinking rationally and start getting desperate." Jake punched a few keys with excess force before he met her gaze again. "Too many good people have been hurt by this guy for me to rest until he's behind bars."

Marnie was reminded of his friendship with Vincent Galway and the fact that Jake had resigned from the force when he had gotten screwed by corrupt cops and "missing" evidence.

"You're really determined to settle this score for Vince, aren't you?" While she admired Jake for being the kind of man who championed his friends, she was reminded of yet another reason that Jake might find it easy to walk away. He hadn't started pursuing Alec to avenge her. When it came right down to it, he had Vince's interests to protect, not hers.

Jake punched a few more keys, but she had the feeling he was mostly avoiding her question.

He wasn't exactly the type of guy to spill his guts.

"Will you ever go back to being a cop?"

He dropped all pretense of working and met her gaze head-on.

"Why? Does it matter that I'm a P.I.?"

He couldn't have broadcast *raw nerve* any more clearly.

"Just curious. I wondered if making things right for Vincent would allow you to go back to a job you traveled halfway across the country to take."

"I don't know," he admitted, the electronic glow casting shadows on his face as he frowned. "Working alone has its benefits."

Did he prefer to be alone in his personal life, too?

Marnie mulled over his statement while she opened her email and read a worried note from her mother asking why she hadn't been at the local community center's pancake breakfast with Santa, an event she normally worked every year. Shoot. She clicked on Reply to explain her whereabouts.

"Doesn't it get lonely?" she asked, wondering suddenly about more than his job. Who would take him out for pancake breakfasts with Santa?

"I'm not the most social guy." He reached for a glass of water by the bed, his bare chest lit by the screen as he leaned.

Right now, she'd like to teach him to be a lot more social. With her. Preferably involving a scenario where she tasted her way down his pecs to his taut, defined abs...

"What about outside work?" She cleared her throat to try to banish her sudden case of hoarseness. "Do you have plans for the holidays?"

"I don't think I'll make it back to Illinois this year since this case isn't closed and we're looking at—" he flipped his wrist so he could see the face of his watch "—December twentieth."

"I can't imagine spending the holidays apart from the people I love." Even if they would all show up for dinner with their happy families while she would be alone. She paused before sending her mom the email. "Although, I do wish I could convince some of them to leave Miami and take a Christmas holiday somewhere up north. The snow is so…pretty."

She'd been about to say romantic, but she could almost picture Jake being allergic to words like that. And she had the feeling all her talk about loved ones and the holidays was scaring him off anyhow. He stared at her from his spot in the armchair, his expression thoughtful.

Foreboding.

"What are you working on?" he asked. The question was so irrelevant to what she'd been saying that she would bet he hadn't listened to a word.

Frowning down at the laptop, she smacked the Send button and tried to keep the hurt out of her voice.

"Just emailing my mom so she doesn't worry about me."

"Wait." He half threw himself over the bed to grab her computer.

"What are you doing?" She didn't mind giving up the laptop, but he yanked the cord out of the back of it, turning the screen black. "That can't be good for it."

"He could have access to your computer." Jake sat on the bed beside her, his bare chest temptingly close.

"Alec?" She stilled as her brain sifted through the implications. "What do you mean? That he could have grabbed it when I wasn't looking? Or—"

"He's got to be great with computers to have pulled off the embezzlement and to frame both you and Lianna." He kept the laptop closed, his grip tight on the case. "So it's very plausible he'd know how to set up remote access to your computer. In fact, he probably did it before the two of you even broke up so that he could keep tabs on you afterward. He certainly knew that you were headed to the Marquis fast enough, right?"

A chill shivered down her spine. Could Alec have been watching her this whole time?

"I let him use my computer on several occasions." She'd never thought twice about it. "You think he...did something to it? Installed spyware?"

"My guess is he did much worse than that. Did you already contact your family tonight?"

"I had just sent an email when you unplugged it."

"Did you tell them where you are right now?" He covered her hand with his, a gesture of comfort that didn't soothe her in the least.

"Yes." She'd written all of three lines, but she'd mentioned the All Tucked Inn by name. "I've traveled alone for my work for years and that's a habit I got into long ago. I always let my family know where I'll be and when to expect to hear from me again."

She'd always thought the system helped protect her safety. But in this case, she had the feeling she'd endangered Jake, Rico and Lianna along with herself.

"We can't stay here." Standing, he shoved her laptop in the case he kept his in, then jammed his alongside it.

"But what about the snowstorm?" She didn't look out the window since Jake had already briefed her earlier on the importance of not making herself a target to anyone watching the building from outside. But she didn't need to look out to know the snow still fell with blizzard force. "We barely made it here and the GPS didn't show another hotel for miles."

The drawback of romantic, snowy mountain regions was that there wasn't a hotel and a Starbucks on every corner. She wasn't in Miami anymore.

"We don't know what he's capable of, Marnie." Jake pulled on his pants over his boxers. "So I'd rather take my chances in the snowstorm than play sitting duck for this guy."

Fear clogged her throat as she began to appreciate how serious this could be. Guilt compounded the sick feeling since it would be her fault if Alec found them.

"I'm sorry about this." She hated that she still hadn't learned enough caution, that Jake was forced to clean up her mistakes.

"I should have thought about the computer before." He shook his head, and the dark expression on his face made it clear he blamed himself. "I'll go next door and explain to Rico and Lianna that we need to leave. Don't use the phone, okay?"

She nodded as she rose from the bed, grateful to him for taking care of her. For looking out for all of them. If not for Jake Brennan, she could easily be behind bars tonight instead of here, falling for a hardened P.I. who might never love her back.

"Thank you," she blurted before he left. "For everything."

Marnie got the full impact of his undivided attention for a long moment, his green eyes inscrutably dark in the firelight.

"I want to keep you safe." He spoke the words like a declaration, with the kind of vehemence you'd expect for a more personal sentiment.

She had an odd, disheartening premonition that this might be as much of a commitment as she ever received from Jake Brennan. She thought about calling him back when he tugged a shirt on and headed for the door, but his name died on her lips when a woman's scream pierced the night.

Jake sprinted through the dark hall of the bed and breakfast.

The scream had faded by the time he tried the handle on Rico and Lianna's room.

Locked.

Pounding on the paneled door, he heard voices from inside. Behind him, he detected Marnie's soft, fast footsteps running toward him in the corridor.

"Go back to the room," he ordered, needing her out of the equation so he could focus on whatever was happening here. "Lock yourself in and don't open it until you're sure it's me."

A quick glance back revealed her worried face as she nodded and backed away. The rest of the floor remained quiet; it appeared they were the only ones renting rooms tonight.

He hated that this was scaring the hell out of her. He'd freaked her out before when he'd run around the blizzard with a weapon in hand, and again when he'd snatched her computer out of her hands. But at this point, it would be better if she was frightened and hiding out than around when trouble erupted.

"Rico, open up." He kept pounding. "It's Jake."

The lock clicked and the door gave way. Rico stood inside with an ashen Lianna under his arm.

"We're okay," the other man assured him. "She saw a man's shadow at the window, I guess."

Jake did a visual sweep of the room, taking in the open suitcase and the still-made bed. Clothes were scattered around the living area. Parted curtains against one window looked out into a darkness lit only by a security light in the front yard, half obscured by the storm.

"We're on the third floor." He propped the door open so he could keep one ear trained for sounds in the hallway. "You sure you saw a person and not just swirling snow or something?"

"I know what I saw," Lianna insisted, still pale, but her voice remained steady. "It was the outline of a man's upper body—from the hips up—as he moved past the window."

"There's a catwalk outside that leads to a fire escape," Rico explained, pointing toward the window in question. "I looked out, but I couldn't see anyone."

Jake crossed the room to check, lifting the shade carefully so as not to give away his position. The light was dim behind him, the glow from the fireplace the only illumination in the room, just like it had been back in the suite he shared with Marnie.

Marnie.

Damn, but this was when not being with a cop sucked. There wasn't a chance in hell he'd be able to obtain police protection for her, especially when they had piss-poor little to go on other than a few strange coincidences. But he felt in his gut that Marnie's former boyfriend wasn't going to just take his money and run. The fact that he'd been angling to meet with Lianna—to spy on Marnie through her—told Jake the guy wasn't done making trouble. Although what exactly he wanted and why remained a mystery.

"I don't see anyone." Peering through the casement, Jake sought signs of movement at the edge of the woods nearby, the backyard lit by a couple of security lights around the perimeter and the glow of red and green decor along the roofline. "But I think that snow on the catwalk might have been disturbed."

Tough to tell with the snow falling thick and heavy. The walkway was a wrought-iron construction with lots of open grates so the snow didn't gather there much.

The phone rang while Jake wedged open the window for a better look out into the frigid night.

"Hello?" Lianna answered while Rico opened another window a few feet away from him, the second cold blast pushing back the flames in the fireplace.

Jake kept one ear tuned into the conversation while he searched the iron path for signs of a footprint. Lianna must have been speaking with the owner of the bed-and-breakfast because she was explaining that she'd seen someone's face at the window and went on to ask if anyone would be working outside their room at this hour.

"Jake, check this out." Rico called to him from the other window, his face barely visible through the falling blanket of white.

Closing his window, Jake moved to the next one, where Rico looked out into the night.

And there, he could see the framework for the fire escape extended beyond the window, around the corner of the building. Leading anyone right to Jake and Marnie's room.

Shit.

Marnie.

Jake pushed away from the sill and plowed over a duffel bag to get out the door. Back to his room.

His feet jackhammered down the hall as hard and loud as his heart, dread pumping through him. He didn't bother knocking, instead using his key card to open the door. When the slide bolt caught—proof she'd double-locked it from the inside—he kicked the thing down. It cracked easily, since the old home didn't contain the steel doors used in big hotels.

"Marnie," he shouted, not seeing her right away. He called again, louder, as he burst into the bathroom.

There, cold wind blew across the empty claw-foot tub. An open window had curtains whipping in the breeze as snow gathered and melted in a pool on the tile floor.

She was gone.

13

"BE VERY, VERY QUIET."

Alec Mason's voice whispered against Marnie's hair as he hauled her across the side lawn of the inn through the blinding snow. The pistol barrel wedged under her jaw and the duct tape strapped across her mouth were far more persuasive than his lowly growled words, however.

She hadn't found one chance to tip off Jake about Alec's return. She'd been so worried about Lianna after the scream that she'd sealed her ear to the exterior door to hear what went on in the room down the hall; Marnie had never heard her ex-boyfriend steal in through the window and right into the suite. God, she hated that she'd let him take her so easily after all the warnings Jake had issued about being vigilant. To think she'd double-locked the door—but who would ever expect someone to climb in a third-story window?

Now, after wrestling her down the narrow fire escape and out into the bitter cold, Alec led her through knee-high snow to the woods. Her slippers had rubber soles, but didn't begin to keep the chill at bay. She shivered in a pink sleep shirt and pajama pants. Behind them, she thought she heard Jake and Rico at the windows, but that might have been wishful thinking. Her heart beat so loudly in her ears she could hear little else.

"Here we go." Alec spoke softly as they arrived at his transportation, his voice puffing clouds in the air. His wiry frame was surprisingly strong, his expensive cologne pungent in her nose. How could she have ever thought for one moment this man was date material?

She stumbled, her slippers not gaining much traction in the snow, and the gun barrel nudged scarily deep. As he yanked her to her feet, she saw where they were headed.

There in the woods, behind a potting shed, sat the horse-drawn sleigh from the Marquis. She recognized the elaborately scrolled tack and the stacks of furs. Except the driver wasn't an inn employee with a sprig of holly in his top hat. It was one of the guys who'd grabbed her and forced her into the tiny hidden room back at the resort. Alec wasn't some lone bad guy. He had backup. An operation.

Marnie had the swelling sense that she was in far deeper than she'd ever imagined. With his knack for adopting aliases, Alec had probably committed more crimes than they'd begun to ferret out.

"Up we go." Alec continued to give her directions as if he were her date instead of her abductor. Still, his iron-clad hold on her never wavered while he handed her up into the sleigh.

As soon as he had her inside, lying sideways on the pile of furs and blankets, he kicked the back of the driver's seat. Fur tickled her nose, but at least the heavy weight of the blankets cut the wind. The creep with the reins in his hand urged the horses forward. As they moved into the forest, they made very little noise, especially with the fresh snow muffling all sound, and there were no lights on the conveyance. Maybe a horse-drawn sleigh wasn't such a crazy choice for a getaway vehicle in a blizzard.

How would Jake ever follow her?

Alec removed the gun from under her chin, but he looped a rope of some kind around her leg, tying her securely to the sleigh with a painful cinch of the cord. Where was he taking her?

New fear set in faster than the cold. What could he possibly gain by hurting her? Then again, what else could he want from a woman he'd set up to take the blame for a felony? His plan for her to be in jail had failed, so maybe he wanted to ensure she never implicated him.

For once, she needed to think like Jake and see all the possible ways this could end badly. Maybe that would help save her somehow.

Beside her, Alec moved up into the bench seat while keeping an eye on her on the floor. Snowflakes gathered on her face, but he covered the rest of her with the excess furs. Her foot remained tied to the sleigh, and her toes were numb through her slippers from the walk through the snow. As her body warmed, her skin burned with the ache of nearly frostbitten skin returning to life.

With the gun resting on his knee, Alec's guard was a bit more relaxed now that they'd put some distance between them and the inn. Her captor pulled out a cell phone and started tapping keys, the electronic glow illuminating his unshaven face. And as she lay there staring up at this man who'd deceived her in more ways than she could count, she tried to imagine what Jake would suggest she do in this situation.

Buy time.

The answer was there so quickly and with such certainty, she would swear she caught the message on a wave of ESP direct from the source. Jake would come for her—she knew that. But she needed to make sure she remained in one piece long enough for him to catch up.

"Mmpf." She braved a small noise behind the duct tape now that his firearm wasn't jammed against an artery.

Alec looked down at her almost as if he'd forgotten she was there, his watery blue eyes visible until he snapped his cell phone shut and cast them in total darkness again.

"Mmpf!" she tried again, pointing to the duct tape and hoping she wasn't pissing him off by reminding him of her existence. But maybe if she could talk to him, she could find out his plans and delay him somehow.

"The lady wishes to speak," he mused, cocking his head sideways so he could look at her more directly in her awkward position on the floor. "I hope if I allow you the freedom of speech you will be kind. You look like a Christmas angel there, wrapped in your furs with that lovely skin. And I hate to lose that image of you with ugly words."

The odd comment made her wonder if Alec might be losing some of his grip on reality. He'd always been charming, but his attempt at gallantry now seemed downright ludicrous.

He must have decided to risk the outburst as he gave a brief nod, indicating she was free to speak.

Gently, she pried up the edges of the tape with one hand, carefully removing the restraint.

"Thank you." Her skin burned from the sticky glue and she didn't feel one bit grateful, but she tried to stay calm so as not to rile him. "Alec, I'm frightened. Where are you taking me?"

She hoped to appeal to his human nature, assuming he still had one underneath his mask of clean-cut, all-American good-guy looks. With his J.Crew clothes and trimmed dark blond hair, he appeared boy-next-door trustworthy when everything about him was a lie.

"We're making a brief stop at the Marquis to change vehicles, then we're lifting off at dawn by plane." He smiled as he spoke, a lock of dark blond hair slipping loose from the navy-blue wool cap on his head. "I know how you like to know your travel particulars. I've missed you, Marnie."

The handgun to her throat was a funny way of showing it. But she tried to keep the conversation more focused on relevant information and less focused on his personal delusions.

She closed her eyes and conjured up a vision of Jake's face. He would find her before Alec did anything crazy. She trusted in that and as far as she was concerned, that wasn't optimistic thinking. That was a logical fact based on everything she knew about Jake Brennan. He'd promised to keep her safe and he would do anything and everything in his power to do so.

She was lucky that he was so committed to his work. Lucky that he didn't just clear her off his suspect list, but also make sure she didn't get framed for someone else's bad deeds. She loved that he put so much of himself and his honorable nature into his work. Hell, she just flat out loved him.

She loved him.

That knowledge was there as sure as her faith in him and the realization of that love gave her the courage to maintain her cool with a desperate criminal.

"You've missed me?" She tried to sound only slightly surprised and not at all accusatory. Finding the right tone, in fact, required one hell of an acting job. "But you broke up with me."

On Facebook, no less. But Christmas angels didn't remind crazy men of things like that when their lives were on the line.

She twisted away from a bough full of snow that dropped suddenly into the sleigh and noticed a little give in the rope around her ankle. Under the cover of her fur blanket, she hitched at the rope with her other foot.

"I needed to distract attention from me for a while until I could hide the movement of the money." He shook his head while he brushed some of the fallen snow from his lap. "It was like a shell game trying to hopscotch the money from one account to the next, creating diversions and dead ends all the time. You know I'm not as organized as you, so it wasn't easy to keep track of it all in my head."

That was why normal people took jobs to make money instead of stealing it! But she stifled that thought, too, and strained for any sign of other sounds in the night besides the dull clop of hooves through the soft snow and the swish of the sleigh runners.

Would Jake return to the Marquis? Or would he try to follow their path through the woods?

She wished she could communicate with him now, to warn him that Alec seemed to have grown a little mad and that a calm, quiet approach might work better so as not to startle him into violence. The thought of anything happening to Jake sent a dark, panicky chill through her, jabbing at a heart still tender from the newfound realization of how much he meant to her. How much she'd lose by never seeing his face again, never feeling his strong, muscled arms around her.

"How did you find me tonight?" She couldn't understand how he came to be lurking around the All Tucked Inn so soon after she'd sent her email. He had to have another way of knowing her movements besides tracking her computer.

"Luckily, the lady lawyer is even more dutiful about reporting in to friends and family than you are. She sent a text message from her phone a couple of hours ago, letting her sister know she was at the charming All Tucked Inn. As luck would have it, I'd been staying there myself this week, keeping an eye on things at the Marquis until a couple of more deals came through for me, so I was very familiar with the layout of the place." He winked at her as he pulled his wool hat down more securely over his ears. "That part worked out so well, you couldn't have planned it better yourself."

Marnie ignored his self-congratulations to focus on what else he'd said. A couple of deals? How many people had he been swindling? She tried not to let her distaste show as she chose her words carefully.

"I'm worried there are a lot of people looking for you," she confided, keeping her voice low so the driver didn't hear her. She couldn't be certain how involved he was in Alec's plans, but she knew from experience that he didn't much care if he hurt her. "You might attract less attention if you put away the gun once we arrive at the hotel."

"Innocent Marnie." Alec tucked the weapon into a holster beneath his wool pea coat. "It's precisely *because* so many people are looking for me that I need to have the piece within easy reach. Your P.I. friend has run me ragged the past two months trying to cover my tracks, but he's not going to win in the end. One bullet keeps him quiet forever."

He patted his coat where the gun rested beneath, and a thick dread rose like bile in her throat. Alec had every intention of killing Jake. A vision of Jake lying cold and lifeless in the snow pierced her heart and chilled her blood in a way no snowstorm could.

The sleigh began to slow as the driver pulled back on the reins.

"Looks like we're nearing our destination." Alec reached down to replace the duct tape on her mouth and haul her up to the seat beside him as the sleigh halted in the woods near the Marquis. The driver jumped to the ground and disappeared into the dark. "You're coming with me until I'm safely out of the country. Your new boyfriend isn't the only one looking for me now."

Marnie's heart dropped at the realization that he'd only taken her to be a hostage.

She might never see Jake again.

Click.

The unmistakable hitch of a weapon being cocked for fire sounded inches behind them.

"I'm the only guy looking for you who counts."

Jake. He stood inches behind the sleigh, his 9 mm pointed at the back of Alec's head. She had no idea where he came from as he'd arrived in total silence, but somehow he was there.

Marnie wanted to warn Jake that Alec had a gun and that there was another guy with him, but Alec held her arms so she couldn't remove the duct tape.

"Let her go," Jake warned. "I've got backup and we've already got your driver and his friend. It's all over."

In the distance, Marnie heard the wail of a siren. Headlights entered the resort parking lot nearby, ringing the sleigh with light.

Thank God. Thank you, Jake.

She sat very still until she felt Alec make a sudden move. Her captor released her to go for his gun, but Jake was in the sleigh and on him in a nanosecond. Three slugs from Jake's fist and he was out cold, slumped and bleeding on the furs.

All at once, the woods were filled with light and sound and people. Rico and his brother arrived. The brother—Raul—had a pair of handcuffs and he took care of dragging Alec out of the sleigh. His ease with the job made her guess he was probably one of the people who had been hunting for Alec.

"Hold still." Jake's arm went around her as he took the seat beside her, his other hand gently peeling the tape away from her mouth. "Are you okay? Did he hurt you?"

"I'm okay." She swallowed hard, still trying to take in what had happened. She wanted to find out how he knew where to find her, how he'd arrived at the Marquis before them. But right now she was just so grateful to see him safe that she flung her arms around his neck and buried her head in his shoulder. "You found me."

Two HOURS LATER, Marnie still looked spooked.

Jake watched her as the local detective finished taking her statement in the lobby of the Marquis at dawn. He'd talked to a half-dozen different departments and task forces that had been investigating crimes linked to Alec Mason. Or at least, it seemed like there had been that many. The cop work was a blur because he hadn't given a damn about closing out an investigation. His one concern was getting Marnie out of here and back home safely as soon as possible.

She wavered on her feet, still wrapped in a fur from the sleigh that bastard had used to abduct her. The damage Jake had done with his fists hadn't come close to satisfying his need to tear the guy apart. When he'd first heard her tell the police that Mason had held a gun to her head, Rico had to keep Jake from hunting down the cop car the scumbag sat in so he could finish him off.

For now, he tried to put that out of his mind to be the kind of man Marnie needed. The kind of man she deserved.

"We're free to go," he told her, sliding an arm around her waist to lead her out of the lobby. "And we've got a safe, quiet room we can stay in here. The police contacted the owner of the Marquis and he's canceling the entertainments for a few days while the cops check out the computer systems. They're assigning a guard to your room to be sure no one bothers you."

Jake had personally made sure of that. He wished he could take her far from here, but the road crews hadn't made much of a dent in clearing the snowfall.

Marnie nodded, allowing him to lead her toward the back of the resort where a handful of rooms overlooked a paddock containing the owner's horses. Jake had checked out the accommodations ahead of time to be sure the windows locked. Logic told him everyone involved with the embezzlement was now in police custody, including the two goons who'd grabbed her in the card room. But for his peace of mind, he'd need windows that locked—preferably, the kind that had bars across them, too.

"How did you find me?" she asked as he opened the door to a suite decked out in Tudor decor.

A marble fireplace rested across the room from a four-poster bed draped in quilted burgundy-colored satin. The tea cart held pewter goblets and silver-domed dishes that likely contained the breakfast he'd requested for her.

"Rico's twin was working undercover here. And actually their names aren't Rico and Raul. They're Rick and

Rafe." Jake locked the suite door and bolted it, then sat her on the edge of the bed before he pushed the tea cart close so she could eat. "Apparently Rafe had been tracking a perp named A. J. Marks."

Marnie ignored the food and the juice goblets to pour herself a cup of hot tea.

"Another alias for Alec." Her dark eyes searched his.

"Right. And he had intel that said Marks was meeting up with his crew here, so he called Rick to let him know he might be following a suspect tonight. The other guy from the closet. And wouldn't you know, Rick and I were just trying to figure out where Alec would have taken you, so we banked on the fact that Alec and A.J. were one and the same."

"But how did you get here faster than the horses?"

"Turns out our bed-and-breakfast hostess keeps some kick-ass snowmobiles in her shed. There's a wide-open trail that follows the power lines between the inn and the resort, so I took off after you on a more direct route to the hotel, closer to the highway. Rick followed with Lianna and they got here about five minutes after me. We made a lot faster time on the sleds in the open fields, not having to guide a horse through the trees."

They'd met up with Rafe, who had already taken care of the other goon after trailing him to the meeting point. Marnie hadn't arrived for about five minutes more after that. The time had stretched so impossibly long that Jake thought he'd lose his mind. He'd second-guessed his decision to head them off here a hundred times in those frigid cold moments while he waited in the snow and the dark.

The kicker was that he wouldn't have even known where to find her if not for Rick's twin working the case from another angle. More proof that he'd failed Marnie.

Something he couldn't afford to do again.

"I wasn't careful enough," Marnie confessed between sips of tea. She must have warmed up a little because the fur blanket fell to the bed, unheeded. "I stayed by the door to listen to what was happening in Lianna's room and because of that, I never heard Alec coming."

"It wasn't your job to be careful." Shaking his head, he buttered a slice of toast and offered it to her. "That's what I was getting paid for."

She accepted the bread, but didn't take a bite.

"No. You were trying to find the embezzler. Protecting me was never part of your responsibility."

"It damn well should have been." He couldn't begin to explain the sick feeling eating away at him because he hadn't kept her safe.

His gaze tracked the delicate curve of her jaw, the fall of her tousled red hair starting to show its warm, natural caramel color at the roots. She wore a pink T-shirt and blue pajama pants with pink hearts. Hell, she'd been dragged through the mountains in those clothes.

"Jake, you were here." Setting down the toast, she reached for him. Brushed a hand along his bicep until his muscle twitched with awareness. "I knew you would find me. The whole time, the only thing that really scared me was the fear that something would happen to you when you came for me."

Her concern melted a warm spot in his chest. The sensation was so strong, so damn real, he had to touch the spot for himself to see if he was still holding together there.

"I'm an ex-Marine. A former cop. And enough of a general badass that people don't tend to worry about me." His forehead tipped to hers of its own accord, his need to be with her so tangible he didn't know how he'd ever be able to walk away from her once they got back home.

"I'm not just anyone," she reminded him, her dark eyes shining. "I care about you, Jake. So much."

Maybe if he'd been better at relationships—or more wise in the way of women—he would have known what to say. But her soft admission caught him off guard.

And scared him far more than any crook with a gun.

Straightening, he tried to find the words that would keep the situation from getting any more awkward.

"Marnie, I—"

Her fingertips brushed his lips, quieting him.

"I need to say this," she assured him. "I know we started out kind of rocky between you thinking I was a felon and all the spying on me without me knowing. But you chose the most efficient means to clear me, and I'm glad now that you did."

Jake's mouth was dry as dust, so interrupting her now wasn't an option. Besides, maybe part of him couldn't believe where she might be headed with all this.

"But something changed for me this week. You made me realize what I felt for Alec—even before we broke up—was just a shadow of how much I could care about someone."

By now, his brain blared with code red sirens and somehow he got his tongue engaged before this situation careened any more out of control.

"Marnie, I can't—that is—I care about you, too." He mirrored her gesture, swiping a finger across her lips. "My lifestyle has always been dangerous. And I like it that way. But this week? When you were at risk? I didn't like that one bit."

He'd never been so freaking scared. And he'd worked some hairy situations in his day.

"I don't understand." She shook her head, her brow furrowed in confusion. "Alec's going to jail. We can go back home—"

"Exactly. We can go back to our lives before all this happened. You'll be safe at your business and you can spend Christmas with your family. And I'll be grateful as hell knowing you're okay."

Far removed from firearms and violence—basically, all the things that had become staples in his life over the past ten years. This was what he was good at. Too bad the job didn't allow him to rope off his personal life and keep it safe from his professional world.

"You want to go back to the way things were before." The softness in her voice was gone. With her shoulders straight and her fingers laced together, she reminded him of the way she looked when she was behind the counter at Lose Yourself. Professional. In control.

And yeah, distant.

Hard to believe that was what he'd been going for. With regret, he kissed her forehead and nudged her breakfast tray closer.

"Yes. I think that would be—" painful "—for the best."

14

"YOU'RE A COP?"

Lianna tried to remind herself this wasn't a cross-examination and that Rick had been instrumental in helping nab a bad guy.

She paced the floor of a freebie suite assigned to her by the owner of the Marquis as a thank-you for her role in capturing a criminal who'd bilked the hotel. Lianna found it frustrating to think that Rick had still been hiding behind a mask the night before when they'd been together.

Her heart had been totally engaged, some long-buried romantic side of her thrilling to the idea that Rick wanted to peel away the pretense and touch the woman beneath. All the while, he'd kept a big part of himself secret.

She'd slept alone for a few hours after they gave their statements to the local police. Rick had told her he needed to help his brother tie up a few loose ends and she'd been so exhausted she hadn't argued. But when he'd knocked at her door a few minutes ago, she'd been ready for answers.

"Technically, yes." Rick sat on the small sofa in her room with its Victorian-gone-deviant decor. Crushed red velvet wallpaper covered the walls between framed ink drawings of antique sex toys. A life-size mannequin of a Victorian nobleman sported a codpiece that would have made for one heck of a conversation starter if she'd been in the mood to discuss that sort of thing. Which she absolutely was not.

Right now, with the realization that Rick had been lying to her all along, her heart ached in a way no libido ever could.

"Meaning?" She had been questioned in a separate room from Rick, so she'd heard only sketchy bits of his statement to local police, and even that had been filtered through the chatter of half a dozen other witnesses to the showdown just before dawn.

"Meaning, that while I happen to be a cop in San Diego, I'm not here in a work capacity. I took a vacation week to help Rafe out. This was personal for him, since Alec swindled his wife out of her savings and duped her into thinking they'd elope." Rick lowered an arm across the back of the small sofa, the heavy rope of muscles drawing her eye and reminding her what it felt like to have his arms around her.

She wanted to know his touch again, to feel the things only he could make her feel. Yet how could she be with someone who withheld the truth from her? Who might have only been with her for the sake of an investigation?

"So Rafe is a police officer, as well." She tried to search for what had been true in the things Rick had told her. "And what you said about coming here with him to forget about the wife who left him was at least partially accurate."

"Well, I thought he'd get over her faster if he found the bastard who'd led her astray so we could send the guy's ass to jail. Yes. True enough." His chin jutted forward, defensive. His jeans and T-shirt were rumpled as if he'd caught a few hours of sleep in a chair in the lobby.

Unfortunately for her, that didn't come close to dimming his appeal. Whereas Alec had been charming and slick, Rick was earthy and real. His dark good looks made it tough to even recall what Alec looked like.

She smoothed her hands over the simple lines of a long, forest-green dress she'd purchased in the boutique that morning since her suitcase remained back at the All Tucked Inn. The ankle-length outfit she wore now could have passed for a modern holiday dress if not for the laced-up cutout all down her back. But since she'd bought a white cashmere pashmina to wear like a sweater, no one could see the hint of skin beneath the laces.

"Then why didn't you tell me the truth last night after you learned Jake was a private investigator?" This was the part she kept coming back to, the idea that upset her most. Alec had used her. And while the two men were different in a fundamental way—one was a cop and one was a crook—she still worried they both saw her as nothing more than a pawn. Her fingers wove through the cashmere, clutching it in her clenched fists. "You must have known that Alec was the same guy you sought."

Rick shook his head.

"Lianna, I wanted to explain everything. But I'd promised Rafe I'd keep cover until we found our guy, and my brother wasn't answering his phone last night for me to clear it with him." He sat forward on the couch, his beautiful sea-blue eyes locked on her. "Besides, maybe I wanted to believe that outside stuff didn't matter. That you and I were already seeing what was real and important in each other. Did it change anything that you're a lawyer and that you live three thousand miles away from me? Or that

I'm a Mexican-Irish cop who will drop everything if my family needs me?"

Rising, he closed the distance between them. Did he know how persuasive he was close up? Ah, who was she kidding? He'd done a damn good job of persuading her from across the room. She had the feeling he'd be equally compelling on a phone call from the west coast, too.

"I don't know." She wasn't sure what to think anymore. "Maybe I'm just scared about getting involved with someone when I don't know them well. I spent half the week waiting to meet up with a guy who turned out to be a total fake."

But Alec had lied to her for months, whereas Rick had only needed a couple of days before being up front with her. And bottom line, Rick moved her in a way Alec never had.

"He didn't tell you who he was because he wanted to take advantage of you." Rick brushed his hands over her shoulders, sweeping them under the pashmina to grip her arms. "I didn't tell you who I was to keep you safe. Now you know everything and my life is an open book for you."

The sincerity in his eyes couldn't be faked. She'd evaluated enough witnesses for trial appearances to know that. But what appealed to her most was the fact that he was still here, and he still wanted to be with her. Much of her worry had stemmed from the fear that his undercover work meant his time with her had all been a lie. That he'd only been with her as part of a job. But obviously, that wasn't the case.

Hope bloomed in her chest.

"Do you really have five brothers?" she asked, curious about the real Rick.

"Yes. My twin and four others, each one a bigger pain

in the ass than the next." The affection in his voice was clear no matter what he said, warmth lighting his gaze as he talked about them.

His touch skimmed down her back, loosening the cashmere around her shoulders as he drew her closer. Her heart rate stepped up a beat, the pace quickening at his nearness.

"Was your dad really a steelworker?"

"Straight from Pittsburgh before he moved out west and settled down. Why would I lie about that?" His strong fingers dipped lower, finding the laces over her spine that exposed bare skin. "And yes, he thinks dancing is for sissies. His words, not mine. Although I think I caught him watching *Dancing with the Stars* once when one of his football heroes competed."

Lianna smiled, wondering about the family that had raised such a warm, wonderful man. A man who didn't care one bit about her past, but seemed—she hoped—interested in her future.

As his touch threaded between the laces down her spine, her skin heated in anticipation.

"My family is scattered all over." Slightly breathless from their talk as much as his touch, she thought a little exchange of information was only fair. "My parents divorced when my sister and I were in college. They both left town to travel and pursue their own dreams and they don't keep in touch more than once a year. My sister is a nurse in Arizona."

He lingered at the small of her back, sketching light circles until her skin hummed with awareness.

"Maybe you could schedule a visit with her when I succeed in bringing you to San Diego for a visit."

"You want to see me again?" she clarified, determined

there would be no more misunderstandings or false pretenses between them.

"I want to spend every second of your vacation with you since you still have a few days off. Then, after we both go back to work and miss each other like crazy, I'll fly you out to Southern California and make you fall in love with warm weather and sunshine."

Just hearing him say it made her realize he was absolutely correct. She would miss him dearly if they were separated. Wrapping her arms around his neck, she let her shawl fall to the ground while she held him close, eyes burning with unshed emotion.

"You want me to fall for the *weather?*"

He grinned, his teeth brilliantly white against his deeply tanned skin.

"Put it this way—I want to be sure you find some reason to keep coming back." He dropped a kiss to her neck, his lips branding a hot reminder into her skin. "Maybe you'll love it so much, you won't be able to leave. They need good lawyers in San Diego, too, you know."

He must have taken her breath away because she couldn't catch it for a long moment. Tenderness unfurled inside her along with a deep desire for that kind of life— that kind of love.

With him.

"I'd really like that." She nodded and the motion jarred a happy tear from her eye.

He caught it with his thumb.

"Are you sure?" He kissed her ear before he whispered in it. "I warned you, I come from a pushy family. If I'm moving too fast for you, I can slow down. I just don't want to leave here without telling you what I'm hoping for."

Stretching up on her toes, she squeezed him tight, savoring his strength and so much more.

"I'm hoping for the same things," she whispered back, her chin brushing his shoulder. "And considering that I'm a trial attorney, I think I'm going to hold my own with you."

This time, she would have a confidence in her personal relationships to match the self-assurance she'd always had in the courtroom. No more being drawn to guys who were bad for her.

He chuckled softly as he rained kisses down her neck. Her skin was on fire by the time a knock vibrated the door to the hotel room.

Rick's soft oath echoed her thoughts, but he came up for air long enough to shout, "Who is it?"

"Jake."

The sharp bark didn't sound pleased.

Lianna leaned down to retrieve her shawl so she could cover up the back of her dress while Rick moved to open the door.

The tension that had marked their early interactions had vanished, she noted. The two of them no longer glared warning signals at each other constantly and they exchanged brief nods before Jake stepped just inside the threshold so Rick could close the door.

"I'm headed back to Miami," he said without prelude. "Just wanted to thank you and Rafe for the help."

"I'm sure Rafe is going to want to thank you, man." Rick clapped him on the shoulder. "He's been itching to can this guy for months."

"Where's Marnie?" Lianna asked, wanting to say goodbye to her. After an awkward beginning, she'd come to respect the way that Marnie had no need for the games and charades that used to entertain Lianna. She seemed to know who she was and what she wanted.

"She…" Jake's jaw tensed "…left about an hour ago."

A long, awkward paused ensued.

"Did she want to fly home?" Lianna knew it wasn't truly her business, but the gritty P.I. who'd scared her half to death when he accused her of embezzling funds now looked so brittle he was ready to break.

Something had gone terribly wrong.

"She decided to take a vacation to recover from her vacation, I guess."

Without him. Lianna tried to put the pieces together in her head, to offer up some words of wisdom for a man who was obviously stinging from whatever had happened between them.

Rick, it seemed, didn't waste time searching for the right words. He forged directly into the breach.

"Dude, don't let her get away." Rick shook his head in obvious disapproval, frowning the whole time. "That woman's crazy about you. And you should be smart enough to know when a good thing comes along."

Lianna was prepared for a sharp retort, but Jake surprised her with a slow shrug of his wide shoulders.

"Seeing her in danger…" He shook his head like the memory was too real. "I couldn't handle that again. And the work—you know how it is. You don't leave it at the office. Some of those cases follow you home."

Was that the life of a police officer? Lianna wondered.

"Hey, don't scare my girl." Rick winked at her as if he'd read her thoughts. "So you get a place outside the city and a big freaking dog. But you can't let that rule you."

"A big dog?" Jake turned toward the door. "That's your answer?"

"Hey." Lianna stepped in, feeling the tension ratchet up in the room. "Jake, I think Rick means that you're a smart guy and you'll figure out how to keep her safe. Because the other alternative isn't an option. If you push someone away because you're afraid you'll lose them, you end up losing them anyway. Even though I don't know Marnie that well, I saw how she cared about you, and I'd bet everything I have that she's hurt like hell. No woman wants a man to let her go like she's…inconsequential."

The way Alec had treated her when it suited him. Rick, on the other hand, came after her when she was scared and alone. One of many reasons she knew this was right. *He* was right.

Jake seemed to take a moment, weighing that statement. And a twitch in his right eye told Lianna he didn't like the idea of hurting Marnie one bit.

He swore softly under his breath, cursing himself, before leaning in to give Lianna a quick thanks and a kiss on the cheek.

Rick growled possessively, pulling her closer to his side. Jake offered him a terse nod before he turned on his heel and left, slamming the door behind him.

As if he had a woman to pursue.

Lianna broke the silence in the aftermath by clearing her throat.

"You weren't kidding about the pushy thing, were you?"

"Hey, I was doing him a favor by pointing out what he can't see. With five brothers, I've learned to recognize when a guy is being pigheaded." Rick stalked back across the room to be close to her. "You watch, he'll thank me one day for that pep talk."

He unwound her shawl from her shoulders and tossed it on the couch. Then, he gathered her hair on one side of her head and tucked it in front of her shoulder, exposing the laces on the back of her dress.

"You think he'll thank you? I think it was me that put a finer point on it than 'Get a big dog.' And if that was a pep talk, by the way, I sure hope you never try to cheer me up."

Spinning her around, Rick halted her so that her back faced him. He slid one finger under the knot that held the ties together.

"I've got an entirely different approach to take when I want to make you feel better." His breath warmed the back of her neck as he leaned close. "Would you care for a demonstration?"

Knees melting beneath her, Lianna couldn't wait.

MARNIE DIDN'T REGRET flying out of Saratoga late that afternoon.

She'd sprung for a flight to get her away from the man who'd broken her heart as fast as possible. Jake had protested, arguing that he could return her to Miami so she could spend the holidays with her family. But he couldn't keep her where she didn't want to be.

And she damn well didn't want to travel anywhere with a man who didn't recognize her right to choose what kind of life she led and who she spent her time with. She couldn't bear one more round of his refrain about her safety.

Did he think she was made of glass?

Now, strapping on a pair of ice skates in the moonlight a day later, Marnie gazed up at her hotel in northern Vermont. More of a ski lodge than a hotel, the Three Chimneys Inn sat on a quiet mountain side with access to cross-country skiing, sledding and a big pond for skating. She'd rented a one-room bungalow outside the main building, unable to return home to all the happy members of her family seated around the holiday table in pairs while she sat alone.

Again.

Inhaling the clean, cold air, she stood on her skates and hoped she remembered how to do this. As it turned out, she needed to lose herself now far more than when she'd been under suspicion for a felony and on the run from the man who framed her. A broken heart trumped all else when it came to reasons for booking a fantasy escape.

She needed this time to figure out how to go on without Jake.

Pushing off on one toe, she leaned forward on the other foot, feeling the blade cut into the bumpy, ungroomed ice. No one else was using the pond tonight, so she had it all to herself. Then again, most people were at home celebrating the holidays with family. Loved ones.

Banishing the thoughts of Jake for the umpteenth time in the past hour, Marnie launched into an upbeat Christmas carol, hoping to sing herself happy.

"It's great to hear you sing."

The deep, familiar voice cut right through her chorus about holly boughs and candles on the tree.

"Jake." She spun to see him standing in the moonlight at the pond's edge and her heart raced as if it were in triple overtime, even though she willed herself to be calm. Composed. "How did you find me?"

Her breath fogged the air in front of her. She was so not ready to revisit the heartache she'd experienced at his hands earlier this week.

"Don't worry." He remained at the edge of the ice, one boot hiked up on the log where she'd sat to lace up her skates. "It didn't involve any hidden cameras or anything. I just called your mom."

Oh. She could just imagine how that conversation went. Her mother had probably bombarded him with nosy questions before assuming he'd be present for Christmas dinner. She was like that with every boyfriend and male acquaintance Marnie had from the time she was thirteen.

"You could have just called me." She tried not to pay attention to the fast trip of her heartbeat. He'd made an impression on her the first time they'd met when he'd built the cabinet for her display at Lose Yourself. And she'd been drawn to him ever since, even when that wasn't wise. Now was no different.

Forcing herself into a small spin on her skates, she hoped the activity would serve as a distraction so she didn't gape at him like a starving woman drooling over Christmas dinner.

"I wasn't sure what kind of reception I'd get and I didn't want to risk you telling me to go take a flying leap or anything like that."

Moonlight spilled over him, his breath huffing white and rising quickly in the cold.

She didn't argue since she wasn't sure what she would have said to him. She still didn't know.

"So why did you want to find me?" Slowing her spin, she took some pleasure in discovering the skating lessons she'd taken as a teen were still stored somewhere in her muscle memory.

Besides, thinking about skating seemed more prudent than letting her imagination run away when it came to Jake.

"For one thing, I wanted to return your laptop." He shoved his hands in his pockets, the snow and the moon surrounding him in white and silhouetting his big, powerful body. "I removed the spyware and cleaned it up for you. It's at the front desk of your hotel."

Stepping out onto the ice, he stalked toward her. She couldn't spin or skate now. All she could do was watch him come closer. And hope that he had far better reasons for trolling around the dark Vermont hillside than to deliver electronics.

"That was thoughtful of you." She kept her cool outwardly, her voice even despite being so unsteady inside. But the closer he came, the more certain she was that he could see how much she missed him. Wanted him.

When only a few inches separated them, he stopped. She was almost eye to eye with him while she wore her skates. His body blocked the wind, sheltering her in a way that made her warmer, yet gave her a shiver, too.

"I figured it was the least I could do to make it up to you for pulling the freak-out show yesterday." His voice, all low and growly and private, sent a jolt of pleasure through her, reminding her of other conversations that had been for her ears only.

She liked the idea that this intense, focused man could have a side he saved just for her. Not that she was getting her hopes up, damn it.

"I'm not sure what you mean." And she wanted to be one hundred percent clear. No more assuming the best because of her optimistic nature.

"Marnie, I'm sorry I went caveman on you yesterday. I kept waiting for you to go into shock after what you'd been through, but I think it was me who went a little crazy afterward." His expression was so serious. Tiny lines fanned around the outside of his eyes as he frowned. "I had no business dictating that we shouldn't be together because

I got scared by this case. Rick pretty much called me a candy ass to my face for acting like that."

"Really?" She tried to picture Jake standing still long enough to take that kind of criticism, and couldn't.

"Yeah." He shook his head, an odd smile lifting one side of his mouth. "He's not such a bad guy. And he was right."

Marnie's skates nearly slid right out from under her.

Apparently, Jake saw her surprise as he reached to steady her, but he kept right on talking.

"I've really put relationships on the back burner for a long time. I had a girlfriend mess around on me while I was on a tour overseas and it sort of cured the itch to have any kind of lasting commitment for a while. I just kept up the happy bachelor thing and devoted the best of myself to the job. Until you."

The night was so still and silent except for his voice. Smoke from some nearby cabins drifted on the breeze. All around them, the fresh fallen snow twinkled in the moonlight. And Marnie had the feeling she would always remember every tiny impression of this moment when Jake had cared about her enough to share something of himself. To open his heart, if only a little.

"I'm sorry some wretched woman cheated on you." She couldn't imagine stabbing a guy in the back like that while he was half a world away, and she knew firsthand what it felt like to be deceived.

"She wasn't The One." Jake took her hands in his, sliding his fingers inside her mittens to touch her skin. Her heart fluttered like a teenager's. "Apparently she was a bump in the road on the way to something better. And I'm not going to be too blind to see the best thing that ever happened to me when she's standing right before my eyes."

Marnie tipped her forehead to his, a profound sense of peace and rightness wrapping around her.

"Jake Brennan, you brought a much better gift than a laptop." She couldn't ask for anything nicer for Christmas than to have him here with her. Tunneling her arms inside his jacket, she wrapped herself around him.

"There's more."

"You're going to stay with me through Christmas?" she guessed, already picturing the fun she'd have unwrapping that particular present.

"I'm very on board with that, if you'll have me." He bent to kiss the top of her head, the rough edge of his un-shaven jaw catching in her hair. "But I also had an early Christmas present to give you."

He reached inside a jacket pocket and pulled out an en-velope that he handed to her.

"A present?"

"You'd better check it out and see if you like it."

Glancing at his face, she tried to guess and came up blank. Opening the envelope, she saw...

"MapQuest directions?" A route had been highlighted from Vermont back to Miami, with stops in between. "Philadelphia? Savannah?"

"I felt bad you didn't get to have much of a vacation so I talked to Vincent Galway, and he helped me figure out some of the Premiere Properties resorts you liked best. I figured you haven't gotten to travel much since you started your own business and while this isn't exactly Paris and Rome—"

Happy sparks showered through her as bright as the Northern Lights. She all but tackled him, squeezing him and her gift tight.

"You gave me a road trip." She'd been envious of the

ones she'd booked for her clients, needing a getaway herself. "It's the best gift."

"Vincent says you can have your job back any time you want it, but at the least, he wanted to give you some comp rooms to apologize for terminating your position with Premiere."

"I'm really happy running my own business." She looked up into his eyes, feeling as if she were still spinning—no, floating—even though her skates remained in place. "But I'll gladly take the comp rooms as long as you're sharing them with me."

Jake nodded as he took the papers back and shoved them back in his pocket.

"I'm part of the deal." He wound an arm around her waist, his hand curving possessively over her hip. "And I'd be glad to take you back to your cabin and show you what an asset I'm going to be during this vacation of yours."

A light, swirling snow started to fall around them, the flakes as fat and glittery as the kind that came in a snow globe.

"Mmm," was all Marnie could manage, happiness and pleasure making her dizzy with wanting him.

"I want you in my life, Marnie. Thank you for giving me another chance."

"Thank you for coming for me." She kissed his cheek, so glad to have the promise of this night with him. This week. A future. "And thanks for making this the best Christmas ever."

Slanting his lips over hers, he met her mouth in a kiss that promised many, many more.

Epilogue

Nine days later

"SMILE FOR THE CAMERA." Marnie stalked her quarry barefoot across the carpet in the hotel room they shared at a historic property on Jekyll Island off the coast of Georgia. They'd spent Christmas together in Vermont before starting their road trip south, straying from the course when the mood suited them.

Now, on New Year's Eve, they'd decided to return to their hotel room, ditching the small champagne party in the dining club downstairs before the clock struck the zero hour. Shortly before midnight, with the sounds of the dance band wafting right through the closed balcony doors, Marnie sashayed around the room in her emerald-green satin cocktail dress, counting her blessings for the year.

Starting with the man in the middle of her zoom lens.

"Not more video." Jake shook his head as he unwound a black silk tie that he'd paired with one of the dinner jackets he'd bought during their stay at the Marquis. With the undone tie looped around his neck, he went for the buttons on his crisp white dress shirt. "Are you still trying to get payback for that hidden camera of mine? I don't think you can possibly capture as much footage of me as I've got of you."

His wicked grin teased her, but she deliberately panned lower on his strong, muscular bod to take in his exposed chest. The taut abs she could start to see as his fingers kept up the work on the buttons.

Would she ever get enough of this man?

They'd spent every moment together since the night he'd followed her to the Vermont skating pond, but she still got breathless when he got close to her. Not just because of the phenomenal heat that sparked between them. She just flat out liked to be with him. To hear about how he'd caught various bad guys. To understand how committed he was to his work. To be a part of his world. Yeah, she had it bad for him. And she couldn't be happier about that.

Especially now that two more witnesses had come forward to make statements about Alec's various schemes. According to Jake, they already had enough evidence to put him away for at least twenty-five years.

And that hadn't been all the good news they'd gotten on their winding road trip south. Lianna had called her two days ago, asking her to book a trip to the California coast for her to see the sights and take in a few neighborhoods for prospective house hunting. Marnie had been only too happy to oblige, spending an afternoon researching fun places for her and Rick to stay.

Right now, she was glad to think about her own future, however. It seemed to be turning out just right with this hot stud of a man in her viewfinder.

"I'm dispensing with the boring bits," she explained "and getting only the juicy parts on tape. So my video archives are going to be way hotter than yours."

Jake stripped off the shirt and her mouth went dry.

"All flash and no substance?" He went for his belt buckle and she had the feeling her gasp of anticipation would be well documented in the audio. "Where's your artistic integrity as a filmmaker?"

Downstairs, she could hear the sudden blare of horns from the dance band and a chorus of shouts. Setting down the video camera, she checked the clock and saw the time.

"It's a new year." Her eyes went to his without the filter of the lens between them.

"To new beginnings." He spoke the words like a toast, but instead of lifting a glass, he stepped toward her. Clamping his hands around her waist, his fingers warmed her skin right through the silky green satin of her dress.

He bent close, the heat of his body kicking up her pulse. She licked her lips in anticipation. Nudged the strap of her slim sheath toward the edge of her shoulder and down. Off.

"Cheers to that," she agreed, her heart and her body so very ready for him.

As she shimmied her way out of her dress, Marnie was glad she'd turned off the camera for what she knew would come next. She had the feeling it would be a New Year's neither of them would ever forget.

* * * * *

MILLS & BOON®

Want to get more from Mills & Boon?

Here's what's available to you if you join the exclusive **Mills & Boon eBook Club** today:

✦ *Convenience – choose your books each month*
✦ *Exclusive – receive your books a month before anywhere else*
✦ *Flexibility – change your subscription at any time*
✦ *Variety – gain access to eBook-only series*
✦ *Value – subscriptions from just £1.99 a month*

So visit **www.millsandboon.co.uk/esubs** today to be a part of this exclusive eBook Club!

4_ST_4